SATAN'S CROSSING

SATAN'S CROSSING
When Walls Won't Work

a novel by R. L. Glinski

To the Migrants who never made it home.

I appreciate ALL (good, bad and ugly) who have shaped my
worldview of human migration.

Prologue

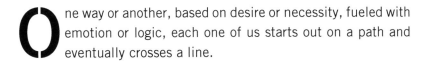

One way or another, based on desire or necessity, fueled with emotion or logic, each one of us starts out on a path and eventually crosses a line.

THE SEARCH

Chapter 1

Both were born in Mexico's rugged Sierra Madre Mountains. The currents of life and circumstance had transported them far to the north. In the distant land one was answering the call of his conquistador blood, hoping to find adventure and livelihood. The other was running on instinct, settling into his new environs.

They met in an isolated canyon in southern Arizona's Atascosa Mountains. Their encounter was a random and brief circumstance; the struggle ended in an instant. One was in the wrong place at the wrong time and afforded enough resources for the other to make it one more week.

Under the cover of a large oak a band of Mexicans huddled together for warmth. The sun had set six hours earlier and now a quarter moon filtered through the canopy, projecting faint shadows on the surrounding wooded hills. The call of a great horned owl boomed in the darkness, alerting the men. They did not like the owl near them. In their tradition it was bad luck. They had enough of that already.

Earlier in the day just after they had crossed into Arizona they lost their scant provisions while scrambling from the U.S. Border Patrol. They needed water. In a few hours they would attempt to find a discarded jug at an old camp and fill it somewhere. But for now the air of an exceptionally chilly February night settled around them, and the fear of being so far from home in a land of so many uncertainties diminished their thirst.

In the expanse of the San Pedro River Valley, Sam Logan was waiting in his truck. With the engine running to heat the cab and the volume turned up to hear any radio traffic, he was primed to doze off. There were twenty-two other patrol vehicles within fifty miles of him. They were strung out strategically across the breadth of the valley with sophisticated gear and special agents from the Tucson Sector of the U.S. Border Patrol. Their goal was to capture illegal crossers.

Sam's briefing to his junior agents had been fairly matter-of-fact: "To the west of us between Nogales and Yuma is some of the hottest and most inhospitable conditions for human survival imaginable. When the crossers came through there last summer we lost about forty, and that's just the bodies we found. There could have been hundreds, we don't know for sure. There's no water in that area. Our presence there is minimal since the environmental conditions offer sufficient 'enforcement' presence. We mainly try to intercept the crossers before their misguided trek becomes fatal. We figure our new program will persuade them to move east of Nogales, into the San Pedro area, where we'll be waiting."

The new program he mentioned entailed a mix of enforcement strategy, fear, and wonder. At the eastern end of this inhospitable region, west of Nogales, about a dozen deaths within the past several years had been labeled "suspicious." Bodies, or remnants, had been stashed in the brush or hidden in caves. Typical remains consisted of weathered and dismembered body parts, and frequently just scattered bones. Very few skulls had been recovered with the bodies, which seemed odd to Border Patrol forensic scientists. This fact also heightened the suspicion of the crossers and fueled a devil myth. Reports of human remains usually came to the Border Patrol from hunters. Mexican crossers seldom made official reports but no doubt encountered many more remains than did hunters. Discoveries by crossers eventually reached law enforcement through a variety of channels as each body was immortalized with exaggerated tales that collectively created an ominous death legend among crossers. That people had died was certain. What had killed them was unknown. Between the certainty and the unknown, the Mexican psyche created a supernatural agent of death, *El Diablo de la Frontera*, the Border Devil. In the minds of many who thought about crossing into the U.S., this demon lurked along the center of Arizona's border with Mexico, an area that became known to crossers as Satan's Crossing.

Initial response of U.S. officials to these fatalities was a mixture of alarm and skepticism. Enforcement officials eventually came to believe a band of thieves was ambushing crossers to steal the money and valuables they carried. Mexican gangs were increasingly becoming a factor in the lives of crossers. Some forcefully kidnapped crossers from the established "coyotes" who originally were hired to lead them across the border. The gangs offered protection and a promise of safe crossing for a fee of $5,000 for delivery to Phoenix.

Whatever the killing agent, the Border Patrol wanted to take advantage of the pause that fear was creating in the mind of the average crosser. So the agency began a mass media campaign in Sonora and Chihuahua, Mexico to further instill fear of the unknown killer in southern Arizona. "Operation El Diablo" was initiated to discourage crossing at the western end of the Tucson Sector and essentially to herd crossers into a relatively narrow area of the border east of Satan's Crossing where focused patrols could increase the number of apprehensions. Publicizing the notion of *El Diablo* took on greater priority with the Border Patrol than pursuing the killer.

This maneuver was successful at creating fear in crossers, which essentially sealed much of the western border. But like a river partly plugged, the pressure of movement from the south kept coming, flowing mostly through other areas of least resistance. Relative economic conditions in the U.S. and Mexico have always mixed with a multitude of other reasons people have for leaving home to seek promises in the north, creating a variety of incentives to cross. Even a landscape that offered a sizeable amount of inhospitable resistance, or an encounter with Satan, could not dissuade everyone...some would always come.

But on this night, across the landscape to the east, the agents found no crossers. "For some reason everyone's laying low tonight." Logan's transmission broke the silence. "Maybe *El Diablo* has decided to visit us in the eastern region. Does anyone want to get out, walk around, and see if he's around?" Witticisms and chuckles echoed through the transmissions that followed, signaling the end of a long night.

Most of the men and women that held the border vigil that night were recent recruits to the Border Patrol. For reasons of safety, new graduates from federal law enforcement training in Glynco, Georgia learned to stay close to the resources housed in their trucks. "Radios, weapons, and sophisticated sensing gear are more useful than legs, eyes, and personal observations...they will save your life," claimed the instructors. Training and attention focused on the functionality of electronics, not the proper fit of boots.

Logan was different, which is why he recently was transferred to the eastern region of the Tucson Sector. He spent thirty years split between the two regions, beginning with his first duty station in Nogales. He never tried to ascend the ranks, preferring to put his energy into knowing the local countryside and residents. He was particularly fond of ranchers, a natural outcome of his rural Texas roots. He was "old school" Border Patrol, and knew how to read the ground and observe sign, which made him a misfit in the modern border enforcement world.

He lived with his wife and three hound dogs in various small towns like Patagonia and Arivaca. Since he and his brother had inherited the sizeable family ranch in west Texas, he did not want to buy property in Arizona. He knew his home and future were in Texas, and his tie to Arizona was the captivating landscapes of its southern reaches. He rented old adobe houses at the fringes of small towns, or farther away if he could. His wife worked odd jobs at banks or stores, and equally enjoyed the footloose, remote lifestyle.

This arrangement made him somewhat of a rebel with the Border Patrol. He had no desire to promote up into an office job. He was a very good field agent and wanted to stay where his skills were exercised. Ambitious ladder-climbers respected these traits and usually gave Logan the lead at making field observations and predictions. However, his partnership with Stayton Sheldon changed everything.

Chapter 2

He was seventy-four years old but had the body of a man half his age. A typical sunbaked southern Arizona rancher, weathered and wiry, his short, combed hair was white and nearly always concealed beneath a cowboy hat. Between that hat and his worn boots, a tall, thin frame was usually draped with a loose-fitting long-sleeved shirt and denim pants. He walked like his feet hurt. Even on flat ground his short, choppy steps suggested he was side-stepping rocks and grass clumps on a rugged hillside. It was obvious Stayton Sheldon had spent more time on horseback than afoot.

He always carried in his shirt pocket a small notebook and pencil that he sharpened with a pocketknife. A fourth-generation rancher whose family had settled the wooded crags at the toe of the Atascosa Mountains southeast of Arivaca, Sheldon had hunted and trapped wildlife, and herded cattle over every square inch of his homeland. He knew the area intimately. That his ranch was in the middle of Satan's Crossing didn't concern him in the least.

Sheldon was respected by both local and regional cattlemen. He was articulate, and the mannerism of his speech was effective at getting and holding attention. He slowly over-pronounced each word, and issued the combination of words with mesmerizing inflection and cadence. Although he was a private man who generally shunned attention, he wisely chose his battles and usually let gentle persuasion win for him.

Sheldon's ranch was one of the last family ranches in the area. The others that were settled at the same time in the 1880s had been sold to investors, land developers, or absentee owners. Banks owned many family ranches after heirs could not pay the inheritance tax. Those waiting in the wings to snatch up the spoils of such misfortune had no care for the land, just an interest in a monetary return.

To manage their "holdings," investors hired drunks who sounded and looked like cowboys, but didn't know one end of a cow from another. They were instructed to spend money on the operation, all tax-deductible. They also complained about the government, which kept them in acceptable standing with the local cattlemen's association. They lacked the power of observation, and any knowledge of range stewardship. They had almost a deathly fear of horses, and of going to places that only a horse could take them. Riding a new, clean pickup on a graded road was their principle activity.

One such character was Jason Downing. By way of fortunate circumstances Downing acquired the title of Ranch Manager of the Sopori Ranch, a 125,000-acre chunk of private land that was part of a Spanish land grant dating back to the middle of the 1800s. The grant entailed surface water in Sopori Creek, upland areas of good soil with plenty of grass, and hills with scattered woodlands sustaining many seeps and springs. White-tailed deer and javelina were numerous, and scenic vistas of incredible landscapes were unmatched.

An investment banker from New York, Jeffrey Berger, acquired the ranch with windfall profits from shady dealings. He had no idea that he possessed a significant gem of Southwestern biological diversity. What he did know was that the Sopori had been on The Nature Conservancy's acquisition radar since the early 1970s. That fact guaranteed a return on his investment, sooner or later. He was content to wait until later, and Downing was his interface with the local culture.

Berger arranged to have potential clients chauffeured from Tucson International to the Sopori, where they met Downing. Listening to the charming tone of his cowboy lingo, they actually took in all he said, believing they were getting a lesson in Western culture and ranch economics. They had no clue that every inch of Downing was counterfeit, and that he was merely regurgitating some of what he had gleaned from his neighbors. Most of what his neighbors thought and said about him he did not recount in his waxing. He buried that under heaps of denial and gallons of booze.

Berger visited the ranch only on rare occasions, usually with an entourage of Easterners who wore new, expensive boots and odd-fitting western hats. They were smart and astute to local scrutiny and worked hard to take on the walk and mannerisms of the locals. The incredible uniqueness of the ranch escaped them...it was only a place for getting away. On their return back East, they especially enjoyed recounting to associates the fact that they were in the area of *El Diablo* in Arizona. Seemed the Border Patrol's publicity had spread east as well as south.

Once Berger showed the Sopori to Larry Thompson, a high-rolling Texas rancher who showed a peculiar affinity for the place. He was not put off by the potential for the drug cartels trespassing with loads of contraband, or by desperate crossers occasionally showing up on the ranch house doorstep. Rather, he seemed intrigued by that possibility. Thompson soon made an offer to purchase the Sopori from Berger.

Stayton Sheldon's Atascosa Ranch bordered the southern extent of the Sopori. About fifteen miles of fence separated the two. His interactions with Jason Downing never lasted more than a couple minutes. Even at the local cattle growers' meeting, he avoided Downing like a disease. His issues with Downing were not with what Downing did or said, but what he always failed to do.

The alignment of fence between the two ranches was unknown to Downing, much less its condition. Sheldon did all the repairs, and within six months he quit informing Downing of his work. He had sent the bills for repair supplies to Downing once and was advised to send them directly to Berger's secretary in New York. Downing was totally out of the loop, not only on the aspect of the ranch condition, but virtually every other operation. Downing "supervised" several hired Mexican *vaqueros* during calf roundup, but he neither rode the herd to monitor or doctor animals, nor realized the need to.

In contrast, Sheldon was pure old-fashioned cowboy. From his posture and gestures, to his conversation and ethic, he reflected a breed that was nearly gone. Hard work had worn out most of them, and there were no replacements from the next generation. Sheldon's kids left the ranch for the city, and his old-time neighbors either died or left when tragedies in the cattle market or family health forced them off the land. That they were replaced with the likes of lazy and ignorant men like Downing was a source of irritation to Sheldon.

Despite the lack of men of his measure, Sheldon was far from lonely. He sought companionship with the majesty of his ranch, and recharged his energy and attitude by frequently riding every inch of fence, and visiting the hideaway springs and seeps of the Atascosas. His livelihood depended on this activity. If the fence needed mending, he knew it. If a spring or seep was going through an annual dry period, he knew the need for a functioning windmill was at hand, as was the need to move his cattle to another pasture. His life was in alignment with the natural world from sunup to sundown, everyday.

He prayed for rain and grass, and cursed the drought. But mostly he was thankful for his role in the world. He never lost sight of this good fortune and health. This was especially true since he lost his wife about five years ago. One consequence of her passing was that he visited the mountains more frequently, remembering the times they had shared those special places. Her memory was always with him, although he never talked about her or his loss. He was a private man who kept his thoughts to himself. The only exception to that personal code of conduct was when he had a conversation with Sam Logan.

Chapter 3

"**W**ell, another night without a fight. That has to be good, even for an old veteran like you, Sam."

Logan closed the truck door just as the fellow agent finished his statement. He instinctively looked around to the backside of his vehicle, then off into the brush. He settled his eyes on the short man standing next to him and said, "Every night in southern Arizona is a good night. But you're right about the fighting. I hate it. I am getting very sympathetic towards crossers…the world has a huge migrant issue and we're seeing only a small fraction of it here along our border. My family was migrants a hundred years ago. Enough of the politics…sorry."

He smiled sincerely, inhaled deeply, and continued, "Nate, this land sure is dry. There isn't even a hint of moisture in the air. The winter rains are missing us again. I didn't even see a jackrabbit on the road in. Did you?"

"Nope."

Logan looked up at the moon, noting how it had progressed across the clear sky, and said, "Must be about three. What time do you have?"

"Two-thirty. Time to call it a night. Will you be in the office in the morning?"

"No, I'm off tomorrow, and I have to meet a guy in the morning. I'm heading home now so I can get a few hours sleep. I'll follow you out."

"10-4. See you on Monday."

Nate Chavez was a young agent from Colorado who had gravitated to Logan when he first came to the Tucson Sector. He liked Sam's style, which reminded him of his grandfather, a man of the woods. He had been on the job less than six months and Nate's supervisor figured his alliance with Logan was due to his youth and inexperience, and his lack of political savvy. Nate asked Sam lots of questions about his stint with the Border Patrol, especially why he had been transferred to the eastern region of the Sector. Sam told him only enough to maintain a mentoring relationship with the young agent. He mostly wanted to protect his friend with practical information about enforcement on the border—the sort that the Border Patrol academy did not afford.

The two men drove along the ridge they had shared that evening and headed for the pavement about ten miles to the northeast. Logan had a thirty-minute drive to his house near Benson. He would be home by three, to bed five minutes later, and up at nine. As he bounced along the dirt road that wound its way through the small mesquites scattered across the flat grassland, he thought about his career. Encounters with young Nate Chavez had that effect on him. He saw a young Agent Logan in Chavez, and smiled at the thought of when his own body was young. However, he relished his older intellect and the differences between the modern Border Patrol and the former agency he claimed. He thought about the life forces that can change a man, no matter his age.

He could see Nate's truck moving along about half a mile ahead, taillights twinkling through the mesquite and the wash of his headlight beams fading into the black of a night sky, occasionally intercepting the airborne desert dirt stirred by Nate's passage. Nate's truck glided within the ghostly sphere of dust and light, which to Logan seemed like a protective shield. He knew that Nate needed protection from so much: the crossers, the bureaucrats, and whatever else might engage the young man's life along the border.

The signs of the drought were everywhere. The lack of good grass cover was one of the many signs, as was the silt that blew into the road ruts, obliterating any sign of passage. All this sort of tracking knowledge Nate would learn with time and a good coach. Logan decided he would be that mentor when he could, but right now his mind was cluttered with other issues. Actually, there was only one thing on his mind. It was the sight of what Sheldon had taken him to last weekend.

When Logan drove up to his house he was welcomed by his side porch light and barking dogs. They were his familiar greeting that added a significant measure of comfort to his life. Stability had not been part of his routine during the past six months, and he treasured the moments when dogs greeted him.

"Quiet," he yelled to the dogs when he exited his truck. As he locked the vehicle's front door, he glanced at his friends, and sure enough, their tails were wagging wildly. They were glad to hear his voice and their gestures pleased him in return.

He stepped up to the porch, unlocked the door, and entered the kitchen. As usual, his wife had left the countertop light on. A covered plate of homemade oatmeal cookies sat to the left of the sink by the phone. Tucked under a portion of the plate was a yellow scrap of paper. "Call Mr. Sheldon first thing in the morning. Love, June."

Sheldon sat on the porch of the house his grandfather had built. He had tried to sleep, and almost succeeded a dozen times. He needed less sleep in his later years, so he was not worried about this restlessness. It occurred often since his wife had passed. But this night was different and he knew it. What he did not know was how wild the ride would be after what happened today. He was not afraid or worried. He was unsettled.

His ranch was fairly isolated from the rest of the sprawling world of southern Arizona's suburbia. At least he could not directly see the lights of Tucson and Green Valley. The looming presence of these cities was evident as a glow on the northeastern horizon. This was especially the case when weather fronts moved through and the clouds enhanced the reflected glow, providing enough light for him to gather tack in the corral well after sunset.

He thought of all the events that led up to today. Why hadn't he noticed anything earlier? Certainly some changes should have been evident. He thought about how age perhaps was taking its toll on his senses, his eyes mainly. He quickly discarded that notion. His vision was still exceptional. He knew the experience that age brought was on his side, enabling him to compare what he was seeing with what he had seen in earlier years. He had always been astute enough to notice gradual changes on the landscape, mainly ushered in by variations in rainfall. He dismissed any failing on his part and resolved that what he had found today was new and totally unique.

Elements of and on the landscape were changing. As the urban centers grew, so did the amount of recreational trespass. There were parents taking the family SUV out for a spin, or ubiquitous kids with quads testing their gear on his hills and in his washes. There was also the increase in drug traffic and illegal immigration. Evidence of the latter was the cut fence lines and camps in the canyons. The drug runners left as little sign as possible so they could escape detection. But those crossing into the U.S. to find a better life made a point of establishing camps littered with items like plastic water jugs and black bags. These things could aid in survival and also mark the passage north, affording a beacon for those who followed.

That there was an increase in illegal activity was without doubt. That it was becoming a more violent activity was also evident. Trafficking in human lives was nearly as lucrative as drug-running. There were almost daily news reports of shootouts on the highway between Nogales and Tucson by rival gangs and coyotes attempting to pirate another's "load." North of Phoenix, law enforcement officials discovered a desert wash along a rural highway that was littered with hundreds of black jackets, pants, and ski masks, all used to blend crossers into the darkness as they scurried between transport trucks and the passenger vans that would take them to some drop house in Phoenix or onto the next leg of their journey north.

Human death along the border was everywhere. There were formal investigations if bodies were discovered before too much decay had set in. Evidence crews, and lately specialized scientists, were sent to the scenes to gather whatever forensic data they could. The cause of death was self-evident usually. But for a dozen or so bodies within the last year or two, that was not the case.

Either Sheldon or Logan, before his transfer to the eastern side of the Tucson Sector, had been the first on the scene in three instances where the cause of death did not appear to be exposure. These incidents occurred during mild seasons of the year when temperature was not a factor. Broken bones suggested violence. But since the bodies had been eaten by coyotes or other vermin and exposed to the weather, a significant amount of sign was lost. All bodies had at least one thing in common: the skulls were missing.

Sheldon and Logan were left thinking that it could have been the work of thieves, *ladrones*, who ambushed and murdered crossers near their remote camps, and took what meager resources and money they carried. But why the absence of skulls? Perhaps the thieves were perpetuating the myth of *El Diablo*, and the victims were crossers who had been their clients. The bottom line was that they were stumped. That is, until they found the first fresh kill. They thought they finally had solved the mystery, but politics reared its head before Logan could present the entirety of his findings. It got Logan transferred, and left Sheldon alone on his porch, wondering.

With the collar of his denim jacket pulled up around his neck he rocked, he thought, and listened. He stopped rocking and looked across the tops of the mesquites at the clear moon as it was setting in the western sky. He began to realize something. He listened more intently to the darkness. What he heard, or failed to hear, began to roll around in his mind. He had not heard the coyotes yipping all winter.

Chapter 4

While buying a supply of food in Sáric, Fernando could not bear to hear talk of dead bodies across the line. With those words his eyes glazed over, and he shut down. At that point he was physically present but emotionally separated and out of touch.

The notion of *El Diablo* created a stir in this small town in northern Sonora, a popular assembly place for Mexicans preparing to cross into the U.S. Many crossers had chosen not to venture into the area of *El Diablo*, which was the landscape from Nogales west to the Baboquivari Mountains west of Sasabe. It consisted of the grassy expanses of Altar Valley north of Sasabe, the beautiful tree-lined valley to the east, through which Arivaca Creek flowed, and surrounding hills and mountains of brush and trees. It was familiar country to Fernando, who crossed it several times in the past two decades. Fernando knew that Border Patrol efforts there had increased significantly as U.S. authorities investigated the mortalities, an action that would greatly increase the chances of getting caught and deported.

Fernando understood the tactics of the Border Patrol and was content with his ability to avoid them. However, when he heard the words "*El Diablo*," he became afraid and angry. Both emotions came rushing to his head in the same instant, competing for expression but finding no voice. Confusion replaced all emotion and created in Fernando a desire to wander, to escape and find release from the conflict.

As a child growing up on a small ranch south of Sáric, Fernando had to compete with eight siblings for the attention of his parents. His efforts always failed. His inability to get along with other kids on the ranch pushed him into the hills where he would go to hide in a world he had created. At times the young *vaqueros* would discover him hiding in the tangle of mesquite trunks or shallow caves along the washes and made sport of attempting to lasso him. When they succeeded in putting a noose around him, they released tension on the tether to avoid dragging him along the rocky ground. But the leather lariats tightened around his body enough to pinch his skin and, at times, draw blood. The physical scars were slight compared to the deep and hidden emotional burdens from this youthful persecution.

Fernando could still hear the words of his beloved teacher, Sister Miriam: "Our Father, in heaven, hallowed be Your name. Your kingdom come, Your will be done on earth as it is in heaven. Give us today our daily bread. Forgive us our debts, as we forgive our debtors. And lead us not into temptation, but deliver us from the evil one." Although the nun intended to comfort him, her face reflected a hopelessness that her touch confirmed as she embraced him on the steps of the schoolhouse during their moments of prayer. Her physicality offered a stark contrast to the words she spoke.

That contrast was what ruled his life, and swirled around his mind as he contemplated crossing again. Was his despair God's will? Could Sister Miriam see into his soul—did she see the root of his temptation, of his sin? Did his suffering somehow justify his actions...would it reduce his penance? Did she really believe that her prayers could deliver Fernando from Satan?

They had not seen each other since a similar voyage about five years ago. Fernando and José again shared the same urge to find new life to the north, to make money and to enjoy life. More so than José, Fernando also wanted to escape the life of Mexico where everything reminded him of his roots. Another trip north would provide the distance, the space for time to help him forget.

The men wouldn't think of hiring a coyote to lead the way. They didn't have the money to pay, but mainly they didn't want the association with crime. In their minds, crossing like in the old days was a way of life, but in modern days with organized guided passage, it was criminal. They didn't want to be a victim at the hand of either *El Diablo* or *El Coyote*.

They talked a little about *El Diablo* and the stepped-up enforcement. They knew lives of their ilk had been altered, probably forever. They decided that getting to Phoenix was better than living an impoverished and fearful life in Mexico. Fernando, in particular, was against staying home. He insisted again, "We need to make some money and to live life!" After that was said, there really wasn't much more to talk about.

José had reservations that centered on *El Diablo*, but they largely went unexpressed. He decided to rest his fears on the back of Fernando as he followed him toward the crossing spot on a chilly night in early February.

Their first night afoot was uneventful. A full moon guided their path and they reached camp just after sunrise. This was average time for the twelve miles they had walked. Both men were in reasonably good shape. What they lacked in strength and endurance, they made up with drive and desire.

They took off their small, black backpacks and stashed them under a cluster of mesquite along a rocky drainage that headed west into the valley. This was camp. It was on the eastern side of the broad valley about a hundred yards from a windmill. They clutched their plastic gallon water jugs, the handles of which bore the marks of their tight grips, and walked toward the windmill.

As Fernando splashed water on his face and filled his jug he looked at José, who was looking at the ground around the windmill.

These men could not read words, but they were masters at understanding the complicated language written in dirt. He said nothing. He and José had noticed the same thing.

The tracks of other crossers were not as prevalent as in past years. Despite the lack of rain, which would have erased such sign, the familiar and comforting evidence of their kind was absent. Perhaps it was the increased enforcement patrols that reduced the number of crossers. But that had never been the case in past years. Most found a way around the enforcement without any major problem. They both acknowledged, silently, each man to himself, that Satan was present here, keeping crossers away.

Where they had left their backpacks was an area usually littered with sign of crossers that had been there a few days earlier. Large black plastic bags, used in the United States for garbage, were an essential element in the life of a border crosser. They were valuable tote bags for clothes and food, and shelter from rain and wind. All that existed in front of them were shredded bags tangled in the grass and low shrubs that had captured their passage in the wind. Most were tattered from months of wind and weather, and essentially useless.

They determined that no one had been here in weeks. Each man commented briefly on the elements of enforcement that could be responsible for what seemed like their isolation in a foreign setting. But there was no sign of the Border Patrol either, an aspect of the land that had always been the target of their search image. Without uttering the words *El Diablo*, they decided to spend only a few hours resting outside the draw next to some large rocks. They would resume their northward journey after eating and napping a little.

A front was moving through southern Arizona, bringing winds and the chance of rain. When clouds began to cover the noonday sun, Fernando and José were about five miles north of where they had stopped at daybreak. They had not intercepted the track of a vehicle or human along the cattle trails, drainage ways, fence lines, and two-track roads they had traversed. These were their normal routes, which in the past, had been littered with indications that others were ahead of them.

The cloud cover thickened and gradually the entire sky was gray and threatening rain. This was a typical pattern of winter storms in the desert, a circumstance they had encountered many times in the past. But this time, things were different. Both men sensed that the landscape now harbored something strange and threatening. They had no definite sign, which in a way was all the evidence they needed to reach that conclusion.

When they approached a large livestock tank, both men were tired from their fast pace. Sweat soaked through the bands of their caps and dripped down their faces and necks. A soft rain was sprinkling the surface of the pond. The gusty wind had subsided, and in the shelter of the earthen dam and large mesquites that surrounded the pond, the raindrops on the water were their only indication of rain. Those spattering on their faces or hands were unfelt amidst the profusion of sweat.

The two men squatted along the edge of the water and looked to the west, the direction from which the storm was coming. They saw a light hazy blue cast to the sky, an indication that this storm would pass by quickly. They knew from experience that there could be a major storm right behind this one. That's the way it was a decade ago, but the drought had diminished the need to cope with wet weather. Their conversation centered on how the dirt tanks had captured so much more water during their earlier treks through this land. It then turned to the lack of human sign at this popular watering hole. A subtle fear once again crept over them and they calculated their next move.

With a weariness tugging at their muscles, they decided to take refuge at the far end of the mesquite thicket, where the trees met the open scrubland away from the pond. They had never set up bivouac there but for unspoken reasons, they concluded that would be a safe place to rest. They would wait to see if the storm intensified and perhaps continue moving after dark. The nighttime had always been the safest time to travel. In summer the night afforded cooler temperatures; during winter it prevented getting cold. During all seasons it made them nearly invisible to the Border Patrol. But this night carried a suspense that was new and different. It was not in their nature to admit fear and surrender to it. Instead, they picked up their packs and filled water jugs, and headed around the pond in search of a bed.

They had kicked the cattle manure off the soft dirt and settled in, each on opposite sides of the large mesquite trunk. Exhaustion, an element that on earlier trips had been eclipsed by thoughts of his destination, was overtaking Fernando. He thought his weariness could be the result of the wear and tear he had exposed his body to over the years. He chose not to give that thought further consideration and closed his eyes.

What awakened him were familiar sounds. The one to his left was a man talking in Spanish over a radio. The other, a vehicle engine accelerating along the flats to his right, was getting louder. He sat up and quickly noticed that José was gone...nowhere to be seen. He paused, instinctively hunching low to the ground. Before he had a chance to get to his feet, the vehicle was forty feet away, crashing through the brush. The Spanish that spewed from the truck's public address system warned him to stay where he was and put his hands in the air. Fernando stayed on his knees. He knew he was caught. A strange sense of relief overcame him. As the Border Patrol agents ran up to him, he was comforted by the fact that he was surrendering to the power of a known entity, one that would not harm him.

Chapter 5

Southeast of the Cerro Colorado Mountains, Steve Black was gripped with fear of the worst-case scenario. As his pickup rolled over the rocky two-track in the rugged Tumacacori Mountains he adjusted the telemetry receiver that kept sliding against his right hip. He had not taken time to put it away before leaving his observation point, and now it was menacing him, breaking his stream of thoughts. He had been subconsciously accelerating to get to the relatively smooth valley road as fast as possible, then had to brake quickly to slow his pace so he wouldn't tear off his oil pan. Exhaustion was affecting his driving, but anxiety was playing a larger role.

He failed to find what he had set out for that morning. After a day of searching, he was positive, almost, that his subject was no longer in the area. Uncertainty was plaguing him. He could not predict the consequences of his disappearance, but past evidence led him to suspect the worst. As a forensic scientist, the sense of ambiguity had never been a problem. Hardly anything in science is certain. Ideas and "facts" are always changing as new data are gathered. However, in this case there was enough information to know that his quarry had moved and his location was unknown. That meant big trouble.

Roy Phillips unzipped the front door of the tent and took in the firmament of a descending moon and muted stars. He walked thirty feet to
the bush he had watered during the night and made one more contribu-
tion before throwing twigs on the smoldering mesquite coals. He lit the
lantern and the stove, and started water boiling and the cast iron
heating. He put a slab of bacon in the pan and went to the fire. With a
few fans of the shovel he ignited the kindling, and then added a fistful
of larger limbs and a few big pieces of wood on the stack. Within a
minute there was a blaze that signaled "wake-up" to the other three in
the tent. It was opening day of the javelina hunt in southern Arizona.

He had performed these acts countless times. He liked being the
first one up, experiencing the pre-dawn alone. This was the time
when owls chattered in the canopies of mesquite along the wash, or
hooted from the numerous cliffs and rocky outcrops around camp.
This canyon in the Cerro Colorados had been their camp for the past
five javelina hunts. It was at the end of a rough dirt road, the kind
that kept others hunters away.

This part of Arizona had always been their favorite hunting area
for javelina and white-tailed deer. The Cerro Colorados are rugged
mountains with steep ridges and numerous rocky canyons and cliffs.
Grass and brush covered most of the ground, except for clumps and
stringers of medium sized oak trees that grew in the areas near
springs, or where water gathered and was sheltered from the drying
influence of the sun. Dozens of little vegetated pockets and alcoves
were scattered along the bases of cliffs or the heads of canyons. Over
the years they learned these out-of-the-way places harbored javelina
and they looked forward to visiting them.

The sun was not even hinting its appearance on the horizon when
the side door to the tent unzipped from the inside and sounds of
laughter signaled the others were up. Henry stepped onto the
doormat, sat down on the stool outside, and put on his boots. He
already had on his camouflage outfit including his belt, which held
his Leatherman and skinning knife.

"Yo, Dad," he said as he walked toward the fire. "I smell bacon!"

"Eggs will be up soon, Budito. You want some hot chocolate?"

"Please!"

This father and son duo was at home in the desert. They had hiked and hunted together since Henry was four. Now sixteen, Henry was an "apple that fell real close to the tree." He had learned to read animal sign, spot game, make good observations, skin a deer, and all the other crafts one learns from a father who spent a lifetime with wildlife in wild places.

The next one out of the tent was Paul. He was a big guy whose voice resounded in the quiet of predawn. He was anxious to get up, and he looked forward to the rugged hike he would make to his favorite area. Mostly he liked to eat and waking up was a prerequisite to that. Since Roy liked being camp cook, they struck up a deal long ago. If Paul brought the food, Roy would cook it. Paul always brought lots of food.

"Pablo, how do you like your eggs?"

"I like 'em!" said Paul, as he took a seat near the fire next to Henry.

Henry smiled as he carefully sipped his hot cocoa. He had heard them exchange that morning greeting many times but still enjoyed their dialogue.

"Here's your coffee. Is James about to get up?"

Paul leaned forward and took the offering with both hands. As he settled back into his chair he said, "He's looking for one of his boots. He should be out in a couple days!"

Roy looked at Henry and they both grinned. "I'll draw him a map of where we're heading from camp, and we'll see if he can find us."

Paul looked into the fire and replied, "I think I better give him a map to his other boot or he'll never make it out of the tent before the sun sets tonight!"

"I smell bacon, I'm almost there!" called a voice from the tent.

"Hurry up, your dad is about to eat your share!" warned Henry.

As the food sizzled, Roy turned down the lantern. He pointed to the west and said, "Look at that moon." It was about to set behind the highest peak in the range. It was full and yellow. "That's worth the trip right there," he said.

They lived in Phoenix and treasured these times away from the city. Roy and Paul had spent much of their lives hunting, hiking and fishing around Arizona. Roy was a wildlife biologist with the state wildlife agency and was outdoors a lot. Paul was an engineer by education and profession, and worked for a company that kept him hopping. These were the only times they could relax together in nature.

"What happened to the lantern?" asked James, as he made his way carefully to the fire.

"Look at that moon," answered Henry.

"It's never that big in the city, is it?" responded James. He took his place by the fire, and Roy walked over to him.

"Good timing, I just finished mixing your cocoa," jabbed Roy as he handed James his cup.

"I planned it that way," countered James. Paul looked at Henry and rolled his eyes. There was a smirk on his face, as there was all around. Fathers and sons bonding was a major enjoyment of their hunts, and it was very present that morning.

"Dad, what will this moon do to the pigs? Will they be bedded down early?" Henry was already engaged in the hunt. As he sat eating his bacon and eggs, he was on the slopes and ridges in his mind.

"They'll be feeding in the moonlight but they'll be around the wet spring areas or the cactus patches nearby. We should be able to find them quickly. But remember, javelina are where you find 'em!"

Henry heard that maxim before and knew exactly what it meant. He was anxious to do what was needed to find a javelina. That meant scouring all the hundreds of nooks and crannies that were out there under rocky overhangs sheltered by clumps of woody catclaw bush. To him, these were very special places, and he relished finding the fresh sign of a herd. He always had the sense when looking into a brush-hidden cave that he was the first human ever to peer into its dark depths.

Chapter 6

Darrel Yost was sitting behind his big desk with a detailed wall map of the border between Arizona and Mexico behind him. He was a 20-year veteran of the Border Patrol who made section chief twelve years out of the academy. He was charged with all Border Patrol activity between Nogales and California. His feet, which were decorated with new cowboy boots that revealed not a nick, were propped on his desk. These dress boots also signaled no intention of going afield that day, which was the usual case. As he would soon learn, that would change. When he arrived at work, there was a message on his phone from the radio dispatcher. "Black needs to talk with you first thing in the morning. He'll call at eight sharp."

Yost had a queer grin on his face. If this thing fell into place the way he had orchestrated it, he could move up the Border Patrol food chain and earn a spot at the state office in Phoenix or even at the regional office in Albuquerque.

"Yes, I know that road. Okay, I'll meet you at the turnoff. I should be there in two hours." Logan didn't even bother to ask Sheldon for details. He knew by the sound of his voice that this was the evidence they were looking for. Last week's evidence was telling, but Logan felt certain that Sheldon now had proof positive. It would justify his actions, the ones that got him transferred. He did not envision the aftermath or any event beyond his vindication.

When his phone rang, Yost almost herniated his gut lifting his legs and reaching for the phone simultaneously. "What's up?" he snapped.

"He moved north into the Pajaritos about eight miles. Then I lost the signal. Either he's headed back south beyond signal reach, or his transmitter has failed. He's nowhere in the country according to his device...if it's working."

"Shit. Where did you look?"

"From the Altar Valley all the way east of Nogales to Douglas. I even got the Apache pilot to cruise the area for an hour. There's no sign of him."

"Well, do you think he went into Mexico and is too far south to pick up, or his transmitter died? Maybe he gave the pack to someone who headed home. I don't know...you're the expert. What's your best guess?"

"I think the transmitter failed, and he's still in the area. Or at least he is not far out of it. I was monitoring his movement north of Nogales then he appeared to head east...but the signal was erratic, like the beginnings of a power failure."

"That unit is brand new, and the battery should last two years. Tell me," Yost sighed, "what's your best guess as to his location right now?"

Steve Black knew that there was a lot riding on his answer. About a year ago they placed the tracking device in a backpack of a crosser they suspected was robbing and killing other crossers. They had meager evidence for their suspicion, mainly the crosser's location near a known cache of stolen property northwest of Nogales, and the possession of a long knife among other curious items he was carrying. They mainly wanted to see if the technique would work, but when circumstantial evidence more clearly linked their man with recent deaths the Border Patrol began to pay more attention to his movements. And that's when Yost invested much effort and hope into the notion that this man was the killer, "*El Diablo*." Tracking this crosser's movements had become Yost's "Plan A," his ticket to a promotion.

Black paused, and carefully said, "I'm not real sure. But if I had to bet, I would say he's heading east. He moved north, and I was expecting him to move west, but he trailed in an easterly direction...assuming the transmitter was working properly. He was at the Santa Cruz about five miles from the border when I lost him. I never got the impression from his movements that returning to Mexico was part of his plan. But there's a chance that he could have gone north and then headed west of Nogales."

"Christ, east...west...which one is it?" Yost seldom expressed frustration so blatantly. "Sorry, I was just about to go into a meeting, and I really cannot even think about this now. Thanks, Steve. I will make some phone calls and get back with you. Will you be home, or on your cell?"

"Either one. Right now, I need some sleep."

"Okay, good job. I'll be in touch."

As Sheldon started his truck to head toward his rendezvous with Logan, he realized he had forgotten his gun. He usually carried it in the pickup to shoot coyotes and rattlesnakes. He had been taking it inside at night ever since last summer when he feared that crossers would steal his truck during their midnight passage through his ranch.

He'd never been fearful of these men before. He grew up with them. His grandfather, father and he had employed them for odd ranch jobs. They were a big part of his labor force when he was

expanding his operations in the 50s. He knew the breed was different now, and more desperate. That's what made him more
apprehensive. And elements of the landscape were acting in mysteri-
ous ways nowadays. Or perhaps these mysteries were accompanying
the new breed of crosser. What he was about to show Logan reflected
these unknowns, and hopefully would add some understanding.

With the motor left running he went inside and retrieved his pistol. He looked at the cylinder to make sure he had all rounds in
place. As he stepped off the back porch and headed to his truck he
heard the cell phone ringing. He had left it on his front seat. He was
a second too late in answering. He pushed some buttons to learn
who had called. It was Logan.

Jay Sharp had just repaired two miles of fence that crossers had cut
at various points over the past month. As he drove his pickup out of
rugged Las Guijas Mountains at the northeastern fringe of the Altar
Valley he thought about fences and human lives. He had helped his
father, long ago deceased, with this same chore thirty-five years ago.
Fencing had become a real problem in the last five years. With the
price of beef diminishing his income and the cost of feeding his
livestock during the drought increasing expenses, the extra burden of
labor and material for fencing was turning his cattle operation into a
losing proposition.

The government didn't seem to have a handle on the situation.
The Border Patrol agents he encountered were never in the backcountry off the roads where all the crossers moved. He despised
seeing their green trucks along the roads. He resisted giving the
Border Patrol keys for access to his private land, but gave in when
threatened by them. They claimed he would be interfering with
federal investigations if he did not cooperate. Sharp avoided the
federal agents, and despised the statistics they posted in the Tucson
newspaper. He made up his mind that they were the biggest part of a
huge problem.

As he headed to his home in Tucson, Sharp thought about when he left the ranch thirty years ago to join the Army. He never went back except to help his dying father. He was an only child and now the sole heir of a ranching operation that once encompassed forty thousand acres of southern Arizona. Between the environmentalists and the crossers, the ranch had shrunk significantly in the last ten years.

The presence of an endangered species forced him to relinquish his twenty thousand acre lease of State land that had been part of the operation since the 1930s. That move essentially cut his income in half. On a federal lease the family had for decades he had to maintain all the improvements like windmills and fences as part of the lease agreement. When they told him he had to cut his herd by fifty percent and just use the land in the winter months, he argued for economic reasons. The crossers were doing the damage, not his cattle. His sky-rocketing expenses were bad enough. When they began cutting into the income side of the ledger he called it quits. A quail conservation group bought his Federal lease, and had regular fence-repair outings for its members to keep the cattle out and the grass available for quail cover.

All Jay Sharp had left was about thirteen thousand acres of parched private land, and a bitter attitude.

Chapter 7

Long shadows from the setting moon were draping the slopes of the western ridges, projecting images of the giant rock pinnacles. These spires were part of the jagged outline of the Cerro Colorados. The band of hunters didn't notice the scene until they reached the ridge top and looked around toward the country they were about to traverse. They all took in deep breaths, and were glad to be on the familiar ridge they would travel toward the west.

They never carried guns with loaded chambers during twilight treks since nothing was visible to shoot. There was a slight hint of lighted sky to the east, and a stirring breeze from the direction of their stalk to the west. They could take the ridgeline west or follow the cliff line at the southern base of the ridge. Either way they would end up at the place they would begin their search for javelina.

They usually stayed together, but that morning Henry wanted to take the lower cliff line route. He had a feeling that he would find some fresh sign in one of the caves. Roy often went with his son's instincts, which had proven fruitful in past hunts. In earlier years he would have escorted him, but that day he thought his son wanted to make the discovery by himself so he let him drop off the southern slope and head west along the lower reaches of the short cliffs.

"We'll meet you at the point just east of Suicide Hill in about an hour. Check your watch. Good luck, Budito," whispered Roy.

Henry nodded and headed down. Paul and James decided to walk along the northern slope about half way down the ridge. As the foursome split up their images, barely visible in that eerie light between a setting full moon and a sunrise, soon blended with the landscape, and then disappeared. Roy was on the ridge top alone.

The moonlight that had guided his footsteps was quickly fading as a pink hue appeared on the eastern horizon. Birds occasionally flitted from the grass and low shrubs. Some were chirping the beginnings of territorial calls, signaling the promise of spring to the desert grasslands of the Cerro Colorados.

Roy walked quickly but quietly westward, wanting to be in position when the others reached the far end of the ridge about a half-mile ahead. His parental instinct caused him to hedge toward the southern side of the ridge so he would be within earshot of any sound from Henry. Although he did not fear for the safety of his son, there was always that fatherly notion.

These mountains had always been their lone hunting grounds, but during the previous year they noticed an influx of others in the area. The crossers were becoming more numerous. Last year they found in many caves and under clumps of dense trees discarded food cans with labels in Spanish and black plastic bags with old clothes and other miscellaneous supplies. One cave was transformed into a fairly sophisticated shelter. A sotol stalk draped with a black plastic bag marked its entrance. The re-purposed trash bag served to keep wind out and warmth inside. It was evident the crossers were spending a significant amount of time in the mountains, perhaps to evade the Border Patrol, which stayed mainly along the roads.

To his left about one hundred yards Roy could see a line of rocks that protruded out of the hill slope. These were the tops of the cliffs that Henry was walking below. He angled toward them, figuring he would find a good spot to check the south valley for javelina. It was getting light enough for his binoculars to gather adequate images and detect wildlife moving in the valley and on the opposite hillside.

As he approached the rocky area, the south valley opened up below him. He could hear bird song in the mesquite growing along the
rocky wash in the valley's depths. He soon found a rock outcrop that
afforded a great perch for observations, and sat down. He didn't
bother to take off his daypack since he planned to stay only a few
minutes. With his binoculars resting on top of his walking stick, he
began to scour the far hillside.

Traversing the slope was difficult in the twilight of early morning.
Henry was athletic, a good football player and track runner. He knew
agility was critical on the rocky surface, and his goal was silence, not
speed. He did not want to spook any javelina he might find along the
base of this ridge. He wanted to locate them before they detected
him. He had discovered the best hideouts during earlier hunts and
was anxious to see what they held on this mild February morning. He
knew stealth was the key to a successful hunt.

As he neared the bottom, he made his way through a mass of
mesquite and large boulders that, eons ago, had tumbled off the
main body of the cliffs to the north. He could see the silhouettes of
these cliffs projecting above him to his right. He had taken this route
many times before, and felt confident he was in the right spot to
begin his search of the caves.

When he approached level ground, he took a deep breath. Although he was far from winded, he wanted to clear his senses in
preparation of what he would find. He knew that javelina hunting was
a combination of being able to smell, see, and hear them. The air
was still, and he knew he would have to be near them to detect their
scent. Since it was a little too dark to see well his strategy over the
next half hour would be to keep alert, stop frequently, and ever so
slowly make his way along the rocks, searching for sign.

As he walked along the base of the ridge's southern aspect, his
attention turned to the ground and a small red object partially
hidden beneath a sparse covering of light brown leaves scattered on

a cluster of rocks. He immediately recognized the "blood bean." About the size of a pinto bean, its common name is Southwest coral bean. Scientists named it *Erythrina flabelliformis*. Henry had learned from his dad that they bring good luck on a hunt. He leaned over and picked up the charm, and with his gloved hand placed it carefully in the pocket of his hunting vest. He gained a sense of confidence from his discovery.

He adjusted the rifle sling on his shoulder, and took a couple of steps forward. From the brush fifty yards ahead Henry saw movement near what appeared to be a shallow cave. It was quick and quiet, and over in an instant. His first impression was that it was not a javelina. They are gregarious and usually spooked en masse, making a woofing noise to communicate danger. He thought he had heard a grunt, or perhaps a guttural noise, but he wasn't sure.

His sense was that the movements of this animal, if indeed it were an animal, were too fluid, not jerky like the start-and-stop motion of a javelina. This creature instantly vanished out of sight into the brush beyond. It had spotted him first, and made its escape in one quick motion.

He decided to play out this encounter and discover what else might be in the rocky shelter. It could have been a lone javelina that had strayed from the group. Since it was early and the light was still dim perhaps he had not registered an accurate view of the event. He decided to stay put for five or ten minutes and wait for better light conditions. Unmoving, he maintained a silent vigil.

When he could clearly see birds as they called from the small trees in the rocky valley to the south he took a few steps forward, bending over to avoid some straggly mesquite limbs that partially blocked his progress. He hugged closely to the cliff base at his right, glancing frequently at the wooded valley to his left. Beyond it was the dry creek bottom with scattered trees on a relatively flat and open plain. He decided to see what was in the shallow cave where he had spotted movement earlier before climbing onto some rocks to get a view of the valley.

His progress was amazingly fast and silent. When he reached the area of the cave he found no obvious sign of javelina, such as tracks in the soft ground. The cave entrance was about eight feet high and twice as wide and deep. As he stepped into the cave he could easily see open and empty food cans, two black plastic bags, and a black jacket that appeared in good shape. A pile of charred sticks indicated that someone had built a fire recently. A white halo of wood ash surrounded the black and burned wood. This scene was reminiscent of the crosser camps they found last year.

He poked at the jacket with his walking stick, and then looked at the soft dirt under the trees farther in the cave. Tracks of either humans or animals were not evident. He could see broken limbs dangling from nearby mesquite and acacia, and evidence of the brush being bent and broken. He thought about what a good camping place this cave afforded. Abundant wood was all around, available for a fire and hiding cover from the Border Patrol.

Last year military helicopters had buzzed low within a mile of their hunt camp, causing Henry's dad to comment that he should be vigilant for crossers when he was out hunting. "They're all around nowadays, and you never can tell how desperate they are," he warned.

Henry's thoughts strayed from javelina, and he began to think of his safety. What would he do if he encountered a band of wayward crossers? He was alone and that question lingered. He paused and glanced around, looking for something he could only vaguely sense. He felt very vulnerable.

He took his rifle from his shoulder, grasping it with both hands in a ready position. His dad had taught him to rack a round in the chamber only after he spotted his quarry, so he was not prepared for a quick shot in self-defense if one were needed. He squatted slightly and moved to the other side of the cave entrance, then looked around and up at the rocks nearby. He thought his best move would be to get onto the rocks for a better view. He was not thinking of javelina.

He stepped out of the cave and looked around. There was a path that headed to a pile of boulders ahead, and he moved quickly along it. He legs were shaking a little as he reached the rocks fifteen feet from the cave. The area was devoid of brush, and he could see the bare soil. There was evidence of something having been dragged along the path. He thought it could have been a large branch gathered for firewood from the base of one of the scattered mesquite trees growing between the rock piles.

As he climbed onto a large rock he felt a little safer. Henry listened for any evidence of life. He heard the flushing of quail from the thornscrub up the valley about two hundred yards. Something had disturbed them. He focused his attention and senses in that area but saw nothing. Part of the cliff blocked his view up the valley, so after couple minutes at his elevated outpost he decided to move to the west, the direction he had been heading, for a better look. If indeed he had spooked a fragmented herd of javelina, perhaps he could spot them wandering among the rocks and scrub of the valley.

He realized the path out to the flatland about twenty feet to the south was covered with a thicket of mature vegetation that required him to crawl underneath it along a trail of sorts. When he got on his knees he spotted a tennis shoe along one side of the passageway beneath an overhang of a small oak. Creeping along toward the shoe his attention was directed five feet to his right. There, beneath the main trunk of a small oak at the base of the rock, was a ball cap partly covered with leaves. The area under the oak had recently been disturbed and sandy ground was abundantly visible, as if the leaves had been scraped onto the cap.

He looked beyond the cap ten feet toward where the bare ground met the rock. His eyes moved toward the cliff base and a string of vegetation that shrouded it. Entangled in a mass of small dead limbs and grass he noticed something that was a mix of red and white and black. He did not recognize the object at first glance but as his vision focused he saw what he thought was an open skull. Rather than an elongated skull of a deer or javelin, with which he was familiar, this was round...melon-shaped. The top of the skull was missing and the exposed white bone was covered with what appeared to be mats of black hair and blood. He then noticed some cloth at the far end of the skull. Puzzled by what he had discovered, his intent gaze into the shadowy undergrowth finally brought into full view what he was seeing. It was a human body.

Henry quickly scrambled through the thicket and rose instantly to his feet on the other side. He immediately chambered a round into his 30-06 rifle and began shouting for his dad, hoping to scare away whatever might be lurking in the caves ahead. Adrenalin was controlling his actions. He was in a fight mood, and instantly alert to any movement nearby.

He scurried away from cliff and onto the flatland, repeatedly calling for his dad. He was terrified by his first view of a mutilated human body. He thought that perhaps he had spooked the killer earlier and that it still might be nearby. He was torn between heading west toward his rendezvous with the others, and backtracking to camp. He kept yelling, "Dad, dad, come here quick!"

The voice coming from below sounded frantic. Roy looked in that direction...his view was blocked by the cliff tops. He was panic-stricken. He knew that Henry was in trouble. He knew that his son had quit hunting, and was threatened by something.

"Henry," he shouted. His voice echoed off the cliffs. He paused for a response, listening, searching with his eyes wide open for any movement below.

"Dad! Where are you?"

"Are you okay? Henry! Are you okay?"

He waited for what seemed an eternity, but detected nothing.

Roy was on his feet and traversing the area above the cliff line when he heard his son again. "Dad, come here, quick."

"Can you hear me?" he responded.

"Dad, come here, hurry!"

"Are you okay?"

"Dad!"

There was urgency in Henry's voice. Henry was fairly mild mannered, and Roy knew it took a lot to get Henry to cry out that way.

"Henry, are you okay?"

His son was terrified. He could tell that Henry had encountered something that rattled him, alarmed him to the core.

"I'm right above you. I'm coming," Roy shouted in Henry's direction. He stumbled on the rocky surface as he scrambled in search of a pathway down. His legs were wobbling with fear, and he realized that he must be careful or he would slip and fall. A fall to his right would be fatal.

"I'm coming," he yelled again. He was not sure whether or not Henry had heard him.

After what seemed like forever, Roy finally found a place where he could scramble down the cliff through a fracture in the rocks. He made the mistake of abandoning his walking stick, choosing instead to grab hold of tree limbs with both hands as he slid down the chute. After wildly skidding about fifty feet, mainly on his butt, and using his feet to break his descent, he came to a ledge. He could go no further. He was stuck, with no hope of readily getting to his son.

He got to his feet and adjusted his pack, which had slid up and was resting high on his back. He limped to the edge of the ledge, realizing that he had sprained his left ankle. His hunting vest was torn, and his nerves shattered. Immediately below him he could see Henry walking away from the cliff and to the west. At first he thought he was in pursuit of javelina since his rifle was pointing forward.

"Henry!" he screamed. "I'm up here."

Henry stopped and looked at the cliff. He instantly saw Roy, waving both arms.

"What's the matter? Are you okay?"

"We gotta get some help...or something! There's a dead body in that cave."

"Are you okay?"

"Yes."

"Don't worry, I'm here." Roy could tell that Henry was on high alert. He had some comfort seeing his son and knowing that with his rifle Roy could afford protection from anything that might put Henry in physical danger. What he did not know was how to provide mental comfort at a distance. He needed to get to him, and fast.

"Henry, it's okay. Can you see a way down from the ledge I'm on?"

Henry did not immediately respond to his question. "I need you to help me get down. Should I go left or right?"

Henry stopped pacing, and stood still. He walked to an area immediately in front of Roy, but he stayed in the open at a distance from the cliffs as he scanned the rocky terrain below Roy.

"Henry, you're safe. Which way should I go to get down from here?"

Standing still and looking briefly to the west, Henry glanced up at his dad. His focus was the precipice below Roy, where he looked into the brush with a wildly intense gaze.

"Can you see a way down?" yelled Roy.

After about thirty seconds, Henry said, "The cliff breaks up that way about a quarter mile. Can you head over there?"

Henry pointed to the west with his walking stick. Roy knew that he would have to climb back up the shoot he had just slid down, and the thought of doing that with his injured ankle was overwhelming. He didn't want to turn his back on his son.

"Can you get up here?" he asked.

"Where are Paul and James?" Henry replied quickly.

"They're to the west waiting for us."

Henry turned his attention to the west. He seemed to want to stay away from the cliffs.

"Did you see anyone else?" asked Roy.

"I don't know for sure...I think so. I'm not sure. Have you seen anyone this morning?"

"No. Henry, don't worry, you're safe. Are you hurt?"

"No, I'm okay."

Roy knew that his son was starting to think strategically, and not react instinctively out of fear.

"Henry, can you get to me on a direct route that will keep us within sight of each other? I sprained my ankle and it's a little stiff. I can walk, but not too well. I'm okay, but can you get up to me?"

Henry focused on the cliff line in front of him. He pointed to a spot about two hundred yards to the west of Roy. Just then, Paul and James appeared up the ridge about fifty yards behind Roy.

"What's the matter? We heard you guys yelling," inquired Paul.

Roy looked up at Paul, then back at Henry. "Pablo, can you get down to Henry? Check to your right, and see if there's a way down to him. I messed up my ankle. Someone needs to get to him."

"Is he okay?"

"I think so. But he's scared about something at the base of these cliffs. He said he found a dead guy."

"A dead guy? Where?"

"I'm not sure. Can you get down to him?"

"I'm sure we can find a way."

Roy looked over at Henry, who had seen Paul and James, but didn't hear any of the conversation. He was moving to the northwest toward the cliff.

"Henry," called Paul. "I'm on my way down."

Henry began to run to the passageway he had described to his dad. He disappeared behind an outcropping of the cliff to the west of Roy. Paul and James were also gone from Roy's view when he looked back up the ridge. There was nothing he could do now but hope they connected on the ridge to the west. He decided he would concentrate on getting to the ridge top, and meet with them up there.

Roy said a prayer for his son and for his friends. He looked around then headed up the cut in the cliff that he had slid down. After about ten minutes he reached the crest of the ridge. It felt good to walk, or limp, on level ground. On the breeze from the west he could hear voices being carried by the wind.

"Paul!" he yelled. "Paul!"

"Here we are."

"Do you have Henry with you?"

"Yah, he's here."

Roy moved into the wind toward the voices. He first spotted their camouflage hats as they progressed among the brush of ocotillo and sotol. Paul was talking with a grin on his face, which immediately draped Roy in a sense of relief. He stopped to get a good look at Henry in his binoculars. His face reflected an amalgam of feelings, calm and joy, and an underlying fear. Roy focused on his son's fear, and walked forward.

As the group approached Roy, he was tucking his binoculars into his shirt. Henry moved to the front of the threesome, and was the first to reach Roy. He extended his arms to his dad, who enfolded him, and began to cry.

Chapter 8

His dogs wriggled at his feet as Logan put down their food dishes. He did not give them their customary head and neck rub, but scooted out the gate as they ate. Luna, his favorite dog, looked at him and wagged her tail as he headed across the lawn to his personal truck. Logan missed her animated good-bye, but he was on a mission. He wanted to know what Sheldon had found, and he was nearly two hours from finding out.

Logan had turned off Interstate 19 at Amado and was headed west along the Arivaca Road when his cell phone rang. "Logan," he answered.

"Sam, can you hear me?"

"Yah, what's up?"

"You're breaking up a little, can you hear me okay?"

"10-4 Nate. What's up?"

"I just wanted to tell you that when I got into the office this morning there was lots of commotion. Yost got a call from his man, Black. They got wind of a pretty fresh body. Seems like there's a chance his man headed northwest, but they lost the signal."

"Where was the last location?"

"I just heard Yost on the phone, so I don't have all the details of the guy they're following. But I did hear Yost use the word 'killed.' I figured you'd want to know that Yost is heading down your way, somewhere in the Cerro Colorados, I think."

"Did he say what the cause of death was?" Logan's cell started breaking and he couldn't hear Chavez's response. The Sierrita Mountains were blocking the phone signal from Tucson.

"Can you hear me, Nate? Nate, are you there?"

The signal faded, and his phone beeped...he lost the signal. Logan knew he would be out of cell range until he returned to Amado. That would be when he headed home, perhaps sometime tomorrow, or later, depending on what Sheldon had found.

Yost was on the track of a different killer even though he had given some credibility to the theory that Logan and Sheldon had formulated. But given half a chance, Yost would try to undermine their efforts. Logan drove on, smiling, knowing he was off duty and that his destination was isolated from the influences of Yost. Sheldon's ranch was locked up, sheltered from invasion by the investigations of Yost and his cohorts. He and Sheldon would be alone, away from government interference, and able to look at the facts in a leisurely manner. If circumstances were just right today could be the day he and Sheldon had been waiting for since last year.

"I guess he did go north and west. Your hunch was right. This body could lend credence to your tracking information, Steve. If he headed across the Pajaritos, he would hit the Cerro Colorados. And if the body is as fresh as they say, the dogs will find him. We could have enough information to end the work of *El Diablo*. We'll lose the big reason why wets aren't crossing as much, but we need to get rid of the public backlash this sick killer is generating. Can you imagine him beheading his victims? He's one deranged wacko. Washington is calling the regional office a couple times a week about it."

Yost made his statement with the conviction and interest of a casual bystander. His goal was not to end the deaths of crossers. He had no particular interest in proving that murder was occurring along the border. He had no sympathy for the thousands of Mexicans who crossed the border. To him, they were merely statistics. His main interest was in promoting up the ranks and getting totally out of the field. He also wanted to be active so that boredom would not settle in. Since he hired Black he was successful in both aspects of his plan.

"He would've had to haul ass to get up there, unless he hitched a ride. We've never had a fresh body to pin this guy to, but now finally we do...I hope. Did you get good directions to the valley?" asked Black.

"Yes, and I have the GPS coordinates and an Apache helicopter if we need it. The chopper is on standby to be the aerial spotter for the dogs. We got the good dogs this time."

"Good deal," Black said, looking out the window to his right.

"You know, it's been three days since you lost the signal. That's plenty of time for him to get up there and do his thing. All he'd have to do is go south from there, and he's at the center of his killing field."

Yost drove along, quietly glowing in the potential rewards for his efforts. He had a tremendous amount of resources at his disposal, and felt confidant that Plan A would pay off, one way or another.

Steve Black looked ahead at the straight road that dipped into all the drainages heading west into Altar Wash. He had come to love this country over the past year since being asked to join Yost's team. He felt that his skills were being put to good use and was comfortable with his standing in the organization.

What he felt uncomfortable about was Yost's silence as they were closing in on potentially indisputable evidence. It seemed Yost was isolating himself from reality. As a scientist, Black had prepared himself to view this corpse as further evidence that would be analyzed and added to the body of existing information. Black knew that Yost had already made up his mind. He knew that when they arrived at their destination, they could be in conflict with the evidence at hand.

Logan drove up to the Texas gate and opened the lock with a key that was stashed in the glove box of his truck. He saw fresh tracks made by Sheldon's pickup as he exited his vehicle to close and lock the gate. He slowly drove along a dry creek bed lined with white oak, and saw Sheldon sitting in his truck about a mile from the gate.

As he pulled up to Sheldon, he noticed a look of fear on the face of his friend. "Howdy, Stayton. Are you okay?"

"Oh ya, I'm fine. I've been thinking a lot about what's out here, and it has me weary. How are you doing?"

"Good. Good. Hey, Chavez called me. Seems Yost has a fresh body in the Cerro Colorados. He's heading there now."

"Huh. This is getting interesting."

"You think we got the answer here, do you?"

"Yes I do. I think we've been right all along. I think we have some real good proof. I'm a little scared of something."

"What's that?" asked Logan

"Well, I don't know what will happen next. This could bring a whole lot of attention down here. I think I'm too old to deal with it."

"I know what you mean. I have that same feeling. But we struck out on this trail and we had good intentions all along the way. If we're near the end that means we did a good job. What happens after that is out of our control. I'm sure that I'll have a lot of answering to do, but that doesn't have me nervous. I want to see what happens next."

"I do too, but I'm still a little bit scared...of lots of things," confessed Sheldon. "You want to take two vehicles? It's just down the road less than a mile."

"Sure, two's fine, why not?"

"I think that's a good idea. Follow me."

The sun was just hitting the canyon bottom as their trucks entered the dry creek bed. The sycamore trees were still dormant and leafless, and the sunlight penetrated their sparse canopy, illuminating the red rocks and bluffs on the lower slopes of the western hills. The effects of this light made the place seem special, surrealistic.

"How could such a place be the site of such a horrific act?" Logan wondered as he followed Sheldon's pickup, rolling slowly over the smooth rocks of the drainage.

Sheldon headed south along the eastern fringe of the creek and then followed its bend to the left. He parked in an opening under a large ash tree, driving forward far enough to allow Logan a spot to pull in behind him. When he exited his truck Logan noticed that Sheldon had his pistol in a belt holster. It had been hidden from view back where they first had met. He was somewhat startled yet comforted by the sight of it.

"It's back in them rocks just outside the creek bed on the other side," said Sheldon. His head was down, watching where he stepped on the river rocks. Logan got the distinct impression that Sheldon was separating himself from what he was about to show him, as if in some state of denial, or disbelief.

Logan waited until Sheldon struck out on a path then followed about ten feet behind. In the dry sand along the parched creek Logan noticed a shoe print. It was a single print, indicating where its maker had stepped off the rocks. He also noticed horse tracks, presumably Sheldon's from yesterday afternoon when he was checking cattle and made his discovery.

Some of the cobblestones had been overturned and the dried sycamore leaves scraped away. As he continued to follow Sheldon out of the drainage and onto a short, gently sloping bench immediately adjacent to it he found more evidence that the ground had been disturbed. The wispy twigs of a giant sycamore limb that rested on the lip of the bench had recently been broken. They had not been used for a fire but were scattered below the large limb.

"Seems like there was a struggle here, Stayton," commented Logan as he looked around.

Sheldon didn't look back, but replied, "You need to see this. You haven't seen anything yet."

Logan stopped his careful inspection and walked more directly to catch up to Sheldon, who was looking off to his right at the base of the red boulders that formed a cave. Thirty feet from the men was a black jacket and black garbage bag full of something, lying at the base of the rim rock that edged the drainage at the toe of the slope. About ten feet away the water had carved out another small cavern that was hidden by short acacia and mesquite shrubs. Freshly broken branches indicated that this shelter had recently been used.

Logan stopped next to Sheldon, who said nothing as he stared straight ahead. Logan eyes followed Sheldon's to the base of the rocky rim between the caves. Logan looked down near his feet at the drag marks leading to where Sheldon was focused. He could see what appeared to be dried blood in the dirt. He followed the drag path forward to the rocks, noting a large pool of dried black liquid – blood.

Under a scrubby oak he saw an arm covered with blue denim. He knelt down, and saw the rest of the human body partly protruding from the left extent of the right cave. The corpse apparently had been dragged into the cave on a trail that started near the rocky creek and went through the brush.

"I didn't go beyond this point. I could see enough from here. But I did find something that proves our case over there at the base of those boulders." Sheldon pointed to the left, where a scattering of large rocks met flat ground. The dark soil was bare of vegetation for several feet. Logan stood up and walked over to the area. Sheldon followed him.

"Look, check out the ground over there," Sheldon said as he gestured to Logan.

Logan slowly walked to the area, watching where he placed his feet. He treated the place like a crime scene, making sure not to destroy any evidence. He proceeded to the bare ground and stopped. Bending over, he placed his hands on his knees and studied the sign.

"That's it, partner. I think we got what we need."

Chapter 9

"Your GPS coordinates were perfect, sir. Thanks. I'm Sergeant Lyons, Border Patrol. This is Officer Johnson."

Roy didn't get up from his camp chair to greet the two men who had exited the Apache helicopter. With his leg propped up on a cooler and a bag of ice draped over his foot he shook hands while remaining seated.

"Good old Garmin 12, the best GPS unit going! We have camp marked so we can find our way back in the dark. Sometimes we get hung up field dressing javelina after sunset." responded Roy. "You guys got here real quick. We just got back to camp. I think I made the call from my cell phone about 8:00 a.m. That's a thirty-minute response time. Did you fly out of Tucson?"

"Yes sir."

"Were you on standby or something?"

"We're always ready for something, sir."

Roy put his hand on Henry's shoulder. They had been sitting close together since returning to camp. Henry had not spoken about his encounter, and Roy was giving him space. He could tell his son was still pretty shaken up.

"This is my son, Henry."

"Pleased to meet you," said Lyons. Johnson stepped forward, shook Henry's hand, then stepped back and remained silent.

"Coffee?" offered Roy.

"No thanks. It messes with my stomach when I fly."

The other agent stood behind Lyons. He smiled and only gestured in response to Roy's offer, and Lyon's answers.

The silent agent looked around, spotting Paul and James coming up the canyon with a load of firewood. He kept watching them as they struggled with their load.

"Those are the other two members of our hunting party," commented Roy, keeping an eye on the quiet one.

"Were they with you at the crime scene?" asked Lyons.

"They were near it, but not actually at the scene. Henry was the only one who saw the body. We wanted to preserve the evidence for you professionals so we avoided the area."

"You're retired law enforcement?" asked Lyons.

"Yes sir. I got out in January 2000 after twenty years. Loved every minute of it."

"State or local?"

"State game and fish."

"Cool. I wanted to get on with fish and game in California, but you need a college degree."

"I hear that a lot. It's the same here."

"This pay's better though, so I'm happy."

"I hear that even more," said Roy, smiling.

Lyons looked over at Paul and James, who were sitting about forty feet away under the kitchen canopy. They were talking to each other, and preparing breakfast. He then knelt down on one knee and focused his attention on Henry, who had avoided eye contact the entire time. "Henry, can you tell me what you saw?"

Roy looked at his son, then at Lyons. "He's still a little shook up," Roy said calmly. "We haven't talked about it ourselves yet. But I understand you need timely information."

Roy moved his hand from Henry's right shoulder and grabbed his thigh. "Budito, are you ready to talk about it?"

Henry choked up a little. He leaned forward and rubbed his face. "All I saw was a body in the brush at the entrance to this cave."

"Had the body been dead for awhile? Was there an odor?"

"No, sir...no odor."

"Could you see what might have caused the death? I mean did the person fall off the cliff?"

"I don't think so. He was kind of tucked in between this little tree and the rocks."

"Was it a man?"

"I'm not sure."

"What was he wearing?"

"All I saw was light blue jacket, like a Levi jacket."

"Could you see any of his body, like his face, or his legs?"

"No, sir...not his face. All I saw was some bones and some muscle with dried blood and hair around it."

"Dry blood is blackish, not red. Are you fairly certain you saw blood?"

"Pretty sure. I've seen dried deer and javelina blood. I think it was blood. It was reddish though, so maybe it was fresh blood."

"And there was absolutely no odor, like of decaying flesh?"

"Not that I could smell."

"Can you pinpoint exactly where this was? Here, I have a pretty detailed map."

Roy was relieved that the interrogation turned from the body to the location. He could tell Henry was getting fairly upset having to recall his ordeal.

"You don't need a map," Roy interjected. "Just get in the chopper and fly over that ridge directly to the right of the highest point." Roy turned around slightly in his chair and pointed to the southwest. "The back side of the ridge is lined with a cliffy rocky area at the bottom. Just land about mid way along the cliff and start looking. You should be able to pick up Henry's boot prints. He has a pretty unique pattern that has 'Rocky' written on it. See," Roy said, pointing to the ground at Henry's feet.

Lyons nodded. "Okay, great. Thanks. I have one last question, Henry. Did you walk around the body very much? How long were you there?"

"I was crawling along on my hands and knees when I saw the body, and took off right away when I realized what it was."

"How far were you from it?"

"Maybe fifteen feet I suppose."

"We really appreciate your call and the information," said Lyons, shaking hands with the hunters. As he turned toward the chopper and began to walk away, Johnson was shaking hands with Roy.

"Can we find out what you discover?" Roy asked Lyons.

"You will read about it in the paper," interrupted Johnson, as he turned to follow Lyons.

The pilot ignited the jet engines as the two men hopped aboard. Within a minute the Apache lifted off the ground about twenty feet, and headed straight for the ridge. When it disappeared from Roy's view he looked at Henry, who was looking at the tracks of his boot soles. They could hear the chopper only for a few seconds after it vanished behind the ridge.

"It's been a tough morning. Sorry you had to go through all that. Are you hungry?"

"Nah. I think I'll go lie down for a bit."

As Paul carried a big chunk of firewood to the pile he watched Henry go toward the tent. He ambled over to Roy, who was still sitting. "Tough day, huh?"

"Real," replied Roy. "Maybe we should find another area to hunt javelina—north of Phoenix!"

Paul nodded and then walked back to the woodpile.

As Henry settled on his cot at the entrance to the tent Roy glanced at him, then at the ridge. He could hear the chopper again momentarily, and then the noise vanished once more. The only sound remaining was of human hands gathering firewood, and a cardinal calling from the mesquite thicket.

Chapter 10

Yost studied his dash-mounted GPS unit, as he pulled off the road next to a patch of ocotillo. "What a bitch of a road," he whined to Black. "The chopper pilot said these coordinates afforded the closest access. I think the hunters' camp is to the north about two miles. We can take this draw down about a quarter mile to the main valley and should find the other guys about half a mile from there."

Both men exited the Blazer, went to the back of the vehicle to grab their packs, then locked up and headed to their destination.

"Do you have any hiking boots, Darrel?" inquired Black.

"I wish I did. I meant to bring them to the office but didn't think I would need them so soon. I'll be alright."

As they departed it was obvious Black was accustomed to the rocky ground along the drainage. He had traveled hundreds of miles through this sort of terrain and his stride and posture indicated he was comfortable. Yost, on the other hand, tripped over every obstacle on the landscape. He kept pulling on the straps of his pack, and finally stopped and said, "I gotta fix this thing. It's driving me nuts."

"Here, let me help you," offered Black as he walked up to Yost. He held the bottom of his pack as Yost adjusted the straps.

"Thanks. I think that'll be better. Let's go."

Yost quit fussing with his pack but his cadence still suggested that he was struggling to walk. His cowboy boots were taking a beating in the brush but he said nothing about it. He didn't want to verbalize his inadequacy. His movements spoke volumes though.

After about fifteen minutes they reached the main drainage. "There they are, on the other side just out of the bottom. See 'em?" Yost said, pointing off to the northwest.

"Yep," replied Black, who had spotted the yellow Border Patrol vests five minutes earlier.

The men turned left up the canyon with Yost in the lead. He was almost running along the dry rocky watercourse, tripping every other step. When he was about a hundred yards away he started yelling, "Here we are! Jake, can you hear me?"

"Darrel, we're right here, just up the wash on the right side."

"Does he think I'm blind?" Yost commented to Black, who just smirked.

Yost crashed through the small brush lining the drainage. He lost his cowboy hat on a mesquite branch. "Damn," he exclaimed. Blood was oozing slightly from a scratch on his forehead. Black retrieved his hat.

"Here you go. Are you okay?" he said as he handed it to Yost.

"Ya, I'm fine. Thanks. Jake, where are you? Lyons, can you hear me?"

"Loud and clear. We're directly across from you on the other side of the mesquite thicket in front of you. I suggest you go to your left and come through that way. It's more open."

Yost was perturbed. The combination of fatigue, scratched boots, and sweat running into the wound on his throbbing head made him uneasy. He walked to his left about fifty yards and found the opening, then turned to Black. "I can't see why any Mexican would leave home to run around this rugged backcountry and struggle for his life. Maybe this sort of existence made our guy go crazy and start killing his own kind. Let's go see what we got."

Jake Lyons had found Henry's tracks and followed them right to the body. He took a quick peek at the corpse then backed away and helped Johnson tape off the area. Then walking toward the helicopter, Lyons signaled the pilot to pick up the forensic team. He took his cell phone from his belt and checked the signal strength. It was strong, so he waited for the chopper to take off and gain distance before calling the houndsman contracted with the Border Patrol to locate the killer.

"I got a real strong signal on the cell from here," he expressed in amazement.

"We're just up the road from Green Valley and civilization," commented Johnson.

"I guess so," added Lyons

Both men had been sitting in the shade of a nearby cave when they heard Yost call them. Waiting for Yost to get through the mass of vegetation, they stood in anticipation of what would follow.

"Where's the body?" asked Yost.

"Right there, under the brush next to the rock face," replied Lyons.

Yost had taken off his pack, and walked over the rocky ground toward the area Lyons was pointing to. He lifted the tape that was strung across the entrance to the alcove then turned around and asked Lyons, "Did you photograph the area?"

"Yes, sir."

"What about tracks?"

"We looked for tracks, but could find only those of the boy who discovered the body. It's tough tracking in these rocks, and there's leaf litter on all the soft ground. We couldn't find any tracks other than the boy's."

Yost glanced at the ground around him then turned toward the body. He walked toward it, bending over as he neared the cliff.

"Shit, his head's gone!" exclaimed Yost. "This killer's a sick bastard. Looks like the rest of the body is intact. Only the head is missing. He must have hit him in the head with a rock or a weapon, and just kept whacking at it. Could you find where this guy was attacked? I don't think he was killed right here. Seems like he was dragged here after he was killed."

"We didn't look around too much. We wanted to wait for forensics to arrive. We didn't want to mess up the crime scene," chided Johnson.

"Good move," replied Yost. "I wonder where the head is...I'm sure forensics will find it. Did you get hold of Hunt?"

"Yes, he's on his way," said Lyons.

"He's bringing his best hounds like I requested, right?"

"Yes, sir. He's bringing his three favorites. They should be here in an hour. I called him about two hours ago. He was in Benson, and had to pick up the dogs at his place in Sonoita. He's coming in the way you did. How was the hike?"

"No problem," said Yost. "If those dogs are as good as Hunt says they are, we should find our guy pretty quick. That Mexican was killed last night." Yost was getting his second wind. After a year of waiting he finally sensed catching *El Diablo* was about to happen.

Yost did not advance further, not wanting to risk getting too much of his scent in the area and hindering the dogs' ability to detect their target. He knew the dry conditions would make the scent trail difficult enough for the dogs to follow. As they were milling around, the sound of the Apache helicopter resounded in the northeast.

"There's forensics. Where's Hunt?"

Chapter 11

Eldon Hunt was born in the rugged Dragoon Mountains of southeastern Arizona. Four generations of Hunts had ranched and hunted the area, and they hunted with dogs during that entire time. Eldon's dad had gathered a pack of hounds for hunting lions that were plaguing his cattle in the '50s. Eldon inherited the pack and over the years improved the quality of his animals. Eldon's interest in working with dogs was much greater than that of his father. He studied techniques and had a sense about each animal. He out-crossed his females with other dogs that he knew were proven trackers.

As a lion hunter he was unmatched. His reputation in Arizona and New Mexico was fairly legendary. For a man in his early forties this was rare. Lion hunters from across the United States paid large fees for his services. He was booked for years in advance, but took a special interest in helping law enforcement. He had been on several murder cases in Tucson and other jurisdictions and made himself available to the Border Patrol. In exchange, his ranch received preferential treatment during the winter months when crosser traffic peaked.

Eldon Hunt was a man of great physical endurance and pleasant personality. He claimed it was because he had spent most of his life hanging around dogs. Whatever the reason, all the agents enjoyed his company. Every movement he made was purposeful and he exuded an amazing conservation of physical energy. This was most evident as he walked behind his dogs.

He was very familiar with nearly all the mountain ranges of Arizona. He knew the area of the Cerro Colorados where the Border Patrol needed his service, and decided that the rocky terrain precluded taking horses. Plus he did not want to bother with the extra fuss horses required. If what Lyons had told him was true the dogs would have a hot track of a man to follow. He felt that he could keep close to his dogs and out walk any man alive.

When he got the call from Yost about a year ago both men agreed that his service would be rendered when a tracking opportunity arose, and that Hunt would try his best to clear his schedule. Hunt's pay would be calculated from "port to port." Wherever he was when he got the call would be the start of his mileage and time claim. He was ready for this first project with Yost.

Hunt detected the faint sound of the helicopter the same time he noticed the black spot in the sky. He had parked his truck near Yost's vehicle and hiked to the confluence of the main drainage, less than half a mile from where he was told to meet Yost. His GPS confirmed this location. When he reached Yost the Apache helicopter was sitting silently in a clearing on the flatland, and there was a stir of conversation near the rocks. His three dogs were surrounding him, tethered with long leather leashes since he had not yet released them to follow a trail. As the hunters approached the group of agents the dogs gathered close to Hunt, occasionally looking to him for instruction.

Hunt called to the men to let them know he had arrived but stayed away from them. He could tell they were conducting their forensic investigation, an activity that did not involve him, and one he chose to avoid. His role was to take off in pursuit once the agents reached a conclusion. In his perfect rural life death was a constant element that he could understand. He knew natural predators like mountain lions and black bears, and accepted them as part of the landscape. But he put murder in the category of deviant behavior, very much unlike any sort of death he encountered in nature. It was beyond his comprehension, and he wanted to keep it that way.

During the half-hour he waited Hunt watered his dogs from a tank the Border Patrol had brought along for him. The dogs were sprawled beneath the mesquite on the soft dirt, sleeping. They knew soon it would be their turn. Hunt sat at the base of the tree, scratching his back on its craggy bark. He whittled on a little chunk of mesquite he had picked up. What he was fashioning had no recognizable form. Rather, it was a nervous habit he began to use 10 years ago to replace his snuff habit.

Yost emerged from the rocks and headed toward Hunt. Four men in white coveralls and plastic gloves lifted a black bag containing the body and headed straight to the chopper. Yost stopped and turned around to talk briefly with the pilot, who had been sitting in the shade of a cliff overhang.

"Perfect timing, Eldon," said Yost. He walked up to Hunt and shook hands. "I am not sure where to start here. We could find no tracks or any visual link to this body. I don't know what to do."

"What we can't see the dogs will find. They'll tell us where to start. Let's begin at the site where the body was discovered. They'll sort everything out then strike out on a line that we cannot even see. How does that sound?"

"It's all yours."

As the two men ended their conversation the jet engine of the Apache ignited. The sound sparked the dogs' attention and they sat up, looking at the object that was dominating the air and getting louder by the second. As it lifted off a light spray of dust headed toward them. Hunt knew that on those airborne particles of ground was the scent his dogs would discover. He would begin his search along the edge of the broad valley, away from the influence of the aircraft rotor. Hopefully the dogs would lead them to boot prints, which would make the tracking easier.

A second chopper was enroute from Tucson with a fresh crew consisting of two spotters who would circle Hunt and his dogs at a distance of a mile or more, ready to descend when Hunt's dogs flushed their target. Yost and Black would board that chopper for a bird's eye view of the operation. Black would attempt to get a signal from the air. If the unit was only transmitting weakly, perhaps an aerial perspective from nearby could pick it up.

"Here's a radio, Eldon. You know the deal. Call me if you have any sign, or if you feel you're in danger. Hopefully, the presence of the Apache in the distance will persuade this nut to hide rather than attack. I may check some likely areas from the air, but if you don't see me, don't worry. I'll be within a minute of you. Let's check the frequency of your transmitter."

"Oh, I'm not worried. I got my .40 caliber if I need it. But these dogs are all the protection I need. They'll tear anything apart if I give them the command. They're good, real good."

Yost nodded his head as he retrieved a small receiver from his pack. He turned it on and a distinct signal boomed from the instrument. "That's you, Eldon. The digital display tells me where you are. The pilot can download the location data, and we'll be right over you in a few seconds."

"That's good to know," replied Hunt as he slipped the transmitter into his shirt pocket. A quirky smile came over him as he realized he was treading between high-powered technology and a dog's nose.

"Well, good luck, amigo," said Yost as he moved away, watching as Hunt began to work his dogs. To the north he could hear the drone of the Apache and he looked over to see it emerge above the backdrop of the Sierrita Mountains. When he looked back Hunt was leading his dogs along the rocky drainage. He headed west up the valley, his dogs ahead of him with noses dragging on the ground and tails wagging wildly. It was evident to Yost that this "combination" was in its element, and he felt hopeful.

The ground was mostly rocky, which would likely yield little track. The area of the sandy flatlands adjacent to the rocky valley bottom would be their only hope for finding sign unless the dogs cut a scent trail. If not, all bets were off. Hunt figured this site had a fifty-fifty chance of yielding scent or tracks, even though the body was fresh. The ground was too dry and any scent had been burned off by the sun, which now was to the west of overhead.

Hunt was a half-mile up the valley when the chopper with Yost lifted off and headed over the ridge to the north. It disappeared, leaving only the sound of its engine. When that mechanical sound faded Hunt could hear his lead dog, Chester, whining about a hundred yards away. Chester was standing, looking back at him with body language that exuded a combination of confusion and anticipation.

Hunt knew Chester did not like this area. There was nothing to track. Chester started toward the cliff line to the north, but Hunt gave a command that checked his direction. Hunt had a hunch himself, a strategy he wanted to employ first. Although he had long ago learned to trust his dogs, especially Chester, he signaled for the dogs to progress westward up the valley.

The valley was narrowing, taking the form of a broad and rocky canyon. After about half a mile of fruitless searching, Hunt decided to let Chester lead. He was curious to learn what the dog had detected. He yelled a command, and all three dogs veered north-easterly, Chester in the lead. Walking was easier out of the rocky canyon bottom. The adjacent flatland was mainly cobblestone with patches of dirt. There was a better chance to find a boot print on this ground while walking along after the dogs.

As Hunt approached the area near the base of the cliffs he saw Chester on the rocks, tail wagging wildly. He was giving an excited muffled howl as the other dogs joined him. Hunt realized Chester had found sign, which was likely not visible on the rocks. He listened for the helicopter as he approached his dogs, and paused. He realized Yost had been out of sight and sound for over ten minutes.

He retrieved the radio from his pocket and pressed the receiver to call Yost. The dogs headed up the ridge and followed scent among the breaks in the cliff.

"Darrel, this is Eldon. Can you hear me?" He waited thirty seconds.

"Darrel, this is Eldon. Yost, can you hear me?" He stood at the base of the cliffy ridge, intermittently watching his dogs re-appear in the jumble of boulders two hundred yards away, mostly hearing their wail of excitement.

"Darrel, can you hear me?"

The sound of the helicopter preceded its appearance over the northern ridge. Yost was busy scanning all the rocky crevices, peering through the brush to discover what might be hiding below. He was consumed with finding his quarry, forgetting that Hunt had a far greater tool to make the discovery.

As the chopper rose over the ridge Yost spotted Hunt standing about twenty feet from the boulders that lined the southern fringe of the ridge. He was waving his arms. Yost tried to get him on the radio, but Hunt kept signaling with his arms.

"Set her down on that flat area. He has something," Yost exclaimed to the pilot.

As the pilot initiated engine shut down, Yost exited after the two spotters had jumped out. Hunt remained where he was, looking in the opposite direction at the ridge. Yost did not see the dogs scrambling wildly in the rocks.

"What ya got?" asked Yost, approaching Hunt. "Is your radio working?"

As Hunt fumbled around his clothing looking for his radio, Yost picked it from Hunt's shirt pocket and asked, "Did you try calling me?"

"Yes. I couldn't raise you."

"I guess the frequency got changed. You were on channel two. I had it set for channel three. Here, that'll work now. What's up?"

"The dogs are on a lion track."

Yost could hear the dogs' excited howls after the helicopter engine stopped. "A lion? How do you know?"

"Look here," Hunt replied. With his feet in the thin layer of sandy soil between slabs of rock, Hunt pointed with his right boot. "It's pretty sketchy, but the way the dogs are acting, I think they're on the scent of a lion. This is the only sign I could find, and it's only part of a print. But I think it's a big tom lion...a really large one at that. It apparently headed into the rocks. The dogs will have a hard time tracking it."

"A lion? Are they around here?"

"You bet. I suspect this country has a good lion population. Just like the rest of southern Arizona."

"Well that screws up everything, doesn't it? Is there any way to get the dogs off the lion scent, and back on to our guy?"

"Apparently the smell of lion is the strongest scent in the area...maybe the only scent at this point. The tracking conditions are real bad with the drought. I didn't find any foot prints along the creek bed, or in the valley bottom."

"Well, where does this leave us?"

"Did you spot anything from the air? Did you pick up a signal?"

"No, nothing."

"I don't know what to tell you, Darrel."

"Shit. I don't know either. I thought we had him."

As Yost prepared to get out of the chopper and into his truck, he instructed Black to search the area visually and with the receiver for a couple hours until the pilot had to head for gas in Tucson. "I left a radio with Hunt so keep an ear out for any traffic as he heads back to his truck with the dogs. He could come across something. I'll monitor your traffic."

Yost adjusted the radio scanner in his Blazer as he backtracked along the rugged and rocky road. It was good to be sitting again, driving along. He was not cut out for walking that country. He glanced at the tires of Hunt's truck as he passed it, wondering what rocky road had chewed up some of the outer tread. He once again thought of the horrid conditions the crossers faced on this landscape. His attention turned to his boots. They were trashed.

He called the forensics lab on his cell. "I'll be there in about an hour and a half," he said.

Chapter 12

Yost had been expecting the call; he was ready. He met the agents in the basement of the Tucson field office. The Senior Field Agent already had briefed him on the elements of the arrest. It seemed like Plan B would be initiated. He had what he needed to initiate the investigation down that path.

Two officers took Fernando into a separate room for interrogation. His fingerprints and DNA were taken. His clothes were confiscated and replaced with a fresh new set. He told the agents where and when he had originated his trip, and where he was heading. The three men discussed Fernando's history of crossings in this region. The agent who spoke Spanish and acted as interpreter was friendly, and Fernando spoke with a calm veracity.

In the other room Yost met with his right-hand man. Walking up to the head of the conference table, Yost began, "Okay, now let's go over what we got. This could very well be our guy. He was in the right area at the right time."

"That's right," said the Senior Field Agent. His name was George Marks and he was very much riding his career on the coattails of Yost. They had known each other for about two years before Marks transferred to Arizona from Texas. Marks had heard about Yost's management style, and concluded their styles were similar and could yield benefits for both men. He took a special interest in Yost's Plan A, to monitor the movements of a specific crosser with a tracking device. He was silently skeptical of the guy they used for the first transmitter and on the lookout for a better candidate. He believed Fernando was that better candidate.

"And here's what else matches perfectly. This guy had a .22 caliber pistol on him, his boot prints matched ones we had found earlier at the cache, and we apprehended him within a quarter mile of the cache on the opposite side of the pond that crossers commonly use. Proximity to the cache of loot is important even though he had none on him...he could have already stashed it. But I think the most important factor is that he was alone."

"We don't know for sure that the murders were the result of a lone killer," Yost interrupted.

"Right, but a lone killer makes sense. If he's as demented as his actions suggest he is, the chances of finding someone else as sick are pretty unlikely. Most mass murderers act alone. They're rogue human beings, solitary predators. I bet this guy killed for the thrill of it, not for all the loot he's garnered. I think the fact that this guy was alone points a bigger finger at him."

"That's right, George. Good input. I think you're exactly right. And he's only 12 miles from that fresh body with the head missing. Do you think this guy is crazy enough to decapitate his victims...like, make it a gruesome scene so all the other crossers get scared?"

"No telling how crazy this guy has become. He may have started killing for the loot, then moved into doing it for the thrill, and now he does it for the macho trip of being *El Diablo* in his own mind. He certainly has fewer potential victims with the *El Diablo* scare, so maybe he does it now more for kicks than for the loot."

Yost had been leaning over the table with his arms extended straight as if looking at a map. He saw his face reflecting off the table's shiny veneer surface. He was thinking about all that Marks had said. The crosser they had put the transmitter on about a year ago had vanished apparently. The only reason Border Patrol suspected he was

El Diablo was because they had apprehended him at the small, hidden cave that housed a large cache of money and valuables. Yost believed that robbery was the motive for the killings and the cave was where the killer stashed the loot taken from his victims. It was a weak link—the guy could have just stumbled onto the cave. Yost knew it was a fragile connection but at the time it was his only tie. But now he had a stronger case, and a plausible *modus operandi*. Fernando was his new suspect.

"Good work, George," said Yost. "Let's see if we get any DNA or boot prints that link Fernando with the body that hunter found."

Marks interjected, "Let me repeat: I think the gun and his proximity to the cache of loot are important, but our big ticket item is the solitary nature of this guy. I cannot remember ever apprehending a lone wet—especially nowadays with the notion of *El Diablo* out there. I think we should go ahead and get him outfitted with the transmitter and let him lead us to the next victim. If he goes to the cache that's good evidence, but we then can use the dogs to backtrack his path to his last victim."

"I agree," concluded Yost. "Bring in Valenzuela and let's see what he's found out about this guy.

Carlos Valenzuela entered the room with a grin, and a posture that held the promise of important information. He was unaware of the factors Yost and Marks had been mulling over. He had his own reason to suspect this was their man.

He sat down at the table across from where Yost was standing. He sat back in his chair, laced his fingers behind his head and looked up at the two men.

"I think this is our guy."

Yost looked at him, paused to savor the moment, then asked, "Why?"

"He has a real detached attitude about *El Diablo*. Either he is in total denial and scared shitless, or he knows there's no such thing. I think it's the latter, and I'll bet my 22 years of interviewing wets on it. This guy has no fear of an unknown killer because he knows he's the killer. He's *El Diablo*. That's his secret, and the only way to keep a secret like that is to operate alone."

Yost looked at Valenzuela for about ten seconds, then pulled up a chair and sat next to him. Valenzuela noticed a hint of a smile on Yost's face and on that of Marks, who also had taken a seat.

Valenzuela continued, "I think you're right. I think he's the guy that's been killing crossers for the past two years. He has the weapon, the proximity to the cache, and he was alone. Only a demented loner would do what we're seeing out there."

Marks interrupted, "I totally agree. The weapon is a weak link since we think he's probably shooting victims in the head then totally removing the skulls...like some demon! We don't have a skull with a bullet hole, so we have absolutely no ballistics match. What he's doing with the skulls is a total mystery."

Yost pushed the chair back and pulled up the socks that were sliding down his ankles inside his boots. He then sat back and said, "You know, this guy really is nuts. Not only does he kill but maybe he tears his victims apart for the coyotes. Maybe he crushes the skulls for the vultures to completely consume. Or maybe he eats the bone meal...I don't know! It seems he can detach himself from all the sadistic aspects of his killings. He is one sick bastard."

Marks interjected again, "This El Diablo phantom that we started suggesting to all the deportees over the past six months has really reduced the number of people crossing the line. Only someone who knew there was nothing to fear would come across, especially alone in the area west of Nogales. Recall that the size of groups we've been intercepting has been significantly larger lately. I think they believe there is safety in numbers. This guy is different. I am willing to hang my hat on this guy mainly because he was alone. The other aspects of him are gravy."

Yost looked at Marks, and then at Valenzuela. He paused only briefly and asked, "Tell me again, what's this guy's name?"

"Fernando."

"10-4. Let's go to Plan B with Fernando."

Chapter 13

Yost stood and opened the box. He pulled out a black backpack and laid it on the counter. "This is what Black put together for me. The tracking device is a special order. It's the latest high-tech satellite GPS...no more second-hand junk from the game and fish boys. It is flat and sewed into the strap; the antenna trails along the padded area of the strap. If we want to do real-time tracking like we've been doing, it has a piggyback unit that signals constantly to conventional ground receiving equipment. Ground tracking range is about 30 miles in typical terrain; it's greater from the air. Black tested it; it works great. I think if we had this set-up on that first guy we were following we wouldn't have lost him. Here, see if you can detect the transmitter," Yost said as he handed the pack to Marks.

"This is good. Nice work. I think it'll work just fine." Marks handed it to Valenzuela. He looked up at Yost and inhaled deeply. "Let's get this guy on the road."

Yost nodded; Marks turned and left the room. Yost looked at Valenzuela and said, "That Fernando, he's creepy isn't he?"

Valenzuela got up and turned his full vision toward Yost. "In a way, yes. But in another way, he's just like all the other scared shitless Mexicans I've ever talked with. But I got the distinct impression that he was not hiding his fear with machismo. I don't think he's numb with fear. I really think he has no fear of *El Diablo*, and the reason is not a deep faith in God. It's got to do with himself. I think he takes comfort in knowing who he is. His problem is that now we do, too."

Fernando was the first one loaded into the green sixteen-passenger Border Patrol van. He had a strange sense of security while in the custody of the Border Patrol. Being deported directly back to his homeland was a welcome episode in his journey. His desire to roam north of the border was absent, at least for the moment. More than he could recall in the past, he was glad to be returning to Mexico.

Fernando was one of fourteen men that had been captured within the past week, given good meals during their incarceration, and driven to Nogales for release to the Mexican officials. This routine was not unusual, but the backpacks were. Since the others also were given new backpacks, he did not feel like his "gift' was any thing more than Valenzuela had described: a new sympathetic gesture of the United States government toward crossers. "It will make your trip home more comfortable."

Yost had purchased about five hundred packs from the same vendor in Mexico that made most of the low-cost backpacks crossers most commonly used, so there was no suspicion. In preparation for the placement of additional tracking units, randomly selected groups of deportees within the last four months had been getting the same treatment.

As the van driver left the border and headed for Tucson he called Yost on his cell phone. "*El Diablo* has been delivered."

"Very good. When Black gets back from Arivaca I'll have him home in on our guy. Thanks."

Yost was on the phone with his wife when the call came in from Black. He abruptly apologized to her then disconnected his wife's call and connected with Black. "Nothing, right?"

"That's right," responded Black. "Eldon found no tracks, and his dogs found no smell. We struck out. Hunt headed home. I flew for about an hour, and even headed to the south and east to see if I could get a signal from our guy—no luck. He's either out of range in Mexico, or the transmitter failed...I think it's the latter."

"Well, don't worry. It's like playing chess. We have another marked piece on the table now."

"A new player...good deal!"

Yost chuckled. "Yes, I just activated Plan B. That guy we picked up near the cache seemed to be a good candidate for Plan B."

"Well, what made this guy a good candidate...and what is Plan B?"

Yost snapped back, "Steve, Plan B is what happens when Plan A fails...it's simple! The first 'beeping Mexican' vanished off our radar, probably due to transmitter failure, right?"

"Yeah, that's what I think."

"Me too. Marks and I think this new guy is a great replacement. The first guy was merely there near the cave. This new guy was there with a personality that could do things like what we're seeing out there. He's ticking as we speak. If the guy from Plan A gets back on our radar, that's all the better. It means we got two pieces to play with then. Remember, it's like chess."

"What's his frequency?"

Black programmed the new transmitter frequency into his unit, and dialed in the tracking mode. Soon a beeping sound filled the room.

Yost was fingering his phone as the beeping sounded. He flipped it shut, looked down at his boots and said to himself, "Steve, sounds like you got him!"

A cloud of confusion began to settle around Fernando, enfolding him like a wet and uncomfortable blanket. He had never before received such cordial treatment from the Border Patrol. He had always accepted that he was a criminal in the eyes of the United States government, and although he believed he contributed to the work force he did not accept any part of the cultural influences from which he made a living. To him the line was as crystal clear as the steel wall that was growing at the northern extreme of his country.

He also recognized that the younger generation of crossers was different. They felt more privileged than he ever had. They were expected, even encouraged to head north by their families, even their government. Booklets published and distributed by the Mexican government advised them how to increase their chances for a successful trek north, and then back home. Their view of the journey was totally different from Fernando's, who had been mentored by the generation before him.

Perhaps it was for this younger generation that the Border Patrol was offering such assistance. Maybe the United States felt compassion for the deaths that were so commonplace just across the line. Whatever the reason, the new hospitality added to the differences and deepened his confusion. It made him consider a route east of his normal one, which had always been to the west of Nogales...the area where *El Diablo* now resided. But he wasn't sure. He knew the western route better.

The only thing Fernando knew for sure is that he would re-enter the U.S. again very soon, and he would not have a companion. He wondered what had happened to José, but when he thought about José, an uncontrollable anger rose up in him.

He was alone as he entered the United States about five miles west of Nogales the first night after his release. He walked for miles along the eastern drainages of the Pajarito Mountains, dipping into canyons with names like Potrero and Alamo, heading in a northwesterly direction. At times he had to ascend small and rocky ridges where the walking was more difficult, but where the cold air had not gathered. He was not certain where he was heading. He just felt the need to move north. At about three in the morning he paused and looked up at the moon. He then sat down and put his head in his hands. He was lost.

He could see the lights of Nogales to the southeast. They were comforting, and seemed to be more of a beacon than the one operating in his head and telling him to head north. If he wanted to continue making good time toward Phoenix he would need to get a ride, or get onto a road. He could see headlights pulling into what seemed like a ranch house in a broad valley only a mile north. Despite the proximity of these people he felt a deep and unsettling divide. He was alone again and that was a comfort and a curse. In his solitude humanity could not harass him. Throughout his life he experienced pain from people...he knew humanity was not a source of comfort for him. And so in southern Arizona the internal struggle began again: solitude and peace, or people and discomfort. Once again the two poles of existence were about to collide in his head. He knew he likely would opt for solitude and acknowledge that people were basically a major source of pain for him.

On his early treks into the U.S. he had always traveled in a group for reasons of companionship. Now, he thought, he should congregate with others for safety. But his experience with life had taught him to build a thick coat of armor for protection from humanity. That armor was getting thicker, hindering his movement and making him bitter. He was torn by a fear of what was around him, and what was now inside him. In so many ways he seemed like another person, or like some entity was inside him, controlling his every move.

There was no clarity in his mind about the events of this journey, or the reasons for it. Should he continue northwesterly, or trek toward the east? Or should he return to Nogales? Or home? When he thought of home he thought of all the persecution, and that made him want to roll further into a ball of pain and confusion...to apply one more coat of armor.

He was paralyzed. His legs locked up on the rocky ridge of the Pajaritos, and his vision vanished. His fear morphed into madness then reverted to fear. Then a rage rose up in him. His sight returned, and he was compelled to move. Whatever was ahead, whatever would threaten him...whatever might want to attack him would be met with his rage...he would kill it before it killed him.

Fernando awoke to the sounds of vehicles and people. He was under a bushy mesquite tree that afforded good cover, so he was not frightened by exposure to his surroundings. As his eyes slowly adjusted to the light of mid-morning, he discovered he was looking at the border wall outside Nogales. He did not remember heading back toward the border or stopping at the wall. But that's where he had hunkered, his pack still on his back and a feeling of deep relief at his core.

Chapter 14

The men were ready to move, especially Fernando. His muscles had not been taxed by the events of last week, but his mind had. He felt a kinship in the presence of old crossing friends that he had found while meandering around Nogales in a mental fog. They too were plagued with restlessness. Men who normally were filled with confidence and determination just milled around as if waiting for something. The border town was bustling with activity that seemed to be going nowhere. It was like a stream that had been dammed...the water volume was growing but flowing nowhere.

During the week since he returned to his country, Fernando encountered many with whom he had crossed in years past. They discussed old times and recent encounters with Border Patrol. What they did not discuss was the cause of their coagulation: *El Diablo*. Their hope for a better day was always present. Their vision was mainly on the present, very little on the past and really not much on the future.

At the same time Fernando was unnerved by the hesitation and trepidation he witnessed in the streets of Nogales. The Mexican males with whom he had crossed the *frontera* in earlier times were different than the present ones. The earlier Mexican men carried the same hopes and feelings that resided in American men 15 decades ago as they conquered the West. They were advancing on the great northern frontier; willing to face the dangers and the adventures, and gather the wealth that loomed just to the north. As Fernando scanned the men around him at the market he felt no connected to their motion. They were strangers to him, not his countrymen.

Two days ago while buying supplies at a store he usually had frequented, he ran into five men from the small town of Sahuaripa in central Sonora. He had crossed with the three old men in the group about ten years ago. They soon began laughing and talking as if they never had split up near Tucson back then. The meeting brought each a sense of kinship that had been absent on their individual journeys since that earlier trek. They kept up the light mood of the reunion as long as they could.

Eventually, talk settled on telling of the events of the past weeks that had brought them to the same place. Well into the night they discussed the recent happenings and the new aura that permeated the borderland. They sat on the eastern outskirts of Nogales, Sonora, quietly assessing their next move, and their collective fate. They briefly considered hiring a coyote to take them cross as so many others were doing since the big *El Diablo* scare surfaced a year ago. But they had confidence in their combined abilities to navigate their way north through any foreign landscape. They decided to make the northern trek together through the eastern corridor. No one in the group had ever taken that route, but any trepidation they individually felt was left unmentioned.

About 2:00 a.m. they crossed the border along the Santa Cruz River about five miles east of Nogales. The crossing was uneventful and by sun-up they made a day camp on a ridge top in the Washington Mountains. They kicked the dry and dusty ground to make soft beds. From what they could see there was no fresh evidence of anyone having been on the ridge in months, perhaps longer.

Three of the men were in their early forties, and had grown up together. They had worked on various ranches throughout the region and
on road crews for the Mexican government. They worked hard when
they had work, but mostly they were idle. The instability of income and
Mexican life in general eventually ushered in the notion that a better
existence was awaiting them to the north in the United States. Despite
initial fears of the unknown, these three seasoned men first crossed
twelve years ago. They no longer considered themselves outlaws or any
sort of criminal. To them, this was their life. It afforded adventure and a
good bit of money to bring home at Christmas. Most men from around
Sahuaripa chose to cross for reasons of economy.

For others the goal was adventure. So it was for the two young
men who were on their first journey north. Now around twenty years
old, they were barely in their teens when they heard the three elders
tell stories of their northward voyages. Under the shade of cotton-
wood trees with cans of beer on Saturday afternoons they had
listened to men talk of their lives in the north. They became inspired
to do the same when they were older.

Fernando honored their special fellowship born from ties to their
common birthplace, and mainly listened as they mentioned someone's name or referenced an earlier time. He was calm by nature,
and this trait plus his attentive demeanor served to make his deci-
sions the ones everyone followed. There was no social order. They
understood that, in reality, it was every man for himself. Yet, with the
bond of unspoken fear holding the group together, they had progressed to the place where that chilly February morning found them:
about twenty miles northeast of Nogales, scattered among the oaks
and junipers on a rocky ridge like a herd of deer.

As the sun began to set they looked east into the San Rafael Valley.
Since they had rested all day and the broad expanse of grass below
seemingly would afford easy walking, they headed down the slope
eastward. The night air was particularly cold in the valley bottom so

they walked at an exceptionally fast pace. The six men reached the center of the valley after several hours of steady, uneventful walking. The only light was from a waning moon on the eastern horizon in a star-filled sky. This place was dark and seemingly uninhabited. In the far distance a dim light twinkled, probably that of a ranch house. The landscape was peculiar...it seemed unlike anywhere else they had ever been north of the border.

As they progressed through the knee-high grass the men came upon a wide, graded dirt road. It headed straight north so they welcomed the easy walking afforded along its hard and even surface. After a couple minutes on the road the men paused and took in the surroundings. To the east about five miles away were the dark and wooded foothills of the Huachuca Mountains that would give shelter from detection by the Border Patrol. The thought of leaving the road and heading across the grass and into the foothills was not appealing. The road seemed safe. If a vehicle appeared on it they would see the lights a long way off, in plenty of time to run into the grass cover for concealment. The walking certainly was easier along the road and they would make good time. So they headed along it, single file.

The road veered to the right then headed up a slight rise. This was a welcome feature in an otherwise flat landscape. From there they would be able to scout their course toward the eastern woodlands, where they would spend the early morning hours before sunrise. The crunching gravel beneath their boots sounded a cadence of determination as they walked up the hill.

Suddenly, the headlights of two vehicles blazed in front of them. An electric blast of "Alto, alto," blared from a speaker. The men began running through the grass toward the east, and down into a ravine lined with large oaks. The Border Patrol vehicle sped toward them, cutting into the grassland in pursuit. The men scurried in an unbridled panic along the dry wash, tripping on the rocks and in the holes dug out seasons ago when the rains last fell in the valley. Areas of soft sand and vegetation hindered their progress.

Running for their lives with wild abandon along ground that was difficult to negotiate resulted in much of their provisions being scattered along their erratic route. Their plastic waster jugs exploded with a splash of water as they tripped and fell along the way. Fortunately, the terrain was too rugged for the Border Patrol vehicles, and the agents did not elect to run after the men on foot. All six men were able to escape the Border Patrol, so they felt lucky.

The group had managed to stay together, but they now had to find water. Their earlier camp was a dry one so they had not replenished their water supply from Mexico. Having lost that most precious and limited commodity in their scramble, they walked through the sea of grass toward the blackish hills to the east, hoping to come across water at a windmill or dirt tank.

When they reached the end of the grassland and the beginning of the woods they began to head north under the light of the crescent moon. It was cattle country so surely would be a watering station somewhere. Weariness from running, and associated sprained ankles and bruises persuaded them to gather under a large, hilltop oak tree and wait for the warmth of sunrise.

They slept very little. An owl around camp was one reason and the chilly air was another. But the greatest reason was the different border mood that permeated the woodland more than the sound and temperature. They were afraid, an emotion they had never known. On this crossing for the first time ever they were aware that north of the line they were outlaws. Whether or not *El Diablo* was creating that notion was uncertain.

Fernando sat on the ground in the sun along the line of oak trees about fifty yards from the windmill. The other men were scattered around him, sleeping or just sitting quietly in the warm sunlight. They had found a windmill and an old plastic jug. Having consumed their fill of water they decided to rest and assess their condition. Later that afternoon they would set foot in a northerly direction in the cover of the woodland.

Fernando had ripped his pack in the scramble through the brush. It had become entangled on a low oak branch last night as he ran from the Border Patrol. The branch had punctured his left shoulder then wedged between his back and the pack strap. With a jerk he broke the limb and kept running. The resultant wound garnered all of his attention. He had not realized the strap was torn.

He had nothing to repair the damaged strap, which was connected to the pack by only an inch of tattered stitching. He had used fence wire for such repairs in the past so he was confident in his ability to mend his pack. He fingered the tear, assessing exactly how much wire to get. The windmill was the place where old fence and baling wire would be available.

Finding a length of wire at the windmill Fernando sat on the cattle trough, pondering how to repair the strap. He pinched its frayed end and attempted to run the wire through the nylon fabric. He couldn't work the wire through the thickness of the inside padding, so he decided to peel open the strap and thread the wire through one side of it.

When he looked inside the strap, he discovered a coated wire. He pulled on it but it would not come out. He felt a hard flat object about six inches up the strap, near the buckle that attached to the strap and adjusted the pack to fit him. He did not know what to make of this object, and as he was contemplating the situation one of the other men yelled out, "Fernando, here comes a pickup."

Fernando instantly scooped the pack from his lap and began running toward the cover of the oaks. All six men moved through the trees and up a rocky drainage, turning right into a side canyon. They ascended a small hill that would give them a view of the approaching vehicle.

The truck stopped at the windmill. A young man stepped out and walked to the tower. He noticed the wire that held the lever to engage the fan had been removed. So he went to the back of the truck and retrieved another piece of wire, engaged the fan, and wired the lever. He looked at the ground for sign and noticed boot prints in the dry, loose dirt. Glancing around as he entered the truck, he closed the door and drove back down the road into the valley of grass.

As the other men were watching the cowboy leave, Fernando was looking at his pack. He had no knowledge of tracking devices or such technology, but he immediately became suspicious and more fearful. He said nothing to his companions as they ambled back toward the windmill to fill the water jug. With a replenished water supply the men would seek the deep cover of oak thickets on the foothills. This would be the place for them to find rest and find peace...all except Fernando.

THE DISCOVERY

Chapter 15

"**A**re you sure?" Yost was incredulous. "This case is getting pretty strange. Gus, I don't have time for a briefing now. Just get a copy of your findings in the file and I'll read it later. Thanks for working on this over the weekend, Gus."

Yost was not a man who could stay on a trail very long. He was the personification of instant gratification. The news from forensics put somewhat of a chill on the trail of his killer. Not a trace of Fernando's DNA was found on the fresh headless body, and animals had fed on the body...he would read all about it later. Also, Black had not been able to locate Fernando after receiving strong signals the first couple days. Hunt had returned to his truck without incident, and called to tell Yost where he would be if needed.

It seemed that Plan B was about to be deemed a failure. Since there was no Plan C Yost decided to go home. Along the way he stopped at the mall to pick up another pair of boots.

When Logan returned to his office on Monday morning there was a short message from Yost: "Call me." Since Logan was in the eastern region of the sector and not under Yost's chain of command he debated what to do. He was not one to run to his supervisor for advice. He trusted his own instinct.

That morning he had a different outlook on his role in the Border Patrol. He had information that his agency needed. The fact that they had treated his skills and instincts so poorly was not within his consciousness. He knew that what mattered most now was for his professionalism to rise up. The choice for him was easy.

"Yost, Logan here," he stated.

"Hey, Sam! How have you been?"

"Fine. What's up?"

"Could I meet you someplace, maybe in Benson? I got some questions I need to run by you."

"Sure, what time?"

"How about nine?"

"I'll meet you at Nancy's truck stop at nine."

"Perfect. See you there."

The phone rang and rang. He tried his house, then his cell with the same result. He redialed the house number since he knew Sheldon had trouble retrieving messages from his cell. "Too many small buttons," he had often complained.

"Stayton, this is Logan. I am heading to meet Yost in Benson. He wants to talk. Here we go! I'll let you know what happens."

When Logan pulled into Nancy's Yost was already there, waiting in his truck. Yost was on his cell, and didn't see him pull up. Logan walked to the driver's window of Yost's Blazer and saw Yost writing something down on a pad of paper. When he looked up and saw Logan he gave a quick smile and gesture that he'd be done soon. Logan wandered into Nancy's and got a table in the corner by the window.

"Sorry about that, Sam," said Yost as he took a seat at the table. "It was a real busy weekend, and the week is starting out the same way. How you been?"

"Good. And you?"

"Okay. How's the eastern half treating you?"

"Just fine. Yost, did you come here to check my mental health, or do you have something else you want to discuss?" Logan had a slight smirk that Yost did not miss.

"Well actually, I wanted to talk about your findings west of Nogales during the last year you were there."

"What findings?"

"Oh, I'm sorry. I'm talking about the murders. You know, the bodies we were finding. What are your current thoughts about the murders...and the killer? You've had a year to think about it, and I was wondering if you still hold to your beliefs."

Logan looked at Yost, and saw a confused and somewhat resigned man. On the drive from his office he had decided he would not reveal anything about what he was continuing to do with Sheldon, or what they had discovered over the weekend.

"Why are you interested in my ideas now?" he asked Yost.

Yost took in a deep breath and exhaled. "We had a body on Friday. A javelina hunter found it. It was a fresh kill. The freshest one we've had an opportunity to examine. I got a lab tech telling me the only evidence he can glean from the body indicates that an animal fed on the guy...maybe even killed him. Since we found the body very soon after death I was wondering if an animal would feed on the body shortly after if was slain by a human."

"What kind of animal?" asked Logan.

"They have absolutely no clue about that. Not even a guess. Could have been a coyote or a mountain lion, they don't know."

"Did he find chew marks that indicated tooth size of the animal?"

"No, I guess there were no real marks of teeth. It was more like fractures to the skull, like the animal had broken off chunks of the skull...like you crack a coconut and get at the meat."

"What was eaten?"

"The skull bone, brains, and the face and eyes."

"No doubt in their mind about teeth marks?" Logan questioned.

"Pretty sure they didn't find any teeth marks, or marks they could relate directly to teeth. There's an outside chance that the guy was killed by *El Diablo* and then eaten by animals. But the evidence points fairly clearly to a scenario that has the poor bastard meeting his maker by way of an animal's grip. Plus we had Eldon Hunt out there with his dogs to track our guy but the only thing his dogs came up with was evidence of a mountain lion. As I recall that was your theory, that *El Diablo* is an animal. So I figured I'd meet you and discuss the cases you worked before you transferred."

"Yost, I did not transfer. I was transferred...remember? And you were the guy who did it. Now you want me to rehash all that I was thinking back then. If you recall I never had a chance to present all my thoughts before you transferred me. Anyhow, I'm over it now."

"Listen, Logan, as far as I knew back then you were way out there with your theories. And your actions with the locals made the Border Patrol look bad in the eyes of everyone we were working with to apprehend crossers, and especially to solve the murders. Now I'm sorry that you couldn't see it that way. I need your help now."

Logan did not fall into the hands of a semi-repenting Yost. He knew Yost was at the end of his wits, but he was not about to bail him out. He knew Yost's mission was to glean as much information from him and supply as little as he could. It was always that way with Yost. And when he got information he held it, as if wanting to control the strategy and outcome.

"Was there evidence of claw marks?" Logan asked.

"I'm not sure. The guy was dragged through some brush, so maybe there were some deep scratches to the body. There were sharp rocks in the area. I don't know. But if it was an animal it chewed the shit out of the guy's head. There was no evidence of a bullet entry, or a blow to the body. There could have been a blow or a bullet to the head, but the head had been chewed up...nearly gone."

Logan stirred more sugar into his coffee and looked out the window at the blue Arizona sky. After about thirty seconds he looked at Yost and said, "Tell me, Yost, was the rest of the body intact?"

"I think so. I saw just the head area...most of the head was gone. The rest of the body was still clothed. I think the only wounds were to the head. Why?"

"Did forensics indicate that any other part of the body was violated, or eaten?"

"No, only the head was damaged. Maybe there were some superficial scratches to the arms or torso. Why?"

"No reason...just curious. When was the time of death?"

"Best guess is that it was last Thursday night. The hunter found it Friday morning. This is the closest we've come to finding a body very shortly after it had been killed." Yost looked down at his hands and asked, "So tell me, Logan, what do you think?"

Logan gazed into his coffee cup then up at Yost. "I think you need to find more bodies and gather more evidence. Sounds like the killer could be using a rock to bash the heads of his victims, and then let animals eat on the remains. That's what it seems like. Don't you believe his motive is to rob crossers? He's just bashing in heads to create a mythical head-eating monster...to draw the attention away from his real motive for the murder, which is to steal the loot."

"Yes, that's the current MO we have for him."

"Then stick with that line of investigation. I think it's a good one. Logan got up from the table, and put a five-dollar bill on the table. "Let me get this one, Yost."

Yost followed Logan's lead and stood up. "So your theory about animals killing crossers is now out the window? You don't believe that anymore?"

"It's been awhile since I thought about it, Yost."

The two men walked outside and headed toward Logan's truck. Logan unlocked and opened the door, and lifted himself onto the seat. Yost hung onto the open door as Logan rolled down the electric window with the push of a button. Yost closed the door as Logan connected his seat belt. "Logan, so you got no theory about these deaths that you want to share anymore?"

"No, I really don't. But I wish you the best of luck."

Logan put the shifter in reverse and began to back out. Yost stepped away and started toward his Blazer. "Hey, Yost," Logan paused, turning down his radio, "I suggest you get a copy of 'Beast in the Garden' and read it from cover to cover. The author discusses animals eating humans. Make some phone calls to some wildlife experts. See if they can give you a hand."

"Beast and the Garden," Yost repeated to Logan. "It's about animals eating humans?"

"Beast IN the Garden. Right, animals eating humans, and a lot more. It's great background for the way your case may be shaping up."

Logan pulled onto the frontage road and headed east toward Benson. As soon as he got to his Blazer, Yost wrote the name of the book next to the notes he had taken from Black earlier. The page read: "Forensics—some large animal chewed on skull. Hunt—sign of mountain lion nearby. Black— Where's *El Diablo*? What's *El Diablo*? Logan—Beast and the garden."

Chapter 16

He trusted the normal gear of past crossings: a black plastic bag filled with clothes and food, and a plastic water jug. The bag protected him and his clothes from the weather, from the wind and bouts of rain. It was like a trusted companion. But now he moved with a deep and troubling fear.

Fernando showed the other men the device he had taken from his pack strap. No one knew exactly what it was but they all concluded that the Border Patrol had put it there for some reason that was not good. Perhaps it was to make him sick and unable to continue crossing. No matter the reason for the wire and strange electronic box, Fernando took his belongings from the pack, positioned the strap on a round rock and with another rock from the creek bed pounded the object inside the strap. He wanted to kill it, and in the process he split open his thumb. Splattered blood was the only initial sign of his injury since once again anger masked any pain he felt. He left the pack in a wadded heap under a pile of rocks in the streambed and covered it with a log and some brush so no one would find it. Then the pain of his smashed thumb began to throb, creating in him a growing anxiety and anger.

He put the Border Patrol in the same category as *El Diablo*, and no longer had a sense of comfort being in the United States. He concluded that his journey through this life was hopeless, and his trek around southern Arizona was useless and without a future. Although the stride of the other men was long and energetic as they progressed north to the Canelo Hills that afternoon, Fernando walked with a choppy hesitance. His legs had become heavy, like his spirit. They were about six miles from where they had stopped earlier that morning when they decided to rest.

Miguel, the youngest of the six, had known a man like Fernando back home. He was especially tuned into Fernando's mood and began taking on his depressed disposition, becoming extremely apprehensive about continuing north. He had never experienced life in the north and didn't have the need for money. He had no wife or children. For him this trip was all about the adventure, the conquest of a land about which he knew so little.

The sun was about three hours from setting in a hazy sky. As the men stopped on a high ridge in the Canelo Hills, Fernando looked south into the San Rafael Valley. He could still see Mexico from that vantage. Once he moved north into the Mustang and Whetstone mountains he knew his homeland would be out of sight. Miguel watched Fernando and knew what was on his mind.

They decided to rest until sundown and then continue northward. The cloud cover would hold in some of the ground warmth that had collected from the filtered sunlight earlier in the day. It would not be so cold. But Fernando's chill was not about the outside conditions. He was chilled to the core of his bones by the events of the last week, and by the suspicion that the Border Patrol had selected him for some reason. Since that reason was not known, his fear ran deeper. Gone were the thoughts of *El Diablo*. That entity was to the west. He felt the Border Patrol now was everywhere, and that he was a marked man.

Trapped under the drudgery of this journey Fernando shared his thoughts and feelings with unusual candor. It was obvious to the others that Fernando was scared and not going to continue northward. So as the sun began to set and the group gathered their gear, Fernando and Miguel wished the others luck and headed back south.

They would backtrack past their morning camp and then continue into the woodlands and the night. Fernando would try to find peace in Mexico. The border and the United States were no longer hospitable for him.

He turned out the bathroom light and snuggled next to his wife in their warm bed. He felt alone with his thoughts, at the end of a thin limb he had climbed onto. His plans had not worked. His body was aching. Yost needed comfort, the presence of another body. He moved toward her but she was asleep. She had left him in the living room an hour ago, a familiar event, and entered a deep, induced sleep, alone as usual.

Yost was trapped between his desire for control and the apparent need to open his investigation for others to examine and contribute. He was trying to handle *El Diablo* alone within the confines of his agency, even resisting attempts by the Sheriff's Office to enter into the search. He wanted all the credit for solving the murders. That his career passion was impacting his marriage went totally unnoticed by him.

Logan had suggested he contact wildlife professionals to interpret his evidence. Yost's first reaction was to mantle the information and run to his Border Patrol resources, but he was beginning to realize the limitations of his organization and consider other options. Earlier in the evening he was struck with the realization that coordinating a task force to review the murders might be the best thing. It would give him control and recognition for his ultimate goal, promotion to the Regional Office. That thought gave him a modicum of relief and a positive outlook for going to work the next morning. It was with that renewed sense of certainty, which was in his mind only, that he listened to the rhythmic, content breathing of his wife. He failed to realize he was not the source of her peace, and fell asleep.

Bob Clawson was a seasoned professional. A thirty-year veteran with the U.S. Fish and Wildlife Service, Clawson was familiar with the issues of wildlife management in Arizona and the Southwest. He had assisted numerous law enforcement cases and always interjected his ecological expertise into legal discussions in a way that afforded helpful and meaningful thought.

When he took the call from Darrel Yost he was very accommodating and agreed to meet with Yost the next morning at his wildlife office in Phoenix.

Yost had done his homework. He had made several calls to the Washington office of Border Patrol to find a federal wildlife official with a law enforcement background. He had not known there was one up the road in Phoenix. Surely Clawson would understand the sensitivity of the information he would reveal and keep it from leaking to the general public and other enforcement agencies. Yost still wanted to make sure his task force was under his control.

It was with this illusion of control that Yost headed to Phoenix. He drove up Interstate 10, past the large and expensive new housing developments on the northwest fringe of Tucson and Marana. It was good to be out of the remote rural areas where crossers toiled through wild and rugged landscapes. Here they were laboring in the construction fields of suburbia or traveling on the interstate highway in vans and trucks toward their ultimate destinations to the north and east...still present but less visible and therefore not as likely to hit Yost's radar. Immigration and Customs Enforcement was responsible for them once they escaped the borderlands, and that was just fine with him.

In the farm fields near Casa Grande Yost could see Mexican workers irrigating fields of cantaloupe and cotton. In about six months the crops would be ready for harvest, which meant more Mexican labor would be required. Mexican men and women would always migrate toward this need. They were not unlike their ancestors who worked

Arizona's copper and silver mines as the region was growing in economic importance. Their work was their life, which enhanced the lives of their families...all of which enriched the fabric of Arizona's landscape.

All these facts escaped his comprehension as Yost drove north. His mind was on his career, his immediate task, and his future. He turned down the heater in his Blazer, turned up the radio, and continued driving northward toward Phoenix.

Chapter 17

"Have a seat, Mr. Yost. Coffee?" inquired Bob Clawson. "Sure, thanks," responded Yost as he sat down. He noticed Clawson's credentials behind his desk hanging from the white walls of his office. Clawson returned with a cup of steaming coffee in mug that said "The Wildlife Society."

"What's the Wildlife Society?" asked Yost.

"It's an organization of wildlife professionals. I was president of the outfit while I was in Texas."

"Are you from Texas?"

"Yes sir. Born and raised in Alpine. Do you know where that is?"

"Sure do…in west Texas. Great part of a great state." Yost actually hated Texans. In his mind they were pushy and tried to take control. All of a sudden he tensed up and put up his guard.

"Now, what can I do for you, Mr. Yost?"

"Well, I have a situation down along the border that may involve something you may know a thing or two about. I need an expert."

"What sort of situation?"

Yost instantly decided that he did not want to risk having Clawson jump right into the case. He would slowly meter information to Clawson and glean as much from him as he could. He now wished he had read Logan's recommended book so he could converse with Clawson with at least some common vocabulary and knowledge.

"We've had a rash of deaths along the border within the last year or so, and we're not sure about the cause. These are not deaths from exposure, which is what we normally encounter. There seems to be an element of foul play. We are trying to sort out whether the killings are caused by man or some other agent."

"Some other agent...like what? What does the evidence suggest?"

The use of the word evidence made Yost even more uncomfortable. He could see Clawson's law enforcement training coming to the front of the conversation. He wished now he was dealing with a guy who had no enforcement background, someone who would just answer questions, and not ask any.

"We're not sure." Yost became illusive, and he felt naked in front of Clawson. "Have you read 'Beast and the Garden'?"

"Beast IN the Garden? Sure. Great book. You know, we had several incidents of mountain lions attacking hikers in Arizona. That's when I got a copy and read it. It's full of good information. There was that incident in Sabino Canyon, in your neck of the woods down in Tucson."

"Yes, I recall," sputtered Yost, trying to remember what he had casually read in the newspaper about two years ago.

Clawson continued, "We know that lions can become accustomed to humans. First they lose their fear of man, and then they can look at man as prey. It's a natural progression of a large predator that can take down most creatures it encounters. Humans are the right size, like a deer. If a lion exhibits no fear of humans and faces shortages in natural prey populations, the jump from deer to people can be expected under certain circumstances."

"What circumstances?"

"Food mainly. If there's a decline in prey base, humans can fill that void. Where are you finding these bodies?"

"Down along the border."

"How many?"

"Well, we're not sure. We've had about twenty show up so far."

"Since when?"

"The first one was about two years ago."

"I take it that you've not scoured the countryside to find them. You just get reports."

"Exactly. The bodies are reported to us, usually by hunters or rock hounds who meander around out in the hills."

"What shape are the bodies in when you encounter them?"

Yost was becoming very uncomfortable. Clawson was acting like the guy in charge, interrogating Yost, who was feeling inadequate since he had few questions of his own. And Yost's answers suggested that he had not done a good job at examining the landscape for more clues. In a two-year period any decent enforcement agent should have been able to solve this mystery he thought. That he had not broken the case yet was now smacking him in the face. He needed to get control of Clawson.

"Various states of decomposition, mainly skeletal remains scattered across the area."

"So this has probably been going on for more than two years if you're finding skeletons. It takes almost a year for all the meat and soft tissue to be eaten by critters and bugs so that the bones can disarticulate."

Yost was becoming stupefied. "Say, Bob, I was wondering if you'd be willing to serve on a task force I'm putting together to solve these deaths, or murders, or whatever they are. I'm assembling experts from a variety of disciplines, and was hoping you'd assist from the wildlife perspective." Yost looked at Clawson, hoping the request for his expertise would stop the barrage of questions.

"Sure, I'd be happy to help. I have a guy on my staff that helped the Forest Service with their lion problem at Sabino. And I know a guy who is real knowledgeable about big cats. He runs dog after them and knows their sign and habits like the back of his hand. You also might want to get the state boys involved. The state game and fish has a lot of lion expertise available."

"Have you ever heard of Eldon Hunt?"

"Sure. He's a fine lion man. Are you getting advice from him?"

"You bet. Eldon was out on a case just this last weekend. He's been a real asset."

"He sure is. That's a good move to involve him."

Yost didn't like Clawson telling him he'd made a good move. It felt too much like a report card. All he wanted was to get out of there and get to a bookstore. He looked at his watch and apologized for having to make this a short meeting. "I have to run now, but I just wanted to touch base. I'll get back with you in a couple days with details of the task force. I hope to have a meeting soon. Do you have any problem meeting in Tucson?"

"No. My Pima County Field Office is in Tucson. I get down there every Tuesday. I can meet next Tuesday if you want."

"That may be just perfect timing. I'll be in touch." Yost pushed back his chair, stood up, and shook Clawson's hand. It was bigger than he remembered it being. "Thanks for your time, Bob. I really appreciate it." As Yost was preparing to leave Clawson's office, the phone on his desk began to ring. Clawson looked at it, and Yost said, "Duty calls. I can find my way out. Thanks again."

Yost left and Clawson picked up the phone, "Clawson here." He glanced over to the coffee he had handed Yost. The cup was still full and steaming.

Having taken directions from the Hispanic clerk, Yost found himself in the natural history section of the bookstore. She said what he was after was in stock, and there should be two copies on the shelf.

He ran his index finger along the books and immediately came to the Bs, and the name David Baron. Sure enough, two copies. He pulled one out and looked at it. "Beast IN the Garden," he mumbled to himself. He didn't bother flipping through the pages. He backtracked to the checkout counter to make his purchase, then walked to his Blazer and headed south to Tucson.

He was resistant to the concept that the border deaths were merely a case of mountain lions killing crossers. Since that scenario was out of his area of expertise he would not give the notion much thought. However he needed to engage the concept just in case lions were

involved, and he felt that leading a group of enforcement professionals to solve the mystery deaths would give the lion theory due
diligence. He opposed the possibility of compromising his path to
promotion by sharing the credit for solving this case with too many
people. His ego was fueling him.

As he navigated the Phoenix traffic he realized how much he hated big cities. His legs still ached, reminding him how much he also
hated the wild areas of the state. His niche was that narrow place
somewhere between the two. His was an uncomfortable and shrink-
ing world that needed constant defense. As he felt his gut boil from
the very thought of battling constantly, he drove along. He was not
sure what his next move would be but he had to make it soon.
Clawson had given him that incentive.

Chapter 18

Steve Black had no direction. He had not heard from Yost since Friday, almost a week ago. After the satellite had failed to pick up Fernando's location he began searching with his ground unit. He concluded his pursuit with a flight from the Cabeza National Wildlife Refuge in the west to the New Mexico line. He heard nothing, not even the hint of a beep from *El Diablo*'s transmitter.

After gathering up the body in the Cerro Colorados it seemed as if the pursuit of *El Diablo* was on hold. He figured Plan B had been abandoned, but there was no announcement of a Plan C. Yost had been out of his office much of the time, and when he was there the door was closed. It was obvious he did not want to be bothered. Black had seen this plenty of times in the past. He knew Yost was sequestered away, planning everyone's next move. Black wondered what that next move had in store for him.

When Yost showed up in his office Black looked surprised. "Hi, Darrel. What's up?"

"Been real busy, Steve. Thanks for the report on your last flight. Say, I got to talk with you. I want to take a new approach. I want to get you together with Hunt. I want you to learn all you can about tracking mountain lions. I want you to go with him for a couple weeks and pick his brain. You need to learn what sign a lion leaves around its kill. I want you to become an expert, and be able to say with one hundred percent certainty that a lion was, or was not, responsible for the death on all future bodies we find. I want you to be the go-to guy on this."

Black was stunned by Yost's display of zeal and trust. This was not the Yost he had known. He immediately began wondering why Yost was placing so much confidence in him. They had worked together for over a year and never had a disagreement. But Black never went against what Yost was thinking or doing so there had never been reason for Yost's retaliation. The example of Sam Logan was always on Black's mind, perhaps making him always dance to the tune Yost was playing.

"That sounds good, Darrel. Is Hunt lined out on this?"

"Yes. Turns out he'll be with clients who have him booked for lion hunts over the next couple weeks. He said you could ride along. There will be plenty of time to ask questions. Can you be in the field for the next week or two? You got any family stuff to deal with?"

"No, I think I'm clear on that front. When will we be leaving?"

"Today...and not me...just you."

"Well, I gotta call my wife and take care of a few things then. Will I ride with Hunt or take one of our vehicles?"

"Yes, take one of ours. I want you to be able to leave when you think you've learned all you need."

"Okay. I presume we're giving up on Plan B?"

"Well, for now. I think there still is some evidence for some crazy crosser bashing the heads of his fellow countrymen and stealing the valuables and money. But recent evidence points toward hungry mountain lions."

"But, Darrel, think about this for a minute. Do you have a little time to go over this now? I have been doing a lot of rehashing about what sent us down the path of a human killer. I think we should review some things before going off on another angle."

In a way this was music to Yost's ears. If there was still a chance of retaining the glory for solving the case with Border Patrol resources alone, Yost was interested. He pulled up a chair and sat along side Black's desk. "Alright, let's go over what you're thinking about."

Black pulled out his field log. It had records of dates, field locations, and evidence gathered at all the bodies they had examined. His notes included all the meetings Yost had convened, and conversations between Black and witnesses and others involved with each visit. This was Black at his scientific best, and Yost recognized it.

Black started his recitation with a calm and confident manner. "Okay, we had our first reported body a little over two years ago. We found a human pelvis and some long bones like a femur and some ribs. No skull. It was reported by some deer hunters who had been archery hunting in the San Luis Mountains."

"Right," responded Yost.

"We had no clue what caused the death so we suspected exposure. Then we had two more bone piles later that month, one in the Atascosas and another in the Las Guijas just out of Arivaca. No skulls. Then one in early February that was more than just bones. It was the one that sparked our attention, making us think that murder could be involved. The February body was about a month old. Our examination discovered a partial hole in the base of the skull...part of the skull actually. That suggestion of a hole was along the fracture edge. It was not well defined and we didn't run ballistics on it, but we concluded that maybe a small caliber bullet had entered the skull at that point."

As Yost listened he recalled the incident as if it happened yesterday. That was the first time he set his sights on the Regional Office in Albuquerque. It was a date burned into his memory.

"Could that hole have been a lion's tooth mark? Maybe. But we weren't even thinking along those lines then. Then we found that cache of money and valuable property that a crosser would carry and that gave us a motive for the murders: theft. So our initial reaction, Plan A, was to find someone near the cache and put a transmitter on him. That was your idea, and it was brilliant. Well, it's been over a year between then and Plan B, and we never found a body fresher than a month or two old." Black was on a roll and he could see a reaction bubbling up in Yost.

He continued, "That cache of clothes, food and money in the cave along Wilbur Canyon in the San Luis Mountains west of Arivaca has meaning...and it's in the heart of the killing field! We cataloged items at the cache and demonstrated new items were being added and some were being removed, most likely taken to sell on the black market. We demonstrated that the guy centered his killing on that cache. He kills, gets his loot and stores it until he has enough for a load and a trip to Mexico or wherever. We believed robbery was the motive for murder. Darrel, that motive is out there. This is way beyond a simple killer lion theory."

Yost looked pleased so Black continued with his reasoning. "We found more bodies, most with the skull missing. We theorized the killer, *El Diablo*, used a small caliber pistol to dispatch his victims, took their stuff and hid it in the cave."

"That's right," interrupted Yost, "and we focused on the lack of skulls, concluding that this was the site of the fatal blow, the place on the body that scavenging animals would eat first. That would hide the evidence of the bullet hole, especially if he bashed in the head later. We had the act of animals eating the head rolled into our theory. It's just that we did not believe animals were doing the killing. Sure, they ate the head and the rest of the body, but they had not killed the guy."

Yost was pensive as he said, "Then we initiated the notion of Plans A and B, wiring a suspect to catch him near the act of murder. We'd spread the word about deaths in Mexico, using *El Diablo* to scare the shit out of the superstitious crossers. Only the one who knew there was no such thing as *El Diablo* would venture into the area of the Altar Valley. We'd find a fresh body and get Hunt's dogs to track him down."

"Right," replied Black. "And that Fernando guy was a good candidate. He was a loner, a guy who fits the profile of a mass murderer. He was near the cache...well, you know all the details."

"You're right, Steve. All indications are that the deaths were human-caused, not animal-caused."

Steve added, "No doubt animals have fed on the bodies, but what else would we expect? Around Arivaca where this is happening probably some of the animals have become pretty habituated to feeding on dead humans. We can expect that to happen. Maybe even some of the large predators have come to depend on dead humans for food...they're now totally scavengers, not killers."

Yost settled back into his dream world, one that had him at the center of the investigation with a firm hand on Steve Black, his main investigator.

"I think *El Diablo* is still alive and well," Steve continued. "Maybe he discovered his transmitter, lost his backpack down a sewer hole somewhere, or gave it to someone who headed back home and way out of range. But no matter the fate of the transmitter, *El Diablo* is still out there."

"Too bad that transmitter messed up. That was a good shot at getting him," said Yost. He liked Black's logic. What he liked more was the fact that Black was a private man, one he could trust with his ideas, knowing that he would not talk to others about his theory. He had a good amount of control over Black, and what control he did not have did not bother him. Black was not a threat.

"I think we should continue trying to find a human killer," said Black. "Call it Plan C if you want. But I think we should systematically search for bodies and then get the dogs on a fresh kill."

"You mean, have an intensive search?" asked Yost. "That would take a lot of manpower. We can't find these bodies from the air. They're usually concealed in the brush and rocks."

"No, but we can have Hunt's dogs find them for us," responded Black.

A sense of relief overcame Yost. He instantly thought of getting Black some sort of Sectional Award. Not a State or Regional Award since he didn't want Black's reputation to eclipse his own. But a local award to cement Black's loyalty. The Plan C that Black had just laid out was perfect. It suggested a stepwise approach, Plans A, B then C, all of which followed Yost's initial line of investigation in a logical sequence. Thoughts of a big Regional, even Washington, desk loomed in his mind as he looked at Black.

"Steve, I like your reasoning. Let's go with the beginnings of a Plan C. While you're with Hunt ask him about the ability of his dogs to find dead bodies. Ask him if they will be able to go from finding a dead man to tracking a live killer."

"10-4, Darrel. I gotta call mama and let her know where I'll be. I'll get ahold of Hunt on his cell and meet him wherever."

"Great. Good luck, Steve." Yost was slipping into deep thought. Not about the case as much as about strategy of another sort. "And, Steve," Yost said, "let's keep everything we discussed here just between you and me. I don't want this getting out. We need to employ information management if we want this thing to work. This may be our last shot."

Chapter 19

Horses were never Steve Black's favorite thing. His legs were strong from hiking but half a day in the saddle following a pack of baying dogs had taken its toll on his butt and legs. His whole body slid off the saddle at the end of the day.

"We'll camp here at the vehicles and get after that lion again in the morning when tracking conditions are better," declared Hunt. "The scent will hold close to the ground and the dogs can get a better line on it." Black and the two hunters from somewhere back East organized their sleeping and personal gear while Hunt took care of the dogs and horses.

Eldon Hunt was in charge and there was no doubt. The dogs obeyed him without as much as an obvious verbal command. They seemed to know what he was thinking. What they were thinking he certainly understood.

Hunt had started a fire as soon as they returned to the tents, which were 30 feet from the truck and four-horse trailer. He had asked Black to add more oak so the fire had lots of coals. The reward for his assistance would be venison stew and "the best peach cobbler this side of the San Pedro River." Black was hungry and looking forward to being served by Eldon. He had already served himself plenty by dismounting that horse.

Black had planned his strategy after an hour in the saddle. He quickly got the gist of lion hunting and didn't need two weeks afield on a horse to learn anymore. He figured Eldon was the expert witness on lion sign so he would be consulted on any body they found. All he really needed to find out from Hunt was the last thing he and Yost had discussed in his office: can his dogs find dead bodies, and could they then trail the killer. Black planned to get that issue settled around camp that evening and be on the road before sun-up while the other three headed out after the lion.

Black could not get a word in edgewise. The two Easterners blabbed and blabbed into the night about their worldly hunting trips. They were fueled by a bottle of bacanora that Hunt had given them. Hunt commented quietly to Black that the special drink from Sonora was almost more important to these Easterners than a lion.

When the two dudes started arguing about who killed the biggest grizzly bear in Alaska Black found his moment.

"Eldon, can your dogs find a dead body? I mean just a plain old dead body stashed in the hills. Are they good enough to find one if you just rode around on horseback with them ranging ahead of you?"

"Never tried that, Steve. I suppose if I conditioned them they could find one, sure. These dogs are basically just a very mobile sniffing apparatus connected to a loud voice box. When they smell what I'm after, they let me know. They tell me how fresh the sign is and how close the target is. It's up to me to train them on a target."

"You mean they can pass all the other scents that's out there and go just after what you program them to seek?"

"Right. They did it today. I bet they crossed a ton of deer and javelina scent this afternoon. They didn't set out after it. They stayed on task because they knew I didn't want a deer or javelina. They do it all the time now. When they were younger they were always getting off-track. But that's just like anything young. These dogs here...they're all real good dogs now."

"So can you train them to find a dead body?"

"I could. But you know, I think for that I would use two dogs that I got about six months ago. They're young and eager, and not set in their ways. These here dogs have been following cats nearly all their lives and they know that routine. The new dogs will be a lot easier to train. Besides, I don't want to get these old dogs off lions. They're very good at that. That bit about not being able to teach an old dog new tricks is true."

"Boy, do I know that! But you think you can teach those new dogs how to find dead bodies along the border? Right?"

"I can give it a shot, sure. I think that's doable."

"Okay. When can you be ready?"

"Give me a month. I got clients for the next two weeks, and I want to try some techniques on those new dogs. I think I could be ready to go in a month."

"Perfect. Thanks, Eldon. I think I'll hit the sack. I'm beat."

"No problem. Will you be going with us in the morning?"

"I think I better head to the office. I got a lot of planning to get done. Will you be alright without me?"

"Well, not really. But we'll try to manage!"

Black was so content after his talk with Hunt that he hobbled over to his bedroll and fell asleep in a heartbeat. Even the howling of two drunk Easterners couldn't keep him awake.

When Yost got the call from Black he was surprised. "How come you're back so soon? Did you fall off your horse?"

"No, no. I wish I did though. Then I wouldn't have had to spend eight hours trying to stay on."

"I know what you mean. How's Hunt?"

"He's great. Boy, he really earned his money with those hunters. Those guys were obnoxious. I mean real obnoxious. I don't see how Eldon can stand them."

"Well, I guess for him it's another day, another dollar. So what did you find out?"

"Hunt said he can train his dogs to find dead bodies, and he can be ready to go in a month."

"Say, that's perfect. We'll officially call this Plan C. I think this is our best idea yet. We could break this case sometime this spring."

"I think so."

"Hey, Steve, I got to make a phone call then run into this meeting before I fly to the Regional Office this afternoon. There's some new big procedural change that I have to get boned up on. Good job with Hunt. I'll call you when I get back."

"Bob Clawson? How are you? This is Darrel Yost."

"Good, good. I wasn't sure what was happening since I hadn't heard from you. How's the case going?"

"Things are moving right along. Say, we've had some new leads that are panning out real well. I think we're close to catching our killer."

"So you don't think lions are involved?"

"No, not with the killing...maybe with scavenging a dead body though. New evidence supports the early findings and it all points toward my first hunch being correct. So we're going to stay on that track for a couple weeks. If everything goes okay we should have this thing wrapped up in a month or two."

"Hey, that's great. Keep in touch, and let me know if there's anything I can do for you."

"Will do. Thanks, Bob"

Chapter 20

Land ownership influences people in a variety of ways. In some it instills a profound sense of responsibility, a noble duty that embodies hard work and a desire for improvements that will make the land better. In others it confers a sense of superiority that transcends the ground, reduces the panoramic landscape to a narrow selfish vision, and numbs the owner's perception of reality.

That later condition permeated the body and mind of Larry Thompson as he poured himself another drink. Watching the setting sun alone from the porch of his Texas ranch, the issue of Mexican migration into the U.S. again occupied his thoughts. As if talking to members of a board around a conference table Thompson declared out loud, "Okay, we've had the Sopori ranch for about three years now and it seems like we're getting a handle on the wetback problem there. Our management practices have worked here in Texas, and I think we shall continue to see benefits from our efforts in Arizona."

Jay Sharp's state of mind was the same as Thompson's, but the experiences leading up to that condition were different. After his father died and his fight with probate court was over he took owner-ship of the ranch his grandfather had built. That is when his battles with the federal government commenced. The use of federal leases that had been a significant part of the ranch were challenged by the government for environmental reasons, and what he didn't lose through regulatory takings he gave up for economic reasons. In his mind that was his land and the government took it.

He sold a chunk of the private remnants of the ranch to a miner for cash needed to pay off the mortgage on his home in Tucson, where he lived alone. The Las Guijas Mountains were rich in miner-als, and residues of past mining operations were strewn across the hills and in the canyons. He was always receiving offers from mining companies and individuals who thought they could strike valuable ore when prices were up. Since his only sources of meager income were the ranch and a small military disability pension, the option to sell some land was a means of comfort, his only means.

About twice a week he made the drive to the ranch. The house there, his birthplace, was barely functional. There always had been intermittent problems with the well, and the drought made that matter permanent. It took a week for enough water to collect in the aquifer to afford a sufficient quantity of water for drinking. If he needed to bathe he had to go to the windmill on the flats where the cattle drank. He was always alone during his wanderings to and around the ranch. He didn't have a dog, which was very unlike any real rancher in the area.

A bum leg, the result of an injury he acquired during his second tour of duty in Viet Nam, always plagued him. He received a Purple Heart for the incident, but he tossed it down one of the deep mine shafts the day he relinquished his last parcel of federal lease. He wanted no part of the federal government in his life. His judgment of the Border Patrol as an inadequate agency enhanced his hatred of the feds even more.

Sharp bought his usual supplies from a feed and tack store on the south side of Tucson. He loaded them into the bed of his pickup except for one box, which he set in the cab on the seat next to him. "*Hecho en Mexico*" was stamped on the brown cardboard. They were cheap leather gloves that worked fine for him. He went through a box of twelve pairs every three months or so. They were symbolic more than functional, part of a ritual he started about a year ago. He stuck the key into his ignition switch and looked at the box, knowing where every glove would end up.

His ranch was on the southwestern fringe of the Las Guijas Mountains. From Tucson he had a choice of two routes to get there. He could go south toward Nogales and halfway to the border head west on the Arivaca Road and then north through the Altar Valley a short ways. If he were in a hurry he could take the road west toward Ajo and go left at Three Points through the Altar Valley. Since he was never in a hurry the choice depended on his mood, which was like the price of beef: variable, but always lower than needed to make a living.

That morning he decided to swing through Arivaca. He had a post office box there and needed to check the mail, which he hadn't done in over three weeks. He often would pass by the post office without as much as a fleeting thought about the mail. His disability check was deposited electronically so nothing there was of interest to him. The electric bill for the ranch was also paid with electronic transfer and he had no other ranch or local supply bills since he paid for everything with cash. He essentially was disconnected from most of the life around him, and he liked it that way.

Sharp knew very few Arivaca residents, mainly the old-timers he had grown up with but they were dying off. Retirees from the growing cities to the east, like Green Valley and Tucac, represented to him all that was bad about the country. They traveled to Arivaca like they were on some sort of safari, gawking at the residents and buildings then returning home and pouring a tall one, toasting their brush with primates and outlaws. In reality Arivaca had not changed much in the past fifty years, other than the developments springing up on its eastern front toward Tucson. Since the homes there seemed to be sucking up all the groundwater he also put those residents on his hate list...a list that seemed to grow with each visit to the ranch.

About two years ago Sharp began reading about *El Diablo* in the Tucson newspaper. He learned that the Border Patrol had concluded *El Diablo* was a psychopath killer who robbed his own countrymen. From the local patrol agents he gleaned that the feds were spreading that conclusion as a means of keeping the crossers from coming through the area, and that they were more interested in keeping up the myth than in finding the killer.

The proximity to Mexico, the relative remoteness of the area, and the presence of nooks and crannies that held water and hiding places made the landscape around Arivaca a natural corridor for Mexican migration. Crossers were a common occurrence in the area, but within the past five years there was a significant rise in crime around Arivaca. Most property owners, especially those who lived on the edge of town and on the surrounding ranches, had things stolen, water gates left open, or extreme littering of everything from trash to abandoned cars. The local citizenry was split on what action to take. Many were sympathetic and wanted to lend a hand to the crossers, while others wanted to form a militia group to round up "wets" that were not being observed by the Border Patrol.

A resident Border Patrol senior agent warned them against militia action. "You cannot make a citizen's arrest because you can't prove to a judge that you were sure they were felons at the time of your arrest," warned Agent Bruce Bean at a meeting of townspeople. "Although it's a felony to enter our country without the proper documentation and to traffic in migrants, you need to be able to articulate to a judge why you suspected such activity...and what observations made you suspect any illegal activity and gave you cause to stop and detain a person. Basically, you need to be an officer of the law to follow the legal process."

That discussion of legal process dampened the vigilante movement so the rest of that summer four years ago the main topic of conversation returned to the drought and hope for a good summer monsoon season. Also *El Diablo* had permeated the area and precluded intervention. Everyone gratefully greeted the absence of crime and stopped talking, or even thinking about some form of local solution to a diminishing problem. Almost everyone.

The experience was new and exciting, and the reward was there. They did it, and he was pleased. Dogs always flashed youthful exuberance when discovering the goal. He responded in a way that further encouraged their senses and instincts. It was this perfect harmony that Eldon Hunt relayed to Steve Black one week earlier than he had promised.

"So it looks like they got the hang of it, Eldon?"

"Yeah, I think they're ready. I was a little concerned about the dogs separating human flesh from other dead animal flesh. The shirt from that latest victim found by those javelina hunters was the only smell of dead human flesh I had, and that was getting pretty old and diluted. I thought it would be over-powered by the scent of dead rabbit and javelina that I got from road-kills, but the dogs had no problem keeping 'em separate.

That's great! I'll tell Darrel that you're ready to go. I'll give you a call, maybe later this afternoon."

Yost and Black launched Plan C. Yost convened a meeting of agents mainly from his western portion of the sector and laid out his latest thoughts. He established his dominance then let Black run most of the meetings. Yost was preoccupied with special assignments from the Regional Office and planned to run a larger sector meeting later in the month, so he was content now to let Black run the smaller get-together of agents mostly under Yost's supervision.

With Black at the helm there had been a significant improvement in data gathering from the field. The agents afforded valuable input.

Most of them had performed follow-up investigations at sites where bodies had been discovered.

Bruce Bean, the seasoned agent who had been stationed in Arivaca for the past five years, offered especially keen insights. He had known the culture of the locals and the crossers prior to the first body being discovered, and as a senior agent he had been present at nearly all the body recovery operations. Most importantly, he was the one who discovered *El Diablo*'s cache of loot west of Arivaca where the foothills of the San Luis Mountains fanned out along the eastern flank of Altar Valley. He had all the body recovery sites located on a detailed topographic map that hung on the den wall at his house.

"If we look at the cache as the center of *El Diablo*'s activity, it's evident that he moves along the east side of the Altar Valley," stated Bean. "Most of the bodies have been discovered south of Arivaca Creek in the foothills of the San Luis Mountains. I think the reason for that is because that's where the hunters are, and the hunters are the ones discovering the bodies. The road access is better there, and there's more public land for hunters to roam. We are getting a skewed picture of the full range of our killer. The foothills of the Las Guijas to the north and east are relatively untouched by hunters because most of it is private land with locked gates. I think we should search that area first to see if indeed *El Diablo* has been operating there. I suspect he has been since the Las Guijas are as close to the cache as the San Luis Mountains."

"So, in other words, we shift the search north," summarized Black.

"Yes, sir. That's my recommendation," responded Bean.

"Very good," concluded Yost, beaming with pride at his local talent, and happy to keep the investigation in house.

Black added, "Aside from these relatively open lands around the Las Guijas and San Luis mountains are the wooded Atascosa Mountains just to the southeast. We don't have any bodies from there but it is mountainous and rugged, and most access is through the large private ranches with locked gates. Bottom line is that we don't know if bodies exist there, undetected." Black's standards for scientific inquiry required that he add that fact to the discussion.

Chapter 21

The call went out for assistance from the entire Tucson Sector. Yost had been able to convince the sector chief to spare ten men from the eastern side for intensive searches for bodies in the rocky hills around Arivaca. In reality he hardly needed to say a word. He had made all the political connections at the Regional Office, which applied pressure on the State Office in Tucson. Yost felt this was his only move, his last chance to show his value to the organization. He had sold himself well. While Hunt had been preparing his dogs, Yost had been setting up his own future.

At the state level the price for applying pressure to the chain of command in the region was potentially high but Yost decided to gamble. If his suspicion was correct and Plan C worked all the bodies they would find would ensnare the killer and all would be forgiven. Or at least his superiors and peers would let him part the waters long enough to make his career progression out of Arizona and toward eastern heights at the Regional Office in Albuquerque.

One of the ten men from the eastern end of the sector assigned to the project was young Nate Chavez. He had relatively little experience at his patrol position so his brains were not as valuable to the eastern mission as his youth and brawn were to the western one. As

Nate sat at the Arivaca Post Office Annex, the site of Yost's tempo-rary operations station, he took notes feverishly.

Yost was taking charge of his Arivaca operation, laying out a scant history of Operation El Diablo and explaining the mission of his Plan C, officially named "Diablo Snare." "We are gathered here to search along rocky terrain of the Las Guijas Mountains for any sign of human mortality," Yost pontificated to the twenty-eight agents in the room. "Here's another mortality site," said Yost, flicking another digital image onto the screen. "Note the similarity of all the sites. They're along the base of a ridge, usually near a rocky area with cliffs. Of the thirty-one bodies we've investigated within the last two years, twenty-two have been in areas like this...that's almost ninety percent!" He showed a graph his secretary had prepared.

As Chavez made a mental note of Yost's math error he looked around the room, discovering that no one held the same zeal for this exercise as Yost. He sensed the other agents all knew this was Yost's gig, his claim to fame. From his body language to his words, Yost essentially was claiming ownership of everything that hopefully would lead to the apprehension of *El Diablo*. He was not giving ownership of any part of this investigation to the agents. This fact was most evident on the face of Steve Black, who was seated near the projector to assist Yost with any technical trouble that might occur.

"Let me recap here," said Yost. "I want to reiterate the founda-tional theory of this investigation. We believe someone is killing Mexicans as they are returning home, and robbing them of the money and possessions they have saved while in the U.S. Or our killer is committing the crime just after crossers leave Mexico with some money to get them to their destination in the states. He might even befriend some people near the border in Mexico, get to know them and what they are carrying, and take 'em out after a day or two of trekking into Arizona. We think this guy has created a devil myth, *El Diablo*, in the western end of the sector. His mythical creature has reduced the number of crossers west of Nogales, which we like since the area gets hot and many Mexicans have succumbed to the high temperatures there. We think *El Diablo*'s intent was to have fewer people around and thus reduce the chance of migrants witness his killings. The signature of an *El Diablo* killing is a headless corpse. About two years ago we began to hear rumors of headless bodies from the Mexican officials and from crossers we rounded up, and already there was a superstitious link between Satan and these deaths."

An agent from the back of the room asked a question that surprised Yost. "Do you think there is only one killer or a group of men, and is the killer a Mexican national or American?"

"I won't go into the details of our analysis," explained Yost. "Let me just say that we are fairly certain the killer is a lone Mexican."

Amid the sound of shuffling chairs and muffled comments Yost scratched something on his note pad then continued his presentation.

"I have decided to begin our systematic search in the Las Guijas Mountains, just a little northwest of here. We will progress westward toward the Altar Valley then skip south into the foothills of the San Luis Mountains. This search will be section by section. We will not leave a section until we have cleared it. We should be able to clear about three to five sections a day with the manpower we have. As you can see, we have about eighty to cover. That's eighty square miles, a lot of country. Our objective is to find a fresh body. We are looking for a fresh corpse that still has the scent of our killer.

"Now, we have some special assistance from Mr. Eldon Hunt. Most of you know Eldon, and many of you have worked with him. He's the best houndsman in the country. He trained two dogs specifically for this mission. They are conditioned to locate a human corpse, and if it's fresh enough and scent of the killer is still present the dogs will be able to track the killer. He will be on horseback with his dogs, searching like you. If you find a fresh body, he will be immediately dispatched to your location and attempt to track down *El Diablo* from that point. The dogs are important, but your eyes looking over the area are critical. You may uncover additional cache sites or who knows what. So please keep your eyes peeled."

Yost asked for the lights and continued his orientation. "On the desk in front of you is a folder with the shift schedule. It will tell you when you're on. All overtime has been cleared at the regional level. When you're on duty you will sleep here on cots that will be delivered this afternoon. I have arranged for several cooks to feed you. We'll have Mexican food for the first go around, then BBQ, and so on. I guarantee you'll like it. Grab a pack...they're sitting in the pile in that back corner. You'll find food and fluids that you can replace at the beginning of your shift. Any questions?"

Hearing none, Yost had one final word. "The land we will be searching is largely private. I have obtained a set of keys from each of the twenty-five or so land landowners. When you get your assignment, you'll be given a key, or sometimes a set of keys. There will be a tag on the key ring with the landowner's name and a number. I want you to know the landowner's name so you can address that person if you run into them while you're in the field. The number corresponds to a grid code."

Like a proud papa Yost looked at the group of young men under his control and concluded, "Okay, check your schedules. Some of you should line up here for your keys now. We'll see the others in a few days. Good luck. Let's get this thing solved."

When Chavez checked the packet on the desk he discovered he had the second shift, which would begin on the forth day. He immediately called Logan and arranged to meet him in Sonoita.

The Border Patrol check station at Sonoita normally operated to stop all traffic coming north from Patagonia. About three months ago it was shut down. As Logan and Chavez sat in the coffee shop at the Sonoita intersection they watched the cars and trucks and vans whiz past the old check point.

"The bad guys are seeing your truck parked outside this coffee shop, then they're taking a left on the Mountain View Road and heading un-impeded to the north toward Interstate 10 and points beyond," said Logan. "Word has spread throughout the community of crossers staging around Nogales that the coast was clear at Sonoita, and the time is right to move." Logan couldn't hide the sarcastic smirk on his face.

"I guess," responded Chavez. "Anyhow, Yost's presentation was all digital. Here's the printout. He looked good...his math was a little off though. There was no time for questions, or even to discuss the strategy. Everyone either took off because they had a later shift, or got in line for their keys."

"He's onto something here, Nate," sighed Logan as he looked at the stack of information lying on the table between them. "At least he's organized. What you guys are doing around Arivaca will be real helpful to learn the full extent of the killings. That's a good thing."

"I guess so...maybe," responded Chavez.

"Did you get a chance to talk to Hunt?"

"No, why?"

"He's a good man. I have lots of respect for him. You can learn a bunch about tracking from that man."

"Yah, I hope so," said Chavez. "He seems like the only one who has a real interest in the actual operation. The agents know this is all about Yost. And Yost has his mind made up."

"You're exactly right. Say, when you get a chance to talk with Hunt I wonder if you can ask him something. Ask him this: when he gets to the site of a fresh kill and his dogs are turned loose to find the killer, will they follow only human scent?"

"Why's that? What else should they be sniffing for?"

"Well, just about everything else that could be killing those crossers. I think he's probably conditioned them against trailing after deer and javelina, but I want to know if his training has limited their search image based on Yost's theory, that *El Diablo* is human."

He had been monitoring the weather for the past week. When he awoke before dawn to feed his dogs he was glad that the weatherman had been right. There was a slow-moving front from California that was just beginning to deliver moisture to the area. A thin layer of clouds was overhead, and to the west was a thicker blanket of darkness that carried rain. The air was calm and it held the smell of moisture. It would perhaps be one of the last of the winter fronts to move through since spring had officially arrived.

"The clouds will keep the temperatures perfect for us, don't you think, Eldon?"

"That's true, Darrel. But the real good thing about this is that the scent will stay along the ground longer. The dogs will have a field day out there. A thousand smells will be hanging around."

"Not too many, right?" asked Yost, pausing to hear Hunt's answer.

"No, not too many. But when there's scent in the air the dogs get a new life. They get real excited."

"Okay, that's good. I just want you to know, Eldon, that I ordered up this weather just for you!"

"You did good, Darrel. You did real good!"

By sun-up the first group of ten agents had been dropped off about three miles west of Arivaca, just north of the road along Arivaca Creek. The Buenos Aires National Wildlife Refuge was the southern boundary of the search effort that morning. The team would head north then swing west after about five miles. The Las Guijas at this point consisted of low rolling hills with some steep ridges. It was all rough and rocky country, with numerous two-track roads and mining tunnels. The sparse cover of ocotillo and mesquite made for easy walking.

Eldon Hunt had started already. His location was about five miles north of the agents, farther up the main mass of the Las Guijas. Here the terrain was steep and deeply incised with canyons. Eldon was not systematically searching the landscape, but high-grading the sections, looking at the best places. He was at the lowest elevation on the landscape that he considered best represented the areas of past killings. This was where rocky ridges fanned out to the south and west, where his dogs could take advantage of any downdrafts of cold air that would be scent laden and slipping downslope, and where the very slight breeze from the western front would bring smells from that direction.

Yost had given him a key to access the land behind the numerous locked gates in the area. The tag attached to the key ring read "Sharp 1-07." His brief observations of the local road use suggested that Mr. Sharp seldom got off the main road and into the backcountry of his ranch, especially on horseback. There was no sign in his headlights this morning of horse tracks along the road or in the numerous washes that crossed the road.

As he sat on his horse watching his dogs work the country, he gently coaxed his gelding into a little draw and away from his pickup and horse trailer. He placed the key into the breast pocket of his leather vest with his gloved hand. He opened the flap of the pocket and peeked in to make sure the key was there, shaking the flap to ensure that it settled at the bottom of the pocket. He lifted the leather flap that covered his saddlebag and looked at the radio clipped to it inside. A red light blinked at him, and the digital volume readout told him it was properly set.

For three hours he followed his dogs. They dipped into the drainages briefly, but quickly ran to the top of the ridges and paused with their noses sampling the air. They headed in a general northwesterly direction. Their stay in the small canyons was brief, and followed quickly by a scurry to the ridgelines. At first Hunt was frustrated that they weren't paying attention to the areas he had suspected would have the best chance of holding the scent of human death. To him, such an area would be in the brushy and rocky bottomlands, not the elevated and relatively barren hillsides.

He knew better than to second-guess them, so he just kept following along their trail, staying about two hundred yards behind. He figured his dogs were getting high on the ridges to catch the breezes that were more prevalent there. They were silent so he knew they had not run across a hot and definite trail. He figured they were running after a very feint stream of intermittent smells. As they got closer to the source of any scent, they would howl out. Then the rodeo would be on.

Chapter 22

When Nate Chavez showed up in Arivaca at 5:00 a.m. on the 25th of March he picked up his key from Bruce Bean. The tag read "Sharp 4-16." He grabbed a pack, which was heavy with water and food, and headed to his Blazer to follow Bean and the others to the beginning of the search field. His main goal was to have a long talk with Eldon Hunt.

His second goal was to discover a body. Thus far, four bodies had been discovered. All were very old, over a year, and consisted of scattered skeletal remains. Yost had not provided daily updates on the results of searches. All available information was from scuttlebutt among the agents. Only Yost, Black, and one or two others in the forensics lab realized one important element common to all the heaps of bones: skulls were absent from the heaps.

As he opened the back of his Blazer and threw in his pack, he noticed Hunt under a light changing a tire on his horse trailer. He quickly closed up his vehicle and ran over to help him.

"Need a hand, sir?" asked Chavez.

"Well, I can't find that dang lug nut in this gravel. You got a flashlight handy?"

"Yes sir, right here." Chavez took the little pen light off his gun belt.

"Where abouts did it get away from you?"

"Somewhere here," responded Hunt, sweeping his hands low over the ground to the left of the flat tire that was lying off to the side.

Chavez found it in a few seconds, picked it up, and handed it to Hunt. "Here ya go, sir."

"Thank you. I gotta get this thing back together and hit the trail. Have we met before? I'm Eldon Hunt."

"Nate Chavez...glad to meet you. I've heard a lot about you. I heard you at a meeting in Tucson awhile back. It's good to be in the field with you."

"The pleasure is mine, thank you. What area will you be in this morning?"

"Sharp 4-16. How about you?"

"If I understand that map Darrel has posted, I think I'm just north of you. You got some pretty tough country to get across today. But it sure is pretty, even though it's bone dry."

Chavez helped Hunt put the flat tire on the spare rack and gather up his tools. "How are the dogs doing?"

"They're doing fine. I'm real pleased with them. They're young and have a lot of go in 'em. That's what a guy wants."

"Have they found any bodies yet?"

"We've been to one pile of bones and found nothing, which is what I expected. I told Darrel that unless it's real fresh don't call me out of the hills to join him. It's a waste of time."

"Has Yost been out here for the searches?"

"Whenever there's a body found he said he wanted to come out, no matter what shape it's in...even if it's just old bones. If you find something today he'll be here. Last time he flew in from Albuquerque in a helicopter. He's real dedicated to this mission."

"I think so," Chavez responded. "Say, will your dogs follow any sign if they get to a fresh body? I mean...do you have them trained to follow just human scent away from the fresh corpse?"

Hunt shut the tack door to his trailer and looked at young Nate. "You know, you're the first one to ask me that. That's a real good question. I have been thinking about that myself. I don't know for sure. I have them trained on the scent of a dead human, and off the scent of the common animals like deer and javelina and coyotes. I've rewarded them for trailing human scent away from the corpse for the past month, but sometimes you just can't tell what they'll chase after. One thing though, if they go after something that's not human, they know they're chasing something different than what I want them to get after, and they won't let out the same sort of howl."

"So you got them trained on human smell, but they kind of have a mind, and nose, of their own."

"That's exactly right. But I can tell the difference by their calls, and I can get them back on the human track. They've come across what I think have been mountain lions by the way they bay, but I can hold them off anything that's not human without any trouble. They're good. Have you been around hounds much?"

"Not much, but one of these days I'd like to get some good dogs and have a try at it."

Hunt was nodding approval of that notion as he checked the back door of the horse trailer. "Well, I'm about ready to roll.

"Well good luck. I hope you find your first fresh body today!" Chavez exclaimed, stepping back as Hunt entered his pickup.

"That would be nice. These dogs have been real interested in the wind from the area where I'll be this morning. They've been that way since we began on Tuesday. I really don't know what to make of it. We've covered a lot of country and they haven't zeroed in on anything in particular yet. But I've learned to be the student with dogs, even young ones. We'll see what they show us today."

"Well good luck. Maybe we'll see you later in the day."

"I hope so. Thanks for the light."

"Yes sir. Any time."

After he finished helping Hunt, Chavez walked to his vehicle and overheard Bean talking to Mr. Sharp. He knew the man was Sharp because Bean had addressed him as "Mr. Sharp." He noted that

Bean was cordial, but not real friendly toward Sharp. Sharp seemed to be in a hurry, and he had the facial expression of one who had just leveled a complaint. Chavez was very familiar with that expression. Locals often complained about what the Border Patrol did or failed to do. Frustration and anger were common facial expressions. Sharp had a mannerism that was beyond a complaint however, one that Chavez suspected was more fear than anything else. He wished he had heard more of the conversation.

Chavez drove up to the first locked gate and looked off to the southeast at a beautiful Arizona sunrise. He could see the vehicle headlights of other agents slowly making their way along the narrow rocky roads to their destinations downslope from him. The operation looked remarkably efficient from his vantage. He was happy to be part of it, and to know that his outdoor skills were being put to good use. He looked at the name, Sharp, written on the tag, and thought about how one goes about life on such rocky ground.

Chavez drove through the gate, locking it afterwards, and stopped at the first wide spot. He exited his Blazer and locked up, adjusted his radio, and put on his backpack. He walked along the ridge top road to a point where it began slipping off into the broad valley. He retrieved the binoculars that were strapped around his neck and tucked into his jacket, and scanned the landscape. Fingers of gently rolling ridges entered the little valley to his north. Beyond the hills was flat land all the way around the western flank of the Cerro Colorados to the southwestern extreme of the Sierritas. All this country drained into the Alter Valley, which was off to his left. Baboquivari Peak stood on its western margin, a landmark monolith that was blaze-orange with the first rays of sunlight.

As Nate tucked away his binoculars and headed off the ridge to the north, he encountered a herd of javelina. He heard them scurry in a small canyon two hundred yards below. He hadn't seen them but their sound was a giveaway as was their smell, which was carried on the slight swirling breeze. Although a short bout of rain had occurred a few days earlier the ground was hard and dry, and he could not help making noise as he walked. He was sure the javelina had detected his sound.

Nate looked to the north before entering the drainage. He could still see the full extent of the country before him. Somewhere out there Eldon Hunt and his dogs were entering their target ground. He had to forget about them for now and walk down the wash for about a mile, then up the ridge to the north and down into the next canyon, eventually heading east. The pattern of washes and ridges in this section was fairly evenly distributed, allowing him to clear it alone. He was grateful for that fact and wouldn't want to share this space with another agent. If he had been assigned to a more complex array of terrain he would have a partner to ensure all the ground was covered.

After Nate made his way up the forth ridge he figured he had walked about two miles. The air was thick with humidity and the smell of rain was all around. A second front was about to pass through southern Arizona, promising more rain than the first. The clouds had thickened. There was an occasional breeze that stirred from a variety of directions, but came mostly from the west.

The washes he had traversed were generally about twenty to fifty yards across with a defined dry watercourse. Along the edges was developed soil that sustained growths of shrubby mesquite and acacia along the streambed of sand and scattered rocks. The drainage ways were wide enough for a vehicle to navigate. He did not see any caves or rock ledges that piqued his desire for a close inspection. For the most part the vegetation cover was sparse enough for him to get a good look at the ground without investigative side trips.

He looked into the wash he had to enter next and found that it was much wider, about a hundred yards across. There was a windmill off to the west about a mile at a point where the ridgeline dipped into the alluvial fan surrounding the hills. Through his binoculars he saw to the left of the windmill an open metal storage tank that was full, and a drinker off to its left inside a little wire-fence corral. He wondered about all the crossers who knew the windmill as a place to drink and replenish their water jugs on their journey north.

He studied the little valley in front of him and slowly scanned eastward, to his right. The vegetation was thicker and some of the mesquite trees were twenty feet tall. There was a road, only intermittently visible from his vantage, winding through the bottomland. As he descended the ridge he was looking forward to learning where the road led, or dead-ended.

Hunt was perplexed. He almost was losing confidence in his dogs. They had an abundance of puppy energy that seemed like wasted movement. Their wandering had been just that, random visits to the narrow little canyon bottoms followed by lengthy pauses on the ridges. They had headed northeast in the early morning but for the past hour were generally southbound. Since they were the only hand he had to play Eldon stayed with the game they were offering, and watched them closely. He was keen on discovering what they were sensing.

He nudged his horse up one ridge then another. The dogs yipped a little from their ridgeline vantage then scooted into the bottoms where they sniffed a bit and headed up the far southern ridge. They were backtracking toward country to the west of where they had been earlier in the week. Hunt paused on the crest of a ridge and took the map out of his vest pocket. He figured he was getting into the northern fringe of Section 16. "I wonder where young Nate Chavez is," he whispered to his horse.

As soon as Chavez approached the road he noticed vehicle tracks. They were not Border Patrol's tread. There was a black pipe partially covered with sand and rock along the left side of the road. He suspected the pipeline originated at the windmill and ended at a watering trough somewhere up the draw. He turned right and headed along the road.

It meandered through the mesquites on the sandy soil. Within five minutes he found the drinker. It was empty. The road continued past it to a locked gate. He tried his key but it didn't work. The lock looked new. The vehicle tracks continued on the road on the other side of the locked gate so he took off his pack and hung it on one of the wooden fence posts. He slid under the fence, retrieved his pack and continued along the road.

About a quarter mile up the road the canyon forked. The road continued to the north along the bottom of the left fork. He knew he was near the northern boundary of his section, and that a turn up the northern fork would likely take him out of his area. He knew he could determine his location for sure with the GPS unit on his belt. However, his curiosity gripped him and he headed along the road.

At a point where old and splintered wooden planks were scattered on the ground among the mesquite the canyon narrowed and the road ended. The trees were crowded together and obstructed his view. A path, perhaps a cattle trail, wound its way through the vegetation.

With a moderate amount of hesitation he slowly began walking along the path. Suddenly the baying of hounds split the air. It was coming from beyond the other side of the trees. He backed up into the open along the road, and knelt down to look under the canopy of the trees.

"Chavez," a voice shouted. It was Hunt, jogging on his horse along the ridge to the northwest about fifty yards. "What's down there? The dogs got something."

Nate stood up, looked at Hunt then back into the trees. "I don't know. I just got here."

Hunt rode down the gentle slope to Chavez. He quickly dismounted and dropped the reins to the ground. His horse, all sweaty and breathing hard, shook and stood right where Hunt had left him. "Let's go see."

The dogs were going crazy with howls and barks out of sight in the area through the trees about forty yards in front of the two men. As Hunt started along the path toward them Chavez followed him, palming the automatic pistol on his belt. The tree limbs had long ago been broken so the men didn't need to bend over as they moved along the trail. Large timbers and rolls of barbed wire were stacked neatly against the rocky margins of the draw.

The mesquite trees were still leafless with gray canopies of dormant branches that were thick and impenetrable at eye level. The men made their way along the path around the large brown tree trunks that were craggy and rough, appearing like erect sentinels in the domain of hazy light. The little grotto was beautiful to the eye, but the sound of the dogs was telling another story.

"That looks like a mine shaft, Nate," commented Hunt as the two men stood at the end of the path. The dogs were standing at the entrance of the shaft, tails whipping and voices howling long and mournful tones. "There's a body in there."

The defused light revealed the texture of the rocky entrance in great detail. No part of the scene was hidden in a shadow. As the men approached the hole they detected the hint of an odor. It was rotting flesh, barely detectible in the still air. Hunt called back his dogs and the two men looked into the blackness.

"You got that flashlight handy, Nate?" asked Hunt.

"Yes," replied Chavez.

Nate moved forward, taking the lead. The hole in front of him was about eight feet across and on the far side of it the rock wall of the ridge had been exposed by past mining operations. The tunnel started at a slight horizontal angle into the hillside at ground level and then immediately took a plunge straight down, following whatever vein of ore the miners pursued. Two large planks had been placed on the litter of red ore that long ago had been heaped up to form a raised crown around the hole.

As Hunt stood still Chavez slowly walked up the crown of ore and peered into the depths of the mine. He quickly glanced at the two dogs that were lying at the base of a nearby mesquite trunk, panting and almost smiling like they knew they finally hit pay dirt. What they had sensed on the wind from the first day was real, and just then becoming tangible to the two men also.

"I can't see a thing, Eldon. This hole is deep, beyond the beam of the light. But it looks like the sides of this hole have been blasted lately," observed Chavez.

Hunt took a step forward. "What do you mean?" he asked.

"Look there, about three feet below the top of the shaft. That rock looks newly exposed, like someone set off a charge just inside the hole."

Hunt replied, "I see what you mean about the new rock near the top there. A tiny explosion here would bury what's at the bottom with fresh debris from the top of the hole."

"I think you're right."

"Well, I know there's a dead body down there. The dogs are saying it's human."

Nate dimmed his flashlight. "I think we need to get hold of Bean."

Chapter 23

Within ten minutes after making the radio call to Bean, Chavez found himself surrounded by the radio chatter of Border Patrol vehicles heading his way. After Nate taped off the area to preserve evidence he and Hunt waited at the dry drinker. They decided not to turn the dogs loose after the scent of the killer at that time, fearing they would disturb any footprints that might be associated with the tire tracks. Instead Nate placed two wooden planks on either side of the vehicle tracks in the road. He picked a spot where the dirt made good prints then protected both the left and right tire tracks. He knew when the Border Patrol vehicles arrived there was the potential to destroy some evidence, so he marked the two sets of planks, each totaling about a ten foot length of track, with evidence tape.

"Good job, Chavez," said Bean, who quickly passed through the gate and toward the mineshaft. Chavez had unstrung the wire gate and slipped the locked chain over the post so the forensics personnel could readily access the site.

Chavez followed Bean and his entourage of other agents. Bean carried a large sealed beam light that would reveal the shaft's contents. Another agent had a length of cave rope and the gear needed to descend into its darkness. Hunt had leashed his dogs to a mesquite and set out food and water. They watched as the parade of Border Patrol passed by, still looking accomplished with their heads resting on the ground along side their front feet.

"I can't see anything but rocks but it sure smells like decaying flesh. Do you think maybe some sort of animal fell down this hole...maybe a deer or javelina?" Bean asked one of the agents.

"That's human smell down there," commented Hunt.

"How do you know that?" asked Bean.

"That's what the dogs are saying. And they can smell what we can't see."

Bean respected Hunt enough to go with that theory for the time being. "Bill, are you ready to go down and check it out?"

Bill Hanna was already suited up with his rappelling gear complete with harnesses and helmet. "Yes sir," he responded.

As two other agents put two ten-feet boards together and centered them across the top of the mine entrance, Hanna secured a double wrap of nylon strap around them and hooked a carabineer onto the strap. He rigged his ascender and sat on the rim of the hole, looking down. Leaning forward, Bill Hanna grabbed the boards as he slowly scooted off the rim. He dangled on the rope for an instant before feeding rope through the apparatus, and slowly entered the shaft.

Hanna's helmet light illuminated the rocky tunnel that surrounded him, and he paused to photograph the walls about four feet from the top. "It sure looks like this rock has been blasted. I'll grab some rock from the bottom to see if it matches," he told Bean as he let go of the camera that dangled around his neck. "It smells bad in here— even through this canister filter."

Bean had measured the depth of the shaft at forty-seven feet. "I think there was a vein of silver that went straight down. The vein could have just quit, or maybe the miner wanted to get at it through another shaft," he wondered to the agents standing at the surface.

"The guy might have wanted to get some bigger equipment out here and enlarge the hole," commented Hunt. "These sort of holes are all over this country. I don't think I've ever seen so many holes in the ground in any other place around the state. It seems most of these ones out here haven't been worked in awhile."

Bean looked at the rope disappearing into the hole. "He must be close to the bottom," he commented. "What ya got down there, Bill?"

"Hold on, I need to get some slack here." Hanna fed rope through his ascender and grabbed hold of the rope overhead as he leaned over to pick up some of the rock littering the bottom of the shaft. "This is fresh rock down here. I think it came from the sides above. I need to dig around and find what's dead down here."

For fifteen minutes Hanna picked up softball size rocks and threw them to the margins of the hole. At the bottom the diameter of the shaft was about ten feet. The air was thick with dust from moving the rocks, and with the stench of death. He dug through about two feet of fresh rocks before he saw something that grabbed his attention. "I got what looks like a Levi jacket down here." He heard no response. "Hey, can you hear me?" he yelled looking up at the gray hole overhead.

"What? Did you say something, Bill?" called Bean. "I think that breathing canister is hindering his communication," he said to the men gathered around him.

"I got a Levi jacket down here. I think there's a body inside it. I have to move more rock."

"Okay," shouted Bean. "Do you need to get out of there and take a breather?"

"No, I'm good. Hold on."

Hanna unhooked his rope so he could move more freely and dig with both hands. He soon had the arms and back of the jacked exposed. The smell became almost unbearable. He stood up and looked toward the opening above, and took in a deep breath. "There's a body down here for sure. Do you want to haul it out?"

"How fresh is it? Will it fall apart, or is it mummified?'

"It's fairly solid. I don't think it will fall apart. It's not that fresh...maybe a couple months old. I'm not sure."

"Yah, let's try to get it out."

"Okay, lower the other rope. I'll tie it around the belt, and get out of here. We can pull it up then."

As Hanna rested near where Chavez and Hunt were sitting on the ground, Bean and two other agents pulled up the body and a helicopter passed overhead. "There's Yost," Bean commented as he struggled with the rope.

The chopper landed in a wide spot in the canyon about a hundred yards from the Border Patrol vehicles. Before the blades quit turning Yost was out and heading to the scene. "Good work, guys," he said as he passed Chavez and Hunt.

He reached the shaft just as Bean was laying the body on the flat ground near the mine entrance. With Yost was Jason Mech, a forensics specialist who had seen many bone piles attributed to *El Diablo*. Mech quickly looked at the body and said, "I can't wait to get him to the lab." The agents called him "*Huesos*," bones in Spanish. He certainly was an expert.

"The headless body is fairly rigid, and fully clothed," Mech dictated into a small voice recorder. "There are no tears in the Levi jacket or pants, and the boots are still laced onto the feet. The shirt and jacket collar are covered with a dried crust that is imbedded with soil. The exposed neck muscles are dried and tattered around the spine and bones of the shoulder area." Mech slipped the recorder into his shirt pocket, buttoned the pocket flap, and then said, "Let's get this body bagged and to the lab. I don't want to start an examination out here. There will be a wealth of information on this guy and I would hate to lose anything."

"Sounds good," said Yost. "How old is this thing?"

"Hard to say. It's winter, and likely fairly cold all the time down in that shaft. I'd say at least two, maybe three months. I can give you a more accurate age when I get him back to the lab. I'll work on this into the evening and have something for you by early morning."

"Perfect." Yost basked in the glory of discovery. He congratulated all the agents around him then looked up to find Hunt.

As the agents bagged the body Yost went over to where Hunt was sitting. "Good deal, Eldon. The body is not as fresh as we'd like, but maybe it's the freshest victim out here. Those dogs sure did good."

"Ya they did. It was our first go around with this sort of thing, and I think I know how to read them now. I think they picked up on this place first thing this week. I held them back a little at the beginning, but I think after today I'll let them range farther. I kept moving from one area to the next, trying to get them into the spot I thought they would discover something. My mistake is that I didn't just follow them."

"I don't think you made a mistake, Eldon," said Chavez. "You and your dogs are a team. You were taking hints from them, and guiding them to get the most of their noses. I think a body in a hole like this would be tough for them to home in on. The scent was not that powerful with all those rocks piled over it."

"You may be right, Nate. Say, Bill, how much rock was on the bodies?" asked Hunt.

"I guess about two feet total, maybe a little more. I got some samples from the bottom, and we took a swab of the hole near the top to test for trace evidence of explosives. I suspect that after the body was dumped the top of the hole was blown to cover it up."

"Are we sure there are no more bodies in that hole?" asked Chavez.

Yost watched the men talking as if he weren't there. He felt a little inadequate not directing the investigation, or asking the important questions. "I'd like you to get back down there and look for more bodies, Bill," he stated. "*El Diablo* could have been using this as his dumping grounds. We need to find out if that's the case. We got a lot more work to do here. This could be just the start of our investigation. We have a spot now that can be the focus of surveillance."

Young Nate Chavez looked at Yost. "Why would *El Diablo* waste a body by putting it in a mineshaft? Why not scatter it in the desert like all the other killings? And where are the heads?" asked Chavez.

"Can't tell you yet, son, but I've been thinking about those things. I got a hunch, but we'll see," responded Yost sharply.

As Yost finished his pronouncement he looked at the dogs. They were deep in sleep. Chavez thought of bringing up the tire tracks but decided against it. He would leave that detail up to Yost. Hunt stood up and said, "No sense me sticking around here. This body is not fresh enough for the ground to hold any scent of the killer. I think I'll head home for a few days and catch up on some chores."

"I think you're right, Eldon," said Yost. "We'll continue our searches per the schedule, and I'll get hold of you if we find something fresher."

"That works for me, Darrel." Hunt's dogs awoke when he stood up and looked at him. He headed to his horse and called his dogs.

"You want a ride to your pickup, Eldon?" asked Chavez.

"Say, that's a good plan. Would you mind? I'll get a high-tie on this horse and leave the old boy here just a bit."

Chavez stood up and walked with Hunt through the open gate and to Hunt's horse. After securing it to a high mesquite limb they went to Nate's Blazer, where Chavez opened the back and Hunt told the dogs to load. The two men got in the front seat and drove down the road toward the windmill.

Yost watched them leave. "Bruce, I'll let you finish up here. I need to head out. This chopper is on loan, and I'm overdue. You need anything?"

"No, we got it under control."

"Sounds good." Yost broadcast a terse blast of congratulatory chatter to the agents then headed for the chopper. He climbed into the front right seat, clicking his boots to shake off the dust they had gathered. He closed the door and the pilot fired up the jet engine. Within twenty minutes after arriving Yost was on his way back to Tucson.

During the ten-minute ride to Hunt's truck, the men thought about what they had discovered. "It's a sad thing, a dead man," Hunt interjected into the silence.

"That was my first one."

"It's always tough. You think about that guy's family...wonder if he had a wife or any kids. It's a bad deal all around."

"Those dogs are good," said Chavez, wanting to change the topic of conversation.

"They were right all along, huh?"

"They were. I mean they had it nailed from the get go. I sure learned a lesson today. Seems I have to learn the same lesson every other year. You'd think I'd have learned it by now. But that's just dogs. They are always teaching me things. I really like working with 'em."

"I think I would too."

"Say, you were right on that body yourself. You did pretty good without dogs. How long had you been there?"

"I just got there. I was on my way toward the mine when you arrived. I heard the dogs then backed off and I looked up when you called out."

"Well we both get credit for that one then."

They reached Hunt's truck and saw another pickup parked next to it. "Who's that?" asked Hunt.

"I don't know," responded Chavez.

Chapter 24

When Yost returned to his office he felt excited and worried. That the investigation had made a major discovery was exciting. That he was not there to lead it first hand was worrisome. He wanted to direct every move, be part of every find. He trusted Bean and the other senior agents but he feared that extending his trust too far would diminish his credit for the operation. He was worried he was not going to be present for the final episode of a story that would significantly influence his future.

He concluded that the timing was bad. He was buried in mid-year budget adjustments that he needed to finalize for his supervisor. He had two agents that needed to make their training requirements by the end of March, and one who needed possible disciplinary action. His role as supervisor was hindering his progression up the chain of command, and lately he resisted opening mail from anyone who had the potential to add to his paperwork pile.

Yost didn't want to stay around the office and dig into the correspondence, but decided such administrative activity would kill the time until he heard from forensics. He picked up the first bit of inter-office mail and his phone rang. It was Bean on his cell. "Have you cleared out of the mine site?" Yost asked.

"Yes, we're back in Arivaca. The guys are whipped. We are on schedule as far as clearing sections."

"Great. What's up?"

"Well, I think you'll be receiving a complaint."

"Shit! From who?"

"Remember that guy Sharp I mentioned?"

"Sure. What's his problem?"

"Chavez ran across him at Hunt's truck. He asked what we were doing and where we had been. Nate told him and he blew up."

"You got permission to search, didn't you?"

"Sure, that's not the problem. He followed Nate back to the mine and when he saw the locked gate had been opened he lost it. He threatened everyone there with legal action. The guy's crazy. We couldn't talk with him. He wouldn't give me a chance to explain what we had. He just kept yelling that he wanted us out of there, that he was calling his lawyer."

"Shit, you should have stuck him in that hole."

"Man, you should have seen him when the guys carried the body past him. He got real quiet, and then just left. He said we were bringing Viet Nam back into his life on his own ranch. He said we'd hear from his lawyer. He got into his pickup and drove off in a hurry."

"Are you done searching on his private property?"

"I think there's just a couple more sections to the northwest that need to be cleared. But we've covered all the best stuff. But we need to get back to that mineshaft and see if there are any more bodies, remember?"

"Yes, that's right. Were the other bodies on his land...the ones found away from the mineshaft?"

"Yes, the four bone piles were on him."

"Do you think he's a potential suspect...could he be *El Diablo*?" asked Yost.

"No, that's real doubtful. He's a long-time resident rancher with a history of just coming and going in the area. He lives in Tucson so I don't think he's really tied to the area."

"Do you think he can give us any trouble with politicians or anyone like that?"

"I don't think so, but he's a rancher and you know how they're all connected to the governor."

"Okay. Well then, how cordial are you with this guy, Bruce? I mean, can you talk with him later and calm him down?"

"I don't know him real well. Like I said, he lives in Tucson and just gets out to the ranch every now and then. He's a strange one. I don't think anyone in town knows him well except some of the old timers. He was born out there. I don't think anyone can calm him down. He was pretty amped up."

"Hell! This is all I need now. Can I get his phone number and call him? I'd like to head this thing off, and see if I can reason with him."

"I have his number at home. I'll get it to you in about half an hour."

"10-4. Thanks, Bruce."

The caller ID read "Unavailable number," so he let the message machine take the call. When Yost identified himself and started giving his phone number, Sharp lifted the receiver. "Hello."

"Mr. Sharp?" Yost inquired.

"Speaking."

"Mr. Sharp, this is Lieutenant Darrel Yost with the Border Patrol. I'm sorry to bother you this evening. Do you have a few minutes to talk?"

"About what?"

"I'd like to explain to you what some of my agents were doing on your property earlier today."

"All I know is that they were trespassing on my land. I bent over backwards to be cooperative with Mr. Bean, and that's the sort of treatment I get. Is that how you guys operate?"

"No sir. We appreciate your cooperation with the search of your private ground. We're trying to solve the murders that are taking place in your area, and your assistance is vital. This morning...."

"I don't care about this morning. I want to know why you went through a locked gate without permission. I gave Bean keys to the areas of the ranch that he could search. That mineshaft is dangerous. I had a hunter threaten to sue me after he almost fell in there a few years ago. I have it locked for a reason."

"Yes, sir, I understand. We...."

"No, you don't understand. Do you know that I am liable for any injuries there? If your agents get hurt the government can take me to the cleaners. Is that what you want? Are you trying to take me to the cleaners, Mr. Yost?"

"No, that is not my intent, Mr. Sharp. All I want to do is solve this murder case. Your ranch contained important clues. We were just in there gathering evidence."

"What sort of evidence can you get from that shaft?"

"The body we pulled out of there can give us a lot of information. We have taken...."

"A body? Was it a hunter? What sort of information can you get? There are probably a whole bunch of them down there. I'll bet lots of wets have fallen down there. That hunter yelled at me for having such a dangerous hole on my property. He was going to sue me! What can that body tell you? I mean, really, what can it tell you?"

"I have to wait for the report from the evidence lab before I can say for sure. I would be happy to share as much as I can once I get the report." Sharp was silent for almost a minute. "Are you still there, Mr. Sharp?"

"Yes, I'm still here. I'm not happy with your procedures. I need to hear that you will not do this again. Can I get your word on that? I need to know that my permission for your operation will not be violated like this again."

"I can tell you that we will not go there again without your permission. We have only about two sections to the northwest of the shaft to clear, then we're done on your property."

"When will you be out of there, and when will I get my key back?"

"We should be finished with those two sections tomorrow, and I am not sure if we'll need to return to the shaft." Yost did not want to reveal that he had every intention of going back to the shaft.

"I want you out totally. No more visits to the shaft. I think I'm pretty lucky no one got hurt today. I don't want to risk a law suit, Mr. Yost."

"I understand. I just can't say for sure if we will need to return. Can you understand that?"

"No I can't. I don't want you on my ground again. Can you understand that?"

"Yes, sir, I can. We will not return unless we absolutely have to."

"No, Mr. Yost. That's not what I said. I said I don't want you back."

"I know...I heard that. But I cannot promise we won't need to get back there until I hear from the evidence people."

"When will you hear from them?"

"Should be first thing tomorrow morning. At least that's what I'm hoping for. I'll call you as soon as I get word from them, okay?"

Sharp said nothing.

"I appreciate your cooperation, Mr. Sharp. I'll get back with you one way or another this evening."

Sharp continued his silence.

"Thank you. I'll call you later," Yost sounded into the emptiness, then closed his cell phone.

As soon as Yost hung up with Sharp his phone rang. "Yost," he answered.

"Darrel, this is Jason. I got some news about the body."

"Great. What ya got?"

"Body was a mid-twenties aged Mexican male, dead about ten weeks. Aside from missing his head the man showed no evidence of trauma other than bruises that he likely suffered from the forty-seven foot fall into the shaft. The head was cut off just below the occipital condyle, the opening for the spinal column at the base of the skull."

"You think someone cut off his head?"

"Yes. There was enough connective tissue present to indicate that it had been sliced with a sharp object."

Yost thought, and then uttered, "The body the hunter found last month was all smashed and lacerated, like an animal had chewed on it. From that evidence we figured *El Diablo* killed the guy with blows to the head, and later an animal chewed on the face and skull. How does this fit into that picture?"

"I'm not saying it does. I'm reporting on the findings of the mineshaft body."

"Right. Anything else?"

"Just one thing. The guy's stomach was full. He had recently eaten a fairly large meal of meat and beans."

"Are you getting any DNA evidence, like hair on his clothes, or maybe the beef so we can try to trace the source of his meat, or something?"

"Yes on the meat; that's standard procedure. We don't know if it's beef yet. We have several hair samples, and perhaps most if not all are from the victim. We'll run them and catalog the results in the database for future comparisons."

"This is getting complicated. We need a fresh body and a direct scent link for the dogs to point to the killer. That's my strategy. I don't want to build a database. I want to catch *El Diablo*."

"Me too. However, this is all I have for now."

"Good job, Jason. I'm getting ready to get out of here. It's been a long day. Thanks for all the information."

THE TRUTH

Chapter 25

"**R**ight. No head. I saw the body myself."

Logan stirred the sugar in his coffee as he pondered the events that Chavez had related. "Were there any other signs of lacerations to the body? Was the clothing torn or punctured? Were the wrists bound...could you see signs of trauma to the wrist area?"

"No, but I didn't really think to check the wrists. I just focused on the dried muscles and exposed bones of the neck. I didn't really think of anything else other than that."

Logan realized this was Nate's first corpse. He couldn't even remember the time he viewed his first dead body. He had no recall of the emotions he felt, or failed to feel. That was over twenty years and many bodies ago.

"So what's Yost think about all this?"

"I have no clue. I heard nothing about the forensic report. After I ran into that Sharp fellow Bean got involved, then Yost got wrapped up and bent out of shape...the next thing I knew we moved the operation south and east of Arivaca Creek into the Atascosas. That's where we found another old skeleton."

"Head missing?"

"I think so, but I'm not sure. I didn't see it, but I think someone said the skull was missing. I don't get this skull thing. Yost never talked about the missing skull deal, never paid much attention to it, or even gave us special instructions to look for skulls when we found the other bones. What's the deal with skulls anyway? He implied he had skulls on his radar though. I think he doesn't know what's on his radar."

"I don't know the deal with the skulls either. Maybe *El Diablo* collects them. Maybe you'll find a cave decorated with skulls. Maybe *El Diablo* has a skull fetish. Who knows? I don't think Yost has a clue. If he did we'd know about it."

"Somebody must have a theory. I think this is a pretty important element of the crimes. That's one of the main reasons all the Mexicans are scared of the deaths, they believe the devil is taking the heads from the bodies."

"I think you're right. I'll bet someone has a pretty good theory but they're holding it close to the vest so Yost won't claim it."

"Who?"

"Ya never know. We'll have to wait and see."

"We can do it at night with stealth lights so he won't see us. Sure, it's no problem. I think you're right. It's been a week, and he's probably calmed down by now." Bean was speaking out of hope, not certitude. He was beginning to agree more and more with Yost's desire to discover all they could about that mineshaft. Bean was somewhat sure Yost didn't think Sharp was involved in any way with the bodies they had found on his ranch. To Bean, Sharp was definitely not a suspect.

"We have to know if there are any more bodies down there," said Yost. "I have advised the Regional Office so they'll take the heat if he calls Washington again. They agree this is our best lead right now."

"I think so."

"When does Hunt get back out there?"

"He'll be here tomorrow. Right now he's with a hunter in the Chiricahua Mountains. He gets home tonight and promised to be here early in the morning."

"Okay. Who do you want to take with you this evening besides Hanna?"

"Chavez just got on again. He's familiar with the site. He's good."

"Okay, let me know what you find. I'll be on my cell all night. And if you run into Sharp, stay cool. But if he gets hostile, arrest him."

Bean pressed his cell off and walked down the ridge to his truck. He wanted to get back into the shaft and was pleased that Yost was willing to take a risk with Sharp's rage. Covert nighttime operations were familiar to him and his agents so he was not concerned about getting detected by Sharp. He also was not reluctant to arrest him if he got out of hand.

The three men took Bill Hanna's vehicle since it contained all the climbing gear. Bean had posted two agents on strategic hills along the south side of Arivaca Creek. Another one was in the hills overlooking the area of Sharp's ranch house. If these sentinels spotted any traffic they would immediately advise Bean. Before sundown the agents were in place and scoping the hills for sign of Sharp's truck driving the roads or sitting along a road.

The agents drove along Arivaca Road to the two-track road leading to the windmill, then up the drainage to the mineshaft. No tracks had overlapped those of the Border Patrol vehicles that had exited the area last week. When they reached the end of the road they quickly shut off the engine and got out. They stood and listened for a minute before Bean radioed the surrounding agents. "Are we clear to begin?" he asked.

All three units responded in the affirmative. "Let's go," he said.

Hanna had already retrieved his gear and was walking along the path with Chavez behind. Bean noted the time: 11:45 p.m.

Everything was the same as Hanna had left it. He centered the planks over the hole, hooked up his line, and descended. The smell of the dead body still lingered at the bottom, which surprised him. "It still stinks down here," he shouted up to Bean.

"That's a sign," Bean replied into the lighted depths.

Hanna removed only about six inches of rock before he found the back of a skull protruding through the rubble. Only the back of the head was visible when he began to photograph the scene. When he swept away the rock debris around the sides of the head with his hands the head shifted and rolled toward him. It was not attached to any body that he could see.

"I got a head down here without a body," yelled Hanna. It's not fresh so I cannot make out any details, but for sure it's a head...all by itself!"

Over the course of the next hour Hanna uncovered three more heads buried beneath a couple feet of rock. As he encountered each one he photographed it in place, then bagged each individually in a sturdy plastic evidence bag. He again took samples of rock to test for explosive chemicals.

As the three men rested to the side of the mound atop the mineshaft, nighthawks called from the surrounding hills. There was no moon, and the place was pitch black except for the glow of Tucson to the northeast.

"Human heads," commented Chavez as he stared at the assembly of distorted human facial expressions barely visible through the bags.

No one responded. Hanna went back down and found two more heads. Below the sixth head was hard rock so he was sure there were no more. He photographed the bottom and then made his final ascent. As Hanna and Chavez dragged the six evidence bags to the truck, Bean was calling Yost on his cell.

"Mission accomplished," he proclaimed. "Good work, boys. Let's get out of here." It was 1:30 in the morning.

Fear was something that Jay Sharp had faced many times in the jungles of Vietnam. He had learned to control it, and keep it from overcoming him. He had played the hand that he sensed was a good move. His private property rights were something easy for him to defend, and calls to the highest levels of the Border Patrol were just his first action. He quickly played the role of a victim, and decided to continue along that course of action.

When Yost showed up at his doorstep in Tucson with another agent Sharp wasn't surprised. He had been expecting them. He calmly invited them inside and offered them a seat around his kitchen table. Yost sat down and noticed that the inside of Sharp's house was neatly kept. And so was the outside. The lush growth of trees that surrounded his place blocked the view of neighbors, which were about fifty yards distance on three sides. The back yard butted up against a hillside. His truck was parked under the carport against a row of oleander bushes. This was a typical quaint neighborhood on Tucson's northwest side, perched along the northern flats of Rillito Creek.

Yost had thoroughly rehearsed his interrogation of Sharp. He was expecting Sharp to fly off the handle when he was informed that the Border Patrol had re-visited the mineshaft and discovered more human remains. The response he got surprised him.

"You should have asked me to help. I have a winch you could have used. Are you sure you don't need to go back? I can help."

"No, we are sure the shaft is empty, Mr. Sharp. Thanks anyhow." Yost didn't want to reveal to Sharp that they found only heads in the shaft on their second visit.

"I got about a dozen mines like that one. Some are twice as deep. Maybe you should check those too. I'll be happy to show you where they are."

Sharp's response put Yost on his heels. He wasn't expecting such cooperation. As Yost began searching for lines of interrogation, Sharp noticed his hesitation and jumped in. "Would you like some coffee?"

"Sure," answered Yost

"Milk? Sugar?"

"No thanks. Black is fine." Yost watched Sharp get up and go to the stove. He was dressed in Levis and boots. "How'd you get into the ranching business?" Yost asked, not really wanting to learn Sharp's history. He was buying time to gather his thoughts.

"Well, that place was my great granddad's. It was a lot bigger and more profitable at one time. Despite the endangered species and the illegals, I am trying to make it work for me but the odds keep getting worse. Between the drought, my expenses, and the price of beef it's a losing proposition nowadays. But it's all I got so I keep at it. It gives me something to do and keeps me out of trouble."

"How often do you get out there?" asked Yost as Sharp walked to the table with the coffee.

"About twice a week. I can't stay out there too long because the well is bad. I have to re-do it. It yields only a dribble. It's old and the perk holes are plugged. I just go there for the day and check fences and waters. I've had to feed with this drought because there's so little feed out there."

"Do you have problems with illegals?"

"Well, doesn't just about everyone have problems with them? It's gotten worse in the past five years. We used to work them when they'd work. We kept a pair of 'em on for a couple years about twenty years ago. They were reliable and knew how to work cattle. But times have changed. The guys nowadays don't know one end of a cow from another. They're city boys."

"Have you used any in the past year or two?" Yost was getting his stride, and kept firing questions at Sharp.

"If you won't bust me, I'll tell you." Sharp smirked as he looked down at his cup.

"I won't bust you. I just want to know about your relationship with all the illegals."

"Sure, I use them. Especially during roundup I try to get a couple to help repair the corrals and loading chute. I have to check out about fifty to find one or two who know what they're doing. But you bet, if they're good and willing, I can use the help every now and then."

Suddenly Yost's cell phone rang. "Excuse me," he said after looking at the display. "I have to take this call." Yost stood up and wandered into the living room area so Sharp couldn't hear the conversation and the other agent began talking to Sharp about the drought. "10-4. You're all clear." He slipped his phone into his pocket and walked back to the kitchen.

"Bureaucracy! Mr. Sharp, you are so lucky you don't have to deal with that. It's the plague of my life! I'm sorry about that," Yost said as he sat down. "Now tell me, do you have any idea how those bodies got into your mineshaft?"

"I think those Mexicans were walking around there at night and fell in. It does get pitch black out there at times."

"I'll bet it does. I'll also bet those guys were killed then thrown in."

"You could be right but I'd be real surprised if you actually found someone who would do that. It seems so far fetched," replied Sharp.

"You've never heard anything out there, have you?"

"Like what? A gun? Screams?"

"Yah, that and any other noises."

"No, not that I can recall."

"How about explosives? Did you ever hear a charge of explosives go off in that area?"

"Heck, the miners around here are always blasting. You can hear a charge go off just about every day. Why?"

"The top of that hole was recently blasted. It seems like the blast was an attempt to cover the bodies."

"Well, that's news. I can't say that I ever heard a blast from down that way. But I'm not there all the time, like I said."

"I sure appreciate your time, Mr. Sharp. I gotta run to the office. That call was about a meeting I thought I was going to be able to get around."

"No such luck, huh? If you boys need any more help with access, just let me know. I'll give you keys to any gate on the place but I'd like to know you're coming. It's good to have your vehicles driving around out there. Maybe it'll help keep my fences intact."

"Thanks again, Mr. Sharp," Yost said as he and the other agent walked out the door and to his Blazer. He got inside and backed out of the driveway. As Yost drove off he wondered why Sharp assumed the bodies from the mineshaft were Mexicans.

Steve Black just turned into the parking lot of the Sector Office in Tucson when his phone rang. "So you got it on okay?" It was Yost.

"10-4. It's snug on the right side of the frame directly below the passenger door handle."

"You're sure that magnet will hold it there, right?"

"Guaranteed. I tested the unit, and he's beeping loud and clear right now!"

Chapter 26

Heading out toward a future of unknowns has always been part of the human spirit. For most it is out of desperation that they begin the journey. For many it's for gold or glory. Some find adventure to be the main pull. These and a multitude of other reasons have motivated millions of Mexicans to enter the United States through a "back door" of the porous *frontera*.

For Jesus Ortiz and his ten young friends their journey was an escapade. There was nothing else to do, and their hometown near Navajoa in Culiacan could not hold them. Each young man was unskilled and without a wife. Collectively they could not imagine any consequences, either pro or con, of crossing into the U.S. illegally. There were neither defined benefits nor major consequences. If they were caught they would be jailed for a while, fed well then returned home. No big deal. It was something to do.

So brash were they that talk of *El Diablo* evoked absolutely no fear in them. If anything it spiced the deal. They represented the gamut of personalities, lacking cohesion for mental strength and experience to guide them. Their only bond was the goal of crossing the border into the United States. After that, they had no common plan.

As the young men walked along the edge of the paved road ten miles north of the border through the Altar Valley, they watched a quarter-moon set behind the landmark precipice of Baboquivari Peak. They were thirsty and decided to find a windmill and re-fill their plastic jugs. They crossed the Arivaca Road about midnight and took a right up the first big wash they encountered. Within an hour they were at Jay Sharp's windmill.

The water was refreshing, and they were tired. There was not much consensus about the next move. The individuality of each was coming to the surface. The dry and dusty ground did nothing to improve their mood. They were like a ship with a sail that was becoming torn and tattered. They never had a rudder. Finally, they agreed to rest under the nearby mesquites and begin walking again in the morning.

As the group fell asleep that night in April, the air was still and totally silent. The absence of the voices of owls, nighthawks and even crickets evaded their notice.

The mix of migrant motivation is as varied as the assortment of responses to crossers at the doorsteps of the residents whose homeland is their destination. For some their arrival, expected or not, is a chance to show compassion and kindness. For others it initiates hate and recalls the creed that a border represents a clear line with laws and regulations that define residency and measure punishment. It is sacrosanct, and it is defended no matter the cost. For this mindset actions at the border are heralded as important necessary means of protecting the ground, the culture and economy...the very lives of all legitimate inhabitants.

But what if it all went "south"? What if political chaos resulted from elections or assassinations or foreign interventions...and what if economic and social disintegration followed? Who goes where? Some are stranded between strife and gunshots; they steal away where they can with very little thought, much less planning.

Those with means and resources pick their next destination with calculated strategy...for better or worse. And so it was with Larry Thompson. He moved between Texas and Arizona with the ease afforded by financial glut and political favors. He had no ties to the land, to people or values. He created his own worlds and mulled them over in the company of whiskey and vodka. His latest acquisition in Arizona had been a priority for a couple years. He wanted to establish a refuge to protect his assets from Mexican migrants. He achieved little success at this endeavor amidst all the private land in Texas and felt that it he would not be able to ride into the sunset of his life in Texas before past actions caught up with him. Desperation was not his motivation, but there certainly was a sense of self-preservation. He liked to handle things his own way, as reflected by his purchase of the Sopori Ranch in southern Arizona.

Being a deceptive escape artist was a point of pride with Jay Sharp. He believed his ability to evade and outsmart the enemy had saved his life in Vietnam. During his solitary ranching practice of the past decade he learned ways to avoid reams of government regulation and taxes. He brought all that skill to the forefront in his latest dealing with the Border Patrol. He was feeling quite accomplished as he drove away from his Tucson house before dawn, certain that the Border Patrol was off his land and out of his business.

He needed to check some fence line and pick up the mail in Arivaca. His plan was to spend some time on the ranch then stop at the post office on his way home. He chose the Ajo Road exit from Tucson. After twenty minutes he took a left onto the Sasabe Road at Three Points and headed up the Alter Valley.

He pulled off the Sasabe Road onto a dirt two-track and opened his locked gate. The day was beginning to break and as he locked the gate behind him he looked up at the early morning light reflecting off the rock mass of Baboquivari Peak. It was a sight that he always had taken in but which never seemed to spark any emotion.

He returned to his pickup, turned off the headlights, and headed to his windmill.

As he approached his watering hole he saw the eleven Mexicans scattered under the trees, sleeping. One of them awoke as Sharp pulled up and turned off his motor. Sharp immediately spoke words of greeting in Spanish and the others lifted their heads. Two of the young men scrambled to their feet and started to run. When they realized Sharp was not the Border Patrol and that his voice was not threatening, they stopped.

Sharp got out of his truck and walked over to the water trough, then to the windmill. He kept an eye on the men as he checked the water and adjusted the float on the trough. He walked over to the gate and opened it. When he returned to his truck he asked them where they were heading. He chatted with them about the best route and commented about the local presence of the Border Patrol. They instantly trusted him as an ally.

After a pause in the conversation he mentioned that he could use one of them to help with some chores. He asked them if they had any experience fixing fence. He reiterated that he had enough work only for one of them, maybe two, but that he could not employ the entire bunch. Sharp had learned long ago that it was possible to select from a group of crossers one or two who would be willing to part with the others for a chance to make some money.

Although no one volunteered any such background, Sharp picked his potential candidate. He had quickly assessed that within this loosely knit group at least one would readily splinter off for the opportunity to work. He was right. The man he had pre-selected said he had fixed fences with his uncle in Sinaloa, and that he would be willing to work for a week. When questioned by the others Jesus said he would meet them later. He said the Catholic Church in Phoenix that they had learned about in Hermosillo was a good rendezvous place, and he would meet them there in a week or so. The group finally had a real plan.

Within five minutes all were in agreement that Jesus would work for Sharp for about a week, then get back on the trail north and meet the others in Phoenix. At this point Sharp said that if Jesus worked out he might be asked to stay on longer. Everyone acknowledged that circumstance. Jesus was particularly effective at convincing the others that this rancher was giving him a great opportunity. Personally, he was fond of the idea of getting a job so close to Mexico, where he could return if he so desired.

So thirty minutes after their encounter Sharp struck a deal with the group and was heading north toward his ranch house with Jesus in the front right seat, waving goodbye to his companions.

Jesus had no clue how to string barbed wire. That was obvious to Sharp but it didn't matter. The fence around the house that Jesus had been assigned to repair would be no worse off for his efforts. Sharp let him continue the fence "repair" until noon. He had disappeared into his house and only occasionally glanced out to monitor Jesus's presence.

As Jesus worked he looked around the ranch house. He looked off to the west at Baboquivari Peak and thought about watching the moon snuggle against it last night. The exertion of yesterday's trek was all but forgotten, and he was refreshed by the good fortune that had come his way only one day into the United States.

Chapter 27

When Jay Sharp showed up along the side of his house he had a plate of beans with tortillas for Jesus. He motioned Jesus to come over to the horse trough for lunch. Sharp said Jesus was welcome to wash up with the water in the trough, so Jesus walked toward the water while he took off his leather gloves. He put the gloves on the concrete edge of the trough next to the plate of food. As he stuck his arms into the water Sharp was putting on a new pair of gloves. Jesus figured it was the patron's turn at the fence, and thought nothing of it.

As he continued to wash up, splashing water on his face, Sharp bent over and picked up a machete that had been lying on the ground on the opposite side of the rectangular trough. The last thing Jesus saw was Sharp heading toward the fence. With one expert and practiced motion Sharp swung the machete at Jesus from behind, severing his spinal cord just below his skull.

Jesus's limp body slumped to the side but stopped short of hitting the ground at the base of the trough. His head hung into the water, and the skin and muscles that had not been cut kept the rest of him from crumpling onto the dirt. With a measured blow Sharp crashed the machete onto the connecting tissue. The sound of metal on concrete rang out, and the head of Jesus splashed into the water as his body collapsed to the ground.

The water turned red with the blood of Jesus, and a pool of blood began to form in the dirt underneath his shoulder. Sharp stood over the gruesome scene, breathing deeply and quickly. His heart rate quickened, and with a surreal hyper vigilance he scanned the surroundings for movement and sound. He was back in the jungles of Vietnam, assessing his status and planning the next move in the midst of death and carnage.

Nate Chavez picked up his assignment early that morning. Bean wanted to brief him personally about a new aspect of the case. "That transmitter we have on Sharp's pickup shows that he's on his ranch. As his route blog shows he started out near the windmill and he's at the house now. He arrived early this morning. I alerted the agents that are in the sections to the south about five miles, and one of them is at an observation point in Vector 3." Bean showed Chavez a map to refresh his memory regarding the "Sharp Reconnaissance Mission."

"Here's your copy of Vector 3 OPs. You need to go directly to this OP, and start your observations on Sharp. He is presently out of sight at the ranch but when he moves call me on the secure channel. Once he gets down his ranch road about half a mile you should be able to see him. If he takes another route away from the ranch, you'll have to move according to the Topographic Visual Corridors the GPS mapping boys have provided. It indicates your sight corridor based on a satellite digital relay of your location. The digital image of Sharp's location will be available on the map function of your receiver."

"Yes, I remember. That's on channel seven, right?"

"Exactly."

"I like having that capability in the vehicles. It's a great tool," commented Chavez.

"I know we went over all this at the briefing last week, but since this is the first time Sharp has visited his ranch since we placed the transmitter I wanted to go over it. You have the best chance of picking up any potentially significant movement by Sharp thus far. Remember, we want to catch him in the act of a crime. Plotting him pass through a crime scene area isn't good enough. Any questions?"

"No sir. I understand this mission thoroughly. I can handle it. Who else is on this shift for backup?"

"You'll have me as a primary contact, and I'll get others to join us as needed."

"10-4. I'm on it," responded Chavez.

"Good deal, Nate. Good luck. Let's see if today's the day we can figure this guy out."

The sun had set over Baboquivari Peak as Nate Chavez continued to monitor his receiver. He sat in the front seat of his Blazer in amazement at the technology the Border Patrol had employed to enforce immigration laws. He was equally amazed that all this gear seemed so ineffective at bringing a halt to the volume of traffic that was occurring, both people and drugs.

He zipped up his jacket to stay warm and thought about how this equipment stacked up against the nose of a hound...suddenly his receiver started beeping. He looked at the monitor and saw a flashing red light on the display. Sharp was moving. A set of numbers in a box next to the light indicated a metric location. He punched a button to place the location on the TVC to see if his vantage afforded a view of Sharp's vehicle. It did. If Sharp continued along his ranch road toward the west he would be in perfect position for good observations.

Right on cue the headlights of Sharp's truck appeared along the ridge about five miles to the northeast. The TVC map indicated he would momentarily disappear for about a quarter mile as he drove through a saddle, but after that Chavez would have an unobstructed view for miles. Sharp's lights disappeared then reappeared after about a minute. He was moving along slowly to the west.

Nate switched the radio to the secure channel and called Bean. "He's moving west toward Sasabe Road. He's got about four miles of dirt until the pavement."

"10-4, Nate. If he turns north on the pavement, let me know and I'll have an agent in Three Points head south to get a visual. He may just be heading home to Tucson. But if he takes a turn on to a dirt road somewhere we want to be right on him. An Apache helicopter is on standby in Tucson and can be here in fifteen minutes."

"Good deal. He's still moving along. I'm on him."

"10-4. Good luck."

Sharp drove along the dirt road with both hands on the wheel and windows rolled down. His thoughts were on his next move. What he had done was gone from his memory. He was operating under jungle rules, on the edge of survival again.

He had wrapped the headless corpse of Jesus in a canvas tarp and put his head in a white plastic paint bucket. He shoved the tarp and bucket toward the front of the truck bed, and stacked rolls of barbed wire and fence posts around and on top of everything so the bucket and canvas were not visible.

Back at the ranch there was no obvious trace of the evidence at the crime scene. He had washed the machete and diluted the ground with water from the trough, then scattered sand over the wet ground from a pile he used to fill low spots that became muddy when it rained. The area blended with the rest of the landscape.

He'd rehearsed the line of conversation he would use if he were stopped: "I'm getting ready to put in a new fence line and wanted to get this material set out tonight. I got a long day tomorrow. If you're in the area, stop by. I can use a hand."

When he reached the pavement of the Sasabe Road he went south toward the Arivaca Road and Sasabe. "He's heading south,

Bruce. I'll have a good view of him at the junction. I'll advise which way he goes."

"10-4. I'm ready to roll here. We should know something soon. He may choose to head home through Arivaca. We'll see."

"10-4. I can see Arivaca from here, so I'll keep you posted."

"10-4."

After a mile Sharp took a left and stopped at a locked gate about a hundred yards east of the road. "He's heading east along the road into Section 16," Chavez reported. "I know that area. I cleared it last month. Right now he's about four miles from the mine. That road goes along the drainage bottom. I'll lose him in about a mile where the wash comes out of the hills."

Bean looked at the receiver in his truck where he also was monitoring Sharp's movements. The only observation point that afforded a view into the drainage was to the east, about five miles northwest of Arivaca. Bean was heading to it as he called Chavez. "Nate, you stay there in case he comes out before I can get to OP 3 in Vector 1. I have Jones and Blakeley in their vehicles right behind me."

"10-4. He's about to disappear from my view."

"That's right, he's about three miles southwest of the mine, parked along the wash in Section 16," Bean explained to Yost. "He was at his ranch all day, left just after sundown, and has been stopped for about forty minutes."

"Who else has his location?" asked Yost.

"Chavez is in Vector 3 to monitor Sharp's movements when he leaves the area. There's only one road in. Jones and Blakeley are here with me. We're about two miles away. I have Sweeny and Brown posted at the Sasabe Road at the junction of the road Sharp took. I plan to intercept Sharp when he returns to that point."

"Can you see anything from your vantage?"

"We're too far for night vision equipment, but with binoculars and spotting scopes we can tell he's walking around with a lantern some of the time. The lights of Tucson are bright enough that he really does not need a light to walk."

"I'm headed to the airport. I'll hang back to the west over the Altar and be available for air support. This could be our moment!" exclaimed Yost.

"I think it is, Darrel. I think the moment has arrived!"

Chapter 28

Sharp reached the gate and got out of his truck to unlock his gate with the aid of his truck headlights. He saw the two Border Patrol vehicles parked along the road about fifty yards north of the gate. At the same time amidst the quiet purr of his truck engine he heard the agents walking up behind him. They had hidden in the brush inside the fence and approached from both sides of his vehicle. Wayne Brown quickly looked in the bed and cab of the truck to make sure Sharp was alone, and stopped just to the right and behind the beam of the headlights about ten feet from the front right fender. "Good evening, Mr. Sharp," he said. "Wayne Brown, Border Patrol, sir."

Sharp turned around, pretending to be startled. The headlights of his truck blinded him. Shielding his eyes from the glare with his hand, he left the gate locked and walked to his left toward the direction of the voice. When he was out of the light beam he saw the two agents. "Good evening. You guys surprised me. What are you boys doing out here?" he inquired.

"Routine patrol, sir. We saw lights back up in the canyon, and came to investigate."

"Good job. I'm getting ready to build some fence back there, and wanted to drop off some material tonight so I could get an early start in the morning."

Brown had programmed his radio so Bean could monitor the conversation as he headed west along Arivaca Road to meet up with them. He could see the Apache coursing low along the Altar Valley about ten miles to the northwest. Chavez was at his post watching the whole scene from his vantage.

"Where are you heading now, Mr. Sharp?"

"I'm heading home. I hope to pick up some supplies this evening...if I get there in time. I have to leave out of Tucson early before the store opens, so I need to get a move on. It took longer to unload the material than I was planning. Guess I'm slowin' down."

Brown knew he didn't have any legal cause to detain Sharp. If they needed to locate him the transmitter would readily allow them to do that. Jones and Sweeny were heading to the area that Sharp had been, and if they found anything Sharp would be apprehended in Tucson.

"Well drive carefully," said Brown.

"I will. You boys be safe. If you guys need some exercise come by at first light. I'll be pounding posts and stringing wire."

"We just might do that, but don't hold your breath! Good evening, sir."

Sharp took off heading north toward Three Points. Within five minutes Bean joined Brown and immediately called Jones. "Anything up there?" he asked.

"We just got here, and there's a pile of fence posts and wire. No tracks leading anywhere from the pile."

"10-4. Photograph the area, and I'll meet you back at the field station in Arivaca. Break, Darrel, did you catch that traffic?"

"10-4 Bruce. Monitor the area in the morning. See if he returns. If he doesn't come back by noon, check out the area thoroughly. You'll have daylight on your side. I can't see that old guy building a fence by himself. Or maybe he really plans to build a fence, I don't know. We're heading back to Tucson."

Yost was obviously frustrated. His best shot thus far at nabbing Sharp had been a wild goose chase. Time was ticking on this case and all the resources he was throwing at it were not paying off. In addition to the body and heads pulled from the mine, a total of eight old bone piles were discovered with the intensive search, six north of Arivaca Creek in the Las Guijas and two in the Atascosa foothills. There were no fresh bodies for Hunt's dogs to work, and his most likely suspect just drove away with a plausible alibi.

Chavez watched as the vehicle lights dispersed through the hills of Arivaca to the north. He felt like a spectator watching the reds and whites moving and stopping, slowing and racing in various directions. He'd heard Yost's voice, but more importantly its tone, and was left uninspired and alone on his hilltop. The hint of April warmth in southern Arizona was quickly replaced after sundown by remnants of winter's chill that resided still in the ground.

Chavez hesitated calling Bean to learn about the rest of his shift. He left the cab of his vehicle and walked around toward the back of his Blazer just for the exercise. The night was dark, and a slight but steady breeze washed up from the bottoms of Altar Valley and over his highland perch. He could see for miles around. He returned to his vehicle, started the engine and, per procedure, left the site without headlights. A tiny light shielded on top and sides was mounted on his front grill, illuminating the road immediately in front of him, permitting a slow and stealthy exit from his position.

When he reached the maze of washes that wound through the hills he pulled on his headlights. In a side drainage dimly illuminated by his headlights immediately to his right a movement caught his attention. He instantly recognized it as a large cat. Mountain lion was his first impression. He saw the animal only for a second as it lunged across the wash and into a thicket of brush along some large rocks. His identification was uncertain since he had never seen a mountain lion. It definitely was large with a long tail. He was not certain of the color, although it appeared darker than the background it was scrambling into.

He stopped to see if the animal would come into view again in the main wash that the road followed. It did not. He didn't even think of getting out of his vehicle to look with his flashlight. He was curious but found himself strangely overcome with caution. Whatever it was would remain a mystery.

As he approached Arivaca he saw a cluster of three Border Patrol vehicles in front of the Post Office. He recognized Bean and Brown, but not the third agent. He pulled over to join them.

"Hey, Nate," called Bean. "Good work. We'll have to wait another day to give Mr. Sharp our attention again."

"Yes, sir. If he's our man, we'll get him."

"Say, Nate, I'd like you to meet John Crow. John's from the Albuquerque Regional Office. He's been with our outfit for forty-six years. He has a lot of field experience and has been detailed here to assist with this case. He just arrived and I was telling him about our efforts with Sharp."

"Pleased to meet you, Mr. Crow," said Chavez as he shook Crow's bare hand. It was large and rough, which matched Crow's voice.

"The pleasure is mine, Nate," responded Crow. "You were the one who discovered the mine shaft with the hound guy, right?"

"Yes, sir. I was just at the right place at the right time. I got there just as Mr. Hunt was arriving with his dogs."

"I'd like to talk with you more about the site. Will you be going to that windmill tomorrow afternoon with us?"

Chavez looked at Bean. "Yes, he's going. He'll be a great help there," interjected Bean.

"Great. Well, I need to head into Tucson. Darrel put me up at the Best Western on the south side of town. I was just checking in when he called to tell me he was hitching a chopper to here, and suggested that I drive down this way in case anything broke tonight. I hope I'm not bad luck!"

"Did you have any trouble finding the station?" Bean asked.

"No, not a bit. Yost said that I better not blink when I got to milepost 1 or I might miss Arivaca!"

Everyone said goodnight and Crow got into his Blazer. As he drove off Bean said, "That guy has a reputation for being able to sense the end of a trail. It's uncanny. He has assisted with hundreds of enforcement cases over nearly every inch of our borderlands, north and south. We're lucky to get him here. He may find something we're overlooking. Yost had to pull some strings to get him here. I guess this case is pretty high up on this agency's priority list."

"I imagine it is," said Brown. "Does he have any hunch with what he knows so far?"

"I don't know. I think he plays everything pretty close to the vest at the beginning. No doubt he has a hunch but he's not saying right now. He's worked a lot with migrant gangs from South and Central America who seem to thrive on violence. Since that could be what we're dealing with here he'll be examining the evidence for signs of their M.O."

"But our focus is on Sharp," injected Chavez. "How could he have a connection with the Central Americans?"

"He probably doesn't," said Bean. "However, we want to leave no stone unturned on this one. Sharp's a big player right now we think. He's our best lead at the moment because his profile is that of a typical 'hater,' and we found the bodies on his ranch. But if his fence story is true and he checks out when we go down there tomorrow afternoon, we need to have another plan of attack. Crow did say he thinks these murders are more like acts of violence than they are acts of theft. The cache of goods we found can't amount to more than a few hundred dollars."

"But the crossers have cash on them, and that's probably the biggest part of the take, not the gear or items they've purchased," replied Chavez.

"True. We haven't found any significant amount of cash yet, so I think our killer is in it for the violence, not the profit. Maybe he stashes the loot as a testament to his conquests. We'll just have to wait and see how it all unravels."

After listening to the conversation Brown stretched and said, "I'm hitting the sack. I'm beat. What time do we head up to Sharp's windmill tomorrow?"

"About three. If Sharp's not there by then he's not coming. We don't want him to catch us there. Jones and Sweeny will be at the OP in Vector 1 at dawn to see if he shows early."

"Very good. Goodnight, gentleman." Brown headed to the field station, leaving Bean and Chavez alone. Bean hadn't had a chance to talk with Chavez alone during the entire operation in Arivaca.

"So, Nate, what do you think?"

"About what?" replied Chavez.

"Well, about how this operation is going. Do you have any insights on this deal? I respect your talent and you've been looking at a lot of ground out here. Do you think Sharp's our killer?"

"There's a good chance he is. Ya, I think I'd put my money on Sharp. The only thing I can't figure out is why he'd do it. What's in it for him?"

"Who knows? Maybe he's just flat crazy, or a hater that has come unhinged. It's hard to figure out what's in another man's head."

"It sure is," responded Chavez. Both men looked at the silhouette of the northern hills against the backdrop of the Tucson glow. They were tired. Bean's thoughts drifted toward his family, wondering how his son did at the track meet. Chavez was reliving the sight of that large cat, trying to extract more detail from the glimpse it had given him.

Chapter 29

"There's not a soul down there."

"10-4. We'll plan to move out in a couple hours. Thanks." Bean turned to Brown and Chavez. "Jones and Sweeny still have no traffic down there. They got the big scope fixed right on that pile of fence material Sharp left. They can see individual barbs on the wire with it. Sharp hasn't been there all morning. We'll leave here at three. Crow should be here by then."

Chavez and Brown nodded, and headed back to their cots. The field station was like military barracks, cold and undecorated, but it was home away from home. Both men had slept in, ate some breakfast, and were anxious to move. Although their shifts had just started the previous day, they were tired of this routine. They could feel a perpetual drain on their physical and mental faculties. Only about ten sections south of Arivaca Creek remained to be cleared, but the focus on Sharp had put that aspect of the duty in second priority. Bean had just four agents, plus Crow, on the clearing operation in the hills surrounding Arivaca now, and he wanted his agents fresh in case Sharp made a move.

Chavez saw the large and bent over form of the man when he passed by a window and headed toward the door. As Crow stepped into the main room off the sleeping quarters Chavez noticed a smile on a sizeable and ruddy face. The brim of his haggard cowboy hat was pulled low over his brow and tilted to the right, shielding that side of his face. It was 2:30 and the mood at the field station suddenly changed.

"Good day, gentleman," rumbled Crow as he removed his hat and slid it onto a nearby table. He unloaded an arm full of briefcase and maps and a large brown envelope. "How are you doing, Mr. Chavez?" he asked.

Nate didn't realize he was the only one within sight of Crow as he walked in. The large meeting room was empty, and Brown and Bean were nowhere to be found. "I'm fine, thank you. And how are you?"

"Couldn't be better. How's the coffee?"

"It's hot. Would you like some?"

"Please."

Chavez walked to the stove across the room from Crow and through a window saw Bean and Brown standing outside between their vehicles, talking. Bean had a map in one hand and a brown envelope tucked under his other arm. "Sugar or cream?" he asked Crow.

"No thanks. Black is fine. You guys have a neat set-up here. How long have you been on this detail?"

"A little under a month."

"What do you think about the killer? Do you think Sharp's our man?" asked Crow.

Chavez grabbed a chair and sat at the square wooden table across from Crow. "I think he's our best lead at this time. How about you, do you have a theory yet?"

"Oh yes. I've looked at all the photos of the remains, and read all the reports, and have concluded that Sharp is the guy."

"What about the violent organized gangs from Mexico and Central America being involved? Is that a possibility?"

He retrieved his hat from the table, set it on the chair next to him and looked up at Chavez with a curious grin. "What do you know about those gangs?" he asked.

"Not much. I know they commit acts of violence, and what we're seeing is pretty violent. I mean, who cuts heads off victims?"

"A crazy man, that's who. Sharp is pretty crazy. If you look at his background, his life style, his stint in Vietnam and the trouble he's had with his ranch, I think he presents a pretty clear picture of someone who has the possibility of losing it."

"So his motive is hatred...of everything?"

"That's exactly right. Besides, those gangs usually act in groups, and they leave sign. They want to get the credit for their violence. They want recognition. They want to instill fear. They don't kill in remote areas and leave the bodies hidden in the brush or buried in a mine shaft."

Chavez looked at the map Crow had spread in front of him and nodded his head.

"Here's a map of all the bodies we've found over the past two years. Twenty-seven scattered around Arivaca within a sixteen-mile radius. It's all within striking distance of Sharp's place."

"And another motive," continued Crow, "could be to perpetuate fear...the *El Diablo* myth. We started that story to instill fear of crossing, and he's keeping it up to keep crossers from messing with his fences and waters."

Chavez thought about how a man could engage both fear and anger as he placed his hand on one corner of the map. "Most of these bodies are south of Sharp's ranch. They occur well into the Atascosa Mountains. Isn't that too far east for him to range?"

"Not really. He wants to take the focus of attention away from himself. He may have killed the wets on his place or along a road somewhere when the opportunity presented itself. But he discarded the bodies away from the center of his operation. This all makes sense."

"I get that he'd put the heads in the mine shaft to keep up the *El Diablo* myth, but what about the body in that shaft?" asked Chavez.

He used the shaft when he couldn't dispose of a body as *El Diablo*. He likely hated crossers enough to just kill when the opportunity arose."

Chavez nodded. At the same time Bean and Brown entered the big room through the back door. "Good afternoon, Mr. Crow," said Bruce Bean. "How was your night?"

"Good afternoon. It was short. I was up at five and going over all the paper I got from Yost. I see you got the same package."

"Yes sir...pretty informative. This is the first summary I've seen of this case. What do you think?"

"I was telling Nate here that I think Mr. Sharp is the killer."

"What about the Central American gangs? Are you ruling them out?"

Crow looked at Chavez, who had a slight smirk on his face. He grinned and responded, "You guys want to leave no stone unturned...that's good! I think that's good. Have you ever run across anyone that you confirmed was from a gang?"

"No, I don't think so."

"Well, if you did you'd realize they are a breed apart. They travel in packs and are all about publicly instilling fear and chaos. Our killer operates with too much stealth. He's a lone killer. He's a beast that seeks protection of the dense jungle, slipping into the open only for a quick kill before dashing back into the cover of darkness. That's our killer...that's Mr. Sharp. The jungles of Vietnam are still running through his veins. I was telling Nate that I have a strong feeling that we will discover something this afternoon."

Nate Chavez stared at Crow as he brought his coffee mug to his lips. The image of a jungle beast stalking his prey played over and over in his mind.

Chapter 30

The four Blazers pulled off along the Sasabe road and Bean got out to open Sharp's locked gate. The key he had kept didn't work, and he noticed the lock was different. "He's changed locks on us," he exclaimed.

Crow heard Bean, and commented, "That's not surprising." He had his left arm leaning on the window frame as he rubbed his face with his right hand. "You need a 'Border Patrol Key'?" he asked Bean.

"You got one handy?"

"Always," Crow replied as he exited his vehicle with a short-handled bolt cutter. With a quick jerk the lock fell to the dirt. Crow picked it up, took a lock from his pocket and said, "Here, replace it with this after we drive through. It'll keep him out of our hair if he returns while we're back there."

Bean expressed astonishment as he looked at Chavez and Brown sitting in their Blazers. He shook his head, smiled and opened the gate for the other agents. That Crow would operate so quickly was expected. That he already was so tuned into Sharp's trail was instructive. Bean maintained his grin as Brown and Chavez drove past, then closed the gate and sealed their entry with the lock Crow had given him.

As they approached the pile of fence material, Bean confirmed the position of Jones and Sweeny. Jones stayed with the vehicles at the OP, and Sweeny walked down the ridge to a point about two hundred yards away under the cover of a mesquite. He had a .223 caliber scoped rifle to cover the agents if they needed protection.

Crow parked about a hundred yards west of the pile and was the first one out. He locked the door of his Blazer and waited for the others to join him. "Let's take a wide path to the south and east of that stuff, and approach it from the east side. We can get a better idea of tracks and other sign with the sun on the opposite side of the scene. And look for trip wires tied to explosives...this guy might try some nasty revenge for our past actions."

Crow led the way, walking along the cobblestone of the wash as he divided his attention between his footing, the pile of material to his left, and the surrounding hills. The hat on his head bobbed as he progressed with short and choppy steps. His Wellington boots, well worn and dusty, and crowned with the folds of his Levis, rolled over the rocks as he moved along with ease, like he was floating.

When he reached a point about fifty yards southeast of the fence material he saw a live limb of a jojoba bush that had been broken off about three feet from the tip of the branch. He picked up the branch carefully and closely inspected it, noticing its worn and tattered tips. The leathery leaves were covered with fine brown dust. "He used this to erase his tracks...to hide his trail. We'll discover where he did this, and that will lead to something very important," stated Crow.

Removing his hat, Crow inspected the soft dirt adjacent to the rocky course he was on. He placed the branch back where he had found it and walked out of the rocky substrate and onto soft adjacent ground. With care he noted each mark on the soil. The track of Sharp's truck had passed by the area in front of them. "He threw the branch out here as he turned around to leave," he commented as he waved his hand for the others to follow directly behind him.

Crow had worked with literally thousands of agents during his tenure with the Border Patrol. He had immense respect for each of them and felt a special bond of brotherhood with each whose path he

had crossed. At this stage in his illustrious career he settled into the
role of a teacher more than anything else. Following a trail was easy,
and he could discuss his strategy as he worked. He knew his own
reputation and didn't let it hinder his open and friendly mannerism.
He also didn't let an agent mess up a crime scene. He always took
charge of his work, directing everyone present with an aura of
authority and purpose.

"Coyotes have been here since Sharp dropped off his load. Maybe
a fox too."

"They came to investigate the new and strange junk in their territory, huh?" commented Chavez.

"Maybe. Or maybe there's something here for them. Maybe
they're conditioned to Sharp's presence. Maybe it's chow time."

"What?" questioned Brown.

"Dinner," said Bean, who was relishing Crow's presence and expertise.

"What's for dinner is what I want to find out," commented Crow
as his sight stayed glued to the ground ahead of him.

When Crow was about ten feet from Sharp's pile of fence material, he stopped. He looked beyond the pile and pointed to the ground
beyond it. There a patch of flat land about ten feet across bordered a
tiny rocky side drainage that passed between two small hills. "See
those coyote tracks? They're on fresh ground. Sharp brushed it with
that limb we found back there. He went up into the hills there along
that little draw. Let's see where he went."

Chavez thought for a second about asking if Crow wanted to photograph the evidence the man had discovered thus far. He kept
quiet, realizing Crow was not about process, but about product. He
was on a trail and didn't want to be sidetracked with busy work. He'd
always been that way.

"Let's all be thinking now. Try to step in my prints as we head
toward that draw. Keep your noses open. I think there'll be a body up
this draw within a quarter mile."

The band of men approached the hills, following Crow in a line.
At the base of the hills mature mesquite trees were scattered among

large boulders. The coarse soil held hardly any sign, but Crow carefully inspected every square foot of it. "There's a scuff mark. It's been brushed over but you can still see it. He probably had a hard time covering his tracks in the dark."

Before moving forward Crow looked for other evidence of Sharp's trail up the draw. "I think he went across that hill there, along side that little gully," he said after a minute of studying the landscape. Crow looked around and finally found what he was looking for. "There's the jojoba bush he got that branch from to cover his track on the way out." He pointed at a plant at the top of the little hill about thirty feet away. "Let's get up there. It should be easy going from there on."

The men walked up the slight incline of the short hill, and directly to the jojoba. A fresh break at the base of the plant indicated that one of the stems had been tugged and twisted off recently. Around the plant Crow scoured the ground. "He came from that direction."

A few weeks earlier Chavez had walked the same ground he now was traversing with the other three men. He was thinking of all the sign he had missed along his route. His thoughts wandered to Logan, whose skills he believed stacked up to those of Crow. He thought about how all that he'd learned at the academy really didn't prepare him for field investigation. This was a science all its own. The electronic gadgets that he had been introduced to were valuable, but relative to walking and inspecting the ground, they were useless. Now all that knowledge seemed like a technological layer between him and what was really important.

Crow was just like one of Hunt's dogs. He had his head to the ground as he walked along slowly. It seemed like nothing escaped his keen eyesight. He directed the other three men to spread out on either side of him and orchestrated their progress without as much as one word. They all kept one eye on him and the other on the rocky soil in front of them.

After about five minutes they reached the top of a low hill and Crow paused. He looked around at the landscape before them. The ridges and washes that fanned out along the southwestern expanse of the Las Guijas lay in front of him. The sparse vegetation clung to the red and tan ground. Crow looked to the north and noticed a raven perched on a sotol stalk that leaned out over a hillside about two hundred yards away. It had been preening its plumage, which glistened a shiny black in the low sunlight, and stopped to look at the gathering of men. It gave a low guttural call, which brought two other ravens up from the wash below. With a final chorus of calls the birds flew off to the east.

"It's over there," Crow said, dipping his head in the direction of the birds.

Chavez looked at Crow, at his hat and his boots. He pondered all the miles of borderland the man had covered, all the things he'd seen. How the culmination of his experience landed him here in Arizona, helping to track down a killer. He thought of his own career, his newness, and his fortune to be mentored by a Border Patrol legend.

Crow took an indirect route to his destination. The others followed. Staying on the ridgeline above the low ground near the ravens he eventually made his way to the hillside across from the raven's sentinel perch. The wash was about fifty yards below them down a rocky hillside that culminated in a jumble of large rocks and broken short rimrock along the bottom. "We've never had a body in this area. That figures," commented Crow. He then lowered his head and exhaled the deep breath he had taken in. For the half-minute that followed he seemed to be praying. He remained silent, almost reverend.

He looked around one final time, then began a slow descent down the hill. The other agents followed, spaced about ten feet apart. It was like a funeral procession.

In a couple minutes they were at the site where the two ravens had flown up, standing next to a clothed and headless body. Crow stood back from the corpse, which had already been half eaten and picked at by a variety of animals. He said nothing.

Chavez thought about Hunt's dogs, and how that strategy was no longer part of the plan. In front of him was the evidence that linked Sharp to the murders. All four men realized this was the end of the trail.

THE WHOLE TRUTH

Chapter 31

This was his first Saturday off in over a month. He had arranged to meet Sam Logan in Sierra Vista and was looking forward to engaging his independent personality. He wanted to get away from anything to do with his job...he needed a break.

The spring season was already giving way to summer's warmth and it felt good to get out of the desert around Tucson. Sierra Vista was spread throughout the upper valley of the San Pedro River. It was a growing community about a mile in elevation, and cool. The early morning chill hit him as he descended into the broad valley so he turned on his heater. He was always amazed by the temperature extremes of southern Arizona. When he first thought about taking a post on the Arizona border straight out of the academy all he could imagine was sand and cactus. He was pleasantly surprised, and mornings like this stoked the fire of his amazement with the state.

He turned off Interstate 10 and onto State Highway 93, then headed for Sierra Vista. The Huachuca Mountains loomed ahead, a "sky island" of woodland and forests surrounded by a sea of grassland. Twenty thousand years ago that was not the case. The climate was much cooler and wetter, and pine trees extended out onto the hills and flats surrounding the slopes where grasses later dominated. As the region became dryer adapted life forms with origins to the south moved into new niches. The Huachucas were a grand mix of tropical and temperate plants and animals. Each was at the border of its range, and constantly crossing that unseen barrier in search of the perfect condition for life. The life assemblages were collectively competing for the opportunity to get a toehold on the landscape, and each organism represented a species that constantly faced an uncertain future.

Chavez understood only slightly all the ecological factors at play in the Southwest. Nonetheless, this assemblage of life intrigued him. He knew that fascinating subtropical plants and wildlife wandered the borderlands and he was anxious to engage it whenever possible. From books Nate had read he knew these mountains were special. He paid homage to them with frequent glances through the windshield.

As he pulled into Sally's Cafe he saw Logan's blue pickup. He was surprised that Logan had driven his personal vehicle. He thought Logan was still on the weekend shift. When Chavez walked into the cafe Logan greeted him with vigor. "How ya doin', young Nate?" Logan quipped.

Chavez was taken aback somewhat by the jovial tone of Logan's voice. "Fine. I got some time off. The world is now a brighter place!"

"I hear you guys did some good work around Arivaca. You solved the big case. That has to feel rewarding. Congratulations."

"All I did was show up. Crow was the man of the hour. That guy really knows how to read the ground. If it weren't for him I think I'd still be out there clearing sections. I got so tired of looking for bones and bodies in the brush."

"I'll bet. How is Yost doing?"

"If he could find Sharp he'd be doing a whole lot better. He figured he had solved the mystery of *El Diablo* and was already basking in the glory of his feat. There are warrants all over the country and in Mexico for Sharp. As soon as he's captured Yost will really celebrate. As it stands now he's on leave in Hawaii for a few weeks. But he's ready to jump on a plane and be in Tucson, or wherever, if they ever capture Sharp."

"I heard that Sharp hung his transmitter on a Swift transport truck that was running between Mexico and the east coast. That's pretty gutsy."

"Yah, and did you hear about the note taped to it? In big bold red letters it read, 'Fuck Off'!"

"The guy has a sense of humor," said Logan with a coy grin. "Does Yost really expect to catch him?"

"I think he's going to give it all the effort he can. He has everyone from the FBI and the entire resources of Homeland Security after Sharp. I imagine he'll surface sooner or later."

"I don't know. That guy's a cross between a desert rat and a jungle bunny. His tour of Vietnam taught him a lot about hiding out. I think it'll take loads of manpower, and even more luck."

Chavez aimlessly fumbled with a menu before asking, "Say, Sam, do you really think it was Sharp that killed all those crossers? What's the count now...over fifty, or seventy?"

Logan looked in his cup and began swirling the coffee. "I don't know. From what I can gather now that the case report is out, Sharp had a hand in some of the murders. I haven't looked at all the remains to see if his M.O. matches all the evidence. He certainly did in that last Mexican you guys found on Sharp's place...plus all the heads in the mineshaft. As for the other remains found over the past two years, I don't think anyone has given that a critical look. From what I can gather that assessment has been taken over by the celebration."

"But you don't think he killed all those guys, do you?"

Logan took a long sip of coffee then enfolded the cup as he lowered it to the table in front of him. He looked at Chavez and said, "Sharp certainly had a lot of hate in him for the government and crossers, for things that were changing his way of life. But there's a major inconsistency between his M.O. and where the bodies have been found across the countryside. Most are in real secluded places that I don't think Sharp would have taken the time to visit. Some places he would have a hard time getting to."

"I was amazed he could carry that last body as far as he did. Sharp's a pretty strong dude," said Chavez.

"He might be, but a mind fueled by hatred can make the body do strange things. The only factor that seems to be common to all the deaths is that the heads were gone. Why do you think Sharp threw those heads in that mineshaft?" asked Logan

"He's a sicko."

"Well, yeah. But maybe he wanted to blend in with the other killer.

"What other killer?" Nate asked.

"I don't have a real clear picture of another killer right now. But I bet when our outfit got the media lined out with the story of *El Diablo* Sharp suddenly had a friend...a role model...and a scapegoat. It was at that point, and not earlier that he started killing crossers. Initially he scattered the headless bodies in the desert like it was the work of *El Diablo*, putting the heads in the mineshaft thinking no one would ever find them. Sometimes he got lazy and threw the whole body down the shaft. That's what I think."

"So our 'Operation El Diablo' was his license to kill."

"It was a license, an idea, a cover...you name it. Without all those elements at his disposal Sharp might not have killed a single person. Another entity started the killing and Sharp was just a copycat."

"So you think *El Diablo*, whatever that is, did the killing...and is still out there? Did you tell anyone else about your theory?"

"Just you know that I'm still exploring the story that pissed off Yost when I worked for him. Back then I said it was an animal, and I still believe that."

"Sweet! I'm honored," responded Nate as he attempted to break the train of thought that Logan had initiated. "So what are you so happy about? You seem somewhat beyond well rested. How long have you been off?"

"Just a few days. I go back tomorrow. Got a meeting in Tucson to bring me back down to reality. I think I'm finally realizing that all the effort a man can put forth is just like a desert monsoon storm: there's a lot of stimulating commotion but when it's all over and the wind quits and the sun shines, a guy realizes that not much rain fell and it's just another beautiful hot day on the ol' desert!"

"I don't know what you mean. You're getting too poetic? You sound like a philosopher."

"An old philosopher, young man. Real old!"

Chapter 32

He was taking a big chance. Since Yost was out of town the risk was substantially reduced. He knew he could call in a favor or two from some old friends in the State Office of the Border Patrol, but he wasn't sure how far he could take it. He stood to lose much if his hunch failed but he was willing to face the consequences.

"Logan, I'm not doing this for you. I'm doing it because you made a formal request as an agent of the U.S. Border Patrol. You got that?"

"Yah, yah, I know. I just need to see the heads and the necks. How many did you say you had?"

"Heads? I have a total of seven. We got Hunt's dogs out there and found a head behind Sharp's ranch house buried in a canvas tarp. That one was from his latest victim. The others were from the mineshaft on Sharp's place. Traces of blood from at least two of the seven victims were found on a machete Sharp had in his house. He chopped off the heads, probably near his ranch house we suspect. We believe he had lured the victims there and killed them, later hauling the bodies to the places where we later discovered them."

Chuck Stevens had been with the Border Patrol's forensics lab for thirty years. Logan had been one of his best customers. Logan used his lab for a variety of tests to pin evidence to numerous crimes. Stevens developed a liking for Logan that lasted through the trials and tribulations Logan had with Yost. The relationship was strengthened by the fact that Stevens had absolutely no respect for Yost, who he saw as a piranha that would feed only on cases or events that served his career goals.

"Chuck, has anyone looked critically at the neck area of the bodies to see if a machete was used to severe the head in all cases? We have some neck vertebrae that indicate the heads were severed with a sharp object, but what about the headless bodies found away from Sharp's ranch? Did anyone examine the neck area of all these bodies for cut marks?"

"No. Yost had the skeletal remains sealed after we took only the usual corpse measurements. No one has reviewed the bodies for features you're talking about."

"As far as Yost is concerned the case is solved," Logan added. "The killer has been identified, and that's that."

"That's right."

"Are the locations of the skeletons recorded?"

"Yes. I set up a database that plotted each body. Here's the map that corresponds to the number of the remains."

"Great. Did many of the skeletal remains include the top of the backbone where it connects to the skull?"

"As I recall, some did and some didn't. Why?"

"I want to see if there's evidence of a machete or some sharp tool being used to decapitate all the victims."

"You mean you want to check each one for marks of a cut?"

"If possible, yes."

"That's a big one, Logan. It will take some time. You know, the Arivaca deaths have been the center of attention but we find dead bodies all the time along the borderland. We have about one fifty believed to be associated with Sharp and another fifty or so that likely died of exposure."

"Those exposure cases have the skulls present and intact?"

"Yes, most of them do have skulls. Remains found south and east of Arivaca generally are headless. Those are the ones we're attributing to

Sharp. The skeletal remains with heads present are mostly from farther to the west. Those western bones are usually older; I'm estimating the western deaths occurred over two or three years ago. Anyhow, I don't think you want to be here while I go over my bone collection so I'll tell you what I'll do. You come back in a few days, or better yet, give me a call next week. I'll go through all the bodies and see which ones have upper vertebrae present. I'll number them so when you come in it will take only an hour or two to find what you're looking for. Will that work?"

"That's perfect, Chuck."

"By the way, what are you looking for?"

"Well, I'm not sure. I need to see what the bones show me. Basically, I want to see if a sharp metal object severed the skull, or something else. What exactly that something else is I'm not quite certain."

Logan decided to return to Benson by way of Sonoita. It was way out of his way but the beautiful grassland bordering the Whetstone and Mustang mountains was spectacular.

As he approached the four-way stop at the crossroads in Sonoita he looked straight along the road to Patagonia. The Border Patrol check-station was still closed. It would not reopen until the marijuana smugglers began making their runs in mid-summer. He decided to get a cold drink at the corner gas station so he turned left at the intersection and drove up to the store. As he pulled into a parking slip a pickup pulled in beside him. An old guy with patched brown pants and a camouflage shirt stepped out of his truck. "Say, I'd like to report a dead body in the area of Parker Canyon Lake," he said.

"When did you find it?" asked Logan.

"This morning. You got a map?"

"Yes, sir. I'm Agent Logan. What's your name?"

"Jack Conrad. Good to meet you. I know you guys don't get out of your trucks anymore, so I figured I'd tell you about this one. You never would have found it."

"That's probably true. What were you doing in the backcountry?"

"Pokin' around looking for Mearn's quail. I hunt 'em in the fall and like to keep track of how many birds survived the winter. Nowadays there are so damned many hunters...and they go back to the same spot and wipe out all the birds in a covey. I am trying to prove to the game and fish boys they need to close down the season. Or at least reduce the bag limit significantly."

"Sounds like you're on a crusade."

"No, I just have an observation that no one wants to believe."

"I know that scenario," responded Logan. "So, what shape's this body in?"

"It's mummified mostly. I've been reading about all the bodies around Arivaca, and think this could be the same deal. There's no head that I could find. Have you had anything like that this far east?"

"No. Not in the Huachucas. Show me exactly where you found this body."

Conrad instantly pointed to the spot. "You can take this road to get back there. The Forest Service has the other road closed off for the fire season. It's dry as a bone out there. The quail are really down in numbers too."

"I know that road. Tell me, Mr. Conrad, was the body clothed?"

"Yah, mostly. The critters have fed on it. There were scraps of pants and a Levi jacket scattered around. Most of the muscle was gone. It's mainly bones with some dried flesh holding the bones together. It's along this draw. There are some rocky outcrops where the drainage cuts left here. The body is just out of the draw next to the rock ledge. Park here and follow the drainage down about half a mile. You can't miss it."

"Very good. Thanks for the tip. Is there a number I can reach you at in case I have any questions?"

"Here, I'll write it down."

As Conrad jotted down his name and phone number Logan studied him. Jack Conrad was a worn man, a fighter in his own arena. He had a passion about him that was unmistakable. He obviously was a good observer, and conveyed his observations with great articulation and some sarcasm. "What do you do for a living, Mr. Conrad?"

"I'm retired, young man. I do a little writing and small game guiding. But mostly I try to show those young biologists that they don't know shit about what they should know a lot about. It's like talking to a tree."

"Are you trained in wildlife biology?"

"University of Arizona. But that's just a degree. A guy needs to wear out his boots to really know something. All these young guys do is read crap on the Internet and use their computer. They don't have a clue."

"Wildlife is your thing, huh?"

"That's right. Why?"

"Just curious about that body. Do you have any opinion about what the cause of death was?"

"No. That guy died months ago. I've looked at thousands of bone piles in my day. I thought it was a deer carcass when I first saw it from about two hundred feet away. I looked for a skull as I approached since that would be the best indication of what sort of animal it was. I could not find one, and it wasn't until I got closer that I realized from the bones it was a human. Plus all the bits of clothing around."

"And you said you couldn't find a skull?"

"No, I never did find a skull. And I looked around quite a bit. But I'm sure those bones are human."

"No skull. That's interesting," said Logan as he folded his map. "Well, thank you, Mr. Conrad. I plan to head out there right now. Take care."

"You bet...no problem. Good luck."

Chapter 33

Stayton Sheldon was busy. The lack of winter rain left his cattle tanks empty, requiring him to feed and check waters daily. He hadn't talked with Logan for weeks, maybe months. He was letting Logan make the next move. He still hadn't found peace in his daily ritual of life. He knew a storm was brewing, not in the firmament over the landscape, but on the human front. That "dog" was sleeping for now, and Sheldon wanted no part in waking him. He also knew it wouldn't sleep forever.

He had just returned home after a morning repairing a float in one of his drinkers when his kitchen phone rang. It was Logan. "The Huachucas? That's pretty far east," said Sheldon as he poured a glass of iced tea.

"It is. I looked at it and took a bunch of photos. I'll check it again in a week to see what changes. That corpse is pretty much like the ones we found on your place."

"What do you make of that? I mean that's fifty miles east."

"Right! I'm not sure what to make of it. I am certain of the marks on the backbone though. We'll have to go over everything soon and see what we got and where we are. We've both been preoccupied with our regular jobs. Say, I gotta get over your way to take my weekly photos of those five bodies. Will you be around Saturday morning?"

"With this drought, I have no choice. What time on Saturday?"

"How about nine at your place?"

"That's fine. See you then."

Logan met Chuck Stevens at 3:00 p.m. as they had planned. Stevens had nine bodies for him to look at. "These are the only ones that had some vertebrae attached to the shoulder area."

As Logan unpacked his personal camera he glanced at the remains Stevens had arranged on a table. At the far end of the table was a map with the dates of collection and exact locations plotted. "You're good, Chuck. You're real good!" said Logan as he looked up at Stevens.

"There's no mark of a machete or sharp instrument on any of them," said Stevens. "What do you make of that?"

Logan closely examined the tip of each backbone. He smiled as he took close-up photos of each one. "See, there's no evidence of any small animal gnawing at the bones...no small chisel marks from rodent teeth. I think the bugs ate all the dried flesh so there was nothing for the small critters to chew on. The only teeth marks present are those made at the time of death, or very shortly thereafter. And they were made by large teeth...very large teeth."

"What does that tell you?" asked Stevens.

"Between you and me, Chuck?" Logan looked up at his friend and paused.

"Between us...it goes no further than this room," Stevens replied.

"I think that whatever it was that killed these guys ate their heads."

"What?" Stevens had come across many weird cases in his thirty years in forensics. But he had never confronted such a situation. As a scientist he was open-minded but Logan was stretching the bounds of open.

"See this end vertebra?" said Logan. "That bone is porous, and when it's alive it's not as hard as the side of a leg bone. It's soft like the joint of a chicken leg bone and you can easily put a tooth mark in it. All these bones show evidence of having been gnawed by an animal with large teeth. Look."

Logan laid out his case to Stevens. On all nine human remains the end vertebrae closest to where the skull had been attached showed signs of teeth scrapes, large teeth.

"Well, there certainly are no marks from a machete or other sharp instrument. What did the chewing?"

"The same animal that did the killing."

Stevens looked closely at the material Logan was inspecting. "You're saying that whatever killed these guys also ate their skulls? What would do that?"

Logan hesitated in answering. He didn't want to divulge everything about what he thought had killed these men. He knew there are no secrets in this world and sooner or later his theory would get out. He didn't want to put Chuck in the compromising position of having to reveal Logan's killer if Yost made an official inquiry, but he also knew Stevens would be an objective filter through which to run his ideas.

"I think it might have been a big cat," Logan said with considerable hesitation.

"Your mountain lion theory again," Stevens said. "The evidence backs that claim but what about the other ninety bodies?"

"Something else got to the carcasses when they were still relatively fresh, and in the process of eating the meat off the back the scavengers ate the entire backbone."

"And you're saying that the killer cat ate the skull?"

"The skull and probably some of the meat elsewhere on the body. But it seems to have a predilection for the skull. It probably likes the brains. There's a lot of nourishment in that organ." Logan watched as Stevens shifted his gaze from one cadaver to another and continued, "There are lots of holes in this notion but the more information I get the more I'm certain it's a mountain lion. The missing skull thing is something I'm not quite sure about. I don't really know how to explain it...I don't know if mountain lions eat brain matter, or if they're even powerful enough to break into a skull. All I know is that nine bodies that have some of the neck vertebrae present show no sign of a sharp object having severed the head. Instead, there are marks of big teeth."

"Well, I certainly can see what you're talking about. If mountain lions do not normally do this then you would suspect that it's the work of one lion that has a preference for brain material. But look at the large area where we're finding bodies. I suspect a mountain lion's territory is a very small fraction of this area.

"Very good point, Chuck...good thinking. One of the things I need to do soon is learn how mountain lions dismantle their prey, and if they typically eat the brain. Maybe they switch to brain material when they take human prey. Whatever the case, I think the mountain lion theory explains many more deaths than the angry rancher theory."

"I can see where you're coming from...I agree," responded Stevens.

"Say, where's the body that young hunter found in the Cerro Colorados? That body was found shortly after death, wasn't it?"

"Right there...it's on that end of the table. It's the freshest carcass found to date. That guy was killed within 12 hours of the time he was discovered."

Logan bent over the carcass that Stevens had pointed out, and very carefully looked at the remnants of skull that surrounded the end of the cervical vertebrae structure. He had the magnifying glass in his right hand but didn't really need it. All the evidence was plainly in front of him. When he stood up and looked down on the corpse a feeling of confirmation and contentment welled up inside. He had seen those teeth marks before.

The glow of twilight was like a halo surrounding the Galiuro Mountains as Logan pulled out of his driveway. He liked to get an early start and be afield before the morning chill vanished. It would take a little over an hour to get to Sheldon's ranch and another half hour to get to his first body.

Logan and Sheldon had found nine bodies around Sheldon's place, and three on the Sopori Ranch. Five of them were fairly fresh, less than a week old when they were discovered. Logan had combed each area for sign, taken photos per forensic standards, and placed video trail cameras triggered by motion sensors at three of the bodies. For the past four months he regularly photographed the bodies to document their rate of deterioration and downloaded the video from his trail cameras. He was hoping to capture the killer on a return visit to the scene.

The only thing he had failed to do was to inform his agency of his activities. It wasn't failure as much as intent based on instinct. Even though he traveled to and from Sheldon's place in his own vehicle and did his investigation on his own time, he knew he was compromising his career with the Border Patrol. Upper management would get him for the offense he was committing. It was a sin of omission. He had not told a soul in his outfit. He trusted no one. Stevens was the only one who knew something. Sheldon knew everything.

As he turned off the pavement and prepared to enter Sheldon's east gate it was straight up six o'clock. Immediately he noticed fresh tracks on the road just the other side of the locked gate. They were tracks of Stayton's pickup entering the area. The dusty road was hard to read but the tracks seemed to be set down from a visit earlier in the week, perhaps when Stayton had entered to check water tanks and feeding stations. He probably left the area through the west or north gate.

What intrigued Logan most were the prints on top of the tire tracks. He had encountered hints of them several times during the past three months but the footprints before him now were very detailed. They also were so much more ominous now, sitting on his friend's track, heading in the same direction along the dirt road. This was the mark of a huge cat, a killer.

Logan drove his truck through the gate and locked it behind him. Before he got back into his pickup he walked over to the cat tracks.

He bent over with his hands on his knees and examined them for about a minute. During Logan's pursuits over the last several months this was the best look at its sign the animal had presented. To Logan the creature was a ghost. He knew it frequented this area because of the carnage it left behind but he had never seen it. He was hoping to capture a glimpse of it on one of the trail cameras. He drove along and noted where the cat tracks left the road and moved onto the dried oak leaves along a rocky drainage.

The sun was beginning to display its energy in the northeast and cast its rays on the tops of the oaks as Logan slowly traveled along his route. It would take him nearly three hours to visit all the evidence stations. He meticulously noted the weekly changes at each site. He wanted to gather information on what happened to the remnants of each body. That these were remains of human beings who had relatives, and at one time had dreams and hopes, no longer entered his mind. At first that was a major issue with him. But as the bits of clothing were blown or carried away and the bones disarticulated into a scattered array, he settled into treating these remains as one essential experiment. He justified his actions by believing his study would eventually enable him to pull all the pieces together and put the deaths into some coherent picture that pointed conclusively to a single killer. And that killer could then be eliminated.

When he finished taking photos and collecting the digital video cards he headed out Sheldon's west gate. The sun had been on the east face of Baboquivari for almost three hours. He was ten minutes from Sheldon's ranch house but his mind was on the cat tracks he had encountered.

Chapter 34

"**S**tayton, you make the best iced tea this side of the San Pedro," exclaimed Logan as he pulled a chair up to the kitchen table. He put his laptop on the chair next to him and took off his hat.

"Well, it's the wettest anyway!" replied Sheldon as he pulled up a chair across from Logan and glanced at the computer. "Well, let's have a look. This is better than Christmas!"

"You're getting pretty impatient, Mr. Sheldon," replied Logan.

"A guy has to find some excitement around here. June is a dog month. I'm tired of checking waters and fence, hauling feed, and searching for bodies. My dogs are getting pretty good at it. I think I'll get out of the cattle business and rent me and my dogs out to the Border Patrol. There's money in that, right? Besides, I'm real tired of checking for rain clouds off to the south. Let's see what we got."

"Okay, okay." Logan took a long sip of tea then lifted the cover of his computer. While he started the machine and stroked the keys, Sheldon looked at the operation in amazement.

"All that stuff passed me by. I mean...I don't have a clue how that thing works. It amazes me."

"Well, it amazes me too, Stayton. And these are old trail cameras compared to the infrared ones available nowadays. Some of 'em get pretty fancy. Anyhow, I downloaded all the camera cards, so we'll see. You ready?"

"Wait," interrupted Sheldon. "Take a sip of that tea before you push those keys to start the video. It's good luck."

"What?"

"Hey, give it a try. It can't hurt anything."

Logan smiled at Sheldon, cocked his head, and then looked at his glass of tea. "It's good tea, but you really think it will give us good luck?"

"It can't hurt!"

Logan gripped his glass, toasted his friend and the computer, and then pushed "enter." "The counter says there's about fifteen total minutes of video. Lots of stuff to look at."

"Two weeks ago we had ten minutes of skunks, foxes, ringtails, and a few seconds of a coyote."

"Yah, and most of the skunk stuff was at night. I think those critters are getting used to the scent of humans."

Logan fast-forwarded the video past a coyote in daylight for about 30 seconds at site one, and past a skunk at site two for three minutes during the night. As the image appeared on the screen at site three, the dim light suggested early morning before sun-up. Logan looked at the lower right of the screen and confirmed that the camera had captured something yesterday morning in the pre-dawn minutes. There was enough light to capture a good image of the animal that began to appear out of the brush to the right of the body.

This was their freshest corpse, found by Sheldon's dogs a week ago Friday. Logan set the camera at this site in hopes of recording what was about to be revealed to them.

Nate Chavez had never formally met Stayton Sheldon. Logan's wife told him that her husband was at Sheldon's place only after Chavez informed her that Sam was in dire trouble and might lose his job. She was still reluctant to tell him how to get to Sheldon's. She wished Sam would answer his phone. She had heard her husband talk about Chavez, and the sincerity of Nate's voice along with the high stakes Nate was presenting made her cooperate with his request.

Logan and Sheldon heard the pickup pull into the drive just about the time the dogs began to bark. "What's Chavez doing here?" wondered Logan out loud.

"Who?" asked Sheldon.

"I think that's Nate Chavez's personal truck. He's an agent in this part of the sector. Have you ever met him?"

"Not that I recall," replied Sheldon. "Is he a good guy?"

"Very good."

Both men left the computer and headed toward the front door. "Nate," exclaimed Logan. "How are you?"

"Good, Sam, good. Sorry to bother you, but I have to talk with you now."

"Sure. Are you okay?"

"I'm fine. But I need to talk with you."

"Nate, this is Stayton Sheldon. He owns the Atascosa Ranch." Chavez shook hands with Sheldon and he cradled his hat to his chest.

"Glad to meet you, Mr. Chavez. Please have a seat. Would you like some tea?"

"Yes, please. Thank you." As Chavez nervously sat down on one of the stretched leather chairs on Sheldon's porch the sound of bull hide on wood emitted its customary squeak. No one spoke for about a minute as Sheldon and Logan moved their drinks from the kitchen to the porch and settled in to hear what Chavez had to say.

Chavez looked at Logan then Sheldon, and then back at Logan, who recognized Nate's reluctance to talk in front of Sheldon. "I've known Stayton for a long time, and anything you have to say to me is okay to say in front of him."

"Well, I don't know where to start," replied Chavez, who hadn't even touched his drink.

"Is this about Border Patrol business?" asked Logan.

"Yes. It's about Yost. He's after you in a big way."

"That's nothing new," responded Logan. "He must be back in town. Does he have a sun tan?" Logan jabbed with a smile.

"He's on his way back from Hawaii right now. From what I hear he's been in touch with Bean and Stevens, and the Regional Office. He is furious from what I heard Bean saying. He's really after you, Sam."

"Do you know what the deal is? What exactly is his problem?"

"Stevens was confronted by Bean about some bodies that you were examining. That's all I know."

"Is Stevens in trouble?"

"I don't think so but I don't know for sure. I was talking with Bean when Stevens returned a call from Bean. Bean was on his cell phone and I could hear some of Steven's answers when Bean wasn't interrupting him."

"How did Stevens get fingered?"

"I don't know that he was fingered by anyone. Maybe he was, I don't know. I really don't know how this whole thing connects, but I do know that Bean talked to Stevens about some bodies you looked at. Bean then talked with Yost. I've never seen Bean so upset."

Logan looked at Sheldon, who was swirling the ice in his glass. He sighed, then picked up his drink and looked at it. "Nate, this is the best tea this side of the San Pedro. Did you realize that?"

Sheldon grinned and said nothing. Chavez glanced at the full glass in front of him and leaned back in his chair. A strange sense of comfort overcame him as the chair again presented its familiar sound. He looked at Logan, who took a long drink and then put the glass on the table.

"I'll tell you exactly what's going on, Nate. But first I want to show you something."

The map on the kitchen wall was littered with red and black dots. As June Logan listened to Chad Everette she glanced at the map. It meant nothing to her. Her husband had put it up months ago and studied it frequently. He didn't share much of his Border Patrol life with her. Their relationship was full in other areas. But as she caught the urgency in the voice of her husband's supervisor, her eyes locked on the word "Arivaca," which was nestled among the dots. She had no clue that every one of the dots represented the remains of a human being.

"Thanks for calling, Chad. I'll have Sam call you as soon as he gets in."

Chapter 35

Among the cool and shady pine-covered crags of Mule Ridge in the Atascosas he rested. He had separated himself from life in the lowlands once again. In a few days he would move down the mountain and begin another search.

The departure from his homeland in Mexico a little over two years ago was traumatic, and now he found himself in this place, which was remarkably similar. His lineage once made a living here, and still there were plenty of resources for his sustenance. Like all living things he had been formed by what his ancestors had experienced, and by what he had learned along the way of his relatively short life.

The significantly changing world that now surrounded him always presented new challenges that were merely part of existing, really not unlike seasonal fluxes. He knew his physicality would enable him to gather what he needed for survival. It also would allow him to detect that which would harm him, and to make good his escape. He was an incomparable blend of instinct and physical might...a grand specimen in every sense. In a few days he once again would escort that constitution down the slopes to the canyons and flatlands below.

———∞———

Nothing could have prepared Nate Chavez for what he was about to see. He followed Logan and Sheldon into the kitchen of Sheldon's house. Without saying a word Logan gestured for Nate to have a seat, and without sitting himself Logan pushed a key on his laptop. The monitor began to display a moving image as Chavez focused his attention on what appeared before him.

The woodland scene was essentially the landscape he had come to know during his tour of duty in southern Arizona. But what soon appeared was like something stepping out of a fairy tale. He said nothing, but just watched the creature move in the low light of pre-dawn. The patterns and colors of its markings were in harmony with its form and movement, all blending perfectly with the setting as it walked slowly into the center of the screen. It punctuated Arizona's wilderness wonderlands and embodied everything he had read about this extraordinary place.

Finally Chavez spoke. In a barely audible voice he said, "A jaguar. That's a jaguar, isn't it?"

"It's a jaguar, Nate. And that drainage is just about three miles from here."

The three men watched as the big cat stopped near the human remains and looked around slowly, its immense head held level with its muscular shoulders. It looked right into the camera for about five seconds before looking straight ahead. After a long stare in front of him he looked down at the carcass. He took two steps to his right toward it, lowered his head and began examining it with his sensitive nose.

"He recognizes everything that has wandered past his kill," said Logan. "It's like that body is his bait to see what's in the area."

The men watched the magnificent animal sniff for nearly three minutes the ground around the shreds of a human form. "Something interests him," commented Sheldon.

"I think so," replied Logan.

Chavez remained silent. A thousand questions whizzed through his head. He didn't know which one to ask first. It was obvious that Logan was not the least bit bothered by the news of Yost's rage.

Exactly what this jaguar had to do with that affair was unclear. The men watched the cat look up from what was holding its attention and move along the ground and out of view like a ghost. No one spoke for a couple minutes. Sheldon fetched more tea from the refrigerator and Logan fussed with his computer. Finally Chavez broke the silence. "What's this all about?" he asked.

Logan touched a key that shut down the computer and Chavez watched the screen go black. As they both sat around the table with Sheldon, Logan said, "Nate, maybe you don't want to know about this. You can walk out right now if you want. If you choose to stay and listen you're part of this deal. Any knowledge I share with you may change your standing with the Border Patrol, maybe for the good but maybe not. Either way, it's your choice. You're either in or you're out."

Chavez really had no idea what Logan had just said. He knew Logan was on the fringe with Border Patrol politics, but he also knew that Logan's attitude about Yost had boundless substance. Chavez trusted Logan more than any mentor he had ever known. That confidence compelled him to say, "I'm here, so I guess I'm in, whatever that means."

"I think you know what that means, Nate. But I'll be more specific," said Logan.

Chavez slowly pushed back his chair and folded his arms across his chest like he was trapped. Logan noticed Nate's discomfort, and wanted him to have an escape route. He looked at his friend and paused. Looking down at the table, he started his explanation. "You know my reputation within the Border Patrol, which is largely based on my past interactions with Yost. I had a theory early on about the border deaths, which Yost only slightly understood. My methods of investigation threatened Yost and he reacted in a way that was guarded. He used his authority to discredit my observations but I did not relent. My actions off-duty led me to the point I'm at now. You had a glimpse of that point. You know where Yost and the Border Patrol stand on this case. As far as they're concerned, it's solved...closed.

"Also, know this," Logan continued. "As a federal law enforcement agent there is no such thing as being 'off-duty' when it comes to investigating a federal case, whether or not it's active. I knew I was hanging way out there. But I also knew there was enough that was unexplained surrounding these deaths to justify further inquiry. I went about it in my own way and now I accept any consequences that come my way. I now know that I was right. You can get up and leave now and say you knew nothing if you want. I don't want you to feel trapped."

Chavez had his eyes on Logan the entire time he gave his introduction. When Logan finished, Nate looked at the computer, which Logan had set aside. Sheldon sat as still as the morning air. Chavez gathered his thoughts and said, "When I found those bodies in that mine shaft and witnessed Yost's actions afterward, I was impressed with the energy he put into this case. He moved more swiftly than I'd ever seen him before. He had the buy-in of his staff, including me. Bean and Yost tracked real well...almost too well. I never suspected that their conclusion was not the reality. I pretty much concluded that Sharp was the killer, and that he was caught with a well-executed enforcement plan." Chavez concluded, "So I guess I don't quite know how to sort out what's good and what's bad here."

Logan looked intensely at him as Chavez explained his consternation. When Nate finished Logan said, "I understand exactly where you are on this. I will present my case in a convincing manner to you and to our agency. I realize that unless I demonstrate clearly that Sharp was a renegade responsible for only a small fraction of the deaths Yost will hang me out to dry. I do believe that Sharp killed some crossers. That is true. But there's some truth, and then there's the rest of the story, the whole truth. I have the rest of the story. You can hear it, or you can choose to leave. If I were you, I would leave and watch the thing unfold from a distance. That way you are not an accomplice in any way, and have plausible deniability in the event of any future witch hunt that Yost may elect to initiate. Again, it's your choice."

Chavez slowly transferred his view from Logan to the computer again. He recalled when he first over-heard the conversation between Yost and Bean he had the sense that he would have to make a choice. When he decided to call Logan, essentially he made his decision. The reality of his position was slapping at him, and he knew what he would do.

Sheldon was perfectly silent as he listened to Logan reveal to Chavez every detail of their investigation on the Atascosa Ranch. The ground he had grown up on was the center of the discussion. He knew every nook and cranny on the place. He had been to all the areas Logan was describing with his father and later with his wife, and recalled events of his life in these places when things were different.

He really admired the work Logan had done. He felt privileged to be part of such an important investigation. He had absolutely no regrets. Although his engagement with life had never exposed him to the politics that Logan had mentioned earlier, he could understand the wasted energy it consumed. If he felt anything about that issue it was disgust for people who used their government positions for personal gain. Sheldon never put Logan in that category. In Sheldon's mind Logan was always after the truth, nothing but the truth.

Sheldon watched as Logan went over all the digital photo records he had taken of the bodies at the forensic lab, and listened to the conviction in his voice. Logan, without trying to sell his case to Chavez, was doing just that. Sheldon realized that Logan was rehearsing his story for a larger and more significant audience, and that Chavez was the perfect sounding board.

After nearly an hour of talking without interruption, Logan rolled the video of the jaguar at site three. The men watched it in silence, alone with their individual thoughts. The animal looked out of place in the Arizona setting yet it looked perfectly at home. It truly was a ghost, appearing in the haze of twilight, and disappearing with an ironically commanding presence.

When the big cat's image faded and Logan turned off the computer, he sat quietly, and deeply satisfied. After half a minute he looked at Chavez and asked, "Any questions?"

"Do jaguars usually attack the head of their prey...and eat it?" asked Nate.

"This one does...great question! If that's normal I don't know. That's what I need to find out next. I thought our killer was a mountain lion. Attacking the head is definitely not their style. Now that I know what sort of predator we're dealing with I need to find out more about them."

Chapter 36

After the two men left Sheldon thought about his chores for that day. First on the list was visiting a fence line that needed mending in two places. However, for the first time in his life he was hesitant about setting foot on his own ground.

He sat on his front porch and looked out at the large mesquites, which were heavy with young beans. He knew the deer and javelina would be feasting in the mesquite grove along the bottomlands of his western boundary. They were prefect prey for a large cat. But the cat that had taken residence on his place was not interested in his deer. It was more interested in him. That fact haunted Sheldon.

He thought back on the time his grandfather had settled this area and started ranching. Back then in the 1860s the Apaches were the most feared element on the landscape. Neighbors banded together for defense, in fact the entire burgeoning livestock industry of southern Arizona lobbied the federal government for protection. Eventually the Apache Wars ended the Indian threat, making the land safe for their industry…almost. It wasn't until the last wolf was killed in the mid 1900s that cattlemen felt fairly well shielded from the risks associated with imposing their foreign livestock on the native landscapes of Arizona.

But the situation was different now. Once again the physical threat was to the rancher, not so much to his cattle. Only three people knew about the new menace and they essentially were the outlaws. They had proof of their claim, but getting that evidence into a court of peers and obtaining some sort of remedy would take months, maybe years. And he had a fence that needed attention right now.

The sun was nearly overhead, which was not a good time to be fixing a fence in early summer. Sheldon thought about his problems and decided to take a nap. He would think about what to do when he awoke. It had been a long and draining morning and he needed to rest. The changing world was hitting him hard and his cocoon of uncertainty and hesitancy offered little comfort.

Chavez drove east along the Arivaca Road to the junction of Interstate 19. He had the day off but didn't want to go home. He had too much on his mind. During such times he enjoyed driving so he headed south on Interstate 19 toward Nogales.

He looked out his left window and glanced at the Santa Rita Mountains, which rose above the desert foothills of the Santa Cruz valley. He wondered if jaguars inhabited those mountains. He looked at the Tumacacori Mountains to his right with the same question. The whole countryside took on a phenomenal yet ominous complexion.

He thought about the ecological significance of jaguars returning to southern Arizona. Lurking in his mind were the practical problems associated with that fact. What sort of predator would attack people...indeed, would select humans instead of deer or other wildlife? That this animal could take down its victim by the head was one aspect of all this that plagued him. One thought gripped his imagination and wouldn't let go. That was the thought of a crosser meeting his end with his head in the jaws of this powerful creature.

He took the Ruby Road turnoff and headed east across the Santa Cruz toward Patagonia, realizing for the first time he was real hungry.

He started out that morning with one mission, encountered a huge decision, and was left with a thousand questions. In Patagonia he would get some food and ponder some of them.

June Logan greeted each day with a joyous sense of wonder and appreciation for the natural world around her. She liked that they lived in rural areas during their stay in Arizona, and that they shared an affinity for nature. They knew each other well and when she met her husband in the driveway the look on her face told him the whole story. He stepped out of his truck and immediately embraced her. With his right arm wrapped around her shoulder he closed the truck door with his left hand and headed to the back door. They silently walked in step with a swaying cadence amidst the clamor of barking dogs. He walked his bride of thirty years into the kitchen and seated her at the table. "We are going to be totally fine, dear. Everything will be okay. When I started out this morning I was only fifty percent sure about that. Now I am one hundred percent sure. We'll be just fine."

"Okay, I trust you. But it's not the first time I got a call from your boss you know. On the phone the pitch of Everette's voice seemed different. He was worried."

"Don't give it another thought. We're on the track of something very interesting. Just wait and see."

On his way home Logan determined he would find out all he could about jaguars. The fact that he was dealing with a new and strange predator excited him. As ideas raced through his brain he settled on the notion that maybe there was something about jaguars in southern Arizona that was unique, that was causing this species to act differently here. He thought about prey selection, about the low numbers of deer during the drought, and about how a predator would naturally switch to alternate food sources like humans under such conditions.

Presently the most common deer-size animal in southern Arizona was a crosser from Mexico. Their numbers were increasing substantially. Perhaps the human head presented an ideal attack point. Cats usually kill by suffocation, and grabbing a small human neck would be harder than a long deer neck. He needed information on the species, its range in Mexico and the New World, its diet and hunting style, and its habitat preferences.

The image of the cat on his computer was burned into his brain. That one animal had a special meaning to him. It was the one that connected him to the species and began turning the wheels of his inquiry. But what about that particular jaguar was really special? What were the factors that brought it to the fringe of the species' range in the Atascosa Mountains of southern Arizona? How long had it been there? Had it developed a predilection for human flesh? Was it the only jaguar in the area?

Chapter 37

When Yost walked into his office on Monday morning he paused. He recalled the events of the past few days as he slowly walked to his desk. One week ago when he took off for Hawaii his world was in order. He had solved the case of his life and was headed for a position in the Regional Office. He'd made the jump from a sector chief all the way to Albuquerque, by-passing the traditional role of heading up the State Office before taking on a major role at regional headquarters. That had not been done before in the history of Border Patrol administration in the Southwest, and he felt special.

Things had changed, or had the potential to. His path could be diverted by the actions of an agent with whom he had many difficult encounters. Logan had been a pain in his side forever it seemed, and now that pain was getting sharper. A fury arose in him as he grabbed the phone. And it reached fever pitch when Logan walked in. He slowly replaced the hand set onto the receiver and stood up.

"Good morning, Mr. Yost," said Logan. He had a smile on his face as he sat in a chair directly in front of Yost. An orderly desk was all that separated the two men.

Yost was speechless for half a minute. He retained the forward seated position he had assumed to reach his phone and remained frozen like a deer in the headlights. "How are you doing, Logan?" was all he could think to say in response.

"Fine. How was Hawaii?"

"Just fine."

"Well, where do you want to begin?" responded Logan.

"With what?"

"Let's not play games, Yost. Everette called my house. I think you have something to say to me."

"Does Everette know you're here?"

"I didn't tell him. I don't know if he does or not. But then, there's a lot that I don't know. Maybe you had him stick a transmitter up my ass and now he knows every move I make. I don't know."

Logan's confidence smacked Yost between the eyes. It left him speechless. It was evident that Logan had gathered substantial information, which raised Yost's anxiety to a point off the charts. Yost reflected a deep and very unsettled fear. He could not confront the boldness with which Logan had approached him. Logan knew it so he pounced first.

"Yost, I'm sick and tired of hiding my thoughts and actions surrounding this *El Diablo* business. You did some good work to uncover Sharp's activities, but you squashed my earlier efforts that pegged the killer as a mountain lion. I have some idea about why you did that, but I'm here to tell you that none of them wash. In my view you took advantage of your authority. You moved me out of your part of the sector to get rid of me. But I'm not made of the stuff you think I am. I don't give up. I would not cower then and I will not run away and hide anymore. You found a guy who killed six crossers that we know about. I know who killed most of the others."

Yost remained hunched over his desk at the edge of his chair. He said nothing. His hands were still on his desk, one on top of the other as he watched Logan. He literally was speechless. Logan recognized his seizure.

"You want to go to Albuquerque. That's fine with me," continued Logan. "But you need to face the facts that I will present my findings to an investigation panel. You can attempt to hinder me but it will cost you. It will cost you your move. In fact, I can guarantee if you try to silence me or discredit my information you'll be looking for crosser footprints in the sand around Yuma through the windshield of an air conditioned Blazer—if you're lucky."

That comment infuriated Yost. But he was still too wary to counter anything Logan was saying. So he propped his elbows on the desk, raised his hands to his chin, and scooted his chair closer to his desk. He remained on the edge of his seat, feeling naked. He let Logan continue without interruption, knowing Logan was holding all the cards in this game, and knowing that Logan knew it too.

"Here's what I want you to do. Get off my ass and get off Steven's ass. And don't get on anyone's ass unless I say it's okay to get on their ass. I hope I am real clear about this, Yost. I mean it. I want full access to all the records and reports and people associated with *El Diablo*. And I want you to be in the background as a support factor."

Logan was somewhat surprised that Yost had not said anything up to this point. He had calculated there might be an outside chance that he would blow up, but Logan's strategy of coming in unannounced and lowering the boom right away was working. He knew he needed to give Yost an out at this point.

Logan continued, "You have a lot to gain if you play your cards right. You can take credit for a form of leadership and innovation in your reach of the sector that led to the ultimate discovery of the real killer. I don't want credit or a promotion. I don't want anything except the freedom to do the field investigation it takes to track down our killer. There's still a lot of work ahead and it's the kind of work that you do best. We'll need to coordinate with several other agencies and individuals to wrap this thing up. But now we're in the driver's seat. The killer has been identified."

Yost jumped at the chance to relax. He needed to be in control of something—of himself at least. He gripped the armrests of his chair and slid back, folding his hands and maintaining silence and his stare at Logan.

Logan liked this change in posture that Yost revealed. He recognized it as a melt down of sorts. "Are there any questions?" he asked.

Yost hesitated, retained his posture and asked, "When can I see your evidence?"

Logan stood up and responded, "Tomorrow morning in the conference room. Have Everette and Bean there, as well as Chavez. This is all the brainpower we'll need to start. We'll decide who else to bring in later."

Chapter 38

"We saw neither hide nor hair of him, but his personality pervaded the wilderness; no living beast forgot his potential presence, for the price of unwariness was death. No deer rounded a bush, or stopped to nibble pods under a mesquite tree, without a premonitory sniff for *el tigre*. No campfire died without talk of him. No dog curled up for the night, save at his master's feet; he needed no telling that the king of cats still ruled the night; that those massive paws could fell an ox, those jaws shear off bones like a guillotine." After reading the passage Logan placed the book on the kitchen table.

"Pretty cool stuff don't you think, June?" Logan had surrounded himself with stacks of literature and was busy learning all he could about jaguars. "Aldo Leopold wrote that. He's considered the father of wildlife management. He wrote those words in 1922 when he was along the delta of the Colorado River. Back then he could still feel the presence of *El Tigre*, the jaguar. It's all changed now. The Colorado doesn't even flow to the Gulf of California any more."

June rarely got involved in Sam's Border Patrol affairs but this case was special. For one thing Logan was more excited about his job than he had been in years, and she liked that. That her husband was enhancing his career was important. She had become accustomed to Logan's bull-headedness and the battles he had with bureaucrats. She always trusted that he knew the limits of how far to go with his convictions, and she knew he had been at the limit. She saw the case he was now preparing as a positive step for Sam and for his agency and everyone involved. "I think that video is all the proof you need, Sam. If you're sure Yost is against the ropes and you gave him a path to his promotion, then I think you have nothing to worry about," she said with some hesitancy.

"Honey, I'm not worried in the least bit. Yost is a puppy dog that's smart enough to know when he has a chance to shine. He went up one step on his ladder with Sharp, and he knows the ladder I am offering him is longer than any he had ever imagined. Trust me. Everything will be alright."

June was intrigued by jaguar biology but she was more interested in knowing that her husband was confident in the path he was on. She cleaned the kitchen as Logan continued to pour over the literature he had checked out of the library. But she remained close by so he could bounce facts and ideas off her. She knew he liked to rehearse with her since she was a good listener. She tried to temper her anxiety so Logan could focus on what he believed was important.

"I gotta get hold of this Joe Gray guy. He was with game and fish and wrote a book on jaguars. I wonder how I can contact him? You know there were about seventy jaguars killed in Arizona in the 1900s? They once ranged all the way to the Grand Canyon in this state. In the last twenty-five years there have been seven jaguars documented by either houndsmen or trail cameras."

"I thought they lived in the jungle."

"They do...in the tropics. But they occur from South America up through Central America into the U.S. along the border. They thrive in different habitats; wherever there's a good supply of food you can expect them. The closest known population to Arizona is a little over a hundred miles away in Sonora, Mexico. They think there about thirty jaguars in that area. I bet that's where our cats are coming from."

"Is someone studying them down there?"

"I bet so. They're an endangered species so someone must be doing a study. That's why I want to get hold of Mr. Gray."

"Joe Gray," answered the voice.

"Is this the Mr. Gray who wrote the book on the jaguar in Arizona?" asked Logan.

"Yes sir."

"Mr. Gray, my name is Sam Logan. I'm an enforcement agent with the Border Patrol. I have some questions about jaguars in southern Arizona. Do you have a minute?"

"You bet."

"Do you know of any jaguars in Arizona right now?"

"There are two jaguars that we know of in the state right now. Why? Did you see one?"

"Well, I'm not sure. I am just curious. Where are these jaguars?"

"One is southwest of Tucson in the Atascosa Mountains and the other is in the Santa Rita Mountains. Are you familiar with these areas?"

"Yes I am. I've spent a good deal of time there."

"Well, the chance of actually seeing a jaguar is slim. They are most active at night or at twilight. But that area is your best shot for seeing one."

"I am very interested in learning what they eat and how they capture it. Where would they hang out in the Atascosas?" asked Logan

"They eat about anything they want...they're a top predator. Their haunts are the rocky and wooded canyons of the mountains, places that offer a hiding place where they can launch a quick surprise attack," responded Gray.

"Tell me. How does a jaguar capture its prey? I mean...does it grab prey with its claws, or with its mouth? How does it bring down a deer? Don't they rely on suffocating their prey like the mountain lion?"

"All the big cats, like mountain lions and jaguars, will employ a suffocation hold on their prey until it dies. They latch on with their front claws, then grab the throat in their jaws and hold on until their quarry quits wiggling. But the jaguar is a little different. It's so big and powerful that once it snares prey with its claws it can bite anywhere on the head and instantly kill the prey. Their huge jaws can inflict a lethal wound just about anywhere on the head. Once they get hold of the head with their teeth it's about over for a deer or javelina. The bite pressure they exert is off the charts, and it punches the long canines easily through the skull bone and directly into the brain. Some people think it's an adaptation to cracking open turtle shells that likely were an abundant prey base for jaguars ten thousand years ago.

"You're saying that a jaguar commonly attacks the head area? Could one specialize in killing its prey by grabbing only the head and crushing the skull?

"It could. That bite would instantly dispatch prey. Jaguars along the Amazon in South America readily kill eight-feet long caiman by grabbing the head and penetrating the reptile's brain with a canine tooth and instantly paralyzing the animal. It might be a little different with an animal like a deer, which has a long throat that offers a much bigger target for suffocation. I suspect with a deer they'd go for the throat and hold on until the deer dies. But those big cats could crush a deer skull with one powerful bite. Do you have something that you think was killed by a jaguar?"

"Well, not really. But I'm not sure. If a jaguar killed by crushing the skull, would it begin feeding on the head and end up eating the entire head before going for more meaty areas like the rump?" As he posed these questions to Gray, Logan was deep in the thought of that jaguar on the video...of the image of it fading into the early morning haze.

"Actually, cats generally like to feast on the organs of freshly killed prey...the heart, liver, that sort of thing. I suspect that if a jaguar killed its prey exclusively by crushing the skull, it could favor eating the brains first. I imagine perhaps it could develop a habit of just crunching the entire skull, eating the brains, eyes, tongue...everything until the entire head is gone."

"Would that be weird?" asked Logan. "I mean, do you think that could really happen?"

"That could happen, sure. A certain specific cat could develop that habit, sure. Remember, each animal is an individual that has learned specific ways to kill and certain ways to break into its prey...that's their calling card. That's how seasoned lion hunters know that they're on the track of a particular cat. Individual animals learn the best way to do things...they develop habits."

"Lion sign is different than jaguar sign, isn't it?"

"That's right, you bet. As far as how each cat kills and breaks into its prey, there are differences. A mountain lion usually will kill with a throat hold, and more so than the jaguar they almost always eat the inside organs first. That's the most nutritious part of the animal. A lion will open it up at the ribs and eat the lungs, heart and liver. If they're hungry they'll eat some of the muscle, but they usually scrape some brush over their kill to cover it, and visit it later in the day or the next day. After the organs are eaten they'll usually break into the shoulder or ham."

"So jaguars don't do that? Is there a way you could distinguish a kill made by a mountain lion as opposed to one made by a jaguar?"

"It's not 100% sure-fire, but usually a jaguar starts eating at some outside area, likely at the site of the fatal wound. They're not as partial to the insides like a lion."

"How about the head? You said you think they could consume the entire head, especially if they liked going after the brain inside the skull?"

"I imagine they would if the skull is not too bony and if that's the focus of their lethal bite. A deer head has little nutrition inside the skull since the brain is relatively small. Plus the bones are dense."

"Do you know of any jaguar prey that offers a good-eating head?"

"Believe it or not, monkeys in Brazil are favorite jaguar prey likely because their heads are perfect for killing and eating. The skull bone composition and shape are the right density and size for cracking with one bite and exposing the sizeable brain. Studies have shown that they select monkey heads if given a choice. It's like a coconut! If they ate people they'd probably have a great meal with our large 'coconuts'!"

"Yeah, right! Do you know of any records of jaguars eating people?"

"There are very few mainly because jaguars tend to stay away from people," replied Gray. "Say, these are some really specific questions. Do you have some evidence of potential jaguar kills?" asked Gray.

"Well, every now and then I run across a carcass that I think was killed by a large predator. There was one with the skull eaten. I was wondering if a mountain lion would do that. I never heard of that so I figured it could be a jaguar."

"It doesn't sound like a mountain lion. But I'm not sure it's necessarily a jaguar. The animal could have died from another cause, and some animal scavenged the carcass."

That's true."

"Say, I have to run now. I teach a class in about two minutes. I hope I was helpful. Let me know if I can be of any more assistance."

"I certainly will. You've been very helpful. Thank you."

"By the way, was that a deer carcass with the head eaten?"

"No. It was a young javelina."

"That makes sense. Well, good luck, Mr. Logan. Stay in touch."

"Will do. Thanks again."

Chapter 39

When Logan showed up at the conference room he had his computer and a brown envelop. In attendance already seated were Bean, Everette, and Chavez. Yost was standing, looking comfortable and in charge, which was a good sign. Logan did not want him nervous and defensive.

As Logan took a seat Yost said, "We're expecting Bob Clawson from the Fish and Wildlife Service. He should be here shortly." Then he walked out of the room.

Logan did not react to Yost's initiative to invite the unexpected guest, but wondered privately why Yost had thought to involve a wildlife professional. *Did he get some background information? Did he pressure someone like Stevens to get an idea of Logan's angle? If so, that was not a surprising move. Actually, I should have expected that*, thought Logan privately.

"Good, he'll be a good addition to the discussion," Logan stated, his words catching Yost as he went through the door. He began to set up his computer.

Chavez sat silently. He was sitting by himself across the table from Bean and Everette. Logan smiled at him when no one could detect the gesture. Chavez was stoic, and did not respond. He looked scared. Logan's smile and posture helped settle Chavez's emotion. He stood up and asked, "You need a hand with that, Sam?"

"No thanks, Nate. I got it," he responded, looking at Nate and smiling again.

Bean and Everette had been seated, chatting to each other, and nodded politely when Logan walked in. They engaged themselves in what appeared to be small talk, hunching together to whisper something then leaning back with smiles and short bouts of laughter. They did not appear anxious but acted like they were at a sporting event waiting for the kick-off, or the first pitch...or the gates of the Roman Coliseum to open. They certainly did not have cheap seats. *They have ringside seats, and they have paid with their dedication to Yost, and with their careers*, Logan mused.

When Yost returned he was accompanied by Clawson. "Bob, this is Lieutenant Bean and Lieutenant Everette, and agents Chavez and Logan."

Clawson was dressed in Fish and Wildlife Service duty uniform, with his agency patch on one shoulder. He carried a brown leather case with loop handles and a rolled up wad of what appeared to be maps. He took a seat between the lieutenants and Chavez, and Yost sat across the table from him. Logan sat next to Chavez.

Before Yost could settle into his seat and while Logan was pulling his chair slightly away from Chavez, Logan asked, "Mr. Clawson, how long have you been in Arizona?" Yost looked up, surprised by hearing a voice other than his own.

"About five years. I came from Texas, where I was raised."

"That's my home state too. It's a wonderful part of the country," said Logan.

"That it is. I hope to get back someday. I still have a family ranch there."

"Me too. I'll return someday also. Where's your place?" asked Logan.

"Along the border near Harlingen. How about yours."

"Around Alpine...in the high country."

"Beautiful area," said Clawson.

"That whole state is beautiful."

"You bet it is."

Yost was seated with his chin resting on his intertwined knuckles as he watched the two Texans exchange pleasantries. It was almost more than he could take and his anxiety was evident. Finally he interrupted, "Thanks for coming down here, Bob. I especially appreciate your response to my short notice. We have some exciting information to share with you."

Logan had not expected Yost to be so liberal with his introduction of a situation about which he had no background. There were only four people who knew about the jaguar; two were at the table. He was fairly certain Chavez had not said anything, which meant that Yost had no clue about this recent development. He likely had figured Logan's new information was more theories about lions. Whatever it was, Logan wanted to hear more so he settled back in his chair and listened.

"The Border Patrol has some data that I think your agency will be very interested in hearing about. I brought these gentlemen together to present this information to you. We may need your assistance. Agent Logan will make the presentation."

Yost could not think of anything else to say. At that point Logan knew that Chavez had revealed nothing and that Yost's introduction had come to an end. Yost did exactly what Logan had assigned him to do. The addition of Clawson's presence and Yost's appearance of control were good touches. Logan decided to let Yost off the hook.

"Thank you, Captain Yost," said Logan, nodding at Yost. "Mr. Clawson, I would like to show you something before I say anything," Logan said. He stood up and pushed a key on his computer. As he walked toward the switch on the wall to extinguish the lights the images he had captured in a dimly lit canyon of the Atascosa Mountains appeared on the projector screen.

NOTHING BUT
THE TRUTH

Chapter 40

Logan walked from his pickup to his house with the usual escort of barking dogs. That sound was interrupted by June's voice. "How did it go?"

"It couldn't have gone better. Yost was paralyzed, Bean and Everette were eating out of my hand, and Chavez and Stevens are now covered. There was this guy from Fish and Wildlife Service who is now my best friend. I think he's going to be a real asset. So I'm feeling pretty good about now. I think I'll still be getting my federal paychecks."

June walked up to Logan and put her arms around him. As so many times in the past her smile indicated she was content. She didn't have to say a word.

"Any word from Sheldon? I need to let him know how it went. We have a meeting with some biologists tomorrow. I'd like Stayton to be there," said Logan as he put his computer on the desk.

"No. No calls."

"That's funny. I called him Sunday to ask if I accidentally left some literature with him. That was two days ago...he usually gets back to me right away."

"He's a busy man this time of year."

"True." Logan sat down at his desk and dialed Sheldon's home phone. No answer. He tried his cell with the same result.

Logan walked to the kitchen table. "June, I need to go pay Sheldon a visit. I cannot raise him on either phone."

"It's almost two o'clock. Wouldn't it be better to go in the morning?"

Logan thought for a few seconds then said, "No. He's as regular as July heat around here. I'm a little worried about him. The days are about as long as they get nowadays, so I got plenty of time to look for him if he's out on the ranch. I should be back by dark. I really want to tell him how today's meeting went."

The two-hour drive would be easy for Logan. It was part of his life. He would use that drive time to think about the events of today and plan his next move. No definite plan had been formulated but Logan felt the ball would be rolling under the direction of Clawson. Various wildlife experts would be brought to discuss Logan's theory and the options for action. Sheldon had to hear the good news.

Logan ate a quick bite of cold chicken, kissed his wife goodbye, and headed out the door. He called to the barking dogs, which raised the level of their excitement even higher. He thought briefly about their loyalty as he got in his truck and headed down the driveway. Sheldon, Chavez, and a handful of humans in his life have been as devoted to him. It's good to have the dogs as a backup just in case everyone else heads south, he thought. He drove off holding that notion and heading for his friend's ranch.

"How are you, John? What a nice surprise to hear from you. Is everything okay in Texas?" Yost was surprised to receive a call from John Crow. He still had not digested everything from his morning meeting. So many thoughts were rolling around in his head that he had not immediately recognized Crow's voice, even though it was unmistakable.

"Everything is fine here in the great state of Texas. Any word on the whereabouts of Sharp yet?" asked Crow.

"No, not a word. I figure we'll snag him when we least expect it. That's usually the way the long arm of the law works, right?"

"That's right. He's on a short rope. So, what can I do for you, Darrel? I got a call from Bob Clawson. He wanted me to call you."

Yost was stunned. The meeting ended just two hours ago and already Clawson was connecting some dots. Yost couldn't even imagine what dot Crow represented. He was so overloaded with information he didn't have the energy to guess Crow's interest in the information Logan had revealed. Yost recognized that his ability to keep everything under his control was rapidly evaporating and that control was something he would lose more of with each passing hour. The fact that at this point he had no control was something that still eluded him.

"About what?" That was the only response Yost could muster.

"About a jaguar case I had in south Texas awhile back. Clawson has a wild hunch there may be a link."

"What sort of link?"

"An enforcement one...that's why Bob asked me to call you."

"Enforcement? What sort of enforcement?" Yost became angry as he mouthed those words. From Crow's response Yost thought his agency had dropped a legal issue regarding jaguar protection in Arizona. Although enforcement of endangered species law was not his responsibility Yost still became defensive. "John, I realize that the jaguar is an endangered species, but we don't have anyone killing jaguars here. We got jaguars killing people."

"I know that. But believe me, there may be a correlation here. Clawson and I discussed this for less than five minutes this morning before we realized this may be a very important piece to your puzzle. Clawson has arranged for me to fly to Tucson this afternoon. He's picking me up at the airport and arranging for a meeting with his biologists tomorrow morning. Oh, he wanted me to invite you to that meeting. It will be at the Fish and Wildlife Service Field Office in Tucson. You know where that is?"

With the phone in his right hand Yost propped the left side of his face with the other. His morning meeting had left him exhausted but now he was over the top with a weariness that exposed his confusion, fear, defense, and maybe his career.

"Sure. What time?" exhaled Yost.

"Clawson has to find out when Logan is available first. Someone will call you."

"Okay. I gotta run, John. I have an angle here I'm trying to run down. See you tomorrow."

"Take care, amigo," responded Crow.

Yost had no angle, no energy, and seemingly no role anymore. After saying his good byes to Crow he hung up the phone and rested his head on the desk. A wave of nausea overcame him as once again he was bitten by his frail grasp on the big picture.

A spattering of raindrop prints covered the dusty driveway at Sheldon's house. The June monsoons were building, offering only a teasing glimpse of meaningful rainfall. But what had fallen was very informative to Logan. The last cloud build-up was Saturday afternoon and evening so any evidence of rain was from that time. The rain-dotted dust was telling Logan that Sheldon had not been in his driveway since Saturday afternoon. That was three days ago.

For the first time Logan realized how alone and separated Sheldon was from the rest of the world. Logan knew of no one who might know Sheldon's whereabouts. He thought of calling Saint Mary's Hospital in Tucson to see if he had been admitted for some accident or ailment.

Suddenly, Logan was struck with a thought that almost paralyzed him. He recalled that Sheldon mentioned he was going to fix some fence Saturday afternoon. The image of the large cat tracks he had seen Saturday morning before he met Sheldon ran through his mind as he quickly returned to his pickup. With trembling hands he put the key in the ignition. Accompanied by hopelessness he backed away from his friend's place and headed for the east gate of Sheldon's ranch.

Thoughts of Sheldon experiencing an ambush by the jaguar they both had observed just days earlier crept into his realm of consciousness. He fought to keep them away but could not eliminate images of an old man fending off the weight of a predator perhaps a hundred pounds heavier, of jaws closing around his friend's face, and of what may have been Sheldon's last gasp of air before all means of inhaling were eliminated. They became more vivid as he subconsciously accelerated along the Arivaca Road.

No one had gone through the east gate since the light rain had left its marks. The pattern of scattered raindrops on the dusty prints of Sheldon's tire track was evident as he opened the gate. Logan read the story displayed before him on the dusty road. Sheldon was here after Logan's trek on Saturday morning. Logan felt more and more certain of the fate that had overcome his friend.

At first he drove slowly along the dusty road but sped up after realizing he was not on a mission to gather data. He also realized he likely was not on a rescue mission. His role was recovery. He did not have his camera but quickly dismissed its absence. What he was expecting to find was something he did not want to record. He reached under his seat to make sure his .40 caliber pistol was there. It was. That was all he really wanted at this point.

Hesitancy gripped him and he settled onto a crawling pace. Instead of focusing on sign along the road he was staring ahead. He engaged his peripheral vision to capture movement in the brush beneath the oak trees. He recognized his defensive mode. He pushed the window buttons to roll the windows up half way. He wanted to be able to detect sound but he also wanted a measure of security from any unwanted entry into his vehicle. His senses were heightened, seemingly extended beyond the limits of anything he had experienced before. In law enforcement vernacular he was in "code red" mode.

When the sound happened he jumped. His survival reaction surprised him, especially when it was in response to such a familiar element of daily life. He quickly grabbed his cell phone to quiet it and looked at the display. It was Chavez.

"Nate, where are you?"

"I'm at Sheldon's east gate. I was passing by and stopped after I noticed your tracks. They look fresh. Are you still on Sheldon's place?"

"Yes. Stay there. I'm heading back to get you. I need some assistance. I'll be there in two minutes."

"10-4."

Chapter 41

Parker Canyon Lake was only a remnant of its normal size. The water pool was ringed by soil and rocks that had been scoured by decades of shoreline wave action and coated with a fine layer of calcium from evaporating water. The drought had exposed more of the blond naked shore than ever before, and it glowed in the faint light of the half-moon. Their destination was the body of life-giving water that was invisible below the illuminated shore. It appeared ominous, like a black hole.

Ricardo Lopez and three companions had crossed about sundown. The heat of the day, still present well past dark, had forced them to drink all the water in their plastic jugs. They were on day two of their trek. Reaching that water was now their sole purpose in life. They looked north toward the lake from one of the long wooded ridges that sloped gently down from the Huachuca Mountains to Campini Mesa. They had less than a mile to go.

Ricardo, who had been crossing since the 1980s, agreed to lead the three young Mexican men into the U.S. The illness and eventual death in March of his mother kept the men from leaving their homes in Sonora during winter, but in Ricardo's mind crossing in summer was good too. The men wanted to make money working the ranches in southeastern Arizona. Ricardo also wanted time away from home to ponder his loss. He was very familiar with ranching tasks and the mannerisms of the ranchers he had served. Doing that work and being with friendly and compassionate employers would offer a moderate amount of comfort, a home away from home.

Ricardo was accompanied by Raul, a twenty-year old nephew who was twenty years his junior, and two of Raul's friends. The three young men had always talked about crossing but never managed to arrange the trip. Ricardo had promised his sister, Raul's mom, that he would show him how to cross and make money. Raul was in it for the adventure, not the money. His two friends didn't have a clue about the work; they were in it to escape their existence in Sonora. Although to Ricardo they were merely baggage without a dream, he kept his sense of duty and humor.

Ricardo was the first to stand up and begin heading toward the lake. The others followed after laboring to their feet and silently having more than second thoughts about their place in this strange land. In single file the three men paraded about fifty yards behind Ricardo. The moonlight on the dry and golden grass was bright enough to allow them to keep their leader in sight. Only when he passed through the oak shadows did Ricardo's form momentarily escape their view.

Just once during the first day of their journey did the topic of *El Diablo* come up. Raul's friends had expressed their concern about dying at the hand of this phantom, and asked Raul to talk with Ricardo about the chance of meeting death at the hand of *El Diablo*. Without having heard about the discoveries of the U.S. officials in Arivaca earlier in the year Ricardo dismissed the cause of their concern. Ricardo's age and experience convinced the young men that if Ricardo wasn't afraid they had nothing to fear. "*El Diablo* is way to the west of us...we're safe," Ricardo said convincingly.

As the young men stumbled over the rocky terrain near the base of the hill and more frequently lost sight of Ricardo, weariness filled them. So huge was their exhaustion there was no room for fear. Or so they thought.

As Logan navigated the slight bend in the dirt road Nate's vehicle appeared in the rear-view mirror in his peripheral vision. At the same time a white object appeared about one hundred yards ahead through the trees and brush. "Sheldon's pickup," he whispered to himself. He slowed to a crawl. He knew what was awaiting him.

"Nate, hold back there, okay?" Some semblance of Logan's old friend loomed somewhere in the near distance and Logan decided that reunion needed to be private.

"10-4." Chavez understood.

The first thing to catch his eye was Sheldon's notebook, lying on the ground about twenty feet from his pickup. The ground was only slightly disturbed where the notebook lay, but the contrast between rain-sprinkled dirt and evidence of a struggle was very evident to Logan's seasoned eyes. Boot tracks dug into the soil and huge paw prints gouged deeper. A dragline streaked with dried blood told the story.

Logan knelt on the soft ground next to Sheldon's notebook. He wanted to pick it up, find his friend and hand it to him, and drive to the ranch house for coffee. That scenario was one that would never happen again and he knew it. He was gripped by what must occur next. He slowly stood up, walked to the road and signaled Chavez to drive forward.

Nate instantly spotted the sign of struggle and said nothing as he exited his vehicle. He walked up to Logan and stopped three feet from his side. He wanted Logan to make the first move along the dragline toward the creek and Sheldon's body. The two men faced the creek and remained motionless for nearly a minute until Logan could no longer contain his emotion. He fell to his knees, bent over and wept silently. Chavez was frozen with his head down and his ears alert to their surroundings.

"I will miss you a lot, Stayton," Logan finally uttered. He rose up and then turned around to face Chavez. "Let's get busy."

Logan went to his truck to get what they needed to process the scene. He walked up to Chavez with some plastic bags and a measuring tape. "Please bring your camera. I'm ready," he said.

"I'm so sorry, Sam," replied Nate. "He was a good man."

Logan nodded and said nothing. Before they walked to the drag-line Nate put his hand on his holstered pistol and looked over to see that extra ammo clips were in the carrier. He then handed his camera to Logan, who photographed the overall scene, took some close-ups of the ground around the notebook, and gradually settled into his forensic chores. He pulled a measuring tape from its round holder and set it below the black pool of old blood before taking the photo. It measured nearly two feet across at its widest point where it had poured over the ground, spilling into a slightly depressed area between two large rocks.

From the pool of blood they could see Sheldon's body thirty feet away under a large hackberry tree. His light blue denim shirt was stained black except on the arms. Logan looked back along the dragline and estimated the jaguar had caught Sheldon as he was returning to his truck. His hat was under some brush about fifteen feet from where the notebook had fallen from his pocket. "That's where the cat got him," he gestured to Chavez. "It pulled him down, dragged him to here and held tight until Stayton expired. He fed under that tree."

"I think you're right, Sam." Chavez paused, and added, "I can take it from here if you want."

"Thanks, Nate. I'm okay. Let's get over to Stayton and get him out of here."

As Logan walked up to the mangled remnants of his dear friend he blocked his mind from thinking about the horror that must have filled Stayton during the last few seconds of his life.

Ricardo barely could hear the young men up the hill who were following along his path through the trees. The dry grass and rocky ground crunched beneath his every step, masking most of the noise his companions made. Only when they lost their footing on the rocks did he hear words and occasional laughter. When he reached the rocky dry creek bed at the foot of the hill he could hear the clear call of poorwills along the hillside adjacent to the creek bed, from which no sound emanated.

He looked around to find the moonlight filtering through the canopy of a large oak. The setting looked inviting. There was no chance that his nephew could get lost so he did not call out to reveal his location. Instead, he walk into the oak shadow and enjoyed the solitude and quite.

He squatted down to stretch his aching back and heard a small rock moving down the slope to his right. As he slowly turned to look behind him he recalled all the times he had pitched pebbles into the brush as he walked with Raul among the hills of their homeland. He smiled, thinking it was pay back time.

He began to stand up when suddenly he was knocked to the ground by a force that was silent, invisible, and dominant. He detected this power only very briefly before his movements were extinguished. As his body crumpled onto the rocks his face was being smothered by the cat's mouth, pulsing wet and warm breaths while maintaining a vice-like grip. The last thing he heard was the grinding crunch of teeth crushing bone, of his face being gouged and shattered. His severed senses could not perceive the weight of what had hit him or the daggers that had stabbed his back and abdomen to prevent his escape.

The jaguar held his death grip on Ricardo, whose body twitched for only a few seconds after the attack. In response to each involuntary movement of Ricardo the cat tightened his hold, wanting to ensure that his prey had no chance to get a breath. As his captor's grip intensified the hideous sounds of Ricardo's teeth fracturing, of his jawbone splintering, and his skull splitting silenced the poorwills.

The jaguar's ears focused on the hillside above. He could hear the other men meandering, clueless of the event that had occurred. When they came within fifty feet, the matchless predator let out a low guttural roar while maintaining his hold on Ricardo, who had attempted his last involuntary breaths and expired. The sound froze the men in their tracks for a split second. Then the terror that had been lurking in the periphery of their minds all along thrust them in panic along the hillside just above the drainage.

Like a herd of wild animals running for their lives they scurried away in the darkness, losing their footing with almost every step. At times resorting to scrambling along on all fours they managed to make progress away from the sound that resonated horror to their very core. They fleetingly wondered if Ricardo had heard the same sound and was making his escape ahead of them.

After five minutes they reached the hilltop from where they could see the glowing sky that marked Nogales. Without formulating any real plan they headed toward that dim light. Raul was convinced in his own mind that they would meet Ricardo there. No one said a word. They were oblivious of the cuts and scrapes that oozed wetness onto their torn pants and shirts, and the pain that emanated from the palms of their hands. For the first time on their journey they had direction.

Maintaining a grip on Ricardo's head the jaguar stood over his quarry. He pulled it from the tangle of the large river rocks into which he had pinned his meal and dragged the limp body twenty feet to the base of the large oak tree. There he released the body and began licking the blood streaming from his prey's face. After a few minutes he began to nibble on the jaw muscles, and lick the brain matter that had oozed from the fractured skull. He nipped at the nose then broke through the facial cartilage, the promise of brain tissue intensifying his eagerness. He put his large left paw on Ricardo's chest. He began cracking the skull with his powerful bite and pulling off chunks of bone and muscle.

As the big cat engaged devouring the head of his prey the noise of crunching bones resonated in the rocky hollow of the creek bed. Amidst this intermittent clamor of a skull being ravaged the poorwills resumed their calls, and the harmony of those sounds pierced the black and boundless space above the wooded hills.

Chapter 42

June Logan carefully chose her words. Her husband had been in a suspended state of existence for the past two days. She knew the reality of Stayton's death was just beginning to sink in. Along with that reality was guilt, self-blame, anger, and resolve. The fact that Sam went straight for his address book after breakfast was a good sign.

"What are your plans for today, dear?" she asked.

"I need to talk with Bob Clawson. How many times has he called since I've been on leave?"

"Well, you've been home for four days, and I think he's called everyday. He mainly wanted to make sure you're okay."

"I got an email from Nate that Yost keeps calling Clawson, who refuses to meet with him until he talks with me. I wonder what's going on?"

"I think it's good that you're ready to talk with him."

Logan looked up from his coffee into the face of his loving wife. "I love you, dear."

At that moment the phone rang. They both looked at it ring a second time. "I got it," said Logan. June smiled.

"Hi, Bob. How are you?" Logan asked as June walked out of the kitchen. "I'm doing fine. Sorry I have not gotten back to you. I needed a break."

"I understand. I'm sorry about Mr. Sheldon."

"He was a good man. I will miss him. I learned a lot from his view of the landscape." Logan took a sip of coffee. "I hear you've been wanting to see me."

"Yes. I would like to meet with you and John Crow. There was a case involving jaguars in Texas that I think may be relevant to the matter that you've uncovered. Since I first talked with John about this he's come up with more information that could link southern Arizona with what we were dealing with in Texas."

"Was it a law enforcement issue in Texas?" asked Logan.

"Yes. I was involved because of the jaguar's endangered status, but it was mainly a legal tangle. And Crow has uncovered a possible connection. Have you ever heard of a guy named Larry Thompson?"

"Sure. He owns the Sopori. What does he have to do with jaguars?"

"That's where the story gets a little fuzzy, but in a nut shell Thompson hunted jaguars in Mexico in the late 1960s before they were protected. They've always fascinated him. He brought at least one live cat up to his Texas ranch. That's where I came into the picture. Crow was the agent who uncovered Thompson's plot soon after the jaguar was listed endangered in the early 1970s. There was rumor going around about why he wanted live jaguars. We never did prove anything because before we could get a court order to go onto his private property he got rid of the animals."

"Why did he want live cats?"

"Like I said, we never did prove anything but we think jaguars were what Thompson used to unleash his hate for the Mexicans who were crossing his ranch on their way north."

"Are you saying they were like his guard dogs?"

"With a fatal bite."

"You said you never did prove anything?"

"No. But like I said, Crow wants to continue the investigation on Thompson. He wants to retrace Thompson's trail from Texas to Arizona to see if there is any evidence of jaguars along that trail. When will you be available to meet?"

"You name the time and place."

"How about this afternoon at 1:00 o'clock at my office? It will be only the three of us. If Thompson is involved with jaguars again his connections in Mexico likely are too powerful and smart to let anything leak out. We need to get our ducks in a row before we make a move."

"I'll be there."

Sam Logan was cut out of the same cloth that produced John Crow nearly a generation earlier. He was a field man that had a sixth sense for understanding his quarry and a knack for reading the ground to gather any evidence it left behind. The only difference was that Crow had been steeped in a culture that appreciated and utilized his talents. Partly that was due to timing. The Border Patrol had not gone high-tech yet. Partly it was due to Crow's supervisors, men who were not threatened by his uncanny ability to find a trail, get on it and produce results.

As the two men took positions next to each other at the conference table in Clawson's office Logan sensed an exciting energy he had not experienced in a long time. That Yost apparently had not been invited made the experience even sweeter.

"Good afternoon, gentlemen," exclaimed Bob Clawson as he pulled out a chair across from the agents.

"Hi, Bob," replied Crow. Logan nodded toward Clawson and continued listening to Crow. "It's good to work with you again." Turning to Logan he said, "Sam, I wanted to say right from the get-go that I'm sorry about Mr. Sheldon. I understand he was your good friend and a real gentleman. Too bad he's not around to help us now. Sounds like he was a big help with your investigation."

"Thanks, John. Yes he was. I will miss the man."

Clawson paused long enough to pay his respects to Crow's gesture, and then started, "Well, I dug up my file on Larry Thompson, Sam. John has the information from his investigation. We'll go over it with a fine-toothed comb, but first I want John to give an overview of what we think is a relationship between Thompson's past activities in Texas, and the situation you documented in Arizona.

"Before he starts though, I want to say that I realize this matter may evolve into a case of homicide. If it does, my involvement will wane and I'll serve both of you in any capacity I can. From where I sit, I think my help will come in the form of providing information on jaguar behavior and status. There may be violations of the Endangered Species Act and the Lacey Act, both of which I have extensive knowledge about. I'll offer my full support in these areas and any other aspect that I can."

"Thanks, Bob. Having worked with you in Texas, I value your knowledge and dedication," replied Crow.

Logan's sense of admiration for these professionals increased immeasurably with the exchange of offerings and compliments, their protocol of respect. He thought of Sheldon for a moment and wished that he could have been around to work with this element of federal investigation.

As Crow reached for a folder in front of him he began. "Back in the 1960s Larry Thompson and his friends would go into the Sierra Madre Mountains of old Mexico to hunt jaguars. It was legal back then. They would hook up with a guide in Hermosillo, Sonora and chase these cats in the thorn scrub just east of there. From what I could find out Thompson shot three jaguars from 1964 through 1967. For some unknown reason he quit going down to hunt jaguars for several years until about 1974. His guide was reluctant to take him out when he returned in the '70s. Apparently this guide, a guy named Armando, was arrested for violating Mexican law with duck hunters near Culiacan in about 1970 and had become weary of scrutiny. The jaguar was protected as endangered in 1972 in accordance with the Endangered Species Conservation Act of 1969, which meant big fines and possible jail time for Armando if he were to get caught accepting clients like Thompson who wanted to shoot jaguars."

Logan listened carefully as Crow spoke. At the proper time he asked, "Isn't all this a customs enforcement issue? Why was Border Patrol involved?"

"Great question," said Crow. Clawson just listened to the two men with his hands folded on the table in front of him. "It gets more complicated. I became involved when Thompson started complaining loudly about crossers on his ranch in 1972. He's the sort of fellow that makes a lot of noise. He began lobbying to his connections in Washington that the Border Patrol wasn't doing its job along the ten-mile stretch of his ranch that comes in contact with Mexico. As a new agent that was my enforcement patrol area back in the day. I agreed there was a problem and that the Border Patrol needed to step up efforts in the area. Well, Thompson is not a man to be denied of his pursuits. When our outfit didn't act as quickly as he wanted us to, he decided to take the law into his own hands. That's when I really got involved."

"How so?" asked Logan.

"One thing Thompson never understood is the old maxim, 'there are no secrets.' His methods of curbing illegal immigration included some pretty far-fetched schemes, all of which sooner or later leaked out to his neighbors. I had pretty good relationships with most of Thompson's neighbors, and I heard a lot about what Thompson was thinking and doing. When I heard that his plans involved jaguars I decided I needed to learn about those big cats. That's when I brought Bob into the investigation."

Logan sat motionless as he listened to Crow unravel the story of Thompson, who was telling his neighbors how he would shoot any wet he found on his ranch and feed the bodies to a caged jaguar. Thompson bragged, "Those big cats will eat every bit of a wet...there'll be nothing left but a pile of clothes and cat shit when they're done."

Finally, Logan asked, "Did you ever find a caged jaguar?"

"No, we didn't," responded Crow. "But I suspect that there's a cage somewhere on his ranch. And even if he never got it up and running in the '70s, I'll bet it's in use now."

Chapter 43

Only yesterday he called to advise Nate to pack for a week in south Texas. On the way to the airport in Tucson Logan gave him stacks of literature to read about jaguars and a file on Larry Thompson. He also gave him several books on large cats shifting their diet from wild game to humans. Included were the 1925 classic *Man-eating Lions of Tsavo* and the recent account entitled *The Man-eaters of Eden*. Both documented African lions feasting on human flesh. The 1944 book by Jim Corbett entitled *Man-eaters of Kumaon* documented how tigers in India shifted their diet to human flesh. *The Beast In the Garden* brought the whole issue closer to home with mountain lions in the western U.S.

Chavez immediately began thumbing through Corbett's intriguing accounts of rogue tigers that developed a predilection for humans in the Indian foothills of the Himalaya Mountains. He did not ask Logan who Larry Thompson was, or why their case had shifted to Texas. He remained engrossed in large cats eating people as their plane descended to land at the Corpus Christi airport. They would rent a car and drive to Harlingen, where a reserved room at the Borderland Motel awaited them.

"Good book, right Nate?" inquired Logan

"Real good. Those tigers petrified those villagers. They're lucky Corbett was around to hunt down those man-eaters."

"He was a pretty brave individual don't you think?"

"I guess. I don't know if I'd have the guts to sleep in a tree and wait for a big cat to stalk a buffalo that I had staked out as bait."

"I know. But it's amazing what a guy will do when there's a need and he has the desire."

Chavez thought about those words and wondered exactly what Logan had said. He continued reading as the plane landed and taxied to the terminal. Neither man mentioned a word about their mission until they were in the rental car heading for Harlingen. Chavez knew that Logan would not volunteer any information so he'd have to ask questions. Logan once told him that people understand things better if the information they are given is in response to questions they ask.

"So," Chavez began, "What are we doing here?"

"Driving along in a rental car at the moment," Logan replied with a grin.

Nate looked at him and smiled. "Really? How does it drive?" Chavez poked back.

"Like a dream. You know the government always makes sure we get the best cars. They spare no expense."

"They gotta keep us happy I guess. That's important, especially if they want us to kill tigers that are eating the residents of Harlingen."

"That's right. The government is always looking after its citizenry," responded Logan

"That's what's so good about our country. We protect everyone, even those dumb enough to get in the way of tigers," quipped Chavez.

"Yes, and Uncle Sam is so benevolent that he looks closely at those man-eaters to see why all of a sudden they have chosen a diet of man over wildlife. Now that's the sign of a competent government."

Chavez was ambushed by the thought, *why were the jaguars of Arizona eating people instead of their natural prey of deer and javelina?*

"What made our cats shift their diet to people, Sam?"

"Larry Thompson...we think."

Chavez picked up the envelope labeled "Larry Thompson." On top of the pile of papers was a large color photo of Mr. Thompson. He appeared old and crusty. Black-rim glasses perched on a noble nose beneath a white western hat, a weathered face that sported the start of a smile, a western shirt with a bolo tie. "He looks like my grandfather in a way with the hat and bolo."

"He's probably like a million grandfathers out there. Except this guy has a cause, and he's radical. He's also very dangerous."

"How old is he?"

"He turns seventy-five tomorrow. And we're going to his birthday party."

"What?"

"I'm an invitee. You're my nephew. See, Nate, we're all one big happy family. That's the way it is in Texas."

Chavez looked ahead at the thorn scrub growing along the road. His mind was racing.

"Now don't get all quiet on me," Logan said. "If I had given you time to think about this you'd have gotten diarrhea and all cramped up. That's not good for a guy. Just relax. It will be fun. We won't even have to lay eyes on the guy. All we want to do is get about five miles west of his ranch house and take a look around. I got all the important areas on a GPS unit. We should be in and out in a couple hours. The tricky thing was getting on his ranch. That's a done deal. All you have to know are the words to 'Happy Birthday'!"

As they pulled up to the Borderland Motel Chavez was still searching for his next question. After Logan checked in he returned to the truck to find Chavez pouring through the two envelopes he had given him in Tucson.

"John Crow is involved. That's pretty special. Will we see him at the party?"

"No sir. Thompson knows Crow. You and I are the only new faces with extensive background on what we've been dealing with in

Arizona. Our mission is to get onto Thompson's ranch with an excuse for being there, get into his holding pen, and find some hair."

"Holding pen for what?"

"For a *Tyrannosaurus rex*, so to speak."

"They didn't have hair," Chavez quipped.

"Oh, you're right. We'll have to look for jaguar hair then."

"Now I'm really lost," said Chavez, who was beginning to really enjoy being around the light-hearted side of Logan. It relaxed him. As he started to immerse himself into their undercover mission, he began to realize that Logan's new behavior must be the way he coped with the stress of playing a covert character. All Chavez knew about undercover work is what he had learned in a few brief hours at the Border Patrol academy.

"Sam, why can't we just get a search warrant and get onto Thompson's ranch legally?"

"Nate, there's nothing illegal about what we're doing. I have a real invitation to the party from Clawson's Uncle Harold, who knows some of Thompson's friends. Harold's my uncle now...one big happy family, remember? They're trying to make this a big party with lots of attendees, and have gotten a little lenient with scrutinizing the invitation list. After talking with Clawson and Crow, I connected some dots and we came up with some mutual friends...and bingo, here we are!"

"Have you ever done this sort of thing before? I mean, work undercover and all?"

"No. Never. How about you?"

"Nope." Chavez knew Logan's question was rhetorical.

"Are you scared?"

"No. It's just new to me."

"You'll do fine. We'll use our own names so when someone calls you by a different name you don't have to remember to respond. This should be a no-brainer. Just remember that I'm here because of my uncle. You are here because you're my nephew from Colorado. Here's the most important thing. We're both State Troopers. I'm retired and you admired me so much you became one in Colorado. So we can talk about what we do for a living, and don't have to get caught in a lie about some different line of work."

"That's a good deal. But, Sam, there's one problem."

"What's that?"

"I'm Hispanic, and you're not!"

"Then you're adopted, Nate. Listen, we probably won't have to talk with anyone. We just need to get into the gate of Thompson's ranch, pretend we got lost while trying to get a good look at a cool bird we saw, get our evidence, grab a beer at the party and say 'hi' to my uncle, and leave. Pretty simple. In fact, we probably won't grab a beer or greet Thompson."

"Sounds simple. I think I can do all that...even if I am adopted!"

"I'm betting on it. The party starts at two in the afternoon tomorrow. Let's get unpacked. I have a few more things I want to go over with you."

"Where did you put that one picture, Jeff?"

"I think it's in that stack there on your right."

Larry Thompson fumbled through the short pile of color prints. "Here we go, Don. Look at this place. I think this is the most prime real estate west of Texas. Everyone's leaving California for Arizona. This place is less than an hour from Tucson, from medical facilities and the university, and anything a guy would want. Tucson International has direct flights to most anywhere in the world."

Don Huff looked at the photo. "Are these oak trees?"

"Yep," replied Thompson. "That shows you it's up out of the hot desert. The views are tremendous. There's Baboquivari Peak to the west, and Wrightson in the Santa Ritas to the east. This deal's worth taking a hard look, Don."

"When did you get the place, Larry?"

"About three years ago Jeff called me about the place. I jumped right on a plane and Jeff gave me a tour the next morning. It was love at first sight for me." Thompson twirled the remnants of scotch and ice in his glass. "Excuse me, gentlemen. Jaime, can you please get us another round of drinks here?"

"Yes sir, Mr. Thompson." Jaime quickly vanished into the den and returned almost immediately to the patio with a silver tray and three full glasses.

"So, give it to me straight, Larry. What's the down side?"

Berger interrupted, "There is none. We've taken care of everything."

"Here's the thing, Don," added Thompson, "I'm too old to take care of this place here and the Sopori in Arizona. I would like to take on a partnership with someone to help manage Sopori or just sell it outright. Jeff has the contract drafted that describes all the options."

The man in the golf sweater paused and looked at his scotch on the rocks. He rolled it around and took a healthy swig. "You know, if I buy land I want it to be where I can build my retirement house. I'm ready to leave Florida. From what I gather California is too crowded also. But a place so close to Mexico nowadays seems risky. Also, Arizona has had lots of wildfires in the past several years. Is the Sopori a fire risk?"

"No fires in decades and the only ones have been small. The Forest Service land just to the south is protected by the full weight of the federal government fire fighters so that's not a big deal," replied Berger.

"What about all the illegals from Mexico? I've had my fill of them in Florida."

"They don't like the Sopori. They've learned that it's not a safe place to be," said Berger.

"What do you mean?"

"Let's just say there's something called *El Diablo* in the region," said Berger. "The Devil. All the wets are scared shitless over it. They won't risk traveling through the area because they're afraid of meeting *El Diablo*!"

"That's right, Don," interjected Thompson. He swirled his glass and took a long sip. "That Devil has moved in and scared them Mexicans away. It's amazing how fast the word spread in Sonora. It cleaned up the border around there. Also, probably won't have many fires now since most were started by wets."

"What's the Devil? I mean, well, what is it? Why are they so afraid?"

"It's a killer unlike anything the wets have known," said Thompson. "It eats them head first, and usually leaves a headless body as its calling card. The Border Patrol has been investigating the killer. At first they thought it was some crazy wetback who was stealing from other wets on their return home with money and goodies from the U.S. Then they found out that it was really a renegade veteran who ranched in the area and was tired of the wets cutting fences and messing with his waters. The guy took matters into his own hands. Border Patrol failed to catch the guy and he's on the loose. I hope he makes good his escape."

"So they haven't caught him yet? How long has he been around there?"

"Oh, for about the last two years. The government has tried, but this guy's clever. I think the government appreciates him. Think of it. He keeps the wet problem under control, and all that's dying is Mexicans."

Berger spoke up, "They got a warrant for this Vietnam vet that they think was doing the killing. His ranch is west of the Sopori about twenty-five miles. They found some heads and bodies on his place. He's a clever fellow and dodged their investigation. They have no idea where he is. He disappeared into thin air."

"He's a good man," interjected Thompson. "He did good in Nam and now he's trying to protect his country in another way. I think he's a good man. They're just Mexicans that he killed...that's all!"

Huff was speechless. He had not realized Thompson was so prejudiced. The scotch was loosening his tongue. Huff thought about what he had heard and decided to push the matter further. "Do you have problems with wets at this ranch here in Texas? You're right on the border."

"We got plenty of problems here. They steal me blind, cut fences, and leave my waters running so my storage tanks go dry. They're pigs. They trash the countryside with litter. I had a big battle with the Border Patrol a few years ago, and lost. They had their eye on me pretty good. I had to cool my actions and just live with the problem."

"Why? Couldn't they see your problem and take action?"

"It don't work that way," said Thompson. All the agents are glued to their trucks and they won't come onto private property anymore. That means all us ranchers that run along the border are stuck with the problem."

"Seems like you could get some help from someone."

"You know, Don, I'm seventy-five tomorrow. I've fought my battles. Back fifty years ago I battled the state of Texas for water rights, forty years ago I had to claw and scratch for the right to use DDT to rid our range of grasshoppers that were eating all the grass. Thirty years ago it was the Endangered Species Act. I'm burned out. Someone else can deal with it now. I'm done."

Huff looked at Thompson as the old man looked into his glass of ice. He saw his friend in a light that was strange and unfamiliar. Slouching in his chair in the setting sun on this beautiful real estate in south Texas, his friend seemed frail and angry.

"It's strange, Larry. I've known you for nearly thirty-five years, and throughout that entire time I have admired the fire and fight in you. I see only a little bit of the fire now, but none of the fight."

Thompson looked up at Huff, then at Berger. He smiled. "Oh, there's some fight left, but I got to pick my battles. I have only a few bullets left." He lifted his glass and proposed a toast, "To the bullets we have left."

"To the bullets," responded Berger.

"And don't forget the fire, gentlemen," snapped Huff.

"That's right, Don. I still got plenty of that left. Sometime it boils over and I have to make sure I let it out."

"How do you do that, Larry?" asked Huff.

Thompson looked at the sunset. A strange and far away look came over his rugged and wrinkled face. He replied, "I pick the right time, the right place, and the right weapon, then I hurl it with a vengeance."

Berger stood up as Huff looked at the sunset. "Excuse me, gentlemen. I need to make a phone call." Berger took off, leaving the two old friends alone.

Huff decided he would not pursue the subject further but a curiosity stirred inside him. What sort of weapon was Thompson talking about? It really didn't matter. Huff returned his gaze to the sunset. "It sure is pretty here, Larry."

Chapter 44

Logan awoke with a smile and a joke. "Hey, Chavez," he barked as he got out of bed. "What's fifty feet long, crooked, and smells like piss?"

Nate rolled over to face Logan. "What?"

"A line dance at the old folks home!"

"I'll have to remember that one."

"What? The joke or the warning?"

"Both."

"While you're storing that on your hard drive, I'm heading for the shower."

Chavez lay in bed thinking about the remains of Sheldon's body in that beautiful canyon of the Atascosa Mountains. Images of Logan weeping over the remnants of his friend lingered in a corner of his mind. Surely that event must have fueled Logan. It now was rubbing off on him. He didn't feel nervous or anxious about the new experience he was about to undertake. He knew that Logan was a trusted friend. He decided his main objective would be to keep a sharp eye on Logan and follow his lead.

As the two agents left the motel a hint of cool air greeted them. "I think fall's around the corner, Nate," commented Logan.

"I better get out my jacket, Sam."

"That's right. Before you know it Christmas will be here. Then Easter. Time flies when you're having fun...are you having fun yet, Nate?"

"Always. Especially with you." Chavez gave Logan a look that revealed his comment was straight from the heart.

Logan stopped in his tracks and looked at Chavez, who stopped slightly ahead and looked back. "Nate, there's no one else I'd rather do this assignment with than you."

Chavez returned the eye contact and said, "Sam, this isn't an assignment, is it? I think this is your show. Yost is out of the picture. It's just you. Maybe Crow and Clawson are in the background...but maybe not. Maybe it's totally just you...and me! And it's for Stayton. That's what I think."

Logan paused only long enough to let Chavez realize that his assumption was correct. "Let's go get breakfast," he said. "I know a good place just up the road. We're going to need some energy today, and *huevos rancheros* will fill that order for me. How about you?"

"Same here, boss."

As they drove to the café, the sights and sounds of Harlingen resounded with its heritage. The men passively took in the influence of Mexico's proximity. Present were old and new cars stuffed with Mexican Americans and Mexican Nationals, sidewalks jammed with people toting fistfuls of plastic shopping bags, and brightly colored store fronts reflecting a great vibrancy and character that was woven into the fabric of this community by the lives lived there.

"Ever been here, Nate?" asked Logan.

"Never been in Texas except along I-40. You know, this town doesn't seem like the typical border town in Arizona, like Nogales. This is nothing like Nogales. There seems to be a feeling here that I don't get in southern Arizona."

"Well, that's right, this is really different. People live here...they don't just pass through. I mean some do of course, but most live here. Nogales is the area that witnessed the first major passage of transient missionaries centuries ago. That trend continues today with the road system that funnels immigrants all the way from Central and South America through Nogales. That's my theory anyway. The only thing I know for sure is that it's different.

"You know," Logan continued, "our ancestors crossed into a new land on the Mayflower. It was adventure with a purpose, much like any guy trekking across the border today. The only difference is that it was legal passage. When they arrived they weren't criminals. They were heroes."

"So is the crosser who gets money back to his family in Mexico," responded Nate.

"Exactly! Well, not exactly. That guy has a shroud of illegality around him and he knows it. So does his family. If we could get rid of that stigma and afford abundant legal passage for them to arrive here to do noble work, things would be different."

"How you gonna do that? The politicians are arguing about that all the time."

"Well, there's one thing we know for sure. That is that walls won't work. My idea is to create a lake right on the border. Maybe build a dam on the Santa Cruz east of Nogales about half a mile north of the line. Then have two migrant stations, one on the shore in Mexico and one near the dam in Arizona. We could build a big-ass boat to bring them across. We'll call it 'Mayflower II.' We welcome them with open arms, they feel good about the experience, and the world gets right again."

Both men pondered that scenario for a bit, then Chavez asked, "What about the crossers here in Texas? Are you saying they don't have any problems with crossers in Texas?"

"No...that's not exactly true. Everything's relative you know. We can deal with tens of thousands of crossings in Arizona. But Texans are different since nearly all the land is privately owned. Along the border some of these Texas families have been on this land for generations. Feelings about heritage and property rights run deep here. One crosser is one too many for some of the guys around here."

"Are we after one of those guys?"

Logan thought briefly about what Chavez did not know yet, and also about how this sharp young agent was beginning to put the puzzle pieces together. "You know the file on Thompson?"

"Sure. There wasn't much in it. There was a photo of him and a page or two about what he does for a living, and what he is doing in Arizona with that Berger fellow. Why?"

"There's a lot more about him that I want to tell you about now. I think what I have to say will answer your question about crossers moving thru rural Texas. What I will tell you I didn't want to commit to a written document...to the record. But it's at the heart of why we're here."

As he sat on his sprawling back porch he could look for miles to the west. The summer rains had left a sea of green grass for the cool morning breezes of early September to bend and sway gently. The bird song had faded with the approach of fall, but Larry Thompson didn't miss it since he had never paid attention to it in spring when it resounded on the plains and woodland before him. He was alone in his mind, and in his typical troubled state.

All the molehills he had made into mountains were now too huge and steep for him to even imagine climbing. As they grew in his imagination his body shrugged under the weight. He carried these self-imposed burdens through his daily existence. His nights were bearable only because he drank himself to sleep. He dreaded waking because that's when his body rebelled against his mind for the burdens it had imposed the night before...and over a lifetime. That war went on daily and Thompson barely existed in the midst of the battlefield.

All the friends that had assembled for his birthday party were staying at two other ranch houses on the place, one two miles away and the other even farther. The party was at his picnic grounds in the woods at the northern portion of his property. Thompson wasn't into this gathering and didn't want it to invade his residence. He had become a recluse for the most part.

The party was Berger's idea, an event to further the real estate dealings he had developed with Thompson. The partnership between the two was typical of Berger's relationships: shallow and pointed. The point was making money. Berger and Thompson had reacquainted after nearly twenty years of hardly any contact. They were brought together by Berger's need for Thompson's extensive array of wealthy contacts.

What surprised Berger was Thompson's instant attraction to the Sopori. The country was more rugged than his Texas Ranch and comparatively not good for livestock, which had been Thompson's livelihood. The one thing Thompson seemed to be especially interested in was the illegal migration of Mexicans across the Sopori. That one issue was a barrier to potential development, a factor that had initially sparked much buyer resistance. The main concern was fire from the camps of crossers in the surrounding federal lands. When Berger mentioned this matter at their first meeting, Thompson seemed to come alive. On hearing an inkling of Thompson's solution to the problem, Berger thought he was joking. He didn't pursue that topic further, but let the lure of the profit numb any budding concern as acquiescence quickly set in.

What followed was only partly known to Berger, who never wanted to know any of the details. After the sale Berger watched from the sidelines as Thompson handpicked the "ranch manager," who would run the meager cattle operation to avoid a huge tax liability. When Berger read articles in the Wall Street Journal about *El Diablo* along the central Arizona border, he cringed. He had brought a monster into that country but he had no desire to learn exactly what that monster looked like.

Chavez looked straight ahead, letting each of Logan's words soak in.

"Thompson is one independent man," said Logan. "He's a lot like many of the folks that inhabit the Texas borderlands. He's a third generation rancher who owns more land than you can ride horseback in a day. Men like him spend a huge amount of effort and resources to guard their ground. To them the land is everything. I don't know if

you can understand that. Having grown up here on a ranch, I understand it real well. Did you have a connection to the land you were
raised on?"

"You bet. I know what you mean."

"Okay, good. The thought of having anyone trespass on your land
is troubling. When they do damage to fences and waters, and
threaten to burn down buildings and pastures and woodlands, the
stakes get even higher. If a guy has a tendency to be bitter or angry
over other events in his life that are out of his control, the act of
someone violating his land may, in his mind, justify him committing
an unthinkable crime. And around here no matter what he chooses to
do his actions will be buffered from law enforcement by miles of
private rangeland.

"You know those ranchers near Lochiel, Arizona who were caught
violating those crossers?"

"Yah, I remember that case," said Nate. "They captured four
Mexicans who were crossing on their ranch, beat them, then sent
them south to warn the others."

"That's right. How stupid can a guy get? There's a legal network
along the Arizona border that is set up so Mexicans can report such
instances, and so the violators of human rights can be brought to
justice."

"Sure. Doesn't the same justice exist along this border?" Nate
asked.

"Yes...well, not entirely. There are large sections of the border
here that are bounded by private land...I mean huge chunks of land
that are surrounded by fences and locked gates. Mexicans work these
ranches for the owners, but they're all legal. The owners play pretty
much straight up. When they have a problem with trespass illegal
migrants they believe in taking care of it themselves. The Mexicans
south of here know it...it's part of the local culture."

"How do the ranchers take care of any problems?"

"By various means. Mostly that depends on the owner's state of
mind. If the guy's from a tradition of grace and giving, and he feels
an obligation to give back for all the blessings he has, then his

methods will be guided by that spirit. But if the family has a troubled past and the current generation fights for property, who knows what extremes they will attempt."

"Thompson is one of the latter, isn't he?"

"The worst kind. He runs his 120,000 acres alone. He cheated his sister out of her share of the inheritance. Since her death about ten years ago all the legal battles have ceased and he got away with theft. He has settled all past matters. He never had any kids so he really has no future. His actions are all about the present. Present taxes, present cattle prices, present rainfall and present problems from crossers."

"Let me put this one together," interjected Chavez. "If a guy's rage can't change the rain or taxes or economy, he'll turn it toward things he can affect. Right?"

"Exactly. In Thompson's case, he developed a horrific wrath to greet the Mexicans that were using his ranch to reach the U.S. He might not have used this elaborate and cruel strategy here, but for sure he employs it in Arizona on the Sopori. He has used the sunset years of his life to inflict pain and suffering. This is when he should be giving back for all his blessings. He's really demented."

"What did he do?"

"When we get to the site where his terrorism began, I'll fill you in. But right now, let's go eat some *huevos rancheros.*"

Chapter 45

Large chunks of mesquite that had been cut and stacked a year ago for special occasions were piled into the bed of the old Chevy pick-up. After the Mexicans finished loading the wood, they drove slowly along the lowland dirt road southwest of the barbeque site. They crept to the first intersection and turned right onto the main ranch road. Their destination was the fire pit, where they would render their load into hot and perfect coals to grill the beef.

Logan and Chavez saw the truck at the same time, a quarter-mile ahead. "What do we do, Sam?"

"Nothing. We're lost out on this big place. Just let me do the talking."

Logan slowed down, pulled off to the right and stopped. He rolled down the window and stuck out his arm as if to signal the oncoming vehicle to stop. It rolled up along side him.

"Good morning, boys. Where's the feast?" inquired Logan with a big smile. "I'm starving."

Logan didn't know if the two middle-aged men in the truck spoke only Spanish, but he didn't want to reveal that he did. When they pointed toward the way he had come, Logan nodded and said,

"Thanks. I gotta get turned around here I guess." He got out of his truck and went around to the open bed where a cooler was sitting. He pulled out four Corona beers and offered two to the Mexicans. "For my *amigos*," he said, still with a wild grin on his weathered face. They took them and thanked him. "Mr. Thompson sure has a fine place here. I haven't seen it in ten years and it's prettier than I remembered."

The Mexicans agreed, thanked him again for the beers, and said they better get going...the coals needed a good start for the barbeque. Logan agreed as he put down his tailgate. "We'll drink these right here before we join the crowd," he said. Chavez opened his door and joined Logan as he waved bye to the Mexicans.

"That was a pretty convincing drunk act, Sam."

"Sitting on the tailgate of a pick-up and drinking beer is something those boys can identify with. They expect that sort of behavior from Thompson's friends. They're cool."

Chavez joined Logan and sat on the tailgate. "Now what?"

Logan took a big swig of beer and spit it out. "Boy, that's good stuff," he said, still smiling. Chavez looked at the bottle in his hand and smiled at it. He looked up at Logan and found a strange sense of security in his partner's confident and easygoing mannerism. He said nothing, knowing that Logan was about to reveal more about Thompson and their mission.

"Nate, what on earth do you think this place has to do with our case in Arizona?"

"I really have no clue. I know that we're here to see what Thompson did to keep crossers from his ranch, but exactly what that is I don't know."

Logan pulled a small GPS unit from his shirt pocket. He turned it on and sat it between the two agents. "We'll let the satellites tell us how far we are from our destination. It should be less than two miles to the south. I have all the road junctions we take to get there. Our first junction is ahead, where our two amigos came from.

Chavez watched as the bars on the GPS display grew longer, indicating that the satellite signals were getting stronger, enabling them to accurately home in on their target. When ten bars had reached their maximum length, Logan picked up the unit and entered a waypoint. An arrow appeared. It pointed south-southwest, and the digital numbers 1.82 appeared in front of the word "miles." Logan grinned. "I have a detailed aerial photo from which I calculated these positions." He punched in the first junction waypoint and the arrow pointed straight along the road in front of their truck. "0.24 miles ahead," said Logan. "This puppy is right on."

"Right on what?" inquired Chavez.

"Right on the path to Mr. Thompson's site of horror...his terror chamber." Logan put the GPS unit into his pocket and looked at his friend. "Nate, Thompson is one twisted son of a bitch. You won't believe what I'm hoping we find just up the road. I waited until now to tell you because if you knew before now and we bumped into Thompson before we got what we're after, I was afraid you wouldn't be able to contain yourself."

Chavez looked at Logan. "Don't you trust me?"

"It's not a matter of trust. It's about strategy. I know that you've never worked undercover before, and on the advice of agents that work that way all the time I decided to keep the pressure off you. I've had to psych myself out for this. It took awhile, but I have been able to get a completely detached attitude about Thompson."

"Maybe that's good, I don't know. You think I'd shoot him on the spot or something?" asked Chavez.

"No, I don't. But if he somehow got you alone you might say something that would compromise this mission. To a certain point it was best that only I know our purpose here. Now it's time for you to know also."

"Fine. What are we after?"

"Hair. Jaguar hair."

"I remember...not *T. rex* hair, but jaguar hair...you were serious!"

"Yes, I was," replied Logan.

"My great grandfather was from Scotland and he went to Ireland to find his bride. The famine of 1850 drove them to America. That's what drove everyone out...there was no food, no future. What was a guy gonna do? They called it the Great Hunger. It left 1.5 million dead and just as many took off for America. There was gold lying on the ground in California and they wanted to get in on that. They became migrants in California and they were welcomed neighbors while the economy was strong. During the Civil War both the Union and Confederate armies relied on their strength. But later, during hard times these same people were cast out and accused of stealing jobs from American workers. Can you imagine that?"

From his seat on the tailgate Logan stretched out his legs, kicked his boots together, then continued, "Some folks were for 'em, and even said that foreigners added much to the wealth and power of the nation... they should be fostered and encouraged. Anyway, my people got part way to California from the east coast but stopped short in Texas to grow beef for people heading west. They were giving away land in the 1880s, so they got as much as they could. And eventually they settled into making a life here and contributing to the good of the country. They helped build this country. My family was proud and made us learn the details of our history.

"The way I heard it from Grandfather, in the1880s steam power shortened the journey to America and immigrants poured in from around the world. The door was especially wide open for Europeans, and for fifty years after steam engines were used a total of almost thirty million people entered the U.S., most of them were from Europe. Nearly one out of ten Norwegians left their homeland for America. But after World War I American attitudes toward immigration really began to change. We became suspicious of foreigners and questioned why they wanted to come to the United States.

"After that we passed laws to hinder immigrants from coming over, but between the depression and World War II there were so many people looking for a better life that there was nothing we could do to hold back the tide. They got rid of the prejudicial way they were treating Europeans and started letting in people from all over.

"We're a strange collection of people. Sometimes we welcome others, sometimes we don't. Most of the time we welcome only certain ones. I can't figure it out...how are the people who want to come here gonna figure it out? It just makes me weak to think about the trouble we've gotten ourselves in with these changing immigration policies. And there is no way we can totally protect our borders from people that want to get here. And we both have seen a twenty-five foot ladder leaning against a twenty-four foot wall...walls won't work."

Chavez listened intently, looking at the various tracks in the dirt on the road as he sat next to Logan on the tailgate.

Logan continued, "Borders are strange things. Look at a political map of the world...all those colors representing all the different countries. Along the lines between the colors is where good and bad happens. Good for some economies, some families...some communities. Bad for others...and it's scary how many times bad people gravitate to those lines. Anyone would surely believe that Satan resides at these lines.

"Around this globe there are many, many regions where people migrate from one place to another to find a better life. I forget the exact figure, but right now somewhere over 65 million people have been forced from their homes and at this very moment are trying to scratch food and shelter out of this earth."

As Logan talked Chavez felt uneasy as some words touched a nerve in him. He knew only a few details of the difficulties his grandparents had getting to the U.S. He realized for the first time that if he knew all the details of that ancestral struggle he might tip...like Sharp, but with the reverse mission. He finally said, "You know, Sam, the Mexicans call this area Satan's Crossing to highlight the point of the deaths. The Border Patrol essentially encourages those deaths, that human suffering, because it helps direct migration the way we want it to go. It serves our purpose. But that greed for our own outcome is no different than the greed of coyotes that charge to escort crossers."

"I think you're exactly right," said Sam after letting Nate's words settle. "No matter where the crossing is, when there is human greed and suffering, I agree that Satan surely has a hand in it. The real tragedy is that crossers are in the middle of it all, and they have no voice...and it's not because of the language barrier. We think they're like dogs that can communicate only with other dogs; to us they are mute. We tell their stories and we interpret their actions. Truth is, we just can't hear them so we really don't have a clue. We don't even listen to them. We're too comfortable with our own lives."

Logan looked across the expanse of Thompson's ranch to the south. After pausing he said, "You know, Nate, I suspect within the hour we will find a creation of one of the most hateful people along this border. But in Arizona we find our own brand of hate...like those guys who cut holes in the cans of beans left by the Samaritans, hoping a hungry crosser would eat them and get really sick. But you also find good at the borderland because there are people who care, like the Samaritans."

Nate nodded and replied, "You heard about that quail hunter who found two young girls at a spring in the middle of no where? He took them all the way to their grandmother in Phoenix. I think the girls were ten and twelve...left by a coyote during cold weather in December, essentially to die."

"Yes. He's a hero to that family. From what I understand the girls' mom had been killed in a traffic accident somewhere in central Mexico and the family wanted the girls with their grandmother in the States."

"Yes, that's what I heard. I think our outfit has a bead on the hunter's vehicle, but I don't know if we'll pursue the case."

"I hope not," responded Logan. "There is good and bad along the border. Just like there's Mexico and the U.S., and really no space in between, that's the way it is with good and evil. All in the same space there's the Samaritan and the can-puncher, the quail hunter and the coyote...there is good and bad right next to each other, touching. Just like our two countries touch. Some people try to see the black and white at this interface, but really it's all gray. At some point the issues of right and wrong need to be addressed, and not just placed on hold as legalities are organized. Most of the time it's a matter of the conscience...we know what's wrong and what's right. It's wrong to punch holes in cans and to leave children in the wilderness to die; it's right to help the needy and turn a blind eye to the legal quagmire."

"You should be a priest, not a Border Patrol agent," exclaimed Chavez.

"Sometimes I think I am. At least I am looking forward to hearing a confession."

"A confession about what...and from whom?" asked Chavez.

"Just pulling your leg, Nate. I'm just a common guy trying to do his best to understand the world."

"I like what you're saying."

Sam continued, "I am telling you this because this is my foundation...perhaps the reason I got into the Border Patrol. I respect the diversity of countries and what citizens from each one bring to the human table. I just want to make the boundaries a little more permeable. Or at least interject some compassion or sympathy into the process of enforcing boundary laws." He paused and lowered his head, then asked Nate, "You think that's reason enough to come over here and root out Thompson?" Without giving Nate a chance to respond he said, "I'll tell you, it isn't. When he killed Stayton that was crossing the line for me."

"Sam, the jaguar killed Stayton...I was there!"

"You wanna get to where this GPS will take us and find some jaguar hair?"

"What's the deal with hair?"

"Just up the road from here is a pen that Thompson used to hold jaguars. We need to prove it by getting hair from the pen."

Chavez looked at Logan in disbelief of what he had just heard. Dozens of questions were colliding in his head. Logan interrupted the flow of Chavez's thoughts with a photograph. Handing it to him he said, "That's Thompson about five years ago next to a jaguar in Mexico."

Chavez slowly took the photo from Logan and uttered, "Did he kill it...was he hunting jaguars?"

"No. It's not dead. He shot it with a tranquillizer dart fired from the rifle on his shoulder. Thompson used to hunt jaguars in Mexico during the '60s and knows the country and guides in Sonora. He talked one of them, a guy named Carlos Luna, into taking him on a jaguar hunt. He told Luna he was setting up a facility on his Texas ranch to breed the animals in captivity for eventual release of the offspring back into the wild. He convinced Luna that he was part of the jaguar conservation effort."

"How did you put all this together?" asked Chavez.

"Even though Thompson paid his guide to keep quiet he made one mistake. He didn't realize that real conservation efforts were just beginning in Sonora. The real conservationists were looking for someone who knew something about jaguars, and word along the Bavispe River was that Carlos Luna was the expert. Luna saw big bucks in being the go-to guy for this legitimate effort, and in the process of convincing his new clients he was their man he spilled the beans on Thompson. He showed them this photo taken by his cousin. He told them about the breeding pen on Thompson's ranch. Crow ended up with the photo."

"Did he use this pen for breeding jaguars?"

"I don't think so. At first Crow thought he might be breeding the cats. Later he suspected Thompson just wanted to have captive jaguars for the fun of it. He never did determine exactly what Thompson was up to five years ago, or if Thompson had live jaguars somewhere in Texas earlier. Crow has a file on Thompson five inches thick. The problem is, he could never get onto Thompson's ranch to prove the existence of a jaguar pen. He had good aerial photos of Thompson's place over a period of years. Anyone can tell from the aerials that something was built and it sure looked like an enclosure of some sort. What it was used for we need to determine."

"How big is it?"

"Oh, it's maybe eight thousand square feet and there are no buildings near it. It's fairly big, I guess...but so are jaguars. We'll see how high the fence is when we get there. I suspect he used chain link, probably fifteen feet high with some structure near the top to keep the cat from climbing out."

"I don't understand why Crow didn't get a search warrant? Don't we need one?

"You don't understand how these old boys operate here. Thompson is so well connected here that there's no way a judge would grant a warrant, or at least a timely warrant that wouldn't give Thompson time to clear the evidence. Thompson's ties with this area run real deep. They protect each other in this neck of the woods. Everyone is against illegal immigration and they all accept taking matters into their own hands if they feel the need. There's a real anti-government attitude here. If Thompson even suspected what we were up to he'd bulldoze the place and we'd never find a trace."

"I understand that sort of mind set. That's the way it is back home. It's the same all over I guess where men are independent and they feel like the government is too close to their business. But I still don't understand the connection between Thompson's actions here and in Mexico and what's going on in Arizona."

"Crow and I are fairly convinced that what Thompson really wanted to do was bring jaguars, several of them, back to his Texas ranch and condition them to kill crossers in Arizona. Perhaps he tried that scheme in Texas a little earlier, but we're not sure about that. Also we're not sure how many jaguars he managed to acquire in the past three to eight years, or how many he actually released in Arizona. I suspect that at least two were released in our state: one in the Atascosas, and the other to the east in the Huachucas. We need to get hair so we can let the DNA give us answers to these questions."

"How would he condition them to eat people?" asked Chavez.

"By feeding them a diet of unfortunate crossers he rounded up on his property here. Get them conditioned to feeding on people rather than their natural diet of game animals."

Chavez was awe struck by the notion and remained silent. The thought of someone implementing such a cruel way to "apprehend" crossers was incomprehensible to Nate. "Why would he do that?" he finally muttered.

"Who knows what devils bounce around in that guy's head? For some reason he has a deep hatred for trespassing Mexicans I guess.

Or maybe he felt frustrated by the incompetence of the Border Patrol and took matters into his own hands."

"So you don't think he tried using jaguars to kill crossers in this area?"

"Not that anyone has ever found, but we're not sure. I don't think he'd use his monsters here because it's too close to home and the law. Plus he already shot off his mouth around here. My guess is that he'd do it far from home. I think that's why he bought the Sopori."

"So you think Arizona is his killing ground?"

"We do." Logan quit swinging his legs beneath the tailgate and said, "Look at the jaguar in that photo real close." Logan took out another small picture from his wallet. "Now look at this photo. These two photos are of the same cat. The pattern of the spots is identical. That's how you can tell it's the same animal. The arrangement of spots on a jaguar's hide is like fingerprints. Each jaguar is unique."

"Yah, I see that. Where's the second cat from?"

"That's the one we photographed on Sheldon's place. It's the one that killed Stayton."

Chapter 46

As the two agents drove along from one road junction waypoint to the next Chavez looked out onto the spectacular landscape that was Thompson's domain. The irony overwhelmed him. "When you see pictures of Hitler's gas chambers there are old buildings with gray skies above them. This place seems too beautiful to be the scene of such horrific acts. Can you imagine what was going through the minds of those crossers when they were dragged into that pen?"

"I'm sure it was over in an instant," replied Logan. "But you're right. It must have been terrible. But what's really terrible is that a guy like Thompson exists. That's what's really the worst part of this whole thing."

Chavez thought about what Logan had said. "You're right. If I ran into Thompson knowing what I now know, I'd kill the son of a bitch...right on the spot!"

Logan said nothing, but nodded. He kept an eye on the GPS unit and the other out the side window. "Look for a two-track road leading off to the right...it will be barely visible because of the new summer grass growth. It's gotta be around here somewhere," he said.

"What's that?" snapped Chavez. He pointed off to the right side of the vehicle where the hint of a road wandered through a tangle of mesquite and low brush.

"That's it, Nate. Good eyes."

Logan drove past then stopped the truck on the left side of the road. As he got out he grabbed a backpack from behind his seat. "Here, Nate. Put this on. We gotta do this like we're on CSI. I got vials and the whole bit. Here's a pair of tweezers for you to pick up hair. Put all you collect in one of these vials."

"We just gonna leave the truck here?"

"Yeah, this way we don't have truck tracks going right to the pen. I'm betting that pen is less than two hundred yards from where we are now. If someone comes to our truck they'll figure we're off on that other side of the road. If they pursue us, we're birdwatching. You know your birds?"

"No!"

"Well, then you'll be a beginning birdwatcher. Let's head off this way for about fifty yards then circle back and cross the road fifty yards up and head to the pen."

As the two men walked up to the pen, Logan readied his camera to photograph the site. Chavez stated, "You were right about this thing. Is that Plexiglas angled down from the top?"

"Looks like it," replied Logan as he took photos from a variety of angles. "How high would you say this is?"

"I guess about twenty feet. What do you think?"

"I'd say you're pretty close," said Logan. "I like the way they wove the chain link mesh together and wrapped it around the horizontal rails at the same time...real strong construction. What, about thirty yards on each side?"

Chavez paced off the side nearest them. "I got thirty-two paces. Here's the gate."

"Is there a lock?"

"No, it's not even closed all the way."

"Good. Let's get some hair." As the two men entered the enclosure, Logan said, "I think the best place to look is on the chain link mesh itself. The cats I watched at the Desert Museum in Tucson paced along the perimeter of their cage. So some hair likely gets snagged on the fence. Also check along the ground for hair that has been rubbed off and fallen to the ground, or washed off with the rain."

Chavez bent over along the fence near the gate and brushed away the green grass with his bare hand. "Sam, check this out."

Sam knelt down along the fence where Chavez was stooping over. "You found a bonanza, Nate!" he proclaimed. "I guess this is the low spot in the pen and all the hair was washed here with the past rains."

Logan photographed the mats of hair against the bottom rail that secured the mesh before it extended underground for an unknown depth. Within five minutes the agents filled ten vials full of hair and dried soil from a variety of points along that side of the pen. "We're out of here, Nate. Good job."

The men stood up and silently looked around. Their forensics science was complete and some human emotion began to creep in. Standing in the pen and looking around at the structure that was encaging him, Logan imagined being there when it was operational. His eyes would gradually focus on a large figure approaching him from a cluster of brush in the corner. It would be walking with steady steps and moving directly toward him, silently with its head lowered and mouth open, revealing long white teeth. Before he could react it would jump up and with the full weight of two men slam him to the ground and grasp his whole head. His very last sense would be the sound of bones shattering just before the jaguar's jaws closed tightly and ended his life.

The squeaky gate brought him back to the present moment, and he looked around to see Nate holding it open for him. "Are we going to the party now?" asked Nate.

"I don't know about you but I got no interest in personally laying eyes on Thompson right now. I'm more interested in getting out of here. What do you say we head for the airport?"

"I'm with you, Sam."

Chapter 47

Neither one said much during the trip back to Tucson. During the entire flight Chavez buried his face in "The Beast In The Garden," keeping his thoughts to himself. As the plane began its long descent westward Logan looked out the window to the south along the desolate U.S.-Mexican border. Over the tops of mountains with names like Chiricahua, Dragoon, and Huachuca, he gazed to the south into the stunning landscape of northern Mexico.

The clear September air transported the vista, enabling him to glimpse well over a hundred miles into that great land. He could distinguish the mountainous terrain incised by the Bavispe River, home of the jaguar population closest to the U.S. The land between there and the Huachucas indeed was wild and untouched by large urban gatherings of humans. It seemed like a great corridor for jaguars to wander north into the U.S. He wondered how many of these great cats have chosen to head north on their own in the last decade without the aid of Thompson.

Logan held that question in the front of his mind as the flight attendant passed by and asked if she could take his drink. "Sure. Thank you," he responded.

Chavez closed his book, sat up in his chair, and looked around. "This book is fascinating, Sam. I would hate to encounter a mountain lion along a trail."

"Me too," replied Logan. "Imagine facing a jaguar. Their mouth is twice as big. They can fit your whole head in it."

"No thanks. Is that how jaguars kill, by attacking the head?"

"You know, I asked a couple experts about that. Jaguars kill like other big cats. They choke their prey to death. They usually grab the throat area of a deer or javelina…they grab monkeys by the head. After talking to all his jaguar people, Clawson thinks the Arizona cats that have turned to human prey just find it easier to grab people by the head. Our necks are too small and protected by our large heads. He suspects they get their death grip on the face area, and hold on until suffocation occurs. This usually breaks the skull, which gives them a taste of the brain. They like to eat organs like the liver and heart, and the brain."

"Do you think Thompson's conditioning changed their hunting or killing styles? Maybe he taught them to attack the head."

"I don't think Thompson taught these animals how to kill. He offered them the chance to shift their diet to human prey, especially crossers, and the major lesson was that humans are dumb prey without senses to detect an attack. Compared to deer, humans are easy. All a jaguar has to do is overcome its innate fear of man. Once that was accomplished Thompson released his conditioned animals into areas where crossers were abundant. They set up territories with all the food they could possibly want. They probably eat one person a week. Unlike a jaguar's natural prey like deer, the human prey base doesn't diminish in a drought. In fact, it drastically increases when the Mexican economy falters."

Chavez shifted his gaze from Logan to the Santa Rita Mountains outside the airline window. "Say, Sam, what's next? I guess you'll be having a meeting with Crow and getting that hair analyzed."

"Yes, I'll get the hair processed and call a meeting to debrief Crow and Clawson. Crow will be glad to learn that his hunch about Thompson is correct. That old boy did import jaguars to his Texas ranch and keep them there."

"Are you going to tell them that you confirmed the identity of the cat that killed Stayton?"

Logan tightened his seat belt in response to orders from the flight attendant over the intercom. He took a deep breath and looked out the window to his left. "Nate, that part of the story is between you and me. All the rest of the world knows is that Thompson held at least one jaguar on his ranch. No one but you and I know this was the cat that killed Sheldon. I'm real curious to learn if the hair we gathered today is from more than just one cat. Remember, we likely have at least two jaguars taking crossers in Arizona. Don't forget the one on the west side of the Huachucas. That's probably a different cat."

"We have the two photos that match," stated Chavez. "Can we get hair from the two Arizona cats to compare DNA with the hair we gathered?"

"That's part of the plan. Clawson has cameras all over southern Arizona now to see how many jaguars are in the state. He hopes to see if the only cats here are from Thompson, or if others are coming here on their own. He's using scent bait from jaguars in zoos to attract the cats. He's also setting out hair traps in hopes of getting hair samples from the Arizona jaguars. He thinks there could be two or three cats along the Arizona border. The hair traps could afford a link with the hair we collected at Thompson's place. "Please, Nate, I'm asking you to keep a tight lip about the two photos I showed you. I don't want anyone to connect those dots right away. If they get hair samples from the cat that killed Stayton and it matches the hair we collected, they'll know what we know. I want to make them discover that on their own right now."

"I hear you. This is personal with you, isn't it?"

"You bet." Logan paused for several seconds then continued, "You know, I think about Stayton every day. He was a kind soul...a generous man. He believed that there is a right way to do things, and that there's the wrong way to go about life. He favored doing the right thing, and frowned on those who did otherwise. When there was uncertainty about what's right and wrong, he always opted for a slow and steady course of kindness and compassion. Stayton did not like injustice...people getting away with doing the wrong thing. Lately I've been wondering a lot about what he would do if the tables were turned...if I were the one killed by that jaguar."

"What do you think he would do?"

"I think revenge would well up in that old man. I believe he would make sure a reckoning occurred."

"Well, you are doing that. We have all the evidence needed to put Thompson away."

"That's one outcome, yes...."

"Do you plan to get Yost involved?"

"No. Old Yost is just about washed up. I think he's slowly going crazy. He was passed up for another promotion at the Regional Office about two weeks ago. He's isolated at his big desk in Albuquerque with nothing to do and no one to see. And he just seems to be getting scarcer every day. He's taking a lot of leave. The State Office is giving me a lot of leeway for special assignments like the one we're on. I don't think I'll have any resistance from the bureaucrats. They're pretty much leaving me alone."

"That's my sense too. That's got to be a good feeling after all the crap you've been through."

"It sure is. Our outfit pretty much has all but forgotten about the border deaths. They figure Sharp was a renegade with his own personal vendetta against illegal immigration, and when they catch him they have enough to put him away. The other killings were by an endangered species, and that's a matter for the Fish and Wildlife Service and the Arizona Game and Fish to deal with."

"Our trip to Texas really links the two though. Isn't that important?"

"It is. But Crow and Clawson are being tight-lipped about this connection. They want more data, evidence, before they reveal Thompson's role. Which means I've got some time and all the resources of the Fish and Wildlife Service to help. The grand finale may be mine to perform."

"What's that involve?"

"I can't say right now. But you'll be the first to know."

Chapter 48

"**S**am, you got a call from Mr. Clawson. He wants you to call him as soon as you can. He said it's real important."

"Thanks, June. Anything Bob Clawson has to say to me nowadays is important," replied Logan.

"Any word on Sheldon's place?"

"I hear the gate's locked. Sheldon's kids decided to lock up the old place until they know what they want to do with it."

"It's been several months now. Those kids must be tormented by the fact that they may have to sell the homestead...but they aren't ranchers are they?"

"No, not in the least. They didn't take an interest in learning the operation, but from what Sheldon told me awhile back, I don't think they want to see it developed. They have their lives in California now, I guess, but it must be tough on them."

"I can't imagine," sighed June.

Logan rolled her words around in his mind. "I can't either."

"The 'bait' worked like a charm," proclaimed Clawson. "Smells from that pen were the magic potion that lured them in."

"Great! What did your DNA tests from Thompson's place indicate?" Logan asked

"That hair you collected from Thompson's place was from three different cats, all males. So the soil you picked up with the hair had scent from three 'strange' jaguars. I think that was the real attraction. You know, the territorial thing. The Arizona cats suddenly thought there were new jaguars in their area."

"Males. We're always the undoing of our own selves, aren't we?" Logan joked.

"I guess that's right. Of the three cats we've lured in we got hair from all of them and a photograph of only one cat."

"The cat in the photo...where was that cat from?"

"East of Nogales in the area east of the Santa Cruz. I believe that was in the Washington Mountains somewhere."

"That's pretty far from the core area of Arivaca. Where are you placing the scent baits?"

"From the Chiricahuas to the Baboquivaris. We figure that's got to be the main corridor into the U.S. Since we got a pretty good amount of funding for this project, we may as well put a lot of effort into it and cover a lot of ground."

"Sounds like a good idea. Strike while the iron's hot."

"Right. That federal iron can get pretty cold real fast."

"Boy, do I know that," Logan replied. "You know, Bob, I just hope that the general public doesn't develop a real paranoia about jaguars because of what Thompson did. He is a deranged man who took control over that animal's power and might. That would be a real tragedy if people feared those assets rather than admired them. After all the reading I've done about this magnificent animal, I'm a big fan, and would like to see the public embrace having them around southern Arizona."

"I know what you mean. Hard tellin' how the public will respond. We'll just have to see how that all plays out."

"Say, what's happening to Thompson? Did you make an arrest yet?" asked Logan.

"We did, but his lawyer bailed him out. We're going to the Grand Jury next month. Endangered species cases are low priority, especially with a political guy like Thompson. His attorney has been doing all the talking for him. Our attorney said it likely would be impossible to pin the *El Diablo* thing on Thompson. All we have is hearsay and Thompson's loud, self-incriminating mouth linking him to the deaths. He said the act of training predators to do horrific deeds seems so far-fetched it would be hard to sell to a jury. I heard Thompson's in Arizona and not available for some of the proceedings in Texas at the moment."

Logan was stunned but said nothing more about the legal matter. "So, no DNA results from the Arizona cat hair yet?"

"No. We have to send that away to Oregon and it'll take awhile. We're low priority on the DNA results schedule. We likely had some wild jaguars not associated with Thompson come across the bait, so we don't expect to get a hundred percent match with the hair from Thompson's. Another reason we're not a priority is that we're not tagging this as a homicide investigation yet. We think media interference could jeopardize things if we prematurely connected the dots between *El Diablo* and Thompson. Our lawyers say there's a good chance we may never attempt to connect those dots."

"Well, it's good to know that your hunch about the best bait for luring a cat has worked," said Logan, wanting to change the subject. "Good luck, and let me know when you get those Arizona DNA results. I plan to be around."

"Sam, I appreciate all you've done thus far. I sure will keep in touch. Take care."

AN EYE FOR AN EYE

Chapter 49

The Sopori Ranch was settled in the 1880s, a time when southern Arizona was wild with Apaches and the vagaries of weather. Cattlemen tried and failed several times to make a go of it but the cultural and environmental resistance was too overwhelming. When the U.S. Army got a good foothold in the territory at the turn of the century ranchers moved back onto the range with their livestock and special brand of living. The Sopori has known about a dozen owners since then.

Logan pulled off the Arivaca Road onto a two-track Forest Service road. He headed east through the National Forest land leased by Sheldon just south of his ranch. After about ten miles he turned left onto a spur road that headed to the southern boundary of the Sopori. The gates into the place were unlocked so he passed through unhindered.

The grass on the Sopori had not been grazed to any significance since Thompson purchased the ground. There were mats of gramma grass on the slopes of drainages that were lined with thickets of sacaton. *This place is a fire waiting to happen*, thought Logan. *No wonder Thompson wanted to get rid of the crossers. They always carry Sterno cans for fires, and don't worry about starting a range fire. Crossers had started most of the fires in this country, and Thompson wanted to remove all risk of property loss...no matter the method.*

Logan sat in his truck and looked at the grand landscape of the Sopori. *This is perfect*, he thought.

He ran his hand along the seat, fingering the scabbard that held his riot shotgun. It was a short barrel 12-gauge loaded with five rounds of OO-buckshot followed by five slugs. He could take down a large black bear with this weapon. It was just the protection he wanted.

He got out and grabbed the shotgun at the same time. He made sure the first round of OO-buckshot was chambered so he could shoot from the hip at a close, moving target. He leaned over to retrieve his backpack, then closed and locked the door. He stood by his vehicle while he looked around. The cool air of a fall morning was just beginning to be tempered by the sun, which shined in a clear blue sky.

He walked into the drainage among the large round rocks, and headed downstream to an area bordered by a jumble of large rocks. There, part of the ridge jutted into the drainage and forced it to bend sharply to the left with an array of short red cliffs. Deer sign was evident, as were human footprints. *Crossers like it here. They probably feel protected by the isolation.*

Logan walked up to the area of the red cliffs and stood watching for signs of movement. He carefully scanned each pile of rock and cluster of brush. *What a great place for El Tigre. If there is a place on the Sopori where he makes his lair, this is it.*

After a couple minutes Logan walked to the tallest cliff and turned to face away from it. He looked around briefly and took off his backpack. All the time he watched his front and the sides. A large slab of rock guarded his back. He knelt down, placing the shotgun along side him with the barrel facing out with the trigger readily available. He knew he could grab his weapon and get off a shot in less than two seconds if the need arose.

He kept his eyes scanning in all directions as he opened his pack and retrieved the vial. Satisfied with the setting, he opened the vial, dipped a cotton swab, then painted a line on the rocks in a place where the sun would warm the scent and carry it up the ridge. He discarded the swab under layers of dried sycamore leaves then returned the vial to his pack.

He stood up and kicked the fallen leaves from the base of the rocks. He then raked the area of bare dirt with a fresh branch of juniper. *If a jaguar comes to investigate the new smell he surely would leave his tracks.* He leaned over and picked up his shotgun. Smiling at his set, he looked around briefly then headed for the truck.

Chapter 50

He put on the uniform shirt and noticed for the first time the frays along the margins of the collar. This shirt has seen quite a bit of action. It's old and tired, and burned out. It's perfect!

Logan walked to the back door. "June, I'll be at Sheldon's place this morning, and at the Tucson office in the afternoon. I should be back by dark. Have a good day, sweetheart."

"Take care, Sam. Love you."

"Love you too," replied Logan as he walked to his truck. He glanced at his resting dogs that were wagging their tails silently. They had nothing to proclaim and no desire to go with Logan. Their instincts were engaged and they could read their master's mind. They knew that his mission was a solitary one.

Logan checked the duffle bag to ensure its contents were present. Satisfied, he closed the passenger side door and walked around to the driver's side. He noticed the air was chilly. The impacts of shorter days had finally taken grip of the southern Arizona temperature. Winter was around the corner. No more threats of hot days.

"Nate? This is Logan. How are things?"

"Good, good. Where you been? I haven't seen you for awhile."

"Around. Taking care of some chores around the house. How's the office culture?"

"I couldn't tell you. I've been busy with the big fall push of crossers hitting the border. The San Pedro has been a real hot spot. And as far as the office goes, I heard that Yost is retiring. Have you heard that?"

"No, that's news to me."

"I guess he finally had enough."

"Actually, he realized finally that he'd never get a place closer to the top," snapped Logan. "I wonder if he ever realized that the bed he's been sleeping in is the one he made for himself. I hope he finds peace in his life out of the Border Patrol."

"Right. Anyhow, what's up?"

"Say, I'm heading to the Sopori. I have a chance to run into Thompson there. I hear he's in Arizona and I think that's his local stomping grounds."

"What you want with him?"

"I have something for him. I'll fill you in later, but I wanted to let you know my location today in case I don't get home tonight. June is expecting me around dark. If all goes well, I'll call you and advise of my status. I'll be in uniform."

"Oh, you're on official business?"

"I'll be in uniform!"

"10-4, Sam. I'll be available if there's any situation you need me for. I get off the river here just after noon, so I'll be home. You can get me on my cell again. If I don't hear from you what should I do?"

"Go to the Sopori headquarters. If no one's there, head to the west gate. I'll have a Border Patrol lock on the gate. Go through it and head along the southern boundary of the Sopori. I'll be near the second gate into the Sopori. Just follow my tracks."

"You in your government rig?"

"Yes."

"I got it, Sam. Be careful."

"Will do."

"Sam, I gotta ask you something."

"What's that?"

"Will Thompson see the sunrise tomorrow?"

Logan paused, realizing he'd revealed more to young Nate that he had realized. "If he's real lucky, he won't."

Chapter 51

The main gate into the Sopori off the Arivaca Road was locked, but Logan could see vehicles at the main house about one hundred yards away. He parked his truck along the fenced entrance, slipped through the gate, and headed to the house. It was a huge adobe surrounded by ancient mesquites. As he approached a dog looked up from its vantage on the covered front porch. It silently watched him advance.

"Can I help you?" a voice asked from the corner of the house.

"Well, perhaps. My name is Sam Logan with the Border Patrol. Is the manager around?"

The man walked toward Logan. He had a stern face with a partial grin. Logan returned the facial gesture. "My name is Downing, Jason Downing. I'm the manager of this outfit. How can I help you?"

As Logan and Downing met they shook hands. "Glad to meet you, Mr. Downing. How's the Sopori holding up?"

"Oh, just fine. I got some cattle to get to the auction this week, so I got some work ahead."

"You got 'em corralled?"

"Yep, they're ready to go. I'm just waiting on the vet to check 'em out, and the brand inspector to give me the paperwork. I was about ready to go unlock that gate so they could get in. I'm expecting them any time now. How can I help you?"

Logan put his hands on his hips, his right thumb bent back and hooked on the belt in front of his holstered .40-caliber pistol. He noticed a new pickup with Texas plates parked along side of the big house out of sight from the road. "I just want to see how things are going here with the illegal traffic. You know, it's getting to be the busy season again. I wanted to make sure you know your government is at your service."

Downing was at a loss for words. Finally he said, "Great. Have you been around these parts long? I don't think we ever crossed paths before."

"I'm new to these parts. I usually patrol the eastern portion of the sector, but with all the activity they're sending guys around to various parts of the line to get a sense of the magnitude of the problem."

"I see. Well, we've just had the usual fence cuttings and trash around the waters. A bunch left a valve on at one of my windmills so I didn't get the water in the tank that I was expecting. You know, the usual problems."

"That all adds up, doesn't it?"

"It sure does. A guy has to be in twenty places at once to make any headway."

"That's for sure. How about your neighbors? Have you heard of any problems from them?"

"No. The old guy to the west died earlier this year and he left a few cattle around. They got through a downed fence onto us about a month ago but my guys ran them back and fixed the fence. I don't know what all is going on over there."

"You're talking about Mr. Sheldon?" asked Logan.

"Yes."

"He got killed in a horse accident, didn't he?"

"That's what I hear. Horse reared up and fell right on top of him. Poor guy. I heard his kids live in California but hardly get over to the place anymore. There's really no one there to look after things."

"So there probably won't be anyone home for me to talk with. I wonder how long that situation will last. It's a shame to waste all that good range."

"Actually, we're trying to buy the place from them. We heard they're in Arizona this week so we're trying to locate them and talk about a purchase."

"That would be a good deal. Are they interested in ranching?"

"I don't have a clue. All I know is that we got plenty to do here without taking on another ranch," complained Downing.

"I bet. It's a lot of work. Guys who have never done it don't have a clue do they."

"That's exactly right. You sound like you've been involved with ranching before."

"I have. Got a family place that I want to work again someday, but, yes, I know what you mean about land barons who think they know about the cattle business."

"I deal with that every day. As if I don't have enough to worry about. I bust my butt, not knowing if I'll have a herd next month."

"That ain't right. There's enough uncertainty without that situation to fret about."

Downing looked over Logan's left shoulder at a pickup that was slowing down near the gate. "There's the vet. I got to run. Nice talking with you, Mr. Logan. I appreciate my government looking out after me, and I really appreciate them hiring guys like you."

"Well, I'm a fast-fading breed, but I try to make it work for folks like you. Good luck. By the way, will you be taking your cattle to Marana?"

"You bet. I usually get the best prices there."

"How are prices nowadays?"

"Same as usual. Down. But that's the cattle business."

"That's right. Well good luck." As he turned to walk away, Logan stopped and asked Downing, "Say, can I use your bathroom real quick?"

"Sure. Go through that door and take a right. That old dog won't bother you."

"I can see that. Thanks."

Logan headed for the porch and Downing walked toward the gate. "Hey, doc, glad you finally made it," he called out to the vet.

Logan did not want to meet the vet, and he didn't care about his truck parked along the road. He hurried toward the front door and quickly entered the large front room of the house. It was dark and filled with leather chairs and western paintings on the pinewood walls. Massive pine poles held up the wooden-beamed ceiling, which supported a veneer of saguaro ribs set in a row. This was classic Southwestern architecture, fitting for a structure built with Eastern money over one hundred years ago.

While Logan's eyes adjusted to the dimly lit room he listened for sounds of life and peered into the depths for more clues. Since the bathroom could be anywhere in the maze of blackness he figured his explorations could be explained, and forgiven. A long hall off the main room seemed to hold the promise of his quest, a room for a land deal, and the man it would likely hold.

Berger let out a sigh of relief when he saw the vet's pickup driving into the yard just in front of him. He wouldn't have to get out of his Cadillac and open the gate. Downing noticed the car arriving and pushed back the gate to let it in. As Berger drove past he waved through the window and drove straight to the house. Downing nodded and closed the gate.

Berger was not the least interested in the ranch's cattle operation or the personnel involved with it. He never called them by their names because he couldn't remember them. The Border Patrol truck parked out front did not register with him. Numbers were his only business here, numbers of dollars.

He quickly exited the Cadillac and locked the door with the remote. The momentary burst of the horn signaled that the security system had engaged, causing the sleeping hound to lift its head, an event that Berger missed as he walked quickly toward the front door. He opened it and saw Logan, who was heading toward him.

"Good morning," said Logan, who had heard the car and moved toward the door.

"Good morning," replied Berger. "Is Thompson up yet?" Logan realized that Berger was oblivious to any social organization at the ranch, including what a Border Patrol agent would be doing there. One clue was Berger's obvious impatience with the light switch near the chair he immediately occupied. The other was his suit and tie.

"I've not seen him," responded Logan, who decided to say nothing else. He moved toward the large window and watched Downing and the vet at the corrals. Berger opened his brief case and fumbled with the contents as Logan remained standing. *Thompson will be here very soon and I'll strike up a conversation with him. As long as Downing stays with the vet, I can say that I asked to speak to the owner about the illegal traffic problem.*

After a minute a door somewhere in the back of the house opened. A shuffling of feet commenced and continued in a progression toward the large room. When he walked through the arched doorway the first thing he saw was Logan standing by a nicely framed replica of a Remington. Berger continued to examine the paperwork in his brief case as Thompson walked toward Logan.

"Can I help you?" Thompson said abruptly in a soft voice.

"Good morning," Logan replied, searching for words to greet Thompson. He turned away from the painting and took a few steps to greet the approaching figure, a short man with a shallow step and a hunched posture. He appeared to have had a rough night. A raspy voice suggested that the bottle had accompanied his night.

"Do I know you?" asked Thompson as he took Logan's outreached right hand and returned the handshake.

"I don't believe so. My name is Logan, Sam Logan. I'm with the Border Patrol and I was just paying a visit to find out first-hand if you're having any problems with the illegal Mexican traffic on your ranch."

Thompson briefly inspected Logan from top to bottom then replied, "We don't have much of a problem. Seems they find their way quickly through our country and then head on. How did you get in here?"

"After I finished talking with Mr. Downing he was gracious enough to direct me to the restroom. You might know how it is after a guy has had about a gallon of coffee already this morning. Your art here captured my attention on the way out," replied Logan, smiling, hoping for the same gesture in return from Thompson.

Somewhat of a sense of ease overtook Thompson as he half-smiled and looked down at Logan's boots. "You walk a lot don't you? Most every Border Patrol agent I know has a rug-burn shine on his britches from sliding in and out of the truck."

Logan chuckled. "The only thing I hate more than the inside of a truck is an office. The bureaucrats try to have everyone tied to trucks for communication, but that's not where the problems are. And Lord only knows that we got plenty of problems in the field."

"That's right," responded Thompson. "Since you dumped some of that coffee, are you ready for a cup?"

"Sure."

"Have a seat and I'll get some. It's already made." Logan watched Thompson amble to the kitchen to where a freshly brewed pot awaited. He poured two cups and brought them to where Logan was standing. He didn't bother asking if Logan wanted sugar or cream, figuring the answer would be negative. Thompson sat down in a stuffed leather chair, and Logan sat in the twin chair next to him.

"So, how's business?" started Thompson.

"Brisk. The season is about to begin. Soon they'll be sneaking back across the line for the holidays, and return in January. From then through the pot crop harvest we'll be real busy."

"They gotta quit talking about building a wall to keep 'em out," said Thompson after taking a slow sip. "Walls won't work. We don't talk about walls in Texas where I'm from. We know that walls won't work!"

"You're exactly right," exclaimed Logan. "If they build a twenty-foot wall there'll be a twenty-one-foot ladder against it. No, I think the answer is personal responsibility. We got to keep them from getting a job here. We have to remove the incentive for them to move north."

"Who's going to do that? It's too political. The economy of our country needs that cheap labor."

"But it's not cheap when you figure all the crime and associated costs. I bet every rancher has several thousand dollars wrapped up in annual repairs to fences and waters. You add the labor to fix all that and it adds up."

"That's true," said Thompson.

"How does it feel to be paying the bill for the cheap labor in Phoenix and points north? It has to be a big burden on your operation."

Thompson looked at Logan as he settled back into his chair. Logan looked back, wondering if Thompson was about to take his bait.

"You have a ranching background, don't you?"

"Yes sir. Born and raised in west Texas."

"Really? That's where I'm from. Whereabouts?"

"My grandfather started a place south of Fort Stockton. My dad took it over and he left it to my brother and me when he passed. I don't get back there too much now but will return when I retire."

"When will that be?" asked Thompson.

"Oh, in about two years. I wish it was sooner...you see, my brother moved to Oklahoma and our lessee does nothing to keep up the place. The wets are overtaking it, and I doubt that the outfit is fit to turn out a cow since the fences and waters are all in disrepair. The wets are ruining us."

Thompson jumped right in. Logan had struck a chord that ran deep in Thompson. It was pay dirt. "Don't you have any connections with the local Border Patrol to get some help?"

"The Border Patrol is the problem! They're too modern to be effective on the ground. All the high tech stuff just keeps agents from walking the backcountry like the wets do. That's the only way to prevent them from overtaking the countryside, by getting out and fighting this war on the front where the action is. I wouldn't give you two cents for two-thirds of the agents working the border," Logan retorted, hoping Thompson would not detect any body language revealing the conflict residing within him over that statement.

Thompson took another sip of coffee; then he took a long look at Logan. Both men felt the pause. Logan knew that the next move had to be Thompson's, and whatever he chose to say or do would dictate the rest of Logan's day.

Chapter 52

Berger fumbled through his papers. "I think we're as ready as we can be. We just need to get with them and see if they're in the right mood."

"Okay, you see if you can track them down while I show Mr. Logan the ranch."

Berger seemed both frustrated and relieved. He obviously didn't enjoy interactions with Thompson and didn't mind Thompson blowing off their meeting. In fact, he would prefer to talk with Sheldon's heirs and their attorney alone without his wrecked partner hovering over the paperwork, which he did not understand in the least. Berger and Thompson both knew that Thompson's interests were in the bottle and the life that he had lost, the life of a free-range rancher that wasn't hindered by a society more complex than his comfort level could tolerate.

As Berger returned to his car Thompson watched him through the window of the house. "He's a pain in the ass," declared Thompson. "The guy knows nothing about the real worth of this land, and why God created it."

"But he's your partner, isn't he?" asked Logan.

"Well, I own this place and he's my partner with our effort to acquire more ranches in the area. Sopori is an investment for me but I don't need the money. This place is giving me something to do. It's not my home. I like it here but nowadays the value of this land is not in cattle, which is what I know. It's in the development potential. That's why I don't want the wets to burn it down. If I lost all the oaks the place would be relatively worthless. Back home fire is good to grow grass. Out here it destroys vistas and assets. That's what I have to protect."

Thompson was in somewhat of a trance as he stared out the window at the back of Berger's departing car. In Thompson's mind Logan was a sounding board for an ideology he could express to no one else. Perhaps Logan's Texas roots engendered Thompson's trust. Whatever it was, Thompson needed a pair of ears to express his true feelings about the life that now surrounded him. Even if that life was now under the shroud of a federal investigation.

"Well, then you really need to see what I have to show you, Mr. Thompson. That wetback camp on your south boundary has the real potential to take out some of the most gorgeous parts of your ranch."

"I know. You got my attention. Let's head out."

As the men walked out the door Thompson looked toward the corral where the vet had parked. There was no sign of Downing, the vet or the cattle. "Where's everyone?" asked Logan.

"Beats me. That manager is useless. He probably forgot to close the gate last night after his workers had the cattle all rounded up. That vet's a good one, though. He'll find them. Berger will be mad because the vet bill will include round up time. That's okay. He has a deep check book."

"Let's take my vehicle since this is government business," interjected Logan.

"That's a good idea. You guys buy a lot of gas don't you? In fact I bet gas is the biggest part of your outfit's budget!"

"I think you're right. That and hemorrhoid medicine," returned Logan. Thompson smiled.

As they drove off Logan asked, "Have you had breakfast? I got some donuts in the back there."

"Donuts! Those things will kill a guy."

"I know, but Border Patrol policy is that you have to consume one for every hundred miles you drive. I figure that's two or three a day."

Thompson looked at Logan and said, "You got your outfit pretty much figured out, don't you?"

"I guess. It's not complicated. Just put in the time, keep quiet, promote and retire after twenty-five years. Pretty simple, actually."

"But you got bigger plans. I can tell. I bet you don't really believe in the way the Border Patrol is going about its job. The way they operate pisses you off, right?"

"Well, the way they operate is not the way I operate. You see, I really don't want illegals in this country. The Border Patrol needs them around. Without them they're out of business, they got no cause to keep the budgets on the upswing. It's all about increasing funding and manpower and technology. What gets done on the ground is only secondary."

"Well, how do you operate, Mr. Logan?" asked Thompson.

Logan looked squarely at Thompson, having rehearsed this line many times in the last several weeks. "Have you ever heard of a guy named Sharp?"

"Sure. Everyone along the borderlands has. He's the guy who cut the heads off those wets on his ranch. Why?"

"He's a very good friend of mine," Logan said, glancing at Thompson as he pulled onto the dirt road at the western boundary of the Sopori. "Listen, I don't know why I'm telling you this. There's something about you that I trust. I think we're alike in some ways...like our attitude about illegals."

Thompson sat up and adjusted his posture on the seat, partly because of the rough road, and partly because Logan had his full attention. He seemed to come alive with the mention of Sharp.

"Tell me about Mr. Sharp. By the way, I think they should declare him a national hero when they find him."

"Trust me, they'll never find him," said Logan.

"Why? Do you know where he is?"

"Sure. Me and a handful of other Border Patrol agents, and one of them is a pretty high ranking guy."

"What's the deal? Are you protecting him?"

"We have to. He was operating on behalf of the Border Patrol, or at least some of us. What he was doing was scaring the hell out of the Mexicans before they ever thought of crossing. His *El Diablo* deal with all the dead and headless bodies made every potential wet think twice about crossing around these parts. Sure, it pushed them to other areas of the line, but we had everything sewed up pretty tight around here."

Thompson posted a look of confusion that Logan instantly recognized as anger. "How did you put all this together? Did you get him to kill those wets and scatter the headless bodies?"

"No we didn't. Actually, two of us caught him in the act of killing wets at his ranch. We just couldn't arrest him when he confessed and explained his side of the story. My partner and I struck up a deal to protect him. A couple other enlightened agents joined us. We believe Sharp has a good solution to a bad problem. Heck, I would do the same thing if I was in his boots. I bet you would too."

Thompson hardly paused before saying, "Hell, I am in his boots. I've done the same thing."

Logan looked straight ahead, not wanting to react to Thompson's budding confession. Instead he began, "You know the law of the West. It's in your blood. You take care of your own...you do what you have to do. You eliminate what you perceive to be the blight on the land. In the days of our grandfathers it was the wolf, throughout time it's been the weather. We could never do anything about the drought. But when the government started being part of the problem, our own democratic government, well that's pretty much when a guy loses it. A guy's got a better chance of making rain than changing a wayward government that ignores the problems, and even adds to them."

"That's right," Thompson said, obviously becoming more engaged with the self-righteous rhetoric expressed by Logan.

Before Thompson could get in another word, Logan continued, "If a guy has a problem with the way the federal government is ignoring illegal immigration, if that inaction costs a man his livelihood, if it chips away at a world that produces a living for raising a family, then a man has to take action. It doesn't matter what the action is at that point. A man has to stand up."

"I believe that. I have stood up," Thompson uttered in disbelief of what he was hearing from his driver.

Logan continued to interrupt Thompson's bulging desire to spill his guts. "When everything calms down we're going to set up Sharp on my ranch in Texas. We'll protect him. He's one of us and we will not let him down."

Thompson was nearly speechless. More to the point, he was verbally constipated. He had so badly wanted to utter affirmations in response to Logan's monologue that the rush of words to his tongue collided, creating a plug at the top of his throat. He needed a drink.

"That's how I see it, Mr. Thompson. How about you?"

Chapter 53

Logan drove under the shadows of the large oaks. Memories of Sheldon were near to him. Thoughts of a man raised in this land, who knew every inch of the landscape and who watched it evolve through the variable seasons of climate and economics and culture. That man was a unique breed, Logan thought. Something in him, maybe his DNA, enabled him to understand his place in the scheme of all this change. Whatever it was, it's a rare trait. For someone to extinguish such character, and be part of the attempt to swindle the heirs of those attributes...it's not right.

"You ever been to these parts of the Sopori, Mr. Thompson?" asked Logan after several minutes. Thompson had been alone with his thoughts also, staring out the windshield, seemingly oblivious to the countryside.

"I've been down this road before, yes. When I first came out here to meet Berger I took him on all these roads to get a look at the country. That guy was so nervous I could barely stand it. He was busy drawing lot lines in his head, scheming the development. I was busy wondering what I was doing with that idiot next to me. Sure is beautiful out here."

Logan realized that Thompson did have an eye for landscapes and an appreciation for them in their natural state. He knew what would corrupt that wonderment.

"Too bad it's being trashed and threatened by the illegals."

"Heck, it's not just the illegals. It's the whole damned country of Mexico. The ones that come across are just symptoms of bigger problems in their heartland. It used to be that you could get a good Mexican to do some good work. I had some in Texas at my place there. They birthed generations on that place. They were good people. That breed is gone nowadays. I got some still but they're only a fraction of what the old ones were."

"Why's that?" asked Logan.

"Hell, it's because there's too many of them nowadays and they're all stuck without any way to make a living. They're crammed in down there like rats on a sinking ship, and they're all jumping at anything that seems like it floats. That government down there sure won't float."

"You're exactly right," said Logan, somewhat surprised at the astuteness of Thompson's answer to his question. He wondered if Thompson had compassion for the situation in Mexico but decided to avoid that topic. Logan had a line of conversation, a rehearsed script that he would follow.

"You know," uttered Thompson, "there comes a time in a man's life when he needs to fight for his space on this planet. There's only so much room on this old globe, and what a man has chiseled out for his home and his family he has to defend at any cost."

Logan thought for a moment then replied, "I don't know about you, but I don't want my land and my life to cost me anything more than I've given in the past. I've already paid my dues. Why should I pay again for something that's already mine?"

"You're exactly right. But fights always cost something."

"I agree. The price of freedom has always been enormous," said Logan.

"This is true, real true. And with each new battle comes a new price, whether or not we like the cost. I think you know exactly what I mean."

"I do," responded Logan. "Yes sir, I do. I am willing to pay the price for new battles. That's what we're doing with Sharp...we're covering his actions and there's a great cost to that. So what's your action?"

Thompson looked around impatiently, giving Logan the impression he was feeling irritated by Logan's questions and comments.

Does he sense that I am baiting him? Logan thought momentarily. *Does he suspect that I believe crossers are fighting for their space on this planet?*

Then Thompson erupted. "I have taken this matter into my own hands. I decided long ago not to rely on my government or anyone to solve the problem I had with illegals trashing my place and burning it to the ground. I've had it with the system...long ago. It's broken." At the height of his raging blurt Thompson gasped, "Who's that?" He pointed out the left side of the windshield. Apparently Logan was so intent on getting Thompson to describe his actions he didn't see the nun crouching behind the trunk of a large oak about 40 yards away.

Logan rolled down the window and called out, "Sister! What are you doing here?" Without looking at him she began running with amazing agility over the rocky terrain. It was very evident that she was familiar with this country.

"Leave her be," said Thompson. "She's one of those do-gooders out here filling watering stations and scouting for wets that are on their last leg and need medical attention."

Logan watched her disappear amidst the tangle of oak and manzanita. "Funny that I've never run into those people all the years I've been kicking around in this country. I heard about them and saw them in town and at the store, but never laid eyes on one in the field."

"Just as well...you haven't missed anything," said Thompson. "If you've ever been down at the Humane Society's dog pound you can see the same sort of person. They are all passionate about their cause. Trouble with this bunch along the border is they got no sense to go along with that passion."

Logan kept quiet and drove along. Thompson seemed like he was about to get into the details of his scheme. Just prior to the nun appearing he seemed like he wanted to climb out of the window as he adjusted his posture and looked around like a caged cat. *He's insane*, thought Logan, who maintained his silence as he slowly continued down the dirt road.

"Logan, I've killed more wets than you can count," Thompson continued without any prompting from Logan. "I did it for my family and my
land. I don't care what the government tries to do...about their new
programs...none of it! I don't care! I took matters into my own hands.
Like you and the other agents you mentioned. We have to do what's
right."

Thompson seemed to relax after his confession of sorts. Logan
made sure he gave Thompson's statements time to bounce around
the cab of the pickup and settle in some obscure place that was
comfortable for both men. He then said, "It's in our DNA, Mr.
Thompson. It's hereditary."

Thompson looked at Logan and grinned. He then settled into his
passenger seat and said, "Sure is beautiful out here. This is God's
country." Thompson felt the start of a kinship for the first time in a
long time.

As Logan gripped the steering wheel he looked at his hands. They
revealed the path of his life, both when he was a kid on the ranch and
as an active and outdoor Border Patrol agent not sheltered from
nature's elements by an office. He glanced at Thompson's hands when
the opportunity presented itself—mostly they were tucked between his
ribs and shirted biceps at the ends of his folded arms. Only remotely
did they resemble the form of hands. They were covered by blackish,
blotched skin approaching the look of a charred marshmallow.

Logan recalled during their initial meeting Thompson's gripping
handshake was firm, but his hand was small. No blood vessels
ventured near the surface, which was covered irregularly with bumps
near the darkened spots. *Perhaps that is the onset of skin cancer,* he
thought. *You can tell a lot about a man by his hands...dad always
told me that. Sheldon had a wonderful pair of hands.*

"Did you ever break horses, Mr. Thompson?" Logan asked.

Without as much as a pause Thompson replied, "We had the best
ranch horses in south Texas. Now there's an art to breaking horses

I'll have you know. It's a lost art nowadays. The Humane Society has seen to that."

Logan knew exactly what Thompson was leading to but he wanted to explore the depth of his knowledge on the subject. "What do you mean?"

"You can get a horse to do anything you want if you let him know when he's real young that you are the master. He has to be afraid of doing what you don't want him to do, otherwise he'll always choose to do what he wants. You have to put the fear of God into him so he will do only what you ask of him...and he will do anything you ask. It's really simple."

"I know exactly what you mean. There's nothing worse than having a horse that has a mind of his own. There's too much horsepower in those animals to let it be around unrestrained. I agree."

"You're right. The gentle approach will not work. That whispering business is something Hollywood invented. It doesn't work in the real world. A horse has to be puckered all the time when you're around, and it has to be totally attentive to what you want it to do. It must be taught that it cannot make a move without you giving a command."

"Otherwise someone will get hurt," Logan interjected. "When you go against something that weighs four times what you do, you need to have control." Thompson nodded his approval. Logan let the thought of animal control linger in the air for a little while and then added another part of his script, "You know, that's the way it is with every animal, even humans. Those wets quit coming up along this stretch of the border when we put out the *El Diablo* scare. That was conditioning just like a guy does with a young horse. And it worked. It works with any animal I suspect. I haven't tried it on anything but horses and wets, but I bet it works with anything. You teach them a new way, take away all the old options, and bingo you got a programmed mind. That's power. Not many people know about mind control but it works on any living creature I bet."

Thompson's whole body was nodding in agreement. "Anything you want to control...you name it...you can control it if you get to its mind. It needs to be re-programmed, just like you said."

"Sounds like you studied this," said Logan in a leading way.

"You bet I have. I started with horses and worked my way up to ranch managers and beyond," inserted Thompson.

Logan registered the word "beyond" before asking, "What do you mean by beyond?"

Thompson looked at Logan with his hands now squarely on his Levi-clad knees. "Mr. Logan, since you're into *El Diablo* and have used him to keep the wets at bay around here, I'll tell you all about *El Diablo*. The Border Patrol can take all the credit for him and you can give your personal amnesty and protection to the guy you think really started the killings that were attributed to *El Diablo*. But I made him...he's my brainchild and creation. I'm glad he was useful to you."

"What do you mean...you created him? Sharp admitted that he was *El Diablo*, the one who was killing and beheading wets around Arivaca." Logan pretended to be confused. "I don't get the connection."

"Mr. Logan, what's the most threatening killer along the borderland? Do you have any idea?"

"Well, not really. We've discovered jaguars killing wets recently, but I suspect that mountain lions have been doing that all along. I mean, they're easier to chase down than a deer or javelina. What's the biggest predator?"

"You hit on it...the jaguar. They have a head twice the size of a mountain lion's, and can kill a man with one bite." Thompson displayed hesitation...he started to say something then stopped.

Logan recognized his pause and let the air rest for a few seconds while he thought about his next question. This whole scenario was playing out exactly the way he had rehearsed it...the way he had hoped it would be. He decided to take the direct approach. "Mr. Thompson, did you condition jaguars to kill Mexicans?" Thompson said nothing. "What a brilliant idea," added Logan. Continuing on without Thompson's affirmative answer, and assuming Thompson's pride and hatred were begging for a chance to explain further, Logan asked, "How did you do it? That's sheer genius."

Chapter 54

Logan spotted the west gate of the Sopori ahead through the oaks. As he pulled up to the spur road that led through the gate he slowed to a crawl and turned left onto the road. The gate was twenty feet in front of the truck. "Have you been down this road?" he asked Thompson.

"Yes, I think so. I was here alone once. Burger decided to draw his lots on aerial maps and never came out with me after our first trip. And that lazy manager he hired can't figure how to open a Texas gate so he's useless out here. Have you been here?"

"Yes sir. I think this is the prettiest part of the Sopori. So do the illegals. It's far enough from the road and that ridge there rises up to the southeast allowing easy escape if they hear the Border Patrol or any other vehicle approach. They've got a big camp just a little ways from here. I'd like to show it to you."

"I've seen a thousand of their camps," replied Thompson. "What's so special about this one?"

"You'll see," Logan replied. "This is a real special place. I'll get the gate."

Logan pulled to a stop at the gate, got out of the pick-up and, leaving his door open, approached the gate. A chain was attached to a pipe that was used as a lever to stretch the Texas gate. Its construction of wire and oak-branches was typical of gates throughout the West. Although it was flimsy it was effective at keeping cattle in and unwanted visitors out. The gate had a closed combination lock hanging from one of the chain links, standing ready to lock the gate if desired for cattle management. Logan used the bar to open the gate, drove through, and returned to the gate to close it. He had pulled a little to the left so Thompson could not see him attach a Border Patrol lock to the chain. He looped the chain around the fence post and the strong oak pole that comprised the end of the gate. *This will prevent anyone from following us...or at least it will signal 'no entry' and make passing through this way difficult*, he thought. Nate has a key.

As he entered the driver side of the truck Thompson said, "I don't think I've ever been here before. Nothing looks familiar. Where does this road go?"

"It drops into the head of Tecolote Canyon, which runs southeast from here into the foothills of the Tumacacori Mountains. Then bends northeast and flows into Sopori Creek about four miles below your headquarters. After about half a mile there's another gate to head south then the road is mostly in the creek bed. It usually washes out real bad but it's really the only way to get a dozer back here to clean out the dirt tanks or to feed. It's an all-day deal if you have to take it though."

As they drove forward Thompson looked straight ahead in anticipation. He seemed nervous and Logan sensed it. "We'll drop into the creek bottom here in a bit and the camp is about a half-mile past that. Isn't this country beautiful?"

Thompson didn't hear what Logan had said. He was intent on their destination. Logan decided to interrupt his thoughts with a topic he knew Thompson wanted to discuss. "So tell me how you condition a jaguar. I suspect that has to be tricky. Where did you get the jaguars?"

Thompson sat back in his seat and rolled down the window. As he prepared to explain his techniques he reached into his leather bag and pulled out a flat container of whiskey. "I know you're on duty, Mr. Logan, but would you care to indulge with me?"

"I would love to, but I'm too close to retirement to drink in a government vehicle. But you go ahead." Logan was relieved by Thompson's gesture because it signaled he was about to calm down.

"So, tell me about those jaguars," Logan said.

"How I got them is a long story that I won't go into. Just know that I've been going down to old Mexico to hunt all my life. I know a lot of people down there. If I need anything I can get it. I used to hunt jaguars there when it was legal and I had contacts that could supply animals. You know, the cowboys down there know exactly where they hang out. Those old boys are good at trapping anything that walks or flies." Thompson took a long swig of whiskey. "I even had them deliver the cats to my ranch through a back road that crosses the border at my place. You know, I didn't want to have to pay any government tariff," he said with a chuckle.

"How much would you pay for a jaguar?"

"Hell, a guy can't get a jaguar nowadays since they're an endangered species!"

"They are?"

"Hell yes. I guess I shot too many of them down there when I was a kid!" exclaimed Thompson.

"So you know the habits of this animal pretty well, do you?"

"I have a way with animals. I can understand them much better than any human I ever met. But I'll tell you, those cats are something special."

"How so?"

"First off, they're big, real big. Especially the head...it's huge. They can fit your head in their mouth and crack your skull with one bite."

"Is that how they kill a deer?"

"Well not really. They're like a mountain lion or any other large cat. They grab the throat and suffocate a deer. First they hook the deer with their claws and hang on until they get a death grip on the throat. With all their weight the deer falls right to the ground and the old jag just lays on it until it dies. I mean, it's something to see."

"So you saw them kill a deer?"

"Yes, I did see one kill a deer one time. I had this big pen built on my ranch to keep the jags in, and I put a deer in there to see how it would kill it. Just like I said, it latched on then went for the throat. Deer was dead in thirty seconds."

"So you kept the one you had shipped to you in a pen? How many cats did you keep?"

"Oh heck, I think I had about six or seven jags over the past few decades. I think I got my first one in the '70s. I had two in there at one time for a while. That wasn't a good deal having more than one in at a time. They're real territorial and spend too much time fighting."

"What did you feed them?"

"Well, you won't believe this, but I fed them Mexicans," Thompson blurted out.

"Illegals?" Logan asked quickly. He was only somewhat surprised by how forthcoming Thompson had been with that comment.

"Exactly. The first time I put a wet in that pen, the young guy was all drunk on bacanora. He tried to fight the jag and lost real bad. But the strange thing is that the cat went right for that guy's head. Straight away, he grabbed him by the head. I guess compared to a deer there was not enough neck on a human for them to get ahold of. Anyway, as soon as he grabbed that head the guy collapsed. Then the old jag latched on real tight and shattered his skull. It was an awful sound. I can still hear that pop."

"Jesus. Did the cat eat the whole guy?"

"No. I don't think they like to mess with clothes. It's not like pealing the hide off a deer I guess. Or maybe they don't like the taste of human meat. I'm not sure."

"Did it eat the head?"

"Well, the jag got up and walked to the far side of the pen and laid down. He looked at that head bleeding like a stuck pig for about half an hour, then went over and started tearing away at his Levis. He ate some of the guy's back and side, then left him and laid down again. I left for the night and by morning that cat had eaten the entire head but no more of the body. They like the brain I guess, and human skulls really aren't hard like the long bones in the legs, so jags just munch down on the whole head. I couldn't believe it."

"Is that what they usually do when they prey on humans?"

"I guess," said Thompson. "That's what these cats did. From my experience, that's pretty much the signature of a jaguar killing a human, a headless carcass. We had one cat that went for the throat, but we trained him to avoid everything but the head. I wanted to create that *diablo* image that Mexicans would make into a mythical killer at the border. You know they're real superstitious people who quickly turn an event into some spiritual thing. A head-eating creature is pretty scary to them."

"How did you train that one jag to eat only the head?"

"Like any cat they like to eat the organs, like the lungs and heart and brain. So they prefer those areas of any prey. But to make sure they stayed on the head we learned that if we put gas on the clothes of the first wet we fed them, they pretty much avoided the gas areas and stayed on the head. Plus when you give them an abundant source of food they can afford to be selective and eat only what they want."

"Great idea! With all the wets along the border there's an endless supply of food. Brilliant! What a way to solve the problem of illegal immigration. And you took the matter into your own hands."

"That's right. And that's the main reason I bought this place. I wanted to take my technique to another place along the border and serve my country in more places than just along my small corner of the world."

"Reports of headless bodies around here are what caused us to create our Operation El Diablo. We didn't know what was really creating all the human remains, and we really didn't realize that the bodies were headless at first."

"That's because the coyotes and other scavengers like foxes and bears will eat the meat and scatter the bones. They can do that within a few days during the summer," added Thompson.

"All I can say is we need more Americans who take matters into their own hands. It is truly my pleasure to meet the creator of *El Diablo*!"

"Just doin' my duty," responded Thompson.

"The limits of the law need to be stretched by bold men like you and me who take justice into our own hands," said Logan. "The judicial system is too inaccurate and costly. In my opinion, when there's a wrong that's been done, it's up to us to settle the score without all that legal process."

"That's exactly right. I agree with you," said Thompson.

Logan had entered the creek bottom while Thompson was revealing the details of his strategy. They were now far enough down the drainage to get out. Logan pulled out of the rocky creek bed onto a flat sandy spot at the base of a rocky ridge. "Here's the spot, Mr. Thompson. The camp's at the base of that rocky area. See that cave just left of that sycamore? That's it."

Thompson took a long sip of whiskey, capped the flask, and tumbled out of the truck. "Yep, this looks like a great place for a wet camp. It also looks like a great place for my jaguars to snack on human heads."

"I think you're right."

Chapter 55

Logan walked to the cave, waiting for Thompson to make his way through the soft sand in his cowboy boots.

"Say, Mr. Logan, I think I deserve a letter of commendation from your outfit for creating the basis for Operation El Diablo. You know, I'd also like to meet that vet you're harboring. If it wasn't for what I started, he wouldn't have had the technique or the gumption to solve his own problems the way he did. Come to think of it, you never told me where you're keeping this guy."

Logan turned around to face Thompson, who was about ten feet away and doing his best to stand straight with a belly full of whiskey. Logan had his hands in his pockets. "I need to let you know something, Mr. Thompson. My outfit had nothing to do with that guy. He's an outlaw just like you, and we'll get him in time. But right now, you're under arrest." Logan pulled his right hand out of his pocket and his service pistol out of its holster.

Thompson's mouth froze in an open gape and his face reflected incredible disbelief as he stared at Logan. "What are you saying...what are you doing? Is this a joke?"

"No joke. I think I'm about to take the legal system into my own hands. We're about to have an extremely shortened process here.

You've called the shots on your ranch, but I'll handle that from now on. For my first duty as executive branch officer, you're under arrest. I find you guilty of killing Stayton Sheldon...that's the judicial process. And I'll have you executed right here...there's the sentencing process. Think of all the money we've just saved the tax payers of this great land."

Thompson said nothing as he watched Logan reach toward the rear of his belt and retrieve a pair of handcuffs. "Now, Mr. Thompson, turn around and face away from me, then drop to your knees. I don't want to shoot you but I will if I have to. I don't plan to execute you myself, but have made plans for an executioner. I do intend to get you ready however."

Thompson just stood there, staring at Logan, who was waiting patiently. After half a minute he said, "You're crazy. You'll never get away with this. You can't just execute me here after your bogus trial. This whole thing is bullshit! Who the hell is this Sheldon guy? I never heard of him."

"You're partner, Berger, is dealing with his daughter to buy the Atascosa Ranch. Her name is no longer Sheldon. You killed her father."

"Are you talking about the guy who got killed in that horse wreck? That was an accident."

"No. Actually one of your jaguars killed him. The horse story was a smoke screen to give us more time to explore the jaguar's role in Stayton's death," replied Logan in a stern voice. "Your jaguar killed Stayton Sheldon. That was your fatal mistake. Mr. Sheldon was a very good friend of mine."

"Listen, if you want me to call off that deal, I'll be happy to. What do you want? I'll let you call the shots."

"Thompson, there's also the matter of you torturing and killing all those defenseless Mexican crossers...those were human beings with lives and families and dreams. All those deaths, which likely number in the hundreds, are other unforgiveable deeds. No, I don't want anything from you. All I want is you gone. And that will happen sometime soon...maybe tonight, or tomorrow. That part's not up to me."

"What do you mean? Who's in charge of that? So you have an accomplice? Is it Sharp?"

"Well, I sort of do. It's not Sharp, but you'll see soon enough. Now turn around and drop to your knees or I'll kick you down. I'd actually like to do that," said Logan. He walked toward Thompson, who took a step backward then tripped over a rock and fell face down. He was helpless. Logan holstered his pistol and grabbed Thompson's right wrist at the same time he attached a handcuff. He pulled that arm behind Thompson's back, and kneeling on his neck grabbed the left wrist and in one motion pulled it to the right one, cuffing the two together. Thompson was motionless on his belly with a face full of sand, breathing heavily, powerless.

Logan stood over the immobile body. "Do you have any last words?" he asked.

Thompson couldn't see Logan as he spit sand from his mouth in preparation to speak. "You're making a fatal mistake. I'll have your ass for this. Just wait."

Logan smiled. "Not exactly what I was expecting to hear from a man in your situation. But have it your way."

Logan walked twenty feet to the truck, returning to Thompson, who was still lying facedown, with a cardboard box and a steel stake about two feet long. Logan took a roll of duct tape from the box, and knelt at Thompson's head to tape his mouth shut. Thompson had struggled through this ordeal so the first few wraps around his head went across his open mouth and the final wraps held his jaw ajar. Thompson was left to breathe only through his nose. He could emit only a low guttural grunt, which he did profusely. He was unable to swallow effectively, and attempting to clear his throat caused him to panic slightly. Logan then retrieved a set of anklecuffs from the box, pulled off Thompson's boots, and bound both of Thompson's legs at the ankles.

Logan remained kneeling over Thompson, watching him struggle. "I hope this fits okay," he said as he pulled a hockey mask from the box. With his bulging, sand-encrusted eyes Thompson tried to look at what Logan was holding. Logan put one knee on Thompson's back as he slipped the mask between the ground and Thompson's face. Logan snugly fastened it to the back of Thompson's head, causing him to groan with pain. He dragged Thompson by one of his encumbered arms to the base of the sycamore tree ten feet away, and sat him against the trunk. Thompson flailed his legs and wriggle wildly, so Logan kicked him in the side. The pain of the blow reverberated through Thompson's body and caused him to lie still.

Logan then sat him against the tree and tied a one-inch strap to his left arm at the elbow. He ran the strap along the opposite side of the trunk from where Thompson was sitting, and slipped the other end around Thompson's right elbow. After running the strap back and through a buckle to secure Thompson's arms, he cinched his waist to the trunk with a second strap so Thompson's lower back was flat against the trunk. He then tightened the upper strap, bringing Thompson's elbows to opposite ends of the trunk. Thompson's handcuffed wrists were stretched to the point of pain when Logan finished buckling the upper strap. He left Thompson sitting securely at the base of the sycamore, with his outstretched legs bound and arms wrapped backwards around the trunk. To render Thompson motionless, Logan pulled a hammer from the box and pounded the steel stake into the ground between Thompson's ankles, hooking a carabineer through the anklecuff chain and a welded loop on the side of the stake. Thompson was totally immobilized, sitting upright at the base of the sycamore tree.

"I want to tell you how special this occasion is, Mr. Thompson. When I was at your jaguar enclosure last September I gathered some hair and soil from that pen. It made a real good concoction that really lures your animals. I have been spreading that bait all around here for several weeks to make sure your friends stay close. I wanted this to be somewhat of a reunion for you...I wanted both of you to meet here in this special place."

Thompson was speechless as he struggled in pain at the base of the sycamore.

"That looks uncomfortable but you'll just have to deal with it. And since I don't want you to miss any of the action I'm going to make sure you keep your head facing forward." Logan ran a length of rope through the sides of the hockey mask and around the trunk to hold Thompson's head up. "There, that's better. Now your friend can't get around to the back of your head, and while he starts to dine you both can be face to face."

Logan walked to the truck with the box and returned with a container of lighter fluid. "Thanks for the tip about the gas. I will have to use charcoal lighter if that's okay. I don't want your jaguar to get confused by this mask and start eating at your body muscles instead of your face. He'll eventually work his way through this mask and get to your face and into your skull." Logan could hear the venom in his voice, an almost cruel tone that had crept into his pronouncements. He continued. "You'll be able to experience for perhaps a couple minutes his hot breath and throaty groans. His actions will probably become more frenzied as he gets closer to tearing off the mask. That should signal your friend is closing in on a meal. Maybe you'll even get to hear some of your bones breaking under the force of those powerful jaws."

Thompson remained silent as Logan stood in front of him. "You killed my best friend," said Logan. "Now you'll pay for that."

Both men were emotionally numb. Each one was at the end of his road.

Chavez's cell rang only once before he answered. "Logan, how are things going?"

"Couldn't be better, Nate. I'm done here," said Logan. "I'll be heading back to my place."

"Okay. You don't need me to head that way or anything, do you?"

"No, it's cool here. In fact I would avoid going onto the Sopori for a couple days...maybe even a week."

"Okay. When can we get together for coffee?"

"Let me get back with you on that."

Made in the USA
Columbia, SC
30 June 2019